Diane Hallisy

HANNAH
MORMON MIDWIFE

H A N N A H

M O R M O N   M I D W I F E

Jaroldeen Asplund Edwards

Shadow Mountain

Library of Congress Cataloging-in-Publication Data

Edwards, Jaroldeen.
    Hannah, Mormon midwife / by Jaroldeen Asplund Edwards.
       p.   cm.
    ISBN 1-57345-280-7 (hardbound)
    1. Frontier and pioneer life—Utah—Fiction. 2. Women pioneers—Utah—Fiction. 3. Mormon women—Utah—Fiction. 4. Midwives—Utah—Fiction. I. Title.
    PS3555.D935H36   1997
    813'.54—dc21   97-28689
                                             CIP

Printed in the United States of America

10 9   8   7   6   5   4   3   2   1   72082

Nothing we do well will ever be wasted.
The Lord will make use of it in His own way
and in His own time.

—*Hannah Childress Fairfield*

CODA

Hannah spent the last summer of her long life in the home of her eldest son, Will. She sat in an old chair that had worn upholstery on the padded arms and the edge of the seat, but it suited her, and so she forbade Will to do anything about recovering it. He and his wife, Nell, endured the chair's shabbiness for the old woman's sake. They had known all their lives that she was not a woman to be argued with. She knew her own mind.

Grandchildren and great-grandchildren came to visit. They kissed her cheek, which was cool and smooth and as finely wrinkled as weathered silk. She sat unmoving, warmed by the golden sunlight spilling through the bank of windows. Her temple-white hair was pulled back into a soft knot at the nape of her neck. Her bones were as transparent as porcelain. She sat straight and silent with her firm jaw, high cheekbones, and snapping dark eyes. Her presence was almost sacred and yet intimidating as well.

The porch had a hushed, reverential spirit. Everyone spoke in whispers, but that was unnecessary because most of the time Hannah simply ignored what was happening about her. There was much quiet conversation among the grown-ups that summer concerning the end of the Second World

1

War. While the grownups talked, the children crept over to stare at her, an inexplicable wonder in their orderly world.

Occasionally this dying woman, who in her childhood had ridden in a covered wagon, would hear the roar of a low-flying plane coming in to land at the city's new airport. A radio was sometimes turned on in the living room, and soft music poured out, filling the air.

But all these modern fripperies were slightly unreal to Hannah. People and things had become distant and removed, as though glimpsed through deep, deep water— shimmery, vague, and silent.

The only things real to her were her thoughts, her memories, and the scriptures. She read for hours every day. The Book of Mormon was still her favorite. She read slowly, savoring, her magnifying glass bringing each word close. How like Lehi and Nephi had been her own mother and father, led from the lands of their birth to a wilderness—a promised land.

Off and on she slept, or seemed to sleep, dozing in her sunlit place. The children tiptoed past her, thinking she was asleep there on the sun porch. How could they know she was not sleeping? That she was not really in her son's home? Her body was there in the chair, but her mind and spirit had flown far away, back to the time when she had found her destiny.

She was a girl again. The wind was blowing, and magic was about to happen. Had it all really begun with a dress— a silly dress? The night she met Adam. Would everything have been different had it not been for the dress? The dress . . . Adam . . . And the dancing at the great house on Childress Avenue. She smiled in her sleep, and her old body was like a discarded dress left empty on the chair as her mind raced with the wind and she was once again young— oh! so young . . .

CHAPTER ONE

The dry cornstalks rustled around Hannah in her hiding place. She sat silent and huddled as a young fox eluding pursuers. Although the early autumn sun was warm on the fields, the wind from Weber Canyon cut through the hidden rows of dead corn with the bite of early snow in its teeth.

Hannah shivered and hugged her knees more tightly to her chest. The sound of the tall, dry corn was like the whispering of old friends, but it was not loud enough to mask the sound of Mama's calling.

Hannah recognized all the signals in her mother's voice. When Mama was happy, she almost sang Hannah's name across the fields, doubling the last syllable, "Ha-nah-ah" on two separate notes.

But when Mama was impatient or angry, she would snap out Hannah's name with an emphatic rising tone that had no melody at all. "Han-*nah!* Han-*nah!*"

Mama's irritation was clear as her voice overrode the wind and the muttering cornstalks. "Han-*nah!* Han-*nah!* Come this minute! We are *leaving!*"

Hannah had no desire to upset her mother, but she was too filled with rebellious and angry feelings to answer the summons. Why couldn't her mother and Eliza just leave without her? She was eighteen years old, after all, and ought to be able to stay home if she wanted to! Why was she required to go to town when Mama knew full well how much she hated these fancy family to-do's at the Big House?

Hannah looked around at the dead cornstalks overdue for stripping, and she had a hopeful thought. Maybe Mama would let her stay home if she promised to clear the field. She would rather be condemned to chopping silage—dusty, splintery work though it was—than spend the next two days talking, eating, socializing, and dancing.

For days she had been trying, unsuccessfully, to explain to her mother why she did not want to go to the family party. Mama had shown not so much as a glimmer of patience or understanding for Hannah's feelings.

It was exasperating, but inevitable, as Hannah had known it would be. How could Mama understand what it felt like to be Hannah? To be young and proud and insecure? How could Mama begin to know how it felt to go into Ogden and see all of the girls of the city families—who were your same age—dressed in fancy city clothes, with elegant city hairdos, and showy city shoes, and exclusive city ways?

Hannah, knowing she was every bit as much a Childress as any of them, resented feeling conspicuously out of place in her secondhand bombazine dress, her old-fashioned farm boots, and her rough, work-hardened hands.

Mama, who gave no notice to material things, had considered Hannah's sentiments nothing more than wrongful pride. "It is time you got over such pettiness," Mama had said in her firm, aristocratic voice. "The Lord does not judge by worldly measures, nor does anyone who is of real worth.

I think you do your family discredit when you assume they make such frivolous judgments."

It was easy for Mama to say such things, Hannah thought morosely. After all, Mama did not have to sit with Constance and the other town girls and endure their veiled condescension.

Feeling unfairly chastised by her mother's words, she reflected that Mama would never understand the problem because Mama was simply not like other people. For some reason that was genuinely unfathomable to Hannah, her mother was completely indifferent to other people's opinions, possessions, or social importance.

It seemed to Hannah that her mother lived by a standard of measures that was hers alone—or rather, hers and the Lord's. As long as Mama and the Lord were in agreement, that was all it took to make Mama happy. That was discouraging to Hannah because most of the time the workings of the minds of both Mama and the Lord were complete mysteries to her. The irony was that these were the two beings she wanted to please more than she wanted anything else in the universe.

"But Mama has a celestial heart, and I despair that I shall ever have one!" Hannah reflected.

She knew that her mother had long ago risen above the things of the world. Service was the thing Mama valued most, and everything she did was weighed against how time and wealth could best be used to give the most to others. Mama was so serene, so complete within herself, that she did not seem to need admiration or recognition.

It frustrated Hannah that she felt herself afflicted with a different spirit altogether. From the time Hannah was a little girl she had hungered after the great, wide world. She perceived the world to be crammed to the brim with wonderful, important, exciting possibilities. She wanted to grab life

5

with both hands. She wanted to wear all the beautiful dresses, pick clean the fields full of flowers, sing a thousand songs, hear ten thousand symphonies, read endless books from a hundred great libraries, see shoreless oceans, breathe the spice-filled air of myriad lands, and talk in golden tongues.

She loved the farm in Riverdale, but what she loved the most about it was that it seemed to spread across fields, streams, mountains, and canyons and bordered on all the mysteries of the vast unknown. It was a place where all the profligate pleasures of nature were spread at her feet, and she relished the abundance of the earth.

Although nature was splendid to Hannah, it was not quite enough. She was painfully aware that the town family members were enjoying the fine things of the world—furniture, clothes, china, and silver—things that were notably lacking at the farm. If the family at the Big House in the city could have beautiful things and still be righteous, Hannah could not see why a little worldly luxury would not be perfectly appropriate for the farm family as well!

Mama, however, adamantly believed the visible display of wealth was both inappropriate and a sign of poor stewardship. So life on the farm stayed mighty simple, which was fine with Hannah most of the time, except when she had to go into town and visit the Big House, and then the contrast made her feel diminished.

Mama had chosen to remain on the farm, even though, after the death of Aunt Adelaide, it had been her right to move into town to the great house. With the sweet confidence that was characteristic of her ways, Mama had told Papa she had grown accustomed to life on the farm.

"Riverdale is the place the Lord has given me to labor. It is my sphere of service and influence. It suits me, dear William. So we shall have no more talk of my moving to

Ogden," she said, when her husband came to help her move. "Let us continue our current arrangement. You shall continue to spend every third week with us, and I will come to town to be with you as often as you ask."

Papa had understood at that moment that the matter was settled. All the family knew there was no point in trying to talk Mama into changing her mind once it was made up.

Hannah was comfortable with her mother's decision. The farm was her beloved home, and she did not covet living at the Big House. Still, she had a compelling and passionate yearning to feel loved, accepted, and respected. Somehow, whenever she went into the family gatherings in town, she felt as though her dowdy clothes symbolized a gulf between her and the rest of the extended family. That sense of being looked down upon made her feel angry and hurt.

Hannah acknowledged to herself that she was sinfully proud, fierce, and overly sensitive, but in spite of her acknowledgment of her own blame, she could not seem to outgrow the feelings. As a matter of fact, much to her horror, at eighteen she still had the occasional unrepentant and decidedly childish desire to smack someone who was being altogether too smug.

She wanted to inform her city-bred peers that none of them would last two days on the farm. If any of those mollycoddles ever came to Riverdale, they would know what it felt to be out of place and ridiculous. Just think of Constance trying to plow a furrow or milk a cow! That would be a sight for sure!

And at a calving? Why, every last one of them would probably faint dead away at the sight of blood and the little calf all wet and mucky! Hannah smiled at the thought of it. When she was younger, these vengeful imaginings had

7

been a defense against her insecurity and awkwardness, but now that she was older, it shamed her that her feelings were much the same.

Every time she went to Papa's Big House she promised herself she would not let such silly things as dresses and fancy ways bother her, but within minutes real or imagined slights would occur. With her feisty nature she found herself struggling through every visit, trying to hold on to her hot temper, bite her quick tongue, and endure through the hours until she could return to the dear, familiar farm.

Today's party would be worse than most—of this Hannah was certain. She hated the dress Mama had insisted she wear. She hated it more than anything she had ever put on her body. It was embarrassing. It was a dress that had been made for Aunt Adelaide—plain, dark blue, old-fashioned, and secondhand. Mama's clever fingers had remade the garment so that it fitted Hannah perfectly, but even Mama's sewing talent could not disguise that it was an older woman's dress and certainly not a ball gown. Everyone with their town-smart eyes would immediately know it was a hand-me-down, and, although no one would be so unkind as to say anything, their expressions would show their thoughts.

Hannah sighed. Blast her dad-gummed pride! Why was she so quick to take offense! Why did she have such unruly passions? She had hoped to grow up to be just like Mama, but now she was convinced there was not a chance in a million of that ever happening, not unless the Lord performed a miracle similar to the casting out of the nine demons from one boy.

A few weeks ago, Papa had bought Mama a caroche. He had driven it into the farmyard with a flourish, looking more like a triumphant little boy than a dignified businessman.

"Julia," he had said, smiling happily at his wife, "I have brought you the finest carriage in the Territory of Utah!"

Hannah knew Mama better than Papa did, for she had looked at the magnificent conveyance and thought, "Not a chance! Mama will never keep it."

For a foolish minute Hannah had indulged in the fantasy of driving up to the Big House in splendor. Wouldn't everyone stare!

Mama, of course, had no such fantasies. "People know who you are and what you are soon enough," she often told her daughters. "Fancy clothes, money, possessions won't fool anyone. The things that make a person worthwhile cannot be bought or pretended."

"William, dear," Mama said quietly, "this buggy is much too grand and impractical for us at the farm. If you want to improve our transportation, a new wagon would be a great blessing."

Papa, as always, had done exactly as Mama asked. He had taken the carriage to the Big House and bought Mama a fine new wagon. Papa would have given Mama anything in this world within his power. It was just that Mama never asked for things for herself.

So now the town family rode in Mama's caroche. The lost carriage had become just one more symbol of everything that rubbed Hannah the wrong way about the inequities in the family.

The new wagon was the best that money could buy. It had strong springs, beautifully painted wheels, comfortable seats, and a leather hood for inclement weather. "So what?" Hannah could not help muttering to herself. "It is still nothing but a wagon, and all the fancy geegaws in the world cannot change a farm wagon into a city carriage any more than all the wishes in the world can change a farm girl into a society lady."

9

CHAPTER TWO

"Han-*nah!*" Mama's voice had grown sharper. Recognizing that it was inevitable, Hannah stood up and waved in capitulation. Her mother saw her across the corn and beckoned for her to hurry.

Hannah knew her mother was too tired to walk across the field. The two of them had worked all morning finishing up the laundry to take into town. Mama had been exhausted when they folded the last batch and had needed to lie down to rest.

As she walked through the corn toward her mother, Hannah felt a jolt of awareness and a sudden realization that her mother had seemed tired for weeks. Mama's usual inexhaustible energy and quick motions had become subdued and almost listless in the past days.

"Even tired," Hannah mused, "Mama gets more work done in a day than any two other women I know." It was a pleasant thought because Hannah knew she was a hard worker as well, and it was one of the few ways in which she was like her mother.

She began to feel a little better.

She and Mama had done all the laundry for the Childress family—both the city and the farm households—

for as long as Hannah could remember. When Hannah was only six years old, Mama had taught her how to put huge batches of laundry through two sudsings, two hot rinses, one cold rinse, a blue rinse, and a final bath of heavy starch. When she got older Hannah helped with boiling the stubborn white things.

Every Monday afternoon of Hannah's life since she could remember, the Childress family's laundry was hung from the vast network of clotheslines in the wash yard at the farm. Year after year, week in, week out, the sparkling white clothes danced in the strong canyon winds. The scent of mountains and meadows was dried in every fold. Then, every Tuesday, Hannah and her mother ironed the starched clothes till they were smooth as satin and crisp as summer air.

This arrangement, begun before Hannah's birth, was an efficient trade of specialties between the branches of the family. The laundry was done at the farm because of the wash sheds, hanging yards, and the freshness of the country air. In return, all of the family baking was produced in the kitchens at the Big House in Ogden.

Every Monday morning someone from town drove a wagon out to the Riverdale farm to deliver the dirty laundry in bulging sacks. Every Tuesday afternoon, someone from the farm drove a wagon back to town and delivered the batch of finished washing to the Big House. The farm wagon was then stacked with freshly baked bread, cakes, cookies, pies, preserves, and cinnamon rolls—enough for the week for everyone at the farm, including the resident laborers and tenant families.

This long-standing arrangement was companionable and practical. Julia Childress, with her pragmatic and efficient mind, had instigated it years ago. She liked doing laundry and was very good at it, but she did not like to cook.

The truth was, Julia was a terrible cook. As a girl in her ancestral estate in the Cotswolds, she had never even seen the kitchens. The kitchens and pantries were the servants' domain, beneath an aristocrat's regard. Julia, in her privileged and protected childhood, had never given a thought to the process by which food appeared in the formal dining room of her family's estate.

When Julia forsook her childhood home and inheritance to journey alone to Utah, she still had no experience preparing food during the months while she sailed across the sea and walked across the plains. By the time she had access to her first kitchen, she had become used to having no interest in the process of cooking.

It had been a true delight and some relief to Julia when her younger daughter, Eliza, had shown an eager interest in cooking. Now, at sixteen, Eliza was a fine hand in the kitchen and had assumed all responsibility for food preparation on the farm.

The delegation of responsibilities was comfortable for everyone. All the cooking at the farm, except for the baking from the Big House, was done competently and happily by Eliza because, unlike her mother and older sister, she did not like to do laundry. Everyone was happy in their chosen task.

Hannah knew the back of the wagon was stacked with the snowy white mounds of clean linens they had laundered. When they finally arrived at the house on Childress Avenue, the waiting family would converge on the laundry baskets. Sisters, aunts, cousins, and daughters would carry everything into the Big House to put it neatly away.

The aunts would snap white damask tablecloths over long tables in the upstairs ballroom in preparation for the coming banquet. The house would have a delicious smell. Great kettles, roasting pans, and work tables would be groaning with food in the steamy kitchen on the first floor.

All the beds would be made up with fresh, billowing sheets, the feather ticks plumped, and the fat pillows stuffed into delicately embroidered cases as white and smooth as satin.

Clean towels would be placed under the washstands. Clothes chests would be filled with dazzling white shirts and blouses, petticoats, and camisoles. The arrival of the linens would be the final touch, and then everything would be ready for the gala event.

"So," Hannah thought, "why can't I just grit my teeth and go enjoy it?"

Large family gatherings at the Big House had been happening all of Hannah's young life, but this time Papa was doing everything in his power to make this week an unforgettable celebration for the visit of Uncle Abner.

Abner Childress was Papa's youngest brother, and he and his family had made the arduous trip down from Idaho where they were settling some of the wildest land in the West—way up by the Continental Divide on the Salmon River. After years of struggle, Uncle Abner had finally established a small fort, a sawmill, and a grazing herd, even though he had been plagued by ferocious weather and equally ferocious Indians. It was almost a miracle that he and his family were still alive.

Papa had not seen his youngest brother for five years, and Hannah knew he wanted this party to express all the love and lonesomeness he felt for his brave brother.

Papa's intense love for every member of his family filled him with an abiding desire to find ways to show that love. Even with the large numbers of his progeny and extended relations, no one in his family ever felt cheated or slighted in his affection. He seemed to have enough love to go around. As a matter of fact, Hannah had an unacknowledged hunch that every one of Papa's children thought he or she was his favorite.

It was hard not to get caught up in the enthusiasm of Papa's affections. He never thought about himself. His whole concern was focused on making others happy.

"I'll never be as saintly as Mama, but I could try hard to be as loving as Papa," Hannah thought. "My soul is full of fiery emotions. I have a burning heart like his. I just need to turn it in better ways."

Thinking of her father and how disappointed he would be if he knew how much his daughter was resisting attending his gala, Hannah felt genuinely remorseful. She began to run, brushing the chaff and dust from her skirts, heading toward her mother, who was standing quietly by the wagon.

Mama was wearing the neat brown coat and felt hat trimmed with pheasant feathers that she had worn for as long as Hannah could remember. Although the hat and coat were old, Mama still looked strikingly beautiful.

Everything about Hannah's mother looked finished and perfect. It was the gift of serenity that Mama had. Hannah did not believe she would ever manage to be serene if she lived to be a hundred—she was too full of untidy heaps of wants and wanting, too full of turbulent thoughts and impassioned, half-understood yearnings, ambitions, and feelings. No, Hannah could not imagine finding out what serenity felt like. Not ever, ever, ever.

"I don't even *look* like I'm Mama's daughter!" Hannah thought with resignation as she drew up, panting, in front of her waiting mother. Instead of looking like a beautiful, delicate rose, as her mother did, Hannah reckoned she looked more like one of those rangy sunflowers at the back of the wash yard—tall and awkward, with petals hanging every which way, always turning to the left and right, never twice the same in a single day. Restless, skinny, and too brightly colored.

"There you are, my dear," Mama said wearily as Hannah rushed out of the cornstalks. "About time! The wagon is packed, and we have been waiting for more than an hour. Didn't you hear me calling?"

Hannah nodded sullenly and moved toward the waiting wagon.

"Look at you!" her mother said, exasperation quickening her tired voice. "Your hair is blown to kingdom come, and your shoes are dusty. What will Papa think of me? He will think I cannot get my own child ready for a party!"

Hannah's exasperation rose hotly to match her mother's. "I do not have *any* desire to go to this party, as you well know. And I am not a child! I am of an age to have gotten myself ready—and everyone can just take me or leave me as I am!" She laughed drily. "I wish you *would* leave me."

Her mother was not amused. "Is all this to-do over the dress you are wearing, Hannah?" Disappointment weighted Mama's voice. "Aunt Adelaide's dress looks very fine on you, especially since I added the Belgian lace collar. Adelaide never even got to wear the dress, and the fabric was very expensive and much too good to waste. Surely you couldn't expect when you have a dress that is perfectly suitable that we should ask Papa to spend money on a new gown? Money that could be far better spent on the needy or on missionary service? To squander money in such unnecessary extravagance would make us poor stewards to the Lord indeed."

Hannah was tired of thinking and talking about the whole subject. "I do not think that my going to a party in

15

one of Aunt Adelaide's old dresses is of the slightest interest to the Lord, let alone pleasing to Him!" she snapped. "And I certainly don't think He'd object if I had a real party dress of my own for once—without my feeling guilty. After all, I am eighteen years old, Mama."

"All the more reason you should understand such things, dear Hannah," Mama said quietly. "When will you learn that worldly things are not the measure of a woman? I know I am right in this. Once I had everything the world had to offer, and I learned it means nothing when compared to the things of eternal value."

"Well," Hannah muttered petulantly, before she could pause to consider her words, "I'd like the chance to find out such things on my own! At least you had the chance when you were young to wear beautiful clothes. Look at this lace collar you brought from England! That is how *you* were dressed when you were a young woman—beautifully! In luxury!"

Shaking her head and compressing her lips in silent reprimand at Hannah's outburst, Mama walked quickly toward the wagon where Eliza was sitting holding the reins and looking more impatient than Mama.

"Quit complaining and get in the wagon, Hannah," Eliza's voice was tremendously annoyed. "We've been waiting for ages and ages, and everyone at the Big House is going to be mad at us for being late. You are acting like you have a bee in your petticoat. What the blazes is wrong with you, Hannah?"

Hannah stepped on the iron foot rest, threw her long leg over the side of the wagon bed, and in one angry, graceful motion dived into the rear of the wagon and buried herself in the laundry.

"What's wrong with you, Liza?" she retorted. "If Papa

heard you swearing, he'd give you a tongue-blistering you wouldn't soon forget."

"'Blazes' is not swearing!" Eliza asserted. "It is what Miss Eldredge calls vernacular speech."

"'Blazes' is just a disguised way of saying 'hell,' because it stands for the fires of damnation, and if 'hell' isn't swearing, I don't know what is! So, you and Miss Eldredge can just keep pretending its 'vernacular,' but everyone who knows anything knows you're swearing," Hannah countered crossly.

"Girls!" Mama said, her voice sounding tired and annoyed. "I do not want to drive all the way to Ogden listening to you quarrel. Eliza, Hannah is right. You should maintain more ladylike speech. And Hannah, don't take your bad temper out on your sister."

Hannah subsided against a bundle of laundry and closed her eyes. She knew she probably should have taken the reins, but the horses knew the way to town by heart and she felt too upset to offer to drive instead of her mother.

After a few minutes, as the plodding of the horses calmed her down, Hannah looked up at her mother's back. For some reason her heart gave a little lurch of fear. The way Mama was sitting, with her shoulders bowed and her head down, made her look frail, tired, and old beyond her years. Hannah trembled at a sudden peculiar realization of how small and alone her mother seemed.

"Let me drive, Mama," Hannah cried, springing up with quick remorse.

"Oh, would you, dear?" Mama turned with a relieved smile. "I think I should like to lie down for a while." Mama pressed her hands against the small of her back and handed over the reins as Hannah clambered into the front seat.

Mama soon fell asleep in the back of the wagon while Hannah and Eliza, their brief quarrel spent, talked quietly

17

of sisterly things and finally were silent, thinking their own separate thoughts, as the sturdy horses plodded toward town.

By midafternoon the team turned, clip-clopping down Childress Avenue, a wide street lined with young elms that led to the spreading lawns of their father's town home.

The sisters could see, even a block away, that members of the family were already gathered on the broad front porch, waiting. One of their nephews spied them. It was Tommy, their half-sister Anne's five-year old. Cries of welcome rang out, and a parade of children came whooping and hollering toward the wagon. Even Hannah in her dowdy dress felt her heart lift as the troop of children ran toward them. After all, this was her family, and though they caused her pain and frustration, still, when all was said and done, she loved them with all the intensity of her impulsive, unbridled heart.

CHAPTER THREE

Their arrival at the Big House was both better and worse than Hannah had anticipated. After the flurry of hugs and kisses and unloading the laundry baskets, her oldest half-sister, Anne, came over to greet her.

"You get prettier every time I see you." Anne's smile was just like her mother's, Aunt Adelaide's, had been: kind, cool, and distant. Anne's compliment was marred by the fact that she always said the same words to Hannah, and the phrasing left the unspoken implication that Hannah had a long way to go before she could be told straightforwardly, "You look pretty."

Anne was small, like her deceased mother, and rather colorless, as though her hair, skin, and eyes had been painted from a single beige palette. Her features were finely chiseled, and the result was what Papa called "a pleasing appearance."

Anne was subdued and her voice quiet and controlled, but her appearance was deceptive, because, in spite of her tiny size, Anne was a woman of daunting efficiency and strong opinions. With determination, duty, and a powerful sense of her rightful place, she had ruled her father's Ogden home with an iron hand since her mother's death.

When Julia had declined to live full-time in the Big House, Anne, with her husband, Cyrus, and their five children in tow, had made the unilateral decision to move in to take care of Papa, his household, and the innumerable visitors, both relatives and guests, that flowed through the doors of the Childress mansion.

Typically, Anne had consulted no one about the decision—not her father, and certainly not her husband. Because Julia had chosen to remain on the farm in Riverdale, Anne felt it was her duty to look after her father's household in Ogden. Anne always did her duty as she saw it.

Cyrus, Anne's patient husband, was a lawyer who handled Papa's business dealings. He and Papa got along well, so the unusual household arrangement worked. The problem for Hannah was that the arrangement made her feel like Anne's guest when she came into town to stay with Papa. "After all," Hannah thought irritably, "we are really just two sisters in our father's home. I belong here as much as she does!"

Hannah supposed she resented Anne's acting as if Papa's house belonged to her and her family. Mama would tell Hannah she was acting like a cat with its tail hanging out, waiting for someone to step on it. "You are looking to take offense," her mother admonished her, with a warning shake of her head.

But it was true. Anne's family occupied the Big House as if they owned it. Anne's two oldest children were away from home, one on a mission and the other at school in Salt Lake, but Anne's three younger children were at home.

Anne's son Edgar was nineteen, short and arrogant and with a cutting wit. He was preparing to leave on a mission, although he was hardly Hannah's idea of a humble, sweet missionary. She liked sparring with Edgar verbally. She was one of the few people who were a match for his quick tongue, but she found his air of arrogant superiority unworthy of him.

Through the years she and Edgar had developed a genuine fondness for each other in spite of their differences, and Hannah knew, if she were honest with herself, that she was going to miss him when he left.

Five-year-old Tommy was Anne's baby. The little boy was growing up surrounded by love, and he greeted the world with open, eager joy. Hannah loved Tommy by far the most of all her nieces, nephews, and cousins.

The real thorn in Hannah's side—the one that never seemed to lose its sharpness—was Anne's daughter Constance, who was Hannah's age and more arrogant than Edgar, if that was possible. Ever since Constance had taken up residence in the Big House, Hannah had found it difficult to be happy there.

Constance and Edgar seemed to bask in the knowledge that their grandfather and their father were two of the leading citizens of the newly emerging city of Ogden. This assumption of entitlement gave Constance and Edgar the conviction that they were part of a privileged caste, as though they had had some kind of royal and personal anointing.

Their unspoken sense of superiority was especially maddening to Hannah because Papa was *her* father, not theirs. It frustrated Hannah no end to be treated on a par with Constance just because of the similarity of their ages. After all, Hannah belonged to a totally different generation of the family. If there was any aristocracy of birth, it was certainly Hannah's in succession, rather than Constance's.

The whole situation of family relationships was confusing and irritating at the same time.

When Anne spoke to Hannah in motherly tones,

Hannah felt it was inappropriate and abrasive rather than endearing. Anne's maternal airs made it hard for Hannah to believe that Anne even acknowledged that they were sisters. Hannah longed for the smallest indication of equality from her older sister, but each encounter left her feeling daunted.

"Now run along, Hannah dear, and find Constance and the other youngsters. I think they are all up in the ballroom hanging grapevine garlands," Anne said, giving Hannah a quick, dismissive kiss on the cheek. As Anne turned back to her work, she saw Julia lifting a laundry basket from the wagon.

With a cry of consternation she ran over to take the laundry basket from Julia's hands. "You mustn't!" she exclaimed. "You know that's too heavy for you."

Julia Childress smiled, and her beautiful face was touched with a sudden flush of pink. "Now, Annie," she murmured self-consciously, "don't make such a fuss. I am perfectly capable of carrying the laundry."

Hannah found herself thinking about the oddness of that interchange as she climbed the porch stairs. It was always a shock to be reminded that Mama and Anne were almost the same age—both in their early forties. Because of her abundant auburn hair, slender waist, and china-pink skin, Mama actually looked younger than Anne.

The two women had respect for each other, but their natures were fundamentally different and their respective roles in the family so complicated that it was hard to think of them being close. Yet Anne's voice had been filled with genuine concern, and Mama had definitely been embarrassed. What did it all mean? Being at the Big House seemed to evoke all kinds of unknown questions and unexpected emotions in Hannah. It was like coming out of a safe, protective shell into a kaleidoscope.

As Hannah walked up the broad, familiar staircase, trailing her hand on the polished mahogany banister, she caught sight of a pair of shoes descending from the third-floor ballroom on the steps above her. In a moment the person wearing the shoes came into view, and with a resigned sigh, Hannah realized her premonitions about the party being a nightmare had come true.

The splendid shoes belonged to Constance. No one else.

"Wouldn't you just know it?" Hannah groaned inwardly. Constance's feet were feminine and tiny, and they were shod in the prettiest little shoes Hannah had ever seen. They were dancing slippers, made of lavender silk to match the ruffled and bustled grandeur of Constance's dress. Buttoned with shiny jets, the dainty shoes had toes of black patent leather topped with velvet bows.

"They are ridiculous shoes," Hannah thought sadly, but they were ridiculously wonderful, and they had the immediate power to make her feel clumsy and stodgy.

She could not bear to look down at the well-worn, side-buttoned black boots that had walked more miles in a week than Constance did in a year—in a lifetime. It was hopeless. Not even Mama's beautiful lace collar could begin to make up for all of Hannah's glaring fashion deficiencies in the face of Constance's splendor.

"Well, if it isn't 'Aunt' Hannah," Constance said, not unkindly. "We thought you were supposed to arrive hours ago."

"Well, if it isn't 'Niece' Constance," Hannah responded with an attempt at a smile. "We're late because we had to finish up the last of that monstrous laundry. What did all of you city folk do? Empty every cupboard and closet? I declare, I didn't know we owned so much washable stuff!"

"It is hardly 'stuff'!" Constance sniffed. "Some of those linens and embroideries have been kept under lock and key

23

for a decade. They were things Grandpapa's mother had owned in Connecticut. Grandpapa brought them across the plains. Some of those linens are generations old. Ma says they are very valuable—heirlooms. I hope you and your mother realized how precious they were and were very careful washing them."

Hannah frowned. "Constance," she said with an edge in her voice, "it's my 'stuff,' too. Remember? Papa and Mama are married to each other, and I am their daughter. Papa's stuff is *our* stuff. Mama's and mine. Of course we were careful laundering it! But even if we weren't, we wouldn't have to answer to you about it."

Constance had the grace to recognize Hannah's rebuke. She dropped her eyes and smoothed the skirt of her beautiful dress with her hands. "Well," she said, recovering the sprightly tone that gave her a carefree and charming air, "sorry. I guess I'd better run down and get the rest of the grape twinings. The ballroom is going to look grand when we're finished decorating."

Continuing up the stairs, Hannah's feet lagged. She regretted that she had let herself be goaded into sharp words. This whole situation was bringing out the worst in her, and she had no desire to join the cluster of family members that would be in the ballroom laughing and gossiping. She knew everyone would be decked out in town finery, like Constance's, and they would be talking about their town friends, whom Hannah did not know. Things were bound to get worse.

"Hannah!" Papa's voice rang with delight. He was walking out of his study at the top of the stairs and spied her. "My precious girl! I am so happy to see you. Where's your dear Mama? Is she tired from the trip?"

Again that odd concern about Mama's health and

well-being—Mama, who was so healthy that Hannah could not remember a day of sickness in her mother's life.

"Maybe she is a little tired, Papa," Hannah said, kissing her father with enthusiasm. "The laundry was huge! She's downstairs with Anne. It is so good to see you! Have Uncle Abner and his family arrived yet?"

Papa gave her a resounding hug. "They are staying at Anne and Cyrus's old house. Gives them a little more privacy. They'll be up here shortly—in time for visiting with the family before the guests arrive for dinner and dancing. Uncle Abner is the picture of health, and his family is growing like a garden around him. Oh, the joys of children!"

With beaming pride, Papa gave Hannah a smiling appraisal. "My beautiful Hannah. You are growing into a magnificent flower before my very eyes. Soon you will grow up and leave me. What shall I do without my little girl?"

Blushing with happiness, Hannah laughed. "Papa, I will always be your little girl. Although a very *tall* little girl, I'm afraid. If I don't stop growing, you are going to think you spawned a young giraffe instead of a daughter."

William Childress looked at the glowing girl in front of him. She was taller than most young women of her age, but the height gave her a regal splendor. Her black hair curled around her smooth forehead and set off the crackling, dark eyes under brows as lovely as raven wings. Her skin was the color of pink-tinged ivory, and her lips were full and red. Every bone in her face was molded with a fineness and beauty that grew more lovely as she matured. The whole effect was one of presence and such impressive loveliness that it amazed him to realize that his daughter did not have any idea how remarkably beautiful she was.

"You get that wonderful height from your Mama's father," Papa said with a smile. "He was an aristocrat, and you show the splendor of his fine bloodline. You are a true thoroughbred."

With a gentle pat on her shoulder, Papa walked past her and hurried down the stairs. "Now I must go find your Mama, but I want you to come to my study as soon as you have finished decorating the ballroom. I have a little surprise for you." Papa gave her a conspiratorial smile and vanished around the landing.

Feeling her spirits refreshed as they always were in her father's presence, Hannah ran up the remaining flight of stairs and burst into the ballroom. "What's going on up here?" she called merrily to the cluster of young people who were busily twining grapevines with wheat, pyracantha berries, and autumn leaves. Everyone turned at the sound of her voice and ran to greet her, laughing as one of the cousins draped a piece of autumn garland around her neck.

The ballroom was a lofty room, filling the third floor of the great house. The room was finished with pine moldings painted dark to simulate mahogany and an oak hardwood floor. Windows topped by fanlights were at each end.

With its unobstructed expanse, the room was used by the family, by the church, and by the community for dances, holidays, banquets, meetings, dramas, and evening musical programs. At one end of the spacious room was a raised platform that could be used as a stage.

"About time you got here, Hannah," Edgar drawled. "We had about given you up for lost and thought we might have to send a rescue party for you."

"I do not need rescuing," Hannah retorted, "but this room certainly does! Dinner's due to be served in two hours, and look at these decorations! This place is a mess."

It was true. The festive autumn garland was snaked

across the floor, half-finished, looking sparse and disheveled.

Betsy, a tender seven-year-old cousin, looked up at Hannah, and a tear trembled in her eye. "We've been waiting for you, Hannah. You always know how to make things work right. We haven't even figured out how to hang this thing."

With a laugh, Uncle Bob's son Jacob said, "Hanging's probably too good for it, anyway!"

Hannah smiled. At least when she was asked to work, she was on ground that was familiar and comfortable. There was a job to be done, and one thing she was good at was getting things done. This decorating project obviously needed firm leadership and organization.

Without hesitating, she started giving orders. "You boys run out to the sedge patch next to the pasture and cut two bushels of long, dry raffia. We'll use it to tie bows around the garland, and then we will have something to hook up to the molding."

She turned to a group of young girls. "I saw masses of dried statice and hydrangea in the field behind the kitchen garden. Get shears and a laundry basket and harvest a bundle for us. The purple flowers will add such nice color. Now hurry. We are running out of time."

Within minutes Hannah had everyone doing a specific task. They twisted the vines and placed nosegays of dried flowers at regular intervals. The statice and raffia proved to be a great hit, and the splendid bows of dried grass gave a full look to the graceful vine, as well as providing a means of attaching it to the nails concealed in the decorative moldings.

As the harvest garland took shape, the room took on a festive beauty, and when the group of young decorators stood back to admire their handiwork, there was a moment of pleasant unity and happy accomplishment. Even Hannah felt pleased. She stooped and kissed the nearest child and then walked over to Anne, who had just entered the room with an armful of tablecloths for the buffet tables.

A dumbwaiter from the kitchens would bring up the food, fresh and hot, and the banquet would be placed directly on the tables without anyone having to carry the heavy serving dishes up three flights of stairs. It was a convenient system and perfect for the big meals required at the family gatherings.

"Would you like me to help you, Anne?" Hannah asked. "I'd be happy to set tables."

"No, no, dear," Anne said. "The garlands look lovely. Thank you for getting that job finished. The aunts will be up in a few minutes to work on fixing the tables, so you have plenty of time to go and get yourself all fancied up for the party. We've got a lot of fine young men from the town coming for the dancing, and you'll want to catch somebody's eye, I know. You are getting to that age."

Anne smiled indulgently and added, "Constance is so excited she can hardly wait for the guests to start arriving. I'm sure she's in her room primping right now—has been since dawn this morning. So run along and get yourself dressed, Hannah. You've got plenty of time."

Hannah felt all the happy feelings rush out of her and a hard lump lodge in her stomach. "I am already ready for the dance, Anne," she said coldly. "This is my party dress."

Anne raised her eyebrows. "If you say so, dear, and very nice it is." Anne gave a distracted shake of her head and walked away toward the tables. "Well, then, run down and visit with Papa. He said he wants to see you about something. Dinner will start at five-thirty."

Knowing she had been dismissed, Hannah walked out of the ballroom and down the stairs toward her father's study on the second floor.

CHAPTER FOUR

Julia had never felt more tired in her life. She supposed the hard morning of doing the laundry, the upset of Hannah's being so obstinate about the party, and the long drive to town had combined to use up all of her energy. She walked into William's large bedroom with its carpet of deep maroon and its high bed made of carved black walnut. The headboard was almost eight feet tall, with an elaborate finial top, and roses carved in heavy clusters. It looked more like a throne than a bed.

At the foot of the bed was a Chippendale sofa with horsehair upholstery. Next to the bed were two large walnut nightstands with marble tops. William's dresser was a highboy made from the finest-grained woods. His enormous armoire stood on the opposite wall, tall enough and deep enough for a committee of three men in top hats to hold a meeting.

Above William's writing table was a portrait of Brigham Young, William's friend and the beloved prophet of the Church. Julia always smiled at the picture because it could not have completely escaped William's notice that he and the prophet looked very much alike.

She had come into the room to put sheets and towels

in the linen press by the window, but as she turned to leave the room, exhaustion invaded her limbs. With a sigh she walked across the carpet and lay down on the red-work coverlet. William's pillow was full and soft under her cheek, and she thought in that fuzzy moment before sleep overtook her that this was really her bed as much as William's, so she need not worry if she mussed it.

"I'll only rest for a moment," she told herself, "and then I'll get back to the kitchen and help with dinner." The words trailed away in her mind, and she slept.

When William hurried into the bedroom to change into his frock coat for the evening guests, he stopped in surprise as he caught sight of Julia asleep on the coverlet. With a tender smile he tiptoed quietly to the chair at the bedside and sat down. He did not make any unnecessary motions in case the rustle of his clothing or a creak of the chair might waken her.

Although he yearned to reach out and stroke her face or touch her hand, he restrained himself. Instead, he sat a few inches from her and caressed her with his eyes, as if he had stumbled on a priceless treasure and was so transfixed by the unexpected wonder of his good fortune that he could not move or speak but only stand and stare to reassure himself that it was not just an illusion.

In her sleep Julia looked as young and beautiful to him as she had that day almost twenty years before when he had first seen her standing, lost and alone, in the tithing yard. He sat contentedly, studying his wife's lovely face, and he let his memory drift back through the years to that long ago morning when he had found Julia Hanford shivering in the snow-laden wind. She had nothing but a thin woolen shawl and her fine-woven poplin dress to shield her from the cold blast of Utah's winter. For nearly four months through the long summer she had been traveling by ox-cart in a company of Saints along the Mormon Trail from Iowa.

It had been almost ten years since the first wagon trains had entered the Salt Lake Valley, and by now the Mormon Trail had become a highway worn deep and wide by the thousands of wagons and tramping feet that had traveled its length.

As William reflected on the journey Julia had made, he recalled that he himself had made the round-trip journey several times in the years since his arrival in the Salt Lake Valley in 1848. He had returned to Connecticut for the wagonloads of goods that had begun his successful mer-chandise stores. He had also helped hundreds of others to immigrate to the valleys of Utah. Since boyhood he had been filled with energy and enthusiasm and a taste for travel and challenge. Those had been great days.

When Julia made the journey a decade after the first pioneers had broken the trail along the entire distance from Iowa to Utah, the roadway was punctuated by wagons going to and coming from Utah with goods and proffered assistance. The traffic was considerable through the sum-mer months. Not like the early days, William remembered, when sometimes his company had traveled for days without sight of another living soul, except perhaps the Indians, who watched always with despairing eyes.

Certainly the trek had become easier, though it was still hazardous, but it was not the bleak, dangerous, and lonely route through untried wilderness that it had been for the original sojourners. For young Julia, however, the passage had been all of those hard things—bleak and dangerous and lonely—because she was alone and penniless and had to earn her keep in the company of the Saints by any means possible. Her journey of faith had offered her a precarious existence at best and an even more uncertain future.

Most of the time she had been able to make herself useful in the wagon company by tending and teaching the children, gathering food, herding milk cattle, and turning her hand to any task, no matter how demeaning or difficult. As a result of her willing and untiring labors, she had been given food, shelter, and friendship by the other members of the company but in a haphazard and uneven way. Even though she had never gone hungry or been left to sleep on the bare ground, she had felt the shadow of those possibilities hanging over her for the entire distance across the plains.

When the wagon company disbanded from the tithing yard at journey's end in Ogden, Julia had said her farewells to those with whom she had become acquainted. One by one she watched her traveling companions filter off to the company of relatives or to other planned destinations. At the end of the day Julia stood alone, a small, delicate young woman with hair the color of the setting sun and a face as fine as bisque china. Her calm brown eyes surveyed the empty yard, and her controlled expression did not betray the panic and fear she was feeling inside.

"What is to become of me?" Julia had felt the question like a sword burning through her heart as she looked around the empty yard and at the bleak mountains that towered in the background. She thought she could hear her father laughing in triumph, far away in England, as though he could see her predicament and relished the fact that his dire predictions had come true. "I told you this would happen to you, my fine girl. This is what your mad, fanatic faith has brought you—penury, servitude, and beggary. Well, you can have your rebellious ways, and be damned! I wash my hands of you forever."

Since her baptism into the Church, she had thought no further than to follow her faith to Utah. Now that she had arrived in Zion, she had no plans, no friends, and no apparent options. Over and over again on this long journey, she had regretted her privileged upbringing and the ignorance of real life it had given her. No one with an ounce of practical experience or knowledge would have ended up in the quandary in which she now stood: friendless, penniless, unskilled, and alone. Why had she not realized that careful planning would be required to make a complete new life for herself?

Julia had slumped down on a nearby flour barrel and shut her eyes, overcome with homesickness and fear. She leaned her head against the shed where the tithing vegetables were stored. Shivering inside her shawl and chilled to the bone, she allowed herself the indulgence, for the first time in months, to think of England and her childhood home at Marymont Chase, the family's ancestral estate in the Cotswolds.

It had been on just such a wintry day as this, Julia remembered, with snow slashing against the windows in the grand salon at Marymont. She had been sitting by the fire roaring in the Georgian fireplace. Her brother, Harold, Viscount Hanford, had come in with steam rising from the shoulders of his caped coat. A swirl of cold air emanated from him as he brought the winter day into the warm, glowing room in the folds of his cloak and the creases of his hat and riding boots.

He stood in front of the fireplace, rubbing his freezing hands and laughing at his sister. "You ought to have come to chapel with me, Julia," he chided her. "You missed quite a sermon!"

"I doubt that Reverend White has ever given a sermon I would regret missing, Harold," Julia responded with quick humor. "I was actually very happy to have a touch of the grippe so that I could excuse myself from Reverend White's inspired tedium."

"Well, there you have it," Harold responded, looking like the cat that ate the cream. "You see, Reverend White did not give the sermon! And, I tell you, the sermon was astonishing! It was given by an American preacher, of all things. An American in a top hat and a black suit who is a follower of some new American religion. Our Reverend Doctor White invited the foreigner to give us a sermon. It was quite the spectacle, and you, my dear sister, missed the whole of it because of your obviously bogus claim of having the grippe."

Julia put down her book and looked at her handsome, rugged brother. He would be the next Earl of Marymont, and he would be a very good one indeed. Harold had a winning way about him.

Her brother had only one more year before his graduation from Cambridge, and he was already accepting more responsibility with the tenant farmers and the family businesses when he was home on holidays. For Julia, though, there were still precious times when she could see traces of the young boy he had been—the older brother who had teased her unmercifully—but who had been her dearest childhood friend.

"Papa will be scandalized!" Julia laughed. "First of all he will be scandalized because Reverend White let an apostate speak from his pulpit, but, more disastrously, he will be scandalized because the man's sermon was entertaining! I think Papa believes there is an absolute rule against anyone enjoying a church meeting."

Harold grinned. "You're too hard on Papa, Julia. Just because he is a serious man and insists that we take our position as stewards of this estate as a responsibility from God himself does not mean that Papa does not have true and tender emotions. He is a man of absolute probity and duty."

"I know," Julia replied soberly. "I'm sorry if I spoke lightly of Father. I would not be disrespectful or hurt him for the world. I was trying to be amusing, and I spoke thoughtlessly."

Harold threw down his coat on a nearby chair, and the footman who had been standing unobtrusively by the door picked up the garment and removed it to the clothespress in the anteroom. Sitting down next to Julia, Harold stretched his boots toward the warmth of the fire and nodded his head.

"We are blessed in our parents, Julia. They are conscious of their duty, and they have taught us well. To be well-born requires that we spend our lives in service to those who are dependent upon us. If sometimes our parents seem rigid and unbending, it is only because they are so aware of their responsibilities to others and to the Lord. They expect us to be the same."

The brother and sister sat quietly for a few moments in the enormous room. The only sound was the snapping of the dry, burning logs in the fire and the rattle of the winter wind against the windows.

"Do you remember when we were little, Harold?" Julia said softly. "I can remember picnics on the lawn and riding on Papa's shoulders and Mama laughing and sitting in the swing. But the years seem to have changed them. They have become so serious and stern. Will that happen to us, too?"

With a shrug Harold contemplated the roaring fire. "I suspect life is a serious thing, Julia," he said. "Papa says the Lord is a stern taskmaster, and we must live above reproach."

"Then you shall certainly have to become serious,

Harold. You shall have to stop teasing me, my dear brother, and serve me by being sympathetic about my sniffles and bringing me hot tea!" Julia challenged playfully.

"I have no intention of being that much above reproach!" Harold retorted. "Besides, I am going for a ride before the sun sets. In truth, dear sister, the gentleman who spoke in church today gave me much to contemplate. In all seriousness, I would like to be alone to ponder on his words."

A shadow of premonition caused Julia to shudder, and she sat up suddenly, with a frown of concern. "Don't go riding, Harold," she admonished, looking out at the flurries of snow and the gray afternoon light. "It is so cold and wet. Stay by the fire and keep me company. You can discuss your thoughts with me. We can ponder together."

Harold hesitated and she thought she had convinced him, but then he jumped to his feet and hurried to the door, calling for his coat and his horse.

"I shall think alone first, and then, when I return from my ride, we shall talk about what I have heard and thought about this American preacher."

In a whirl of motion and a blast of cold air from the front door, Harold was gone. Julia heard the clatter of his horse's hooves on the paving stones in the front courtyard, and then the gray afternoon descended once again.

They found her brother's body long after dark. His horse had returned at twilight, riderless, and the farm laborers and tenant farmers, dressed in their rumpled woolen coats, with caps, gloves and scarves warding off the freezing wind, had taken their lanterns and followed the horse's tracks across the snow-dusted fields until they came to the low rock fence where the horse had fallen on an ice slick and thrown Harold across the stones. His neck was cleanly broken.

Not a day had passed since that Julia had not thought of her brother's smiling, handsome face. It had seemed to her on that cold winter day that the world had become forever less bright without Harold.

Lord and Lady Hanford believed that mourning should be a private, individual matter, with no public display of any kind. Self-discipline, faith, and tradition required that no one should speak of Harold aloud or mention his death. It was the most cruel ritual of aristocratic behavior that Julia had ever experienced.

Every morning and evening the three of them—the last of the Hanfords—sat in the massive dining hall at the ancient banquet table with its elaborate place settings and golden service. Parents and daughter sat in their own agonized solitude, speaking in courteous tones of the weather, the servants, the events of the day. Most of each meal was passed in silence as their heavy hearts strained to speak of the massive burden of grief. But not one word was uttered.

As the weeks went by, and the earth began to melt into spring, Julia felt she could not bear another day of this interminable agony of silent suffering. The heavy mourning in her heart was like a wild beast tearing her apart. Her father and mother spent hours each day kneeling in their private chapel, apparently seeking private solace. Julia had tried to reach God in the same way, but her prayers rang hollow and empty.

If there was a God, how could he have been so cruel as to take the life of a young man like Harold, who was so good and fine and sought only to serve Him? Julia could not quiet the questions and suffering in her heart and mind.

Trapped in loss and the remorseless grip of doubt and confusion, Julia finally decided to break the unwritten law of silent grief. She determined that she would go to the Reverend White and seek spiritual guidance to help her find comfort and faith. Not wanting her parents to know she was not strong enough to maintain the discipline of silence, Julia waited until a late afternoon after her parents left for their annual fortnight's stay at their lodge at Tillhurst Farm, a day's journey away.

Shyly, and with a guilty sense of doing something of which her parents would not approve, Julia approached the rectory, the home on the Marymont grounds where the resident clergyman, Doctor White, lived with his small family. She felt she would die if she could not speak aloud of her pain and her questions about Harold's death. Her only hope was the Reverend White. Surely he could explain to her what had become of Harold's soul, what possibilities there were for life after death, and why the Lord had turned a deaf ear to her prayers.

When she knocked softly at the rectory door, much to her surprise the door was opened by the Reverend White himself. He was dressed all in white, and Julia's eyes opened in astonishment. The churchman seemed equally astounded by her unexpected presence on his doorstep, and for a brief moment the two stood staring at each other, at a loss for words.

"C-come i-in, Lady Julia," the Reverend White stammered, remembering his manners. "What can I do for you, my lady?"

Totally at a loss to comprehend or explain what she was feeling, Julia stood motionless at the doorway. Tears welled in her eyes. "I need to understand," she whispered. "I need to know."

The Reverend White immediately reached out his hand and gently led her into the house. "So do we all, my dear lady. So do we all. Without answers, our life is but a shadow."

She nodded eagerly. "Yes! Oh, I knew you would understand!"

She walked into his small sitting room and suddenly stopped and stared. In the room sat the Reverend White's wife and his two young children. They, too, were dressed in white, and a man—a stranger—also in white, stood in front of the fireplace with a book in his hand as though he had been reading aloud.

"Don't be afraid," the Reverend White said reassuringly. "This is Elder Croft, and he has come from America to bring us the truth of the restored gospel of our Savior, Jesus Christ. Through him you may learn the answers to the questions that are heavy in your heart."

"I don't understand," Julia said, shaking her head in confusion, but she sat down. In the next few hours in the cozy quiet of that little parlor she heard, for the first time, the promises of eternity.

That night, after dark, she went with a handful of the faithful to the pond behind the nutting woods, and there she witnessed the baptism of the White family. She remembered the smell of apple blossoms in the back gardens as she slipped into Marymont Hall after midnight and retired to her room to sleep a full night for the first time since her brother's death.

In the next week Julia spent every waking moment talking with the Reverend White or with Elder Croft and watched with heartbreak and yearning as the Whites packed their belongings and prepared to go to Liverpool, where they would join a company of newly baptized Saints who were heading for Zion somewhere in the western reaches of an unknown continent across the ocean.

The more she heard of the promise that loved ones could be together forever and that Heavenly Father regarded his children with love, not with wrath, and desired their joy, not their suffering, the more Julia was sure she had discovered the truth and that all her questions could be answered through study and prayer.

She read the Book of Mormon nightly, as well as the Bible, and she saw the wonderful fulfillment those two great books created when read together. For the first time in her life she felt a closeness to the Lord that spread comfort and hope through her heart and mind like a sweet and healing salve.

The Reverend White and his family left for Zion one week before her parents' return from the farm. When Julia's father entered Marymont Hall, the butler handed him a letter in which the reverend explained his family's abrupt departure. It was a letter of apology, a request for forgiveness, and a stirring testimony of the Reverend White's new faith.

Julia's father turned pale with rage. "May he rot in hell and his family with him! How could a man of the cloth so lose himself in heresy that he would bring his wife and children into the awful and eternal fire of God's punishment? He has made a pact with the devil. How could he have so deceived me—posing as a man of God? His name is never to be spoken before me again. He has brought a blot on the spiritual instruction of every member of our Marymont congregation, and neither I nor the Lord shall ever forgive him!"

"But, Father," Julia protested without thinking, "our Lord and Savior requires that we forgive all men. By that judgment whereby we judge, we shall also be judged. Don't you think it might be worth at least finding out what this new faith has to offer that a man as strong in the Lord as the Reverend White should be moved to give up everything for it?"

The face her father turned upon Julia was one of such anger and suspicion that she did not recognize him.

"How dare you champion such a heretic and ingrate? How dare you question my decision?" her father thundered. Suddenly Lord Hanford grabbed his daughter by the shoulders and looked into her face. "Have you been listening to this man's poison? Have you put your own immortal soul at risk?" he shouted.

Something in her face must have betrayed her, because her father whirled on his feet and called to the upstairs maid. "Go at once and search her ladyship's room. If you discover any books or papers there, bring them to me immediately!"

The Book of Mormon was brought from Julia's bedroom to her father's study, and he confronted his daughter with the evidence of her guilt. Oddly enough, instead of feeling afraid, Julia felt relief that her search was out in the open.

"Papa," she cried, "I have wanted you and Mama to know what I have learned. This gospel tells us we will see Harold again—that he will be cared for and loved until we are reunited. It tells us that the Lord watches over us with love and that everything that happens in our lives happens for good. Oh, don't you see, Papa? All the good you do is rewarded not just in heaven but here on earth. We are meant to be happy and to love one another—not to be frightened, or angry, or joyless. Punishment is not the measure of life. Love is. Oh, Papa, you must read this book, and you will not have to carry your tears for Harold in secret in your heart. He can be with us . . ."

Before she could say another word, her father flung the book into the fire. "Not another word!" he shouted. "You will not speak of such things to me! Ever! Do you hear? If you wish to remain in this house, if you wish to remain my daughter, you will immediately give me your word that you will never speak of this religion again. You will not speak of your brother or his death. It is unseemly. You must

41

promise you will have no contact with those who espouse this evil faith. You will never touch a piece of writing or literature concerning it, and you will declare to me, with your hand on the Bible, that you know that all you have said and learned is a fraud and a lie."

She gasped. The coldness of his fury was more convincing than if he had struck her. She knew he meant every word he said, and she stood staring at him. Then she turned to look at her mother, and she felt her heart break. Her mother, too, was stony-faced, as adamant in her rejection as Julia's father.

With a terrible shudder, Julia stepped backward. "I cannot in good faith take such an oath. Papa, I know I have found the truth and, if I deny it, I shall be truly damned, not only by you but by a Heavenly Father who has led me to his truth. I love you and Mama, and it cuts me to the heart to lose you and to lose this home that I love, but if I turn from what I know is right, I will lose you and Harold for all eternity."

Julia packed that night and left the house. For a week she stayed in the village with a family of converts. At the end of the week, she was baptized and then journeyed with Elder Croft and a small group of Saints to London. There Julia sold the pearl necklace that her parents had given her on her eighteenth birthday. She knew she was paid only a small fraction of what the necklace was worth, but the money was enough to pay her passage across the ocean and to secure a place on a wagon train to Utah.

She had arrived in Utah at last. She sat cold and alone in the wilderness, with little money and no knowledge of what to do or where to go.

CHAPTER FIVE

Brigham Young himself had assigned William Childress to meet immigrant companies when they arrived at the Ogden tithing yard in order to render any assistance that was required. William had received word late that a new wagon train had reached town that morning. By the time he arrived at the yard, most of the immigrants had already been met by relatives and had gone.

As he rushed into the tithing yard, William saw the lone figure of a young woman, and something in the sight of her tugged at his compassionate heart. She looked dignified and grave, and he had the immediate sense that he was looking at one of the great women of Zion. He felt the power of her resolve and the courage of her loneliness reaching out to him. He stopped and then walked toward her.

In the following weeks William became Julia's mentor. He found her a situation as a governess with the Poulsen family just four blocks from Childress Avenue and introduced her into the community. With characteristic generosity he lent her a riding horse and arranged for the sisters of the Relief Society to provide her with adequate clothing for the coming winter.

He could see her discomfort with her need for assistance, and after three months she went to him with payment in full for all she had received. William knew the money represented every penny she had earned since coming to Utah and that she had sold her few possessions to be free of debt.

"Thank you for your help, Brother Childress," she said with the calm dignity he found so appealing. "I have been taught that my life was given to me to serve others, not to be served. I have been a grateful recipient of your help when I could not have survived without it. Now I make you a promise that with the help of the Lord I shall never be a burden to anyone again."

He knew her words were true, and in the following months he watched the frugal simplicity with which she lived. She never allowed herself an indulgence of any kind. All of her efforts went into saving and using her means for the help and succor of others. It was as though she consciously whittled her own needs into the simplest and barest necessities, and everything else was the Lord's surplus.

Nonetheless, even though Julia wore the plainest clothing, without frills or decoration, her magnificent coloring and the fine features of her face made her beauty shine in any gathering. Even among the most elegantly dressed women, she stood out like a swan in a field of peacocks.

It was Brigham Young who told William to marry Julia. William, in obedience and with a pounding heart, had asked the beautiful young Englishwoman to be his wife. He never dreamed she would say yes. How could a young woman of Julia's loveliness and intelligence feel love toward a man old enough to be her father?

When she accepted his proposal, William could scarcely believe his ears. He married her with his heart brimming with love and admiration, and from the day of their wedding he could not look at her without marveling that such a blessing should have been given to him.

After the wedding he purchased the farm in Riverdale for her. "I grew up knowing of farming life, and I think I could run a farm very well, William," she told her new husband when he offered to build her a house in town. "I would prefer to live in the country. I do not think I am suited to town living. I want to have tenants for whom I am responsible. Send me new arrivals who have no land of their own or who do not know how to work the soil. I will teach them and employ them and help them until they can cultivate their own farms and be successful. That is my dream, to help build this place—this Zion—a few families at a time."

"You are very wise, Julia," William responded. "If Zion does not succeed economically, it will not succeed spiritually. Deseret must have strong and successful workers who know how to help this place blossom like a rose. Many of our converts come from Europe where they were teachers, or clerks, or factory workers. Here they must learn how to turn a wilderness—a desert—into productive land on a large scale. It is a daunting task."

Julia nodded. "But I watched my father manage his lands from the time I was a little girl. I understand the land. I understand laborers. I believe I can train men to work the soil. At least, I would like to try."

In the years that followed, William continued to run his far-flung mercantile enterprises from the growing town of Ogden, and Julia used the farm to welcome, train, and develop dozens of whole families. These people left Julia's stewardship in Riverdale to establish productive and successful farms of their own throughout the valley. In her quiet way Julia became a significant influence in the rapidly growing territory.

As the years of their marriage passed, William's love, admiration, and respect for Julia became as deep as a river. It flowed through him like a life-giving stream, and yet he still could not say he completely understood his wife. She was a continuing mystery to him—more complex and private than anyone he had ever known.

He wished with all his heart that she would leave the farm and come to live with him in the Big House. At night he often wakened and longed to reach out and pull her into his arms, but she remained at the farm because, in some profound way, she had become a part of the land, and it had become a part of her. Some instinct told him she would not be happy as the mistress of the Big House in Ogden.

In Riverdale, at the farm, Julia knew her life had purpose and meaning, and she clung to it. William knew his wife loved him, but he was wise enough to recognize that she could not leave the life she had created or the Riverdale farm that had been her home for nearly twenty years. He smiled at the flow of his memories.

Julia's eyes opened sleepily, and without moving she looked sweetly at her husband sitting next to her at the side of the bed. "Dear William," she smiled with joy at the sight of him. "Dear, dear William. Have you been sitting there long? Are you thinking that I am a lazy excuse for a wife? Napping in the middle of the day!"

She laughed, but she did not rise.

William chuckled fondly.

"I wish you would stay here forever, Julia. Right where you are now. I would like to stay here beside you as well!"

Julia reached out her hand and patted the bed. "Lie next

to me for a moment then," she whispered. "If they have not missed us yet, a few more minutes will not matter."

Taking her hand in his, he kissed it gently, and then removed his house slippers and lay down next to her.

"Sweet Julia," he whispered against her silken hair. "How I miss you. Can I not talk you into coming to live here in town, at least for the next few months? It is going to be a harsh winter. I feel it in my bones. Please come so that I might care for you every day—every moment. You will need that care, I think."

She raised her face and kissed him tenderly. "I would love to be under your care every day, William, but you have many, many responsibilities and people who need your daily attention. You must know that I could not be happy living here in this house with Annie in charge, dear as she is, and I would not displace her for the world. She has been so good to you and is much better as a hostess than I would ever be. I'm just not good at dinners, banquets, and such. No, no—our current arrangement is much better as it is, dear William. When you come to the farm I have you all to myself for a few precious days, and when you are not there I have my own work to do."

"Yes, Julia, but surely now. Just for these next few months . . ."

Julia laid her finger softly across his mouth. "Sh-h-h. Speak no more of it. I want to rear my girls away from wealth and worldly things. I want them to learn their own value and develop confidence in their own strength and the power of labor. I want them to know and understand the land, because it is the land that is the source of the Lord's blessings in our lives. Please do not ask me to leave those things, William. I am very, very content."

William sighed and kissed her again. As he felt her small, sweetly formed body, he pulled her against him tightly, and his heart groaned with longing. "Oh my dear, I miss you so!"

"And I miss you, too, dear William. Oh, I do!" There were tears in her eyes, and her hands stroked his shoulders. "With all my heart I miss you day and night, but surely the Lord requires of us that we do what we have been led to do, and only through obedience to our duty will we earn the right to be together for eternity. I want that, William, even more than to be together every day of our mortality."

He listened to her passionate whisper, and he embraced her hungrily, kissing her with all the yearning of his mighty heart.

Just then there was an urgent knock at the door, and Hannah's voice called, "Papa, are you in there? You asked me to come see you."

Flushing scarlet, Julia sat up and tried to smooth her unruly hair into a semblance of order. William swung his legs over the side of the bed and slipped his house slippers back on.

"Yes, Hannah, dear," he called out. "I shall be with you in a moment." He hurried over to the door, straightening his coat, while Julia rose from the bed and patted the covers straight.

When Papa opened the door to his bedroom, Hannah was astonished to see her mother with disheveled hair and flushed cheeks rapidly putting the bed in order. Papa, too, looked strangely rumpled and nonplused. It was so seldom that Hannah saw the two of them together in private circumstances that for a moment she was at a loss for words, as if she had come upon something that ought not to be seen. She blushed in confusion.

"If . . . if you like, I could come back later," she stammered. "I mean . . . if you are busy. Or if I am interrupting."

Julia walked briskly toward the door. "No, no, Hannah.

48

Come right in. Your papa wants to talk to you, and I must get down to help with the banquet. I'm sure Annie is exhausted from carrying all the responsibility. I was just resting for a few moments."

With a kiss on Hannah's cheek, Julia left the room and hurried down the front stairs. Hannah stood uncertainly by the door as she watched her father's face. His eyes followed her mother's retreating form as if he were a man in darkness watching a lantern leave. Hannah did not understand the look completely, but she knew it made her feel both sad and happy at the same time. Her mother and father's relationship was unfathomable to her.

"Well, my dear girl," Papa said cheerily, turning to face Hannah. "I am so glad to have a few minutes with you. I had hoped to get this to you sooner, but I could not get out to the farm this week because of an unexpected trip to Salt Lake City. Better late than never!"

Papa walked over to his wardrobe and pulled out a large box. "I hope it fits because there will be no time for alterations. Your mother sent me your measurements, so it ought to be right."

With an excited gasp, Hannah opened the box. It contained a dress of crimson taffeta shot with black, with a magnificently draped and pleated skirt and a tight bodice trimmed with braid and jet buttons. Tucked next to the dress were a pair of kidskin, high-top shoes with red cutwork trim. Hannah knew instinctively that the dress would suit her coloring and figure perfectly.

"Papa!" She could not speak above a whisper, for so many emotions crowded into her heart and mind. "Thank you. Thank you. It—it's overwhelming—and so beautiful!"

Her father laughed. "I am glad if you like it, Hannah. I want this to be a very happy evening for you. I know that sometimes, living on the farm, away from me, you might feel . . . left out." Papa paused. It was the first time Hannah had seen him seemingly at a loss for words.

He cleared his throat. "I want you to know, Hannah, my dear daughter, that even though we are often apart, I am mindful of you always. I admire and believe in you. You have much of your mother in you, and someday you will be a woman who will leave a mark upon the world—a mark of righteousness. I know this, Hannah. There is greatness in you."

Realizing how serious the moment was becoming, Papa smiled and gave her a quick hug. "What I am trying to say is that now, while you are young, I want you to have the joy of being young. I have no control over the challenges and adversities that will be yours to face in your adult life, but it is my greatest desire for all of my children that I make their childhood and youthful days as happy as possible while I am able to do so."

"Oh, Papa!" Hannah cried, throwing her arms around his neck. "Being your daughter is the happiest thing I can imagine. You don't have to do anything more for me than that!"

As she said the words she realized they were true—true to her very heart. She realized her father's love was like a great rock, a foundation on which she could build forever. Suddenly the absolute knowledge of her father's regard for her was more precious than she had ever known or imagined. His unconditional fatherly love made her feel she really was everything he believed her to be—strong, independent, full of faith, and—yes—beautiful!

Carrying the box with its splendid dress, and overwhelmed by the sense of having comprehended something important and real about her life, Hannah went downstairs to the back bedroom. It was the room that she and Eliza always shared when they came into town.

Eliza was already in the room, standing in front of the pier-glass mirror and turning this way and that. Her chestnut-colored hair was piled on top of her head, and her china-blue eyes were dancing with happiness. She was wearing a dress of robin's-egg blue silk that made her eyes look like pieces of the sky in her rosy face.

"Eliza!" Hannah exclaimed in admiration. "You are the prettiest sight I have ever seen! Did Papa buy you a dress, too?"

"Oh, yes, Hannah! Did you know he had our dresses made in Salt Lake to our own measurements? He sent all the way to St. Louis for the fabrics, and the styles are the very, very latest from the East! I *am* beautiful, aren't I!"

Eliza pivoted in front of Hannah, and her flashing skirt flew up to reveal dancing slippers made of matching blue kidskin. "We are going to be the belles at the ball!" Eliza bubbled. "Do let me see your dress, Hannah. I'm sure it is every bit as lovely as mine!"

Diffidently, Hannah raised the lid of her dress box, and with a scream of ecstasy, Eliza gathered the cascading gown out of its tissues and held it up.

"It is so grownup and absolutely gorgeous, Hannah! Oh my, won't every other girl at the dance feel dowdy! I can't wait until Constance and the other town girls see what their country relatives look like at the ball tonight! Then we shall see who's going to lord it over who!"

"Over whom," Hannah corrected automatically.

Eliza laughed. "All right. Over whom, then. But when we are dressed in these elegant clothes, our grammar shouldn't matter. We are above such paltry things! We are above *everything!*" Eliza continued, prattling on in her excitement about the party and who was coming and how much fun it was to look so sophisticated.

As Hannah half-listened to her sister's happy

ramblings, she felt her own excitement begin to drain out of her. She heard Eliza's voice, but her mind was hearing none of the words. Her thoughts grew reflective and serious as she began to evaluate all the experiences of the day. She was trying to understand the sweep of her emotions from the beginning of the day as she sat in the cornfield until now.

" . . . and Papa's dresses are just the thing to make us as important as everyone else. No one can doubt Papa loves us when they see how much time and money he has spent to make us presentable . . ." Eliza's delight in her new dress had turned on a spate of words that could not be stopped.

"Eliza," Hannah said softly, "we do not need new dresses to know that Papa loves us. He shows it in a hundred genuine ways. I am just beginning to see the truth of that."

"Of course, Hannah," Eliza answered lightly, scarcely listening. She looked at her sister with a frown of concern. "Oh, do hurry! If you don't get your new dress on soon, you will be late for dinner. Naturally that would mean a grand entrance, but I'm not sure Mama would approve."

Eliza turned Hannah around. "Here, I'll help you undo your buttons. Aren't you just dying to try on your gorgeous new gown? It is going to make you a different person! All your sulking was for nothing. Aren't you glad you came now?"

At a loss to explain what she was feeling, Hannah shook off Eliza's helpful hand. "No. Thanks anyway, Liza," she said softly. "I want to wait a few minutes before I dress. I— I need to think about all of this. It's all happening so suddenly! I'm not sure I want to be a different person."

Puzzled by Hannah's subdued demeanor, Eliza stood back and gave her sister a long look. "You're a tough one to figure out, Hannah. This morning you didn't want to come to the party because of your old dress, and now you have the most magnificent dress in the world and you are still acting as if you want to hide in the cornfield. What will it take to make you happy?"

Suddenly Hannah came out of her reverie. She shook herself, and a huge smile lit her face like a lantern. "Eliza, I just realized—this very minute—I just realized that I don't need anything to make me happy. Everything I need I already have."

"Honestly, Hannah!" Eliza gave an exasperated sigh. "You would drive a Saint to drink! Half the time I can't even figure out what you are talking about, let alone what you are thinking. But you do seem happy for the first time in days. I just can't wait another minute to have Mama see my new dress, so I'm going to leave you to dress on your own. And, for land's sake, do something with that wild hair of yours—it's as tangled as a bush!"

Eliza slipped out the door, and Hannah sat down heavily on the bed, staring at the splendor of her new dress spread out across the counterpane. Slowly her hand stroked the crisp folds of the silk taffeta. The faint rustle of the fabric sounded rich and luxurious, like the whisper of gold-dusted leaves.

She picked up the dress. With a sigh of pleasure, she held it in front of herself and looked at her image in the mirror. Even without putting on the dress she could tell it made her look as magnificent as a sunset. The flashes of crimson brought out the rosy glow in her ivory skin, and the onyx buttons flashed as bright as her eyes. If she wore that gown she would be the best-dressed girl at the party.

CHAPTER SIX

Henley Finlayson had put together a dance band from the groups of converts pouring into Ogden. There were many talented performers and musicians, and he always made it his business to find out who played what instrument. Often he discovered the new musicians were classically trained, and he needed to convince them that the Lord thought it was important for His people to dance and be cheerful. Finally, with his well-honed gifts of persuasion, Henley convinced even the most high-brow musicians to turn their gifts to the music of the ballroom.

As a result of his determined efforts, Henley's musical ensemble played wonderfully, and they performed everything from baroque chamber music to the latest dance hall merriments. The Henley Finlayson Ensemble was much in demand, but they always made a place in their schedule for any event at William Childress's home. Tonight they were playing the supper music.

Abner turned to his older brother William as they stood side by side in the ballroom. The tables were laden with food, the decorations glowed in the light of dozens of lamps, and the music was as sweet as a summer morning.

The two brothers were enjoying the wonder of their reunion after so many years.

"William, I have never seen such hospitality. Indeed, in my years in the Salmon Valley, I had almost forgotten such pleasantness existed. In the years since you entered the valley you have created a new Jerusalem. I fear I am laboring in the wilderness of Sinai."

"Abner, the Lord asked you to go to one of the most difficult spots in this untried land, and you will leave a mark on that outpost that will serve as a beacon to all who follow. What you do battling the loneliness, the elements, and our hostile Lamanite brothers is the work of Joshua. How I wish I could do more to help."

With a hearty laugh Abner clapped his brother on the shoulder. "We can talk of such matters at another time. Tonight let us just revel in the eternal joy of watching our family rejoice. It is seldom enough that we have such occasions."

William laughed. "I could not have said it better, brother. Do you still dance a lively reel?"

"That I do!" Abner proclaimed. "But not until I have eaten some of this bounteous feast."

Leaving Abner to help his younger children fill their plates, William wandered over to the table where Julia was serving slices of sweet potato pie. "Shouldn't you be sitting down, my dear?" he asked anxiously. "You have had a tiring day."

Her face softened in a beautiful smile. "Do not be concerned for me, William. I am fine. And please do not attract attention to my condition by being overly attentive."

With great dignity he bent and kissed her on the cheek. "I care not a fig for what others may think. My concern is for you alone."

"Well, then, go and see what your daughters are up to!"

Julia laughed. "There is Eliza, surrounded by young men, but I cannot see Hannah anywhere."

"She will make a dazzling entrance," William predicted. "What a beauty she has become."

"I suppose she is pretty," Julia answered distractedly, "but my concern is not with her beauty but that she become a useful woman in our Heavenly Father's kingdom. That will not happen until she understands that her purpose and worth are far more important than her appearance."

"Perhaps," William said with a smile, "but beauty in a woman is a hard thing to hide. It is a gift like any other, and not one to be ashamed of or hidden. I, for one, cannot wait to see her decked out. It will be quite a moment. She is going to bowl this room over!"

Julia frowned slightly. "But will it be Hannah or the dress that people will be impressed by?"

Adam Fairfield dismounted slowly from his horse. His chestnut stallion, Ensign, shook his forelock impatiently and pranced away from the reins. "Easy boy," said Adam as he reached out a strong, tanned hand and smoothed the horse's blaze. "Easy does it, fella," he crooned softly as he pulled the animal toward the hitching rail.

Ensign pulled his ears back at the sight of the other horses, and Adam sighed. "You're going to give me trouble, aren't you? All you've got to do is stand out here in this lovely, cool night, and eat oats and fresh hay, and drink water, and rest. I've got to go in there and meet people, and dance, and be charming. I'm the one that ought to be kicking over the traces, not you!"

He led the horse down to the far end of the Childresses' yard to a length of fence by the carriage house where he could tie the animal away from the others. Adam took off the saddle, wiped Ensign with a piece of wool blanket from the saddlebag, and then placed water and feed near him.

"With any luck, I won't be gone long," Adam whispered. "So, behave yourself."

It had been almost fourteen years since Adam had seen the Childress home. As a young boy growing up in Ogden he had watched the great house spring up like a mushroom on the large lot in the middle of Childress Avenue. He could remember climbing through the fence with a group of boys to steal carrots from the sprawling kitchen garden at the back of the property. They had run away, scared, when they saw the black crepe on the door and guessed that someone inside the house had died.

He supposed that had been when Sister Adelaide Childress had passed away. He never really knew her because she seldom left her bed. It was said she had suffered so much during her journey across the plains in the third party of pioneers to enter the Salt Lake Valley that she had never recovered.

Sister Adelaide had lived for years as an invalid. The large house had always seemed intimidating and mysterious, and all Adam could really remember about the Childress family was the oldest daughter, Annie, who seemed as old as his mother and who always bore her testimony on Thursdays at fast meeting. The other brothers and sisters kept to themselves and always seemed to be going off on missions or to school or to get married.

Adam did remember Brother Childress very distinctly. He had always been one of the leaders in the community, but even when he was a little boy, Adam could remember the kindly, bearded man calling him by his first name. Brother Childress seemed to know everyone by name, and he cared about people as if they were his main concern. As a child Adam had always imagined that Brother Childress was some kind of special assistant to the Lord.

How else could it be that Brother Childress seemed to be everywhere? The Childress stores, where people could always get credit and help; the Childress land grants, where people were helped to build homes and to get their gardens thriving; the Childress irrigation system that made water freely available. Now Brother Childress had been asked to engineer the town's reservoir and water supply, and Adam had been hired to return to the community of his boyhood, as a newly graduated civil engineer, to help.

Adam racked his brain to dredge up more of the details of the Childress family. Brother and Sister Childress had arrived early in the Salt Lake Valley and were immediately sent north to settle the Ogden area. Although his first wife was sick and frail, William's older children had been old enough to help, and the Childress family had thrived from the very beginning, taking care of themselves and others.

It had helped, Adam supposed, that William Childress was an educated man with funds of his own from back East. Apparently the Childress family was one of prominence and wealth in Connecticut.

Adam grinned. His family, the Fairfields, had been New Englanders for many generations before his parents joined the Church. Adam's mother and father, converted in upstate New York, were also educated and had a modest resource of family funds and heirlooms. It had not taken long for Adam's parents to become good friends with William Childress.

The Fairfields built their first home in Utah on property near the four-block square the Childress family had acquired when the city of Ogden was being laid out. When Adam turned twelve, his father and mother closed up their Ogden house and moved to Farmington, where they opened a small academy. His parents were trained as educators, and they quickly assembled a group of nearly fifty students. His father bought and farmed a small parcel of land in their new community, and so the Fairfields lived comfortably and became staunch citizens of the growing town of Farmington. Their house in Ogden had remained closed up for more than a decade, but Adam's father was reluctant to sell it.

Occasionally, at general conference time or when he went to Salt Lake City on Church business, Adam's father, John Fairfield, and William Childress met each other and renewed their friendship, catching up on news of each other's families and the growth of the towns in which they lived. Had it not been for the high value John Fairfield placed on his old and treasured friendship with William Childress, Adam would not have been preparing to cross the threshold of this large home with its decorations, lights, and fancy music. Such elaborate social occasions were things to be avoided, in Adam's estimation.

During his mission in the Carolinas he had observed the ruins of the Southern civilization after the Civil War. It was a bitter end to a society of highly inbred, wealthy landowners who had lived in pride, social frivolity, and contrived isolation from the very people who made their wealth possible. Adam wanted no such echoes of a rarified social order in Zion or in his personal life.

He did not fault Brother Childress for his splendid home or his festivities, for he knew the man did not have an arrogant bone in his body. William Childress used everything he owned to serve other people and the Lord. Still, Adam felt any display of wealth was a threat to the humility and simplicity of the gospel.

Adam had finished his mission with the Lamanites in the southern states. During his mission he had watched a people and a way of life melt away into the landscape, almost as though they had never existed. The ancient Indian tribes were shrinking farther and farther into the bayous and wilderness, or were rotting hopelessly on reservations, or were mingling with squatters on creeks and in small villages, where they were lost to themselves forever. He felt the sadness of those once-noble Israelites, now lost a second time.

After his mission, he had not returned to Utah but had gone to New York to complete his training as an engineer at the new university in Cornell. He had come back to Utah only this summer, employed by the territorial government to help build the dams that would create a water system throughout the central valleys of the territory.

Adam's first assignment had brought him to Ogden to assist in creating the plans for the new reservoir.

"You may live in our old house off Childress Avenue," his father said when Adam told him where he would be working. "The place is rather small, but I think you will find it adequate for your needs. Do you remember the house at all?"

Adam had smiled, "Of course. I remember quite a bit. After all, I wasn't a babbling youngster when we left."

"Well," his father said, "it is good to have you back in Utah. We have missed you, and it will be nice to have you living nearby. Brother Childress wrote me when he heard you would be working in Ogden. He is delighted to have you employed on his water project. He also says he is giving a harvest ball next Friday in honor of his brother Abner, and he would be pleased if you could attend."

"I'm not much of one for parties, Pa," Adam said dismissively.

"Then, if you will not go for yourself, please attend on

my behalf," his father answered, "as a courtesy to my old friend."

Adam, trapped in filial duty, had promised his father he would indeed go to the party, but he did not commit himself to any length of stay. So, on his first night back to his boyhood home here he was, walking up the half-remembered steps of the Childress mansion, facing the massive double doors that now wore festive wreaths of autumn garlands instead of the black crepe he had remembered from so long ago.

Light, music, and laughter spilled out of the crowded house, and Adam could see children playing tag in the wide foyer. Dignified men and women were mounting the broad staircase toward the ballroom, and, on the spreading porch at the sides of the house, he could see in the curving shadows slender young women and ardent young men in shy and daring seclusion.

"I am too old for this and too young for it, as well," Adam thought, and for an urgent moment he wanted to turn around, mount Ensign, and ride like the wind through the crisp autumn night until the world melted away and he was part of the air and the dark and the stars.

As he stood uncertainly in the light spilling out from the entryway, a young woman appeared at the open door and peered at him intensely. "Who are you?" she asked. Her voice, though charming, had a haughty ring. "Are you by any chance lurking?"

He laughed and stepped inside the foyer. "No, ma'am," he said. "I am not lurking. I am looking."

She was wearing a violet silk dress that was altogether too fancy for her rather plain face framed by light brown hair with curls that were far too tight and elaborate. Still, she gazed at him with a confidence that gave her presence, and he smiled back politely, removing his hat.

"Adam Fairfield, at your service," he said. "I am here at the invitation of Brother Childress."

"Oh my goodness!" Constance squealed, pleased to know that this handsome young man was a genuinely invited guest. Her delight at being the first to capture him was hard for her to disguise. "I am Constance, and I live here. I am William Childress's granddaughter. You must come with me, and I shall introduce you to everyone that is worth knowing."

He laughed and followed her up the stairs. She paused every two or three steps to introduce him to other people moving upwards, and even in those first few minutes he felt she had assumed a proprietary air toward him, as though, by the simple act of inviting him into the house she had made him her own possession.

"Adam Fairfield," one older man laughed, as Constance introduced him. "I recollect you very well, my lad. I believe you are the very boy that threw a ball through my kitchen window."

Adam laughed in return. "That's the problem with returning to the scene of your youthful crimes. Someone is bound to remember."

Another man said, "Your father told me you were on a mission in the Carolinas."

Adam nodded but said nothing. His mission experiences were still difficult for him to talk about in a casual setting. They were too personal and intense.

Constance took his arm and led him through the press of guests. He did not protest, but he could not wait until he could politely disengage himself from this imperious escort. Faces began to blur, and, by the time they reached the ballroom, he felt hot and cornered. The sound from the party was not reassuring. The music had grown lively, and he could hear the thump of feet dancing a Virginia reel. The overheated air and the crush of those eating at the buffet, the sound of conversation, laughter, and merriment were like a wall of bricks falling on top of him, trapping and smothering him.

Nevertheless, he collected his manners and asked Constance to take him to her father so that he might greet him. As soon as he had spoken to William Childress, he could slip away into the night, having fulfilled his promise to his father.

William was delighted to see the son of his old friend, and with open arms he welcomed the tall, muscular young man. "I knew you'd grow up to be a great man—or a wastrel!" William laughed. "You were far too full of life to be mediocre at whatever you did!"

"My father wanted me to be a scholar or a doctor—or even a lawyer," Adam smiled. "He was not pleased with my choice to be an engineer. I think he thinks I am a bit of a wastrel. But I am a man of action. A man for the out-of-doors. I could no more think of a sedentary profession than I could think of eating grass if there is bread to be had. My father is the scholar in our family; I am a man of the earth."

William Childress nodded. "I made the same decision about my profession as you did—and for much the same reason—when I was a young man. Since then I have discovered it is possible to be both: to live with the earth, to use it and to understand it, and also to be a student. A student of the earth. A student of people. A student of books. Such a life makes one a scholar."

Adam smiled. "I will think on that."

Constance took his arm in hers and pouted at her grandfather. "Grandpapa, you are being far too serious with Mr. Fairfield. Don't you think you should be inviting him to dance with me or to eat, rather than telling him he should become a scholar?"

"All right, you two young ones, off to the dance floor!" William waved his hand in dismissal, and Adam could tell that Brother Childress was assuming he and Constance were to be partners. With a sigh Adam turned to invite her to join him in the next dance. Constance looked up at him with satisfied expectation on her face, but just then, over the young woman's moire-clad shoulder, he caught sight of something, and his mind stopped mid-thought. The invitation to Constance died on his lips.

CHAPTER SEVEN

It had not been an easy decision. Hannah stood looking in the mirror, staring at the transformation that had occurred when she put on the new gown. It was as though the story of Cinderella had come true. The dress fit perfectly and made her waist look as slender as a handspan. The luxurious fabric and design made her seem everything she thought she longed to be—rich, confident, enviable, and triumphant.

It was a heady sight. So why wasn't she happy? Her logical, analytical mind was not fooled. "Inside that dress you are still the same person you have always been." Why should putting on a fancy dress make her more valuable? If she wore the elegant dress, she was admitting that Constance and Edgar were right—that how she looked was more important than what she was. Unbidden questions tumbled in her mind. If the prince could not love you as Cinderella, if he could only love you when you wore a splendid dress, did he really love you at all, or was he in love with the dress?

After all, it was Papa who had bought the dress for her, and he was not a man of superficiality. Was it some obstinate pride or stubbornness that made her resist giving in?

What part of this dilemma was copper-plated pride and what part was genuine humility? It was all confusing, but in the end she decided as she knew she must—let the chips fall where they may.

Once she decided, she finished getting ready quickly, but she was very late and the party was in full swing when she arrived at the ballroom. She stood hesitantly in the doorway, searching for a glimpse of her father and mother.

The dance set had just finished, and the musicians were taking a short break. As the floor cleared, the revelers parted, moving to the sides of the room to cluster around the buffet table and the punch bowl. Hannah remained standing in the doorway, unaware that as the crowd dispersed they created a clear path that pointed straight toward her. She stood framed like an actress in the proscenium arch of a spotlighted stage, silent, expectant, as though preparing to speak her first lines.

Across the floor, Adam had the sensation that a shaft of light had cut through the crowded room and by a tunnel in space he was suddenly joined to the breathtakingly lovely young woman who paused in the doorway, still as a portrait, bathed in the glow of the ballroom's lamplight.

She was tall and slender, with black hair that glinted with burgundy red like sunset hidden in its shining folds. Her abundant hair was gathered into a loose knot at the top of her head, but tendrils sprang out and curled around her face in a cloud of beauty.

In a room full of women dressed in bustles, pleats, crinolines, shawls, and brocades, this girl wore the simplest of clothes. A dark, plain dress lay on her body gently and hung to the floor in a graceful line. Around her neck was a collar of dazzling white lace. Everything about her—her quiet, erect posture, the natural set of her shoulders, her poise and stillness—conspired to lift the eye to her face, as surely as the stem of a magnificent rose points to the beauty of the blossom.

This girl's face was a flower, warm with pink and golden tones. Her bones and features were as perfect as a statue's, but her dark, brilliant eyes and delicate brow were alive with intelligence and vitality.

"Who is she?" Adam breathed, scarcely believing the vision he was seeing and not realizing he had spoken out loud.

Constance, puzzled and irritated by Adam's preoccupied behavior, glanced over her shoulder in the direction he was looking and clucked her tongue in impatience. There was Hannah, a scarecrow as usual in that dowdy hand-me-down. Late as usual, too.

"That's Hannah," Constance said dismissively.

"Hannah who?" Adam persisted.

"Hannah Childress," Constance snapped. "She's my mother's half-sister. You don't want to bother with her. She's kind of a tomboy and no fun at all. She doesn't know anyone who's worth knowing. She doesn't even live in the city. She and her mother and sister live like hermits out on the farm. Kind of eccentric. If you want to be part of the social circle . . ."

Adam laughed. "Constance, engineers don't go in much for circles. We're more inclined to straight lines. Would you introduce me to her?"

Without waiting for Constance's reply, Adam began walking across the room toward Hannah, but at that moment Hannah spied her father and darted from the doorway toward the corner where William was visiting with some of his guests.

"Papa," Hannah said softly, touching her father's sleeve. William turned and glanced at his daughter. When he caught sight of Hannah's old dress, a puzzled frown passed over his face.

"Didn't your new dress fit, Hannah, my dear?" he asked with concern.

"It fit perfectly." Hannah flushed with the awkwardness of trying to explain. "I love the dress, Papa, I really do. It is so beautiful, and I wanted to wear it more than you can ever know. That's the problem. I wanted to wear it too much—for all the wrong reasons. You see, Papa, I have to prove to myself that I don't have to wear it."

She peered anxiously into her father's face, praying that he would comprehend what she was trying to explain.

He smiled fondly at her and shook his head in resignation. "Hannah," he laughed, "If I live to be a hundred years old I will never completely understand you or your blessed mother." Chuckling, he pointed to the dance floor where the young people were gathering for a polka. "Try to be more like Eliza. Life is simple and uncomplicated for her. There she is in her new dress, dancing the night away without a single heavy thought in her pretty head. Go and be part of the party, Hannah. Be young. Have fun. Joy is part of righteousness, too, you know. Don't worry so much."

She kissed her father on the cheek. "Thank you, Papa," she laughed, her heart as light as a bird's. "I'll wear my dress to the family dinner tomorrow night, I promise."

Feeling freer than she had for a long time, Hannah whirled around and prepared to join the group of young people that Edgar was gathering for the next dance set.

She had taken only a few steps when Constance stepped in front of her.

"You look very pretty tonight, Constance," Hannah said sincerely.

Constance, a petulant, annoyed look on her face, did not even acknowledge Hannah's compliment. "This is Adam

Fairfield," Constance said abruptly, gesturing toward the man who was standing next to her. "He wants to meet you."

With that Constance turned on her heel and walked angrily away.

Hannah raised her eyebrows. "Well, you certainly made a conquest in Constance!" she said with a wry smile.

Adam grinned. "I am afraid I do not have the appropriate reverence for social circles to suit Constance. I think she has given up on me—and on very short acquaintance, I might add."

With a mischievous smile Hannah shook her head. "Not so short acquaintance as all that."

He looked at her inquiringly. "What do you mean? I met the girl only half an hour ago."

"Adam Fairfield, you are too young to have such a poor memory." Hannah's voice held a light, teasing challenge, and it made Adam look at her quizzically. Everything about Hannah seemed intriguing and enchanting to him. He raised his eyebrows in questioning surprise.

"You really don't remember?" Hannah was suddenly serious, and she peered into his eyes gravely. "How could you possibly have forgotten?"

Adam shook his head, a baffled half-smile playing about his lips.

"Don't you remember playing hide-and-seek here at the Big House?" she reminded him. "Almost every evening you older children from the neighborhood would come play in our yard—and you would let Constance and me join in, even though you thought we were far too young, because you knew if you didn't we would make a huge fuss."

Adam was quiet as he stretched his mind back to those long-ago summer evenings.

Hannah continued. "One afternoon, Constance was 'it,'

and everyone was scattering while she counted. You dived into my favorite hiding place in the pile of logs behind the summer house right on top of me! You nearly mashed me flat, and you don't even have the grace to recall it."

Adam was watching her face as she told the story, only half-listening, marveling at the wonder of her, and yearning to know if she felt any part of the swirl of emotions he was experiencing.

He shook his head, and she continued her story. "Well, you did! You plunked down in the wood chips, and you put your hand over my mouth so I wouldn't yell in surprise. But I wasn't surprised or frightened—I was mad. Mad as a wet hen! I hissed at you, 'This is *my* hiding place! You go find your own!' But Constance had counted to ten and was starting across the lawn. She was heading straight toward our log pile. I said, 'I bet she peeked!' and then you said— and this is a direct quote—'Don't worry. I'll protect you. I promise. I'll protect you always.' That's what you said, Adam Fairfield. Those were your very words. And now you have admitted that you have forgotten your forever promise."

Adam stared into Hannah's laughing dark eyes, and suddenly he remembered a little girl with a mass of curling, unruly black hair who came to play at the Big House once in a while. He recalled how fast she was at games, almost as strong and quick as a boy—and just as fearless. As his memory came back, he could also visualize how she always seemed not quite to belong, with her countrified clothes and sturdy work boots. The town children recognized that she was a farm girl, but they also recognized something steady and reassuring about her that made them like her. She was different, that was all. And she was still different. In any crowd, she would always stand out.

"I remember it," Adam whispered, amazed. "We

hooked little fingers and made a pledge." He reached out his hand. Blushing, Hannah reached up her hand, and they hooked their little fingers together.

"'I promise, Hannah. I will protect you always.' That is what I said," Adam's voice was so quiet she could hardly hear him. "And then you said . . ."

Hannah laughed and finished the sentence. "And then I said—'me, too! I'll protect you always, too, Adam!'"

"I had forgotten." Adam smiled and shook his head. "Until this moment, I had completely forgotten. If I'd known you were going to be this beautiful when you grew up, I would have written that promise in granite and tied you to it."

She was confused by the intensity of his expression and his complimentary words. She blushed and said awkwardly, "Well, it was just a silly childhood memory. It is nice to have you back after all these years. I suppose now that you are a serious grown-up, I ought to call you Brother Fairfield. If you like, I can take you around the room and reintroduce you to some of your old neighbors, although I don't know everybody myself."

"No, thank you," Adam said. "That won't be necessary. Constance made the same offer, but I have just met the only person here I want to know." He looked at her squarely.

Again Hannah felt herself blushing scarlet, and she was at a loss for words. "Surely you will want to meet the community leaders and the bishop and some of those lovely girls," she stammered.

He took her hand and led her toward the table. "No, not tonight. But I am hungry. Let's eat first, and talk, and then, if we feel like it, we can dance until morning."

She hesitated, and for the first time Adam realized how impetuous he was being. He was acting as if the two of them were alone when in reality they were at a large

71

gathering in Hannah's house. Perhaps she had hostess duties—or a beau. His presumption overwhelmed him, and he paused uncertainly.

"I mean, I would like to spend every minute of this evening with you, but I recognize that if you have other obligations . . ."

Hannah felt him turning away, and everything in her wanted him to stay. She remembered how it had felt that long-ago day when they had crouched in the stack of wood in the little enclosure where they were hidden from the world. They could peek through the chinks and see Constance coming closer and closer, but no one knew where they were.

"I'm going to make a run for 'home'," Adam had whispered those long years ago. How she remembered that big, strong boy! He wasn't like the other children. He never teased her or made her feel she did not belong. Everyone liked him and wanted to be on his team because he told you when you did well and never made fun of you when you made a mistake. He was bigger and older than she was, but he did not send her away or make her feel like a baby. He had always been kind to her.

"You stay right here, hidden in the woodpile," he had told her. "I'll run like the dickens. I can get home easy before Constance tags me. She'll see me come out of the woodpile, and she will think no one else is in here. When she runs after me, you'll be safe."

With that Adam had leaped over the log pile and made a dash for home base. She remembered how lonely the hiding place had seemed after he was gone.

She wanted him never to leave again.

Putting her hand on Adam's arm, she smiled. "I do not have any obligation in the world except to protect you. I promised when I was six, remember? And I always keep my promises."

He laughed and put his hand over hers. She looked down at his tanned, muscled hand sprinkled with fine hairs as bright as gold dust, and she felt her heart open and pour happiness to the very tips of her fingers.

He bent and whispered in her ear. "You are the most beautiful woman in this room tonight. The most beautiful woman I have ever seen."

"Oh," she breathed, more to herself than to him, "what an extraordinary thing for you to say to me—especially tonight."

He looked at her with a puzzled frown. "What do you mean?"

She smiled mysteriously. "I'll explain it to you some day. But right now there is one thing I know for certain: I shall love this plain, hand-me-down dress for as long as I live."

CHAPTER EIGHT

Eliza was bouncing up and down on the bed. "Wake up, Hannah! Wake up! You've been asleep for hours, and we have to go down to help with breakfast soon. I want to talk!"

Hannah rolled over reluctantly and punched up the pillow under her head so that she could get a better view of her sister. Eliza was kneeling on the counterpane. The room was chilly with the encroaching cold of the season.

"Get back under the covers, you ninny, or you will catch your death of cold. I don't want to talk. I want to sleep until I have to get up." Hannah pulled up the covers and closed her eyes.

"No you don't!" Eliza began jumping again. "I want to talk!"

"About what?" Hannah yawned. "I did not even see you all last night. You must have been having a wonderful time at the party."

"Oh yes indeed!" Eliza said indignantly. "Of course you didn't see me last night! You didn't see anyone! All you could see was Adam Fairfield. The whole room was buzzing about it, and Constance was fuming. She says she got Adam first and then you stole him away from her!"

74

Eliza could not stop. Her questions came rolling out like marbles from a tipped jar. "Why didn't you wear your new dress? Was Papa upset at you? How did you meet Adam? What is he like? What did he tell you about his Lamanite mission and about the university and about his new job and . . ."

Hannah sat up in bed, and the two girls put their heads together and talked away the dawn, laughing and sharing their thoughts and confidences. They had brushed out their party hairdos, and their long hair hung in single braids down their backs.

They were wearing long, white, flannel nightgowns with full sleeves and high collars, but after a few minutes, the cold room got to be too much for Eliza, and she climbed back into bed. The sisters pulled the quilts over their shoulders and continued whispering and giggling as the morning light filled the room.

Suddenly there was a rattling of stones thrown against their window.

"What's that?" Eliza squealed, ducking her head under the sheets.

"I don't know," Hannah replied. She put her feet out of the bed tentatively and ran across the cold floor to look out the window into the backyard.

In the pale morning light she saw Adam standing in the gravel by the frost-silvered rose garden. He was holding the reins of a magnificent chestnut stallion, and plumes of steaming vapor were rising as he and the horse breathed. Adam stooped to pick up more stones.

She pushed open the window, and a blast of icy air made her gasp. "What are you doing out there?" she called down. "You'll catch your death of cold!"

Hannah supposed it was immodest to be talking to Adam in her nightgown, but the window casing hid most of her from view, and she was so astonished to see him that she could not refrain from questioning him.

"Come down, come down!" he called, trying to whisper, as if the whole house could not see him from any window on that side of the building. "I want to take you riding. You've already wasted too much time sleeping."

"I have not wasted a minute. I've had only six hours of sleep!" she protested.

"Any time we are apart is time wasted," Adam replied, his voice getting stronger as he recognized the futility of keeping his presence a secret. "Shall I go ask your father if you can go riding?" he persisted.

"No, no!" she protested. "He must be resting. Don't bother him. I have to help with breakfast this morning . . . You'd better come back later. I—I . . ."

She suddenly became very conscious that she was leaning out the window in her nightgown with her untamed hair escaping from its braid in the morning breeze.

"Go home, Adam," she ordered him, "and come back and call at a proper time."

"I told you last night," he replied. "I don't know how to do things properly . . ."

Just then another voice joined the conversation. It was Papa's, speaking from the casement window in the study. "Young man!" his voice was stern but not unkind. "You have wakened the entire household. Now take your steed and go home. Get a hot breakfast, unpack your bags, go register at the land and water office, and then you may come back to see my daughter and have dinner with us. Is that clear?"

Adam turned formally toward William Childress's window and bowed slightly. "Yes, sir. I will do as you advise. At what hour may I return?"

"At a decent hour, young man!" William roared. "At a

calling hour. At five o'clock in the evening. Is that satisfactory?"

With a flourish, Adam put on his wide-brimmed hat. "Yes, sir!" he said emphatically. Then, as William closed his window, Adam turned back to Hannah, who was still shivering by her open casement. "It will seem like an eternity until five o'clock," Adam called to her. "Think about me until then." He was off in a shower of gravel, as his horse pounded down the driveway.

Hannah watched until he was out of sight, and then she closed the window and ran toward the bed. She felt blue with cold. As she dived into the bed she heard Eliza laughing softly. "Oh my," Eliza said. "This is all so romantic!"

Shivering, Hannah snuggled down under the covers, but she got the last word. "Yes," she said, speaking the simple truth. "It is."

CHAPTER NINE

The day that Uncle Abner and his family left to return to Idaho was a gray and blustery day with wisps of snow in the air and a bone-chilling dampness in the wind.

There was grayness in the hearts of the families as well, because the future stretched before them with uncertainty and hardship. "We shall meet again soon, brother Abner," William said, embracing his younger brother's broad, work-hardened shoulders. "As soon, perhaps, as this summer. If I am able, I will make the trip to see your settlement in Idaho."

Abner smiled wistfully, and both brothers knew that the possibility of William's being able to leave his Church and civic duties in the near future was unlikely. But William had given Abner a wagon train of supplies for the winter, and he had also called several young men from the surrounding area to join the expedition back to Idaho.

"You've done more than I deserve or expected, William," Abner thanked his brother warmly. "We return with a much greater chance of success on account of your generosity."

"Generosity's easy," William rejoined. "It is courage that

makes the difference. Your courage is what will create your success. Go with God, and may he see you safely home."

The brothers embraced again, and with tears and heavy hearts the families bade farewell. Hannah stood with the other relatives in the front yard of the Big House and waved her apron until the slow-moving wagons were out of sight.

Adam accompanied Abner's party until they reached the north fork at the head of the canyon. It was late that night when he galloped back into town, but the lights were still burning in the windows of the Childress house when he mounted the porch two steps at a time and knocked on the door.

William Childress came to the door with an anxious look on his face. When he saw Adam he asked urgently, "Is everything all right?"

"Yes, sir," Adam replied. "Brother Abner and his party are well started. With any kind of luck—and the blessings of the Lord—they will make it to their valley in Idaho before the heavy snows."

William nodded absently. "Even if they run afoul of a storm or two, they are well supplied, and winter will not establish itself before they have time to get back to their home. Still, I shall rest better when I know they are back in their little fort."

"Fort?" Adam queried.

"Yes," William replied. "The Indians in that territory have been fed terrible lies by the mountain men, and they are fiercely opposed to a Mormon presence in that area. There have been several raids on the family by the natives. Rather half-hearted attacks—but still, there have been a few wounded and one death. I won't feel at ease until there is a larger number of white settlers in the Salmon Valley."

"Our relationship to the Indian tribes is difficult to sort out," Adam said. "Philosophically, politically, religiously, humanly—any way you want to think about it, the situation with our Lamanite brethren presents nothing but questions and mighty puzzling answers, as I learned on my mission."

William nodded. "That's true, young man, very true. But when the Indians are facing you with bows and arrows or guns, it does focus the questions with admirable swiftness."

Adam shrugged his shoulders. "For the moment, yes. But our need to defend ourselves still begs the question of whose fault it is that we are fighting over the same piece of land in the first place. We are, after all, the interlopers."

"Sent by God." William's voice closed the subject. Then he reached out and pulled Adam into the house. "Come in out of the cold, and tell me why you are banging on my door at this hour. Surely not to discuss the philosophical aspects of our relationship to our brothers the Lamanites."

"Brother Childress, I've come to ask if I have your permission to call upon Sister Hannah, your daughter." Adam cleared his throat nervously, but he stood his ground firmly and looked Hannah's father straight in the eye.

"Upon my honor," William laughed, "of course you do! I'll warn you, the girl has a mind of her own. She's like her mother. I heartily give you permission to call on her, but I have no control over what her feelings will be on the subject."

Adam smiled. "I have reason to believe she will not be displeased."

William laughed and ushered Adam back toward the door. "Well then, young man, it is time for both of us to get some rest. I will tell Hannah that you will call tomorrow at five. At the proper time." William's voice was warm, but it was also firm.

"Five o'clock it is, sir!" Adam ran down the stairs and mounted Ensign in a single leap.

When Mama and Eliza went back to the farm, Hannah asked her parents for permission to stay in town, and they both agreed. Eliza thought she should be allowed to stay, too. "The farm will be a graveyard without you, Hannah!" Eliza complained. "I don't see why we can't all stay in town!"

But Mama was anxious about the farm and insisted on hurrying back. Papa told Eliza that Mama could not be left alone and it was her duty to accompany her. With a heavy heart, but trying to be cheerfully obedient, Eliza left in the farm wagon, sitting next to Mama, with a load of delicious baked goods giving the trip a sweet aroma. When the wagon was several yards down Childress Avenue, Eliza turned around on her seat and stared at Hannah, who was still waving good-bye. With a look of resentment and resignation, Eliza stuck her tongue out at her sister and then turned back to face the road.

Through the months of October and November Hannah lived at the Big House, and Adam Fairfield came to visit her every day. Her father gave her a riding horse, and she and Adam rode in the autumn evenings out into the country, up the canyons, and, in the first snows of the season, they braved the elements to make fresh tracks in the empty square of the city park.

Several times Adam hired a buggy, and the two of them drove out to the farm to visit Mama and Eliza and have dinner with them. Eliza and Adam liked each other, and Hannah could tell that Mama approved of Adam as well. Mama listened to the young man gravely when he discussed the doctrines of the Church and the political future of Utah.

In early November Papa asked the young couple to ride out to the farm to take Mama the news that a courier had come from Idaho with a letter from Abner. The news was that Abner and his party were back at their settlement in Salmon Valley and were very grateful for the supplies and extra men that William had sent. Abner wrote that his family felt securely settled for the coming winter in the fort they had named Lemhi.

"So far," Abner's letter read, "we have seen only a little evidence of Indian unrest. Some of our stores were broken into while we were gone, and several sacks of grain were stolen. A small shed outside the walls of the fort was burned, and a few of our grazing stock have been killed. Now that we have returned, however, things have been very quiet. Winter is coming, and perhaps most of the tribes have gone to their winter hunting grounds. Let us pray they have gone, for the cruelty of the long winter is a hard enough battle. We ask the Lord that all will be well with you and yours. Abner."

Mama sat quietly when she heard the news. "He is a brave man, that Abner. It is important that we establish the corners of Zion. Outposts like his will be necessary if we are to preserve ourselves from the world."

"I do not think continued isolation will be possible for us or for the Church, Sister Childress," Adam said quietly. "The world is already at our doorstep. When California became a part of the United States, it was inevitable that Utah would become a stopping-off place for the highways of the nation. California's gold strike ensured a continuing exodus from east to west. This territory will never be ours alone. We will need to learn to live with Gentiles and still keep the faith."

Julia's face showed concern. "But surely, Adam, the Lord will keep us a peculiar people. We cannot ever let what happened in Nauvoo, or Missouri, or with Johnston's Army—those things must never happen again. We must have our own place—our own land—"

Adam saw the alarm in Julia's eyes, and he touched her arm gently to reassure her. "Those terrible things won't happen again, Sister Childress. We are too strong for that, but the day will come when we will need to live surrounded by the real world. We will need to learn that the only safe place for the gospel to be preserved and to prosper is within our own hearts and our own lives. Zion is not a geographical place.

"When we understand the principle of personal testimony," he continued, "our people will be able to live anywhere and still keep the Church alive and well. We just need to learn to believe in the restored Church with all our hearts and to live better and better."

Julia smiled. "You are an idealist, Adam. My brother was an idealist, and he was, perhaps, the finest man I ever knew—except for my husband, of course."

When Adam and Hannah drove back to the Big House that night, they jounced along in the little buggy Adam had rented and watched tiny silver snowflakes, no bigger than motes of dust, twisting in the moonlight.

"The reason Mama dreads the outside world so much is that I was born when she had to retreat from Johnston's Army. Brigham Young called Papa to gather everyone from Ogden and evacuate down to Payson," Hannah explained.

"Mama said it was a terrifying time. They left everything they owned. Just closed their doors—some people even left their meals at the table—and got into wagons and headed south. Everyone was afraid the army was going to pillage and burn and destroy, as the mobs had done in Missouri and Nauvoo.

"In the end, nothing happened. But the fear was as

damaging as a wound. After a few weeks Brigham Young sent word that everyone could return to their homes. During the expulsion, Mama gave birth to me in a flat wagon bed in an open field on a rainy night. She brought me home to Riverdale when I was three weeks old."

The horses had slowed, and Adam drew them gently to a halt.

He was silent for a long time, and Hannah grew uncomfortable in the indigo and silver light of the winter night. "Adam," she whispered, trying to see his face, "I'm freezing. What is it?"

She could see the outline of his head. It was bowed, but its noble lines and the strong bearing of his shoulders touched her with a sudden rush of tenderness, and she wanted to reach out and stroke his hair.

Suddenly he turned to her and grasped her mittened hand. With such slow and careful fingers that she could scarcely feel his touch, he drew the mitten from her hand and held her sweet, warm palm with his cold fingers. Tenderly he stroked the soft skin, turning her hand over in his as if it were a rare volume of precious antiquity, too delicate for mortal handling. Then, with infinite slowness, he raised her fingers to his smooth, cool lips and kissed each one with quiet longing.

"Hannah," he whispered, "tomorrow I will ask your father for your hand in marriage. I know it is a very short courtship, but I cannot live without you. You have become as necessary to me as the air I breathe, and I believe you have feelings for me, too. I am not a man who is patient or subtle. From the moment I saw you in the doorway of the ballroom, I have wanted you to be my wife, and every moment that we are together only confirms that feeling."

With a shuddering breath, Hannah pulled her hand

away from his grip and with shaking fingers put her mitten back on. "I don't know what to say, Adam."

"Say that you feel it, too!" he exclaimed. "Oh, Hannah. Surely a man cannot feel the kind of fire that burns inside me whenever you are near and not have some similar warmth ignite in the woman next to him! Please tell me that I am not mistaken, that you, too, feel some of the yearnings that are tearing at me."

"I—I—" Hannah stammered, uncertain and over-whelmed by the intensity of Adam's words.

"I'm sorry. I should restrain myself," Adam said, more quietly. "I find it hard to express my feelings, but once I begin I seem unable to stop myself. Of course, I am not such a fool that I do not understand that women of honor do not feel the same passions as men. I should not have asked such an intrusive question."

There was a long moment of awkward silence, and finally Adam gave a resigned sigh and reached for the reins. Hannah's hand flew out and caught his. "No, Adam! Please, let's stay another moment. I want to answer your question, but I can only do it here, in the dark."

She drew a long breath. Then she folded his hand in her two mittened hands and held it against her breast. "I feel everything that you are feeling, Adam. It is like our hearts are one heart, and I feel the fire and the pain and the joy. Perhaps that means I am not a woman of honor. I don't know. All I know is that I love you and I need you—and I want you."

With a shout of joy, Adam threw his arms around Hannah and kissed her soundly on her soft, red mouth. Her cheeks were as cold and smooth as marble, but her mouth was as warm as the heart of the sun. Adam held her in an embrace as old and as certain as the promise of Eden, and the two remained locked in that chaste and affirming posture as though they had, at last, found the place where they had always belonged.

The horse, uncertain what to do without the guidance of human hands on the reins, began to meander along the road to town, wearily plodding his way toward home and the warm, hay-scented stable.

In the days that followed Hannah experienced moments of both the greatest joy and the greatest disappointment of her life.

William Childress was delighted at the prospect of his daughter marrying Adam Fairfield. He knew the young man well. Not only was Adam working with William on planning the district water systems, but he had known Adam's parents for many years. Hannah could not have found a more suitable husband, William was certain, but the unseemly swiftness of the courtship was a little disturbing to him, and it was devastating to Hannah's prim and proper sister Anne. Anne did not hesitate to make her feelings known.

"Papa," Anne snapped, "it is disgraceful for Hannah to meet a young man and plan to be married in only a month's time! Such behavior will attract all kinds of unsavory gossip. You are not in a position to let a member of our family set such a precedent. You know it will cause talk!"

"Now, Anne, other people's gossip is not a good criterion for making a decision. Anyone who knows Hannah and Adam will know they are intelligent and upright young people, and such a decisive action on their part will come as no surprise."

"It is almost Christmas," Anne went on, still outraged. "We already have an enormous amount of entertaining planned at the house and so many obligations that it will be impossible to add a wedding party to the festivities."

William frowned. "Anne," he said impatiently, with an edge to his voice, "whenever the wedding takes place, the wedding party will be held here at the Big House—no other event would take precedence. You are a very conscientious woman, Anne, but these are matters which do not concern you. They are between Julia, Hannah, Adam, and me."

Feeling chastised and offended, Anne flounced out of the room.

It was not only Anne's less-than-gracious response that proved a problem, however. The real resistance came from a source that Hannah had not expected. A few days after Adam's proposal, Hannah rode out to the farm alone to visit with her mother and ask her opinion about the wedding plans. Arriving at the house in the early afternoon, she shook the snow off her scarf and coat and took off her outer shoes. The house was chilly and dim in the early winter darkness and very, very quiet.

"Where is everybody?" Hannah called, as she heard footsteps overhead. Eliza came swiftly down the narrow staircase.

"Oh, sister!" Eliza exclaimed. "I'm so glad you are here. I sent Brother Warren to town to fetch you and Papa. Mama is not well, and I don't know what to do!"

Hannah ran up the stairs and into her mother's room. "What is it, Mama?" she cried. "Are you hurt? Are you sick?"

It was odd, she thought, that by now everyone knew Mama was going to have a baby. It had become physically obvious, and, even though Mama stayed in seclusion, anyone who saw her could not fail to notice that she was pregnant. Still, no word was said by anyone because, as apparent as her pregnancy was, it would be a terrible social indiscretion to say anything about it. No one could properly acknowledge her condition or mention it out loud!

How funny people are! Hannah thought. Having babies is as natural a part of living as breathing or eating, but for some reason it must be hidden and concealed—as though it were something to be ashamed of in polite society. Hannah could not think of any purpose or value in such secrecy. It seemed damaging and unnatural to her.

Hannah had attended the birth of hundreds of animals and had watched cows, horses, dogs, cats, sheep, pigs, and goats give birth. Beginning at age ten she had been trained to care for and help the farm animals in delivery. She had an intense interest in medical care and nursing: both of animals and of people. It was a skill that came naturally to her, and she had a great feeling of love for the newborn creatures of both barn and field.

Since lambing time was always difficult, and every pair of trained hands was necessary, Hannah had begun her training during lambing season. For some reason the Lord had created sheep to give birth in the cold, cold days of early spring. Each year the skin on Hannah's hands became raw from her work in the lambing sheds, but she never tired of the miracle of birth.

Over and over again she watched as each wet, young lamb—by some incredible act of heavenly knowledge—found its own mother, who licked the matted wool on the wobbly infant and guided it to eat. Each maternal tableau was filled with all the wonder of life.

The farm's lambing crews had come to count on Hannah for help because her small hands were able to reach inside the ewes when a presentation was wrong. She could often unwind a cord or grasp a tiny hoof—saving both lamb and ewe. Everyone on the farm took such events as a matter of course.

Yet here was her own mother, many months pregnant from the look of her, and no one within the family had spoken a word of the matter. Surely her mother would break the code of silence and say something to Hannah now, when she was apparently having difficulties, opening the subject so that Hannah would be free to ask honest questions.

Instead, Julia lifted a white, thin face from the pillow. "Don't be alarmed, Hannah dear. I'm a little tired, that's all. As I have told Eliza, I just need some rest. I'll be fine in a day or two."

It was clear that Mama had no intention of speaking of her pregnancy. Her Victorian sense of decency and propriety could not be breeched.

Julia belonged to a generation that thought carrying a child was a disgraceful thing—an evidence of original sin, a weakness of the human condition. Mama pretended to herself and everyone else that her pregnancy was concealed. To speak of the pregnancy would be to shatter her illusion and force her to acknowledge that the world was perfectly aware that she had known a man in secret and intimate ways.

To approach her before she herself had spoken openly of her condition would be a social and personal insult. So, even though Julia was not well, no one could openly discuss the cause of her illness without specific permission— not even her own daughter.

Hannah realized immediately that things were not going well, not for Mama, and not for the farm. Her mother looked truly ill, and already the house and farm had taken on an air of sad neglect. Eliza looked lonely, overwhelmed, and helpless.

With the boy who drove the supply wagon, Hannah sent word back to the Big House that she would be staying at the farm to help her mother. She requested that Papa send her things out to the farm with the next wagon. The following evening, when Adam was told the news, he galloped out to Riverdale and pounded on the farmhouse door.

"What's going on?" he demanded anxiously, as Hannah invited him in. The rooms of the farmhouse were cold and cheerless. Eliza and Hannah had spent much of the day in their mother's bedroom, watching her still, white face as she slept, not knowing what to do. The house had the strange, neglected feeling that comes when there is serious illness.

"Mama is not well," Hannah whispered. "I am so sorry, Adam, but I have to stay here until things are better. There's no one else who knows the farm well enough to run it, and Mama needs a great deal of nursing."

It had taken Hannah several hours of careful observation and discreet questioning to figure out what was wrong with her mother. Julia had developed an infection in her kidneys. She was in a great deal of pain, with blood in her urine and the need to be helped to the chamber pot with great frequency. Hannah was frightened by her mother's condition, which seemed to worsen overnight.

The next morning Julia had become feverish and started vomiting. "Boil some willow tea," Julia had whispered to her daughter. "And I will also need some alum. You will find it in my herb chest."

Hannah had prepared the remedies as her mother directed. Julia sipped the hot brew and shuddered as she took the alum, but the medicine and rest seemed to help. Finally, in the early afternoon, Mama had fallen into a fitful doze. Now Adam had come, and even though she had not sent for him, Hannah felt the relief of his presence as if it were a soothing balm.

Hannah knew it would be highly improper to discuss anything about her mother's condition, but she felt so close to Adam that there was nothing she feared to say to him, and she had to talk to someone whose judgment she could trust or she felt she would go mad.

"Mama's really sick, Adam," Hannah's voice shook. "It may be months before she is better. I'll have to stay until I know she's all right."

"When is the baby due?" Adam asked with a directness that both astonished and reassured Hannah. She should have known Adam would not be deterred by absurd rules of secrecy or social decorum. He had no patience for the shrouds of delicacy.

"She won't even discuss it with me," Hannah sighed. "She thinks that being with child is a disgrace and should be hidden."

"The attitudes of Queen Victoria have infected the known world!" Adam exclaimed. "The Queen believes it is improper to be perceived carrying a child. Strangely, she is both proud and delighted to announce the arrival of the new baby. But the infant is to have appeared by abstraction with nothing physical involved. Such secrecy surrounding times of confinement cannot be healthy for women or their babies."

It was such a relief to speak of her concerns that Hannah put her head on Adam's shoulder and began to cry. "How can I help Mama if she believes she cannot even talk about her condition without impropriety?"

"Darling girl," Adam said, "you must do what the Spirit directs you to do. Even if it makes your mother angry, you must speak to her frankly and find the proper medical help for her."

His arms were around her slender shoulders. Adam held Hannah against his heart and thought her the sweetest thing the Lord had ever given to him. The opportunity to hold, comfort, and advise this wonderful young woman was already dearer to him than his own life.

"Adam," she gulped back her tears. "I'm getting your coat all wet." He handed her a large, white, linen handkerchief and reluctantly released her from his embrace.

She looked at him with a woebegone expression, her eyes filled with worry and disappointment. "I think it's going to be a long time before the baby is born. Probably three or four months. Mama needs me, Adam. You can see that I cannot leave her. We'll have to put off the wedding until she is well."

Adam tried to keep the pain out of his own eyes. "I understand, dearest," he whispered. "I know she needs you. We'll pray the time goes by quickly. You must not worry about a thing. I will come out to visit you as often as I can."

When Adam mounted Ensign that night, the snow began falling steadily, and Hannah handed him a baked potato, fresh and hot from the oven. "Put that inside your coat," she said, "and it will keep you warm."

Adam bent down from the saddle and kissed her upturned face. "The thought of you will keep me warm," he said. "I will bring the doctor tomorrow. Take care."

For a long time after Adam left, Hannah stood looking down the narrow road as it filled with white and silent snow, and the moon rose like a silver lantern.

CHAPTER TEN

The next evening Doctor Morgan arrived with Adam and William Childress. The doctor was in Julia's room for nearly an hour, and when he came out and looked at the upturned faces of the family, his expression was grave.

"Julia will need to remain in bed until this crisis is completely passed. She is retaining water in her extremities and needs to be kept absolutely quiet. Her liquid intake should be restricted, and salt must be eliminated from her diet. Aside from that, and making her comfortable, there is little we can do."

The long weeks began. Hannah read everything she could find on child-bearing and its complications. Doctor Morgan lent her anatomy and obstetrical texts, and she sent for medical pamphlets. The library at the Big House yielded a medical handbook with a few chapters on childbirth and its complications. Over and over again she was astonished at how meager the information was. It was a subject on which even the medical journals seemed determined to keep a discreet and—as Hannah was beginning to feel—a deadly silence.

Her own helplessness as she watched her mother grow thin and pale, with puffy hands and feet that ached and

93

split, was a source of agony to Hannah. Willow tea seemed to afford some relief, and, as long as her mother remained resting and still, her condition did not measurably worsen. Some days were better than others, but Hannah could tell that her mother was growing weaker and more exhausted as the weeks passed.

Although Christmas was approaching, the house remained silent and bleak. Neither Eliza nor Hannah felt any desire to decorate or cook treats. Few visitors, except Adam and William, made the journey to the farm in the winter weather. Most people were too busy preparing for their holiday festivities to give a thought to the little family struggling in the isolation of the farm.

William spent every weekend at Julia's side, unless the weather was too extreme to allow travel or the demands of his work and Church responsibilities kept him in town. Adam, however, came to visit Hannah at least two or three times a week as well as on the weekends, bringing news of the family, the community, and of the progress of the planning for the reservoir and water system.

Two weeks before Christmas, Adam came bursting through the farmhouse door, bringing a swirl of cold air and snow with him. "The roads are so bad that Ensign barely made it," Adam announced. "There will be no wagons or buggies coming down that road until this blizzard slows down."

"Then you must not try to return tonight, Adam," Julia said softly. She had come down to the kitchen and was sitting in the rocking chair. It was one of her better days, and she was feeling a little stronger. Adam was alarmed to see how poor Julia's color was and how swollen her little feet were in the soft house slippers she was wearing.

With a laugh, Adam walked over to the stove. "Well, I'll worry about the return journey when the time comes. In the meantime, Hannah, your firebox is practically empty. Come outside and help me gather some firewood."

Eagerly, Hannah grabbed her coat and shawl. "We'll only be a minute!" she told Julia and Eliza as she followed Adam out the door. As soon as they were around the corner by the woodpile, Adam swept Hannah into his arms and kissed her with such yearning passion that tears came to her eyes.

He held her in his arms and pressed his face into her hair. "The days seem endless without you, Hannah. It seems like the only time I am really alive is when I am here with you. Constance keeps trying to involve me in parties and socials, and sometimes I can't refuse without seeming completely ungracious. But it is never any use. Everything is empty without you."

A little thrill of fear touched Hannah's spine. "Constance?" she repeated. "You are spending time with Constance?"

Adam laughed at her discomfort. "Listen, you silly girl. Of course I see Constance. I'm working with your father, remember? I go to see him in his office at the Big House every day. I can't always avoid Constance. It would look ridiculous. Hey! Is this a spot of jealousy? I think I like it."

She turned away from him with an impatient toss of her head. Quickly he put his arm around her shoulders and pulled her to him. "It means absolutely nothing. Everything I do when I am away from you is just filling in time."

"I know, Adam," she whispered breathlessly. "I feel that way, too. I don't want to be away from you, but Mama needs me more than ever. She is growing weaker and weaker as the baby grows larger. I am bound here until this is over."

"When do you think the baby will be born?" Adam asked.

"It can only be a few more weeks," Hannah answered, her voice breaking. "Mama can't survive much longer than that, I'm afraid. I still don't know when for sure, because she will not discuss it with me."

Adam held Hannah against himself as though he would never let her go, and then he took a deep breath and released her. Looking into her eyes he gave a determinedly light-hearted laugh. "Well, all this nursing drudgery has done something to your looks."

Hannah flushed, and her hands flew to her cheeks. "Oh, I know! I must look terrible. I don't have time or inclination to fix my hair, or tend my clothes . . ."

"No," Adam said seriously, "it's not that. What it is— is—that you look prettier than ever, and I'm trying to figure out how that is possible. Either worry and work are becoming to you, or I just forget between visits how beautiful you really are!"

Hannah laughed out loud with surprised happiness at his outrageous compliment. "You are better than a tonic, Adam. I thought I had forgotten how to laugh."

"I think all three of you have forgotten how to laugh," Adam said quietly. "Since it seems I may be marooned here by the weather, I think I will go about teaching you how again."

They carried heavy loads of kindling and logs into the house and stacked them in the kitchen and by the fireplace in the dark, unused sitting room.

Adam looked around at the gloom. "No wonder all of you have grown glum," he said sternly. "You've forgotten how to make a house come alive. It is Christmas, you know."

Hannah rubbed her back and stretched her neck. "I know," she said, "but the days seem to run into one another, and besides, there doesn't seem to be much to celebrate this year."

"That," said Adam, "is exactly the time when you should make the greatest effort."

Adam built a huge fire in the fireplace in the front room, and, when the room had grown bright and toasty, he lighted the lamps, carried Julia into the room, and placed her on the deep horsehair sofa. Putting a book in her hands, he asked Julia if she would be all right alone for a while. She responded with a tender smile, "Of course I will, dear Adam. You and the girls run along and enjoy the fresh snow."

The three young people put on coats and mittens and, carrying a lantern, went out to check the barn animals. They placed feed and water in the stalls and locked the barns and sheds against the steady drift of falling snow.

The snowfall was heavy, but the wind was not cold, and the flakes were thick and white as feathers. It was a magical night. Eliza, Hannah, and Adam stood in the barnyard after their chores were finished and shivered in the beauty of it all. Even the house looked beautiful with smoke rising from the chimney and the lamps softly glowing in the windows.

"Time to bring a little Christmas into your lives," Adam shouted, running through the soft drifts of snow toward a wooded copse beyond the kitchen field. They ran after him, laughing, and in the next hour they collected branches of cedar, clumps of mountain laurel, and clusters of mistletoe from the dying oaks. Their arms laden with the bounty of the winter woodland, they staggered back to the house through the deepening snow.

As they entered the house, warmth from the roaring fire reached out to them, and, for the first time in weeks,

Hannah felt like the farm was home, not just a place of sorrow and sickness.

As Julia watched, the three young people festooned the quiet house with Christmas greenery. They sang carols as they worked, and the fire crackled in the hearth. Hannah watched happily as she saw two bright pink spots appear on her mother's pale cheeks, and, for the first time since she had come home, she saw her mother's face glowing with happiness.

On impulse Hannah went over and put her arms around her mother. "Everything is going to be all right," she said, tears coming to her eyes. "I know it, Mama. We'll get through this, I promise, and you'll be putting up the decorations yourself next year."

Julia patted her daughter's hand. "You take such good care of me, Hannah. I am very, very grateful. I know how hard this long delay is for you and Adam. I wish it were not so . . ." Her voice trailed off.

"No, no, Mama! Don't worry about such things. All we want is to see you well once again. There will be time enough for Adam and me." Hannah's voice was reassuring and resolute, but sometimes she felt trapped, as though she were condemned to live Julia's life, when her own life beckoned. With determination Hannah put away the unworthy thoughts. Certainly Mama would never have chosen to be sick. Mama was trapped in this circumstance as much as she was.

The house looked festive and alive and the hours passed more swiftly than any time Hannah could remember since returning to the farm. As the evening progressed, Julia began to pale, and Eliza started yawning outright.

Adam went over to Julia. "Time for you to call it a night, I think, Sister Childress. Let me carry you to your room."

He wrapped Julia carefully in her woolen shawl, lifted her easily, and carried her up the stairs.

Eliza and Hannah followed. Hannah had prepared the bedwarmer with some coals from the fire, and she passed the heated pan across the sheets of her mother's bed. Then Adam tenderly placed Julia between the covers.

With gentle hands Hannah pulled up the coverlets, and Julia fell back thankfully against the deep pillows. "I think I shall sleep very well tonight," Julia murmured. "Thank you for a lovely evening."

"Goodnight, Mama," the girls said, and kissed her on the cheek. Adam waited quietly outside the door while they settled their mother for the night. When Hannah and Eliza came out of the room, Eliza said, "I think it would be best if Adam slept downstairs in the daybed in the kitchen. The guest room is freezing and the bed is not made up."

Hannah agreed. "You can keep the fires going downstairs if you don't mind, Adam, and the house will stay warm through the storm."

"Happy to," Adam answered cheerfully. "I'll be very comfortable in the kitchen. I know that Ensign, too, is thankful to be in the warm barn tonight instead of fighting his way through a wall of snow."

"I'll get Adam's bed made up, Eliza," Hannah said. "I'll be up in a minute, as soon as Adam is settled."

Eliza giggled. "No hurry!"

Hannah went to the cupboard and pulled sheets, blankets, and pillows onto the floor. Adam gathered them up. Laughing, stacked high with bedding, they made their way down the stairway and into the kitchen.

While Hannah pulled the daybed nearer the stove and put the bedclothes on it, Adam stoked up the fire and adjusted the dampers. The kitchen was warm and had a sweet, yeasty smell as though all the past years of hearty foods and laden tables had left the air perfumed with plenty.

In the dim light of the dying fire, Hannah became aware of the intimacy of the situation, and she suddenly felt self-conscious. The bed lay between the two of them, smooth and inviting with its white sheets and thick, feather pillows and soft quilts.

"I'll leave you now, Adam. You must be tired. It's been a long day." Hannah turned and started to go, but Adam reached across the bed and caught her hand. At his touch she became as still as a startled rabbit. For a moment she felt his hand tight against hers, as though he had to will it to refrain from pulling her down onto the bed that lay so temptingly beneath their joined hands.

If he did pull her toward the bed, Hannah thought, she did not know how she would react. Her heart was beating like a wild thing, and she felt the blood rushing to her head. In a moment of terrible clarity she knew she wanted him to pull her down. She wanted to lie down beside him, to feel his arms around her, to seize the comfort of sleeping next to his strong, lean body while his hands and his kisses caressed all the loneliness and fear out of her.

She could not meet his eyes. For a moment they stood silently—each fighting a silent battle with desires stronger than either had ever known. Then she heard a great breath expel from his lungs. With firmness he pulled her beyond the bed and toward the darkened sitting room, where he gently guided her to the sofa. The fireplace glowed with the dying embers of the huge fire, and the room was still warm. The decorative greenery gave off the fresh scent of pine and bayberry, and Hannah felt the two of them had escaped a moment of real peril.

Adam bent in matter-of-fact fashion to put a fresh log on the fire, and then he went to stand by the window.

Hannah felt he was trying to reestablish the normal balance of their relationship and to quiet the dark temptations that had almost overwhelmed them both in the kitchen.

The room was dark so they could see out into the night quite clearly. The snow was falling more heavily than before.

"This is going to be a serious storm," Adam said. "It's possible that the farm may be snowed in for several days. You don't suppose your reputation will be damaged if I am an extended guest, do you?"

Adam's voice was light, but she sensed that he understood the seriousness of the question.

She thought for a moment. "Not with Mama here—and Eliza. Besides, the snow is an impeccable excuse." She took a deep breath. "I miss you so much, Adam."

Adam laughed. "Bless the snow!" he said.

They were silent for several minutes, both thinking of the empty bed in the other room, and yet both knowing they would do nothing about it. There was too much at stake that was of infinite value, and as strong as their desires for one another were, their sense of honor was stronger.

"Adam," Hannah whispered fervently, "I have nothing to give you for Christmas except all my thoughts—all my heart—everything I am or hope to be—all of myself—you may have all of that. I do love you, Adam."

An ember in the fire snapped and flared, and then there was silence. Hannah sat on the sofa wondering if she had said too much. Had she opened her heart in a way that was too forward? Perhaps Adam was tired of waiting for her. Maybe he was already interested in someone else. Constance was right there, under his very feet. He must be tired of the long ride out to the farm.

Suddenly, in the quiet room, Hannah felt frightened and

foolish. Was she too obvious in her love for him? Didn't she have enough sense to flirt and play hard-to-get? Had she misjudged the depth of Adam's feelings for her? Should she have kept silent? His quiet remoteness suddenly frightened her.

Adam continued standing at the window with his back toward her, looking out at the snow whirling and glinting against the darkness. When he spoke his voice was low and serious. "I love you, too, Hannah. More than you can ever know. You must believe that. I want to marry you more than I want life itself, but there is something I must tell you, and I cannot put it off any longer. Please say nothing until I'm finished, and then, if you want me to go, I will go."

With a gasp of apprehension, Hannah clasped her throat. Fear almost choked her. What was Adam saying? Was he trying to find a way to tell her kindly that he had met someone else during the long weeks she had been sequestered at the farm? Was it Constance after all? Her heart pounded, and she waited in dread.

CHAPTER ELEVEN

Adam began quietly, still not looking at Hannah, but staring out the window at the blizzard. "When I left on my mission to the Lamanites in the southern states, I was told by Brigham Young himself that I was to find a way into the heart of the Indian tribes. It was the wish of the Lord. 'They are a people lost to their own heritage,' President Young said. 'You are called to bring them back to it, and the Lord will show you the way.'

"I went into the Blue Mountains and followed the hills southward, stopping at Indian villages and encampments and carrying a knapsack with copies of the Book of Mormon.

"Everywhere I went I found remnants of tribes. The ancestral Indian villages were a thing of the past. Lodges had caved in, and the pathways had become overgrown with vines and undergrowth. Those Lamanites who had not been relocated to reservations were living in nomadic clans or had gravitated toward white settlements and were living on the fringes of the frontier as dependents on the dregs of our society.

"Finally, I found a small clan of Chickasaw that had managed to keep the old ways. They had built a village after the old traditions, with lodges and wickiups, close to a deep, swift stream. They lived by fishing and hunting and by cultivating yams, corn, and beans.

"The old chief's name was Mantoowam, and for some reason he took a liking to me. I stayed with the village through my first winter. It was cold and wet, with heavy mud and chilling rains that made the old lodges seem luxurious with their rich, smokey air and the warmth of fire and bodies. I spent many a rainy day sitting around the chief's fire with the men of the village, speaking of the meanings of life, while his wives and daughters chatted and giggled at their tasks.

"I spoke to the men of the Great Spirit. Of the coming of Moroni. Of the record of the Lamanite people, which was restored to the earth. The men of the tribe listened to me. I earned their respect.

"They taught me how to hunt and fish and invited me to go with them to their summer hunting grounds. At the end of the winter, I had almost forgotten I was not Chickasaw. I had lived with the tribe for so long that their thinking, their voices, their way of life had seeped into me. When Chief Mantoowam asked me if I wished to be adopted into the tribe in the week before they prepared to move to their summer place, I accepted his invitation.

"It seemed to me that this was a sign from the Lord. If I was to have an influence on these people, I would need to be one of them, and so I went through the ceremony of adoption. After five days of dancing, fasting, and trial by fire . . ."

Here Adam paused and walked over to where Hannah sat, as still as if she had been turned to stone. He opened his shirt, and, in the flickering firelight, he showed her three straight scars across his chest. "The marks of initiation," he said.

He continued his story, but now he was sitting at the

104

other end of the settee, his earnest eyes in the semidarkness searching her face as if he wanted to memorize it, as if he wanted to see every thought she was thinking.

"What I did not realize, Hannah—I swear to you I did not know it—was the end of the initiation and adoption. As I stood by the fire dressed in my gift robe of painted leather, beads, and feathers, they brought the chief's daughter to me. Princess Taconah. She was the final gift. The chief married us that night. I believed at the time that it was the Lord's way of telling me what I must do—that this action was the fulfillment of my commandment from Brigham Young, the true beginning of my mission among the Lamanites.

"For over a year I lived their ways. Taconah, my wife, stayed with me and cooked my food and shared my bed. Gradually I was able to teach many of the tribe, and some of them were baptized. In all that time I had heard nothing from the Church headquarters. Not one single word. I sent letters to the Brethren whenever I could by any foot travelers who passed our way, but I had no way of knowing if my letters had reached Salt Lake.

"Since the time I had received my calling and been sent to the southern Indian nations, it was as if I had been cut off from the rest of the world, from everyone in my former life: my family, the Church, my friends. That world had ceased to exist. I simply had faith that I was doing the work I had been called to do and that the Lord knew where I was and was directing my work.

"At the end of that year my wife gave birth to a baby. Our baby. A little girl."

Hannah drew a shuddering breath, and tears came to her eyes, but she did not otherwise move or speak. Adam reached out his hand to touch her and then pulled back, uncertain how she would react to his touch.

"The baby did not live out the night of its birth. The

next morning Taconah rose from our bed and said to me, 'You are not true Chickasaw. The Great Spirit tells me this,' she said. 'I return to the lodge of my father.' Then she spoke the words of denunciation over me and picked up her deerskin bag with all her belongings.

"I begged her to stay, to let me take care of her. But she said not another word to me. It was as if I did not exist. She had wrapped our dead baby in her blanket, and she lifted it in her arms, slipped silently out of our lodge, and never returned.

"Divorce and marriage are that simple, swift, and final in the tribes. When Taconah said the sentence 'I return to the lodge of my father,' the marriage was completely erased, just as if it had never occurred. It is the Indian way.

"For days I did not know what to do. I had not loved her, at least not in the sense that I understand love now, but I cared about her and felt a great responsibility toward her. I felt that in taking her as a wife, I had been obedient to the will of the Lord, and yet the union had not proved to be a blessing for us or for the tribe.

"The chief welcomed Taconah back into his lodge as indifferently as he had let her go, and it was as if nothing had happened. No one spoke of the marriage, or the child, or the separation. A year of my life had simply been washed away.

"Suddenly I knew that I did not understand these people. Their emotions and their customs were alien to everything I was feeling. My heart was on fire with grief and a sense of failure, and they were impassive. It seemed to me at that moment that if I lived with them forever, I would still be a stranger to their ways. Taconah was right. I was not Chickasaw.

"Completely without guidance from any higher authority but desperately wondering why I had heard nothing from the Brethren in all that time, I determined that I would make my way back to the railhead and return to Utah. I would go see Brother Brigham, and, if he sent me back to the nations again, I would go. I would stay there the rest of my life—an alien being in an alien land—if that was what I was called to do by the Lord. But, in my despair, I had to know what my calling was.

"When I arrived in Utah, I went directly to the Beehive House and was given immediate audience with the president. When he heard my story he said, 'Brother Fairfield, we had lost track of your location and have been anxious about where you were for many months. Now the Lord has brought you home to us. You have served an honorable mission and have done everything that the Lord has desired of you. Now, return to your university studies in the East and then come home and help build Zion.'"

Adam stopped speaking.

Silence lay between Adam and Hannah like a thicket. Neither dared to speak for fear of not finding the right path through the tangle of emotions and thoughts that overwhelmed them.

It was Hannah who spoke first. Her voice sounded rusty, as if it had lost its use. "Why did you tell this to me?"

Adam's voice was fervent. "Because you are part of me, and I could not let any secret stand in the way of our completeness. It was selfish of me to unburden this on your innocent shoulders, and yet I could not bear keeping secret something that you have every right to know.

"I did not want you to think that I come to you with the same gifts of innocence that you bring to our union. It is your right to know my past. There can be no empty spaces between us."

She thought about his words for a moment, and then

she bowed her head. "Yes," she affirmed, "that is true. There can be no secrets between us."

Moments passed, and then she raised her eyes to his. "You must have loved Taconah some."

There was another long silence before Adam answered. "I don't know if it was love. I accepted her. I grew comfortable with her and . . ." He cleared his throat. " . . . and I found physical and emotional comfort with her. Perhaps that is a form of love, but it is nothing—I tell you, Hannah—it is nothing compared to the feeling I have for you. Nothing. The two emotions cannot compare. That is the truth."

The passion of Adam's voice filled the room as he continued. "Had I known what true love was, had I known you and what was waiting for me in your splendid untouched heart, I swear that if an angel had appeared in person and commanded me to marry Taconah, I would not have done so."

Hannah's voice was shocked. "Hush, Adam. That is a defiant and unrighteous thing to say."

Adam groaned. "You're right. Since I feel that God has given you to me as the greatest gift a man could wish, then surely I would have to say that I would do anything for Him in return, and yet I have, in His name, done something you may never be able to forgive. In being obedient to Him, I may have lost you."

Another silence. "Did President Young think you had done the righteous thing in accepting Taconah as your wife?" Hannah asked softly.

"Yes. Yes, he did," Adam replied quietly. "He said I had fulfilled my commission in the fulness of the spirit and the letter. He told me that the marriage was the Lord's way of giving me an opportunity to teach my Lamanite brethren. He said it was the will of God."

"Then I, too, say so," Hannah said, firmly and quietly.

108

"Adam, I do not know what the Lord had in mind when He gave Taconah to you, but I believe you did exactly what He required of you. I am only thankful that He has sent you back to me."

There was a long moment of silence, and then Hannah said softly, "I know how hard it must have been for you to speak of these things. Thank you, Adam. This is the best gift you have ever given me—to trust me with the burden of your past. To be unafraid to tell me things which are so seldom talked about out loud.

"I am desperate to be able to speak openly of matters that touch the most tender and private parts of life. I am tired of secrets and primness and false modesties and manners that make us afraid to express our deepest, most important thoughts and experiences. I know there are matters which need to be discreet and intimate—but between husband and wife, there should be no barriers."

Adam stood up and walked back to the night-dark window. The room was growing cold as the fire died down. He was so silent that Hannah grew alarmed, and she walked over and placed her hand gently on his arm. He turned toward her, and, in the light from the moon she could see tears glistening on his strong, manly face.

"Hannah," he said, his voice rough with overwhelming emotion, "I did not know what love was until I met you. I will spend my life caring for you, watching over you, and, if God will let me, I will see that nothing will ever hurt you again."

She put her arms around him and they stood locked in a solid, comforting embrace. "Sh-h-h, Adam," she murmured soothingly. "You have not hurt me. I am grateful for this shared confidence, for it binds me to you more strongly than ever by ties of trust and truth as well as love. All is well, dear love, all is well."

CHAPTER TWELVE

Christmas Day was as quiet and tedious as fast meeting day. Adam had left several days earlier, and another storm had come in from the east on Christmas Eve to drop its heavy load. The farm was snowbound, shrouded in a thick, silent blanket of snow. The only color that could be seen from the kitchen window was white, with the blue, shadowed indentations of Hannah's booted feet looking like stitches from the kitchen to the barn where she had walked to feed and water the animals.

On the horizon the two young sisters could see the lazy smoke rising from the chimneys of the farm workers' cabins, but, aside from the trails of smoke, the Christmas morning sky was swept clean and icy blue. Nothing stirred as far as the eye could see, and Hannah and Eliza could only imagine the laughter, the opening of presents, and the warm smells in other kitchens.

Their own breakfast was the usual oatmeal, with a bit of coarse sugar and the foamy milk that Hannah had stripped from Maizie's teats when she had done the chores at the barn earlier in the morning.

The girls took up a tray to their mother, with a sprig of mistletoe, wished her Merry Christmas, and sang a chorus of "The Boar's Head," the carol their mother had sung to them when they were little. "It reminds me of my childhood," Julia told them. "We always sang that carol on Christmas Eve in the great hall when the servants brought in the Christmas feast."

When Eliza and Hannah were little girls they had sat at their mother's feet in round-eyed wonder as Julia described the richness and beauty of her childhood Christmases in England. It still seemed to them that those stories were more like a fairy tale than any real experience or any part of their dear, familiar mother's life.

Christmas Day dragged endlessly. No presents and no company. The roads from Ogden were snowed in, so Adam and William did not come. Not even sleighs could make the journey out to the farm because horses would have foundered in the deep drifts.

In the days following Christmas, a stiff wind and warming temperatures cleared the snow enough that Papa and Adam were able to plow their way out to the farm. The happy group spent a wonderful evening in Mama's room talking, singing, opening presents, and enjoying the treats that had been sent from the Big House. It was three days after Christmas.

The visit tired Mama quickly, and she fell asleep before Adam and Papa had to start back. The two men hurried out to the sleigh in the twilight, intent on getting back to town before the night air grew too cold for traveling. Wrapped to their ears in heavy mufflers, with Papa wearing a coat of buffalo skins and Adam in a thick, woolen greatcoat, the two men looked more like bears than humans, and Eliza and Hannah watched them go with great yearning.

Papa had explained to the girls how work on the blueprints for the water system was going. The work of engineering the far-reaching project was a complex design

111

problem, and Adam was spending hours drawing up plans that would anticipate all objections and contingencies.

The political and civic challenges of the project were almost as great as the difficulties of the design. Long meetings, differing opinions, opposition in raising bond issues and capital were debated hotly and at length. William Childress was the only man who seemed able to generate consensus, and Adam was the only one with enough training to prepare the engineering designs. The two men were overwhelmed with work and responsibility. All in all, it was a much greater undertaking than either of them had imagined, and the plans had to be completed before the spring thaws or the project would be delayed another year.

"Dear Julia," Papa exclaimed with anguish, "how I wish we had kept you at the Big House, but now it is impossible for you to travel. Though I want to stay here with you through these last weeks until your confinement, I simply cannot. I have a solemn duty given me by the Lord, by Brother Brigham, and by the people of the community . . ." William's face reflected the strain of the awful dilemma he found himself in, and Julia reached out and grasped his hand.

"William, you must go back to town and do what you must do, and I must stay here and do what I must do. I know your heart is here with me, and you will come whenever you can. The girls are here, and I am well cared for."

With a heartfelt sigh, William bent and kissed Julia with infinite tenderness. "The doctor says you must call Sister Burgess if anything happens. She lives less than a mile away. If there is a storm or emergency that prevents Doctor Morgan from coming to you, he says she is a very competent midwife. You are not to worry."

It was still a matter of amazement to Hannah that neither her mother nor her father ever actually spoke directly

112

of the fact that Julia was going to have a baby. Her condition was always referred to in oblique, courteous phrases, and the dissembling of the situation made Hannah feel almost desperate with frustration.

Why can't we talk about pregnancy? her angry thoughts cried. Why can't I ask Mama direct questions about what she is feeling and how the baby is progressing. I don't even have any idea when the baby is due. And I don't dare ask her!

Still the unspoken code of silence was observed, and the days continued to pass. Mama seemed to grow weaker, but her body outlined under the bedcovers was becoming rounder as the baby grew. The swelling in her face and hands was no worse, but it was not any better, either.

Because Mama was having trouble breathing, Hannah had propped her up on fat, feather pillows, and she could only sleep half-sitting up. She grew more tired by the day.

On the night of the last day of January, a dreary and seemingly endless month—the loneliest time Hannah could remember in her entire life—Hannah was wakened just after midnight.

A scream tore through the house and lingered in an echo of desperation: "Hannah! Hannah!"

It was Mama's voice, but it was scarcely recognizable. Hannah and Eliza leaped out of bed onto the ice-cold floor and raced down the hall to Mama's room. Julia was lying half out of bed, turned on her side, with her knees drawn up. She was groaning in a horrible, panting, ragged way so unlike her dignified, quiet nature that both girls stopped at the door in shock.

In less than a second, Hannah recovered herself. She sprang to her mother's side and grasped her hand. "What is it, Mama?" she asked steadily. "Tell me what I must do."

Julia took some huge gulps of air and seemed calmer. "I

am in labor. Please get Sister Burgess at once." No sooner were the words out of Mama's mouth than she grew rigid with pain, and between her gritted teeth another long groan escaped.

Outside the January air was cold as iron, and the ground was frozen solid. Even with a lantern in the dark, it would take more than half an hour to walk to the Burgess place, and although Sister Burgess might well drive back in her sleigh, it would certainly take some time for her to get ready and come to Julia's aid.

"I'll go," Hannah said, turning to Eliza. "You stay here and help Mama."

Eliza's eyes were huge with terror. "No, Hannah! You can't leave me alone with Mama! I don't know what to do! What if she is dying? I'll go for the midwife. Please let me go!"

Mama had relaxed, but her face was pale and perspiration bathed her forehead and upper lip. "Stay, Hannah," she whispered. "I need you. Eliza, hurry! Hurry as fast as you can!"

Eliza spun on her heel and ran back to her room. Within minutes she was back in the doorway again, wrapped in a greatcoat and muffler, with warm boots on her feet and a lantern in her mittened hand.

"I'll get back with help as soon as possible," Eliza assured her mother. Her voice was clear with courage, and her pretty face shone pale in the heavy frame of the woolen scarf. She looked young and resolute.

Hannah ran and kissed her sister. "The Lord will walk with you," she whispered. A groan from Mama made her turn her head toward the bed, and when she looked back at the door, Eliza was gone.

Her mother's pains were wrenching. In all the animal deliveries she had watched, Hannah had never seen such

114

agony. It was as if her mother's body was being twisted and assaulted from within, and all that Hannah could think to do was mop her mother's brow with a warm, damp cloth and give her sips of water between contractions. When the pain was at its height, Mama gripped Hannah's hand and clung to it like a dying woman being swept out to sea on a brutal tide.

Mama's grasp was so fierce that Hannah felt her blood vessels bursting and her skin tearing as her mother's hands clenched with superhuman strength. If her mother's hand-clasp was a meter of the level of pain, then, Hannah thought, Mama's pain must be close to unbearable.

"Why aren't they here?" Mama groaned over and over again as the pains came stronger and closer together. "What's keeping them?"

Hannah felt a calmness come over her. She knew she could help her mother more if she did not allow herself to become stupefied by the press of her own emotions—of her pity and love. Gently, she raised her mother into a more comfortable position. Instinctively Hannah sensed that if her mother were sitting upright the baby could progress through the birth canal more easily.

She lifted her mother higher, pausing for another contraction. With Mama in this better position, Hannah had the satisfaction of seeing her mother take a long, deep breath and seem to get a new burst of energy.

By now Hannah's hands were raw and bleeding. She pulled an old sheet from the clothes press, tore it into strips, and tied heavy knots in it. Then she attached the strips to the headboard.

"Mama," she said softly, wiping her mother's face dry with a soft towel and waiting for her eyes to open. "Take these knots in your hands, and when you feel the contraction coming, pull as hard as you can." Hannah took the knotted strands and placed them in her mother's hands as another pain began to build. Her mother's eyes opened wide with terror.

"I can't do it!" her mother moaned. "Not again. Not so soon."

Hannah was beginning to see the pattern of the birth process. She put her hand over her mother's as Julia strained against the knots. "Yes, you can, Mama," she said in a soft, reassuring voice. "You've done it before, and you can do it again."

The sound of Hannah's voice had a calming effect. The pain passed, and Julia relaxed. In between pains, when Julia was strong enough, she talked to Hannah.

"If the baby is a boy, he is to be named after my brother, Harold."

"Not after Papa?" Hannah asked, surprised.

"No." Mama's voice was adamant. "After my brother. Without my brother I never would have had my life here in Utah—the Church, your father, or all these blessings. My brother was the finest man, next to your father, that I have ever known. I want his name remembered. I want his name spoken. I want his name passed on!"

The last word was a suppressed scream as another labor pain tore into Julia's weakened, wasted body.

"The baby is too big," Julia cried, her head thrashing on the pillow. "I am too weak, and I can't make it move."

"No, no," Hannah's voice was soothing. "Everything is going to be fine, Mama. Just fine. You are doing such a good job. Your body will remember how."

The passage of time was grinding and slow, and Hannah tried hard not to let her mother see that she, too, was wondering desperately where Eliza and Sister Burgess were.

Just as the window began to show the light of early

dawn, Hannah heard the downstairs door open, and Eliza's voice anxiously urging, "Hurry, Sister Burgess, please. She needed you hours ago!"

Hannah could hear the heavy creak of the stairs as though a ponderous presence were making its way toward her. Eliza flew through the bedroom door. "Is Mama all right?" she cried, her face was filled with worry and despair. "I couldn't get Sister Burgess to move! She delivered another baby earlier today, and she said she had to have some rest. I had to wait while she napped. Then she had to eat something and—oh, Hannah! She just wouldn't hurry! Has it been awful? Is the baby here?"

Just then Julia opened her eyes. "Eliza?" she whispered. "Did you bring help?"

Eliza ran to the bed and buried her face beside her mother's exhausted body. "Oh yes, Mama. I brought her as soon as she would come. Sister Burgess kept saying there was no hurry, and I couldn't convince her. But she's here now!"

Just then a stout, disheveled woman stepped through the doorway of the bedroom. Her dark gray hair was pulled into a sloppy bun at the back of her head, and loose, greasy strands straggled around her face. She was dressed in a dark serge dress over which she had pulled a stained apron. In the pockets of the apron were some instruments, whose handles protruded like weapons of war.

Sister Burgess's face was stained with sleep, and her hands had dirty nails. "Well, Julia," the woman said gruffly, walking over to the bed, "so you and William forgot your age and station, and now you are paying the price. And wouldn't you know it? Not a man in sight at the final reckoning."

Julia opened her eyes and looked at the midwife with

117

angry dignity. "Sarah, you forget yourself. My daughters are present."

The midwife put a rough hand on Julia's abdomen and felt the outline of the child through the delicate skin. The touch of the woman's cold hand sent a spasm through Julia's body, and she immediately twisted in another contraction.

"This little one's sure tryin' to get out," the midwife said, "but it's not makin' much progress. You are too old for this sort of thing, Julia, and that's the truth. Mary Kenyon had a boy last night. She's but thirty years old, and I reckon she won't live out the day. Another baby too big for the mama, and that looks to be your problem, too, as I live and breathe."

Hannah was horrified. She grasped the older woman by the arm and pulled her toward the door. "Don't say such things to Mama!" she hissed. "You are frightening her."

"Ain't nothin' but the truth, missy," the midwife replied. "Don't get all uppity on me. When it comes to havin' babies, everyone does it the same way, and there ain't nothin' elegant about it. It is pure hard work, and messy, and so don't think it's ever different, 'cause it ain't. Not for fancy folk like your Mama—not even for Queen Victoria herself."

The midwife glared at Hannah and walked back over to the bedside. "Yer daughter thinks she knows enough to tell me what to do!" she said to Julia, with a shake of her head. "Well, I've delivered over three hundred babies in this valley, and I reckon a slip of a girl can't tell me my business."

Julia groaned and strained against the knots and fell back, exhausted. The midwife pulled up a chair next to the bed, took a piece of careless knitting from the pouch bag she had carried in, and began to click away. The sun continued to rise, and the room grew brighter. The midwife knitted calmly.

With the next pain, Julia gave a stifled scream, and the girls flew to her side. Hannah glared at the midwife. "Can't you do something? Mama is suffering something awful. She has been for hours!"

"Ain't nothin' anyone can do at this stage. Your ma has to do it all. Do it, or die. That's it. I can't do anythin' until she starts bearin' down. All this pain is just openin' things up." The woman pulled the gray yarn around her stubby fingers and continued to knit. "I coulda slept another hour or two."

Hannah looked at her mother, and some instinct told her that her mother was too tired to continue. She turned with instant decision and ran downstairs. With trembling hands she prepared a cup of herbal tea with sugar and milk and set a kettle with leftover beef broth to boil. Running upstairs, she lifted her mother's head and helped her sip the tea. She watched as Julia revived a little.

"Eliza, in a few minutes, go downstairs and bring Mother a bowl of hot broth. We need to keep up her strength, or she will give up."

The midwife looked at the two girls in their ministrations, shook her head with disdain, and continued her indifferent knitting.

At last the transition period of labor began. If the girls had thought the early contractions were terrifying, they trembled with shock as Julia caught her breath in an awful silent gasp and held it until her face was the color of night.

Her silence was more awful than her groans. No screams escaped Julia's closed mouth, but Hannah saw where her mother's lips were almost bitten through in her attempt to stifle those unvoiced screams.

Sister Burgess put down her knitting and stood up with

a heavy sigh. "Reckon it's time for me to begin, Julia," she said. "We've got a passel of work to do. Your youngun's fair stuck!"

The woman laughed at her own joke, but Julia had started another wrenching contraction and this time it did not stop. Hannah watched in silent misery as her mother's face contorted with strain, and every muscle in her mother's body pushed downward. Blood vessels broke and blossomed on her mother's forehead.

The midwife ripped off the bedclothes with brisk indifference, and Julia was exposed to view. Her nightgown was drenched, and her legs were drawn up. The girls shuddered in pity as their beautiful mother's dignity and modesty were so rudely stripped away. Eliza turned her head in a wash of embarrassment, but Hannah resolutely walked over to the bed.

"Push, Julia!" the midwife yelled angrily at the laboring woman. "Push harder. You ain't tryin'. Push harder. Don't keep us waitin'." The woman's voice was strident and demanding.

The contraction seemed to last for an eternity, but at last her mother's body relaxed, and Julia took a deep, gasping breath. Julia slumped against the pillows looking like a lifeless rag doll. She seemed only half-conscious.

Hannah knew instinctively that if her mother lost consciousness now, in her weakened state, it would be a tragic and terrible thing. She grasped her mother's hand. "Mama!" she cried, "Mama! Don't let go! Don't drift away. It won't be much longer. Hold on!"

With cloudy eyes, Julia tried to focus on her daughter. "Too tired," she murmured. "Let me sleep!"

Suddenly blood spread across the sheets.

"I knew it," the midwife said in exasperation. "The baby's too big, and it's tearing her clean through. I'm just goin' to have to get it out myself. Whatever way it comes out now, there's goin' to be hell to pay, so we may as well speed things up."

Sister Burgess reached into her apron pocket and drew out a long-handled iron instrument that she proceeded to lubricate with her unclean hands from an evil-smelling jar in the other pocket.

"Had to use the instruments on Mary Kenyon, too. Baby was twice too big for that tiny woman. If I'd a' let it come on its own, it would've taken till next Monday. Still got her blood all over me. Didn't even have time to clean up proper before Eliza here comes running for me. I tell you it's a woman's lot. In pain and suffering we bear our children. That's how the Lord punishes us, and He sure sees that His curse comes true. Half the time there's nothin' to be done but get these babes out the best we can and then pray."

Hannah stood and watched with sick horror as Sister Burgess prepared to violate her mother's body with what looked like an instrument of torture. She stared at the woman's dirty hands, the ugly forceps, the midwife's calloused expression, the filthy lubricant.

Sister Burgess approached Hannah's mother's bedside as emotionless as if she were facing the task of cleaning a chicken. Hannah could not endure it.

"No!" Hannah shouted, knocking the instrument out of Sister Burgess's hands. "You will rip Mama to shreds with that thing! How dare you touch her with unwashed hands! What are you thinking?"

Sister Burgess was outraged. "What do you mean, missy! My hands don't need to be clean. They just need to know what they are doing—which is more than you do. Why should I worry about clean hands? I'm workin' on the filthiest part of the human body—I don't see how my hands could make it any dirtier. Now get out of my way!"

Mama had started another contraction, and the blood was running redder as she pushed in silent effort. Sarah Burgess yelled at the laboring woman, "You ain't gettin' nothin' done with that weak pushin'! Push, Julia! Push! If you don't push, you're goin' to be sorry! Ain't no time to be ladylike."

In an agony of indecision Hannah watched Sister Burgess pick the forceps off the floor. Eliza stood with tears running down her face. "Don't make things worse, Hannah!" she pleaded. "Just let her do what has to be done." Hannah looked at the midwife and thought things could not possibly get worse.

"You wouldn't put your dirty hands in someone's mouth!" she shouted at Sister Burgess. "Why would you think it is all right to put them in any other part of the body? I know what you are doing is wrong. I just know it. You are going to kill my mother."

"No, I ain't going to kill her," the midwife retorted. "This baby is."

"I won't let them die!" Hannah cried. "They can't die!"

With towering fury she faced the midwife. "Do not touch my mother. Do you hear me? You are not to touch her—not with those hands and not with that filthy instrument!" The words sounded horrible even to Hannah, as though she had sentenced all of them in the room to some terrible purgatory. The midwife stalked over to the corner of the room where she sat glowering at the girls.

"Mama," Hannah whispered with tears streaming down her face. Julia reached weakly for her daughter's hand and held it briefly.

"I trust you, Hannah," her mother murmured. "We'll do it together. You and I."

CHAPTER THIRTEEN

"Let's pray, Mama," Hannah said and beckoned to Eliza, who came over and stood on the other side of the bed. Each girl took one of their mother's hands, and they bowed their heads in silent prayer. Hannah could feel the tension in her mother's hand and arm, and, as she prayed, she clearly recalled the animals as they delivered their young. Animals seemed to know instinctively that they needed to relax and let their body have its way. They resigned themselves to the process.

In fact, Hannah had seen cows and horses fall asleep between labor contractions, their whole bodies as relaxed as though they were sunning themselves in a meadow.

Hannah's eyes flew open, and she looked carefully at her mother. Julia's brows were knit tightly in fear and concentration. Every muscle in her mother's body was tense and anxious, waiting for the next pain. Mama's breathing was quick and shallow with fear.

Hannah's hands went to her mother's brow, and she began to gently massage her temples. "Take slow, deep breaths, Mama," she urged persuasively, "slow, quiet, deep." Hannah kept her voice soft and sweet. "Let your body relax. Let it do its own work."

The touch of Hannah's firm young hands was soothing. Julia did as her daughter requested and tried to take calm, deep breaths.

"That's right, Mama," Hannah encouraged, "there's no hurry. Give your body time to open and relax."

Julia began to shiver. "I'm so tired and cold," she said in a small voice. Another pain began, and again her mother's body became fiercely concentrated. Hannah could see Mama straining down with as much force as her depleted energy could create.

"Good!" Hannah whispered. "Good work, Mama. It won't be long. Now rest. Take long breaths and close your eyes. Just rest."

Quickly Hannah signaled to Eliza. "Run down and warm a flannel blanket on the stove and bring it up to wrap around Mama so we can get this shivering stopped."

Eliza flew to the task. While she was gone, Hannah placed a soft shawl across her mother's body, gently massaging Julia's shoulders as she encouraged her to breathe slowly. The shivering abated slightly, and the tension in Julia's face lessened.

"She's already ripped inside," the sullen midwife said. "All this nonsense is just adding to her misery. We need to pull that baby out of her."

"And rip her more!" Hannah shook her head. "No. I believe the baby and she need time to . . . to . . . labor."

"Let the tragedy be on yer head, Hannah! I ain't goin' to have nothin' to do with it. You are nothin' but an ignorant girl prolonging your ma's misery."

Just then Eliza entered the room with the warmed blanket, and the two young women placed it around their mother's upper body. The welcome warmth made Julia smile, and relief was apparent in the softening of the lines in her face.

"Your body can do this," Hannah said confidently as Julia started the next contraction. "You've done it twice before. You can do it again, Mama! You are doing just fine."

The contraction was long and hard, and as Julia again took a deep breath, she grasped Hannah's hand. "I felt the baby!" Julia exclaimed. "The baby's moving. It is almost here!"

With only a few seconds' break, Julia's voice rose with pain and excitement, and then there was the long, hard silence again as she pushed until the veins in her face stood out like ink. This time, Hannah watched as her mother paused for a second, and then, with a huge intake of air, continued in exhaustive concentration.

Hannah saw the thick, black thatch of the baby's hair and, in an instant, the head and then a shoulder. After another enormous breath, her mother delivered the child, and Hannah lifted the baby up from the bed.

It was a perfect baby boy, already pink. He was large and plump but too quiet. The baby made a little mewing sound, not really a cry, and Hannah felt a pang of fear. Her mother was laughing and crying at the same time. There was blood and water and the long rope of the cord. Hannah took care of tying the cord, a little clumsily, and delivering the placenta, having only an idea of what needed to be done but feeling that she was being directed by some certain inner voice.

After the baby was cleaned, Hannah wrapped her newborn brother in the soft blanket she and Eliza had embroidered, and then she placed him in their mother's arms. While Mama stared at the miracle of the baby, with gentle hands Hannah bathed and cleaned Mama, and changed the bed linens.

Sister Burgess stood up and picked up her satchel with a sour expression. "She tore bad, Hannah, and that's a fact.

That young'un was just too big for her tiny body. I don't have much hope for either of 'em, but since you don't want my help, I'm headin' out of here. And don't come callin' for me when things turn sour, 'cause I won't come."

Hannah felt sick at heart. She could tell that neither Mama nor the baby was in good shape, and she wondered if her interference had contributed to the difficult delivery. Still, as she looked at the unkempt midwife, her common sense confirmed that she had been right to prevent her from removing the baby with the filthy instruments.

"Good-bye, Sister Burgess. I know you must be tired," Hannah said coldly, and she saw the woman to the door. As the midwife turned to go down the snowy walk, Hannah handed her a smoked ham and a small bag of coins.

"We pay our debts," Hannah said, "and you did come as we requested, so you are deserving of your fee. But, Sister Burgess, I know I am right. You should clean your hands and your instruments before you deliver a baby. It is the respectful thing to do."

Offended again, the midwife took the money and food without comment and tramped toward her sleigh and the dejected horses she had left tethered to it. Hannah sighed and turned back into the house. With a heavy heart she prepared to return to her mother's side. How she wished she could hear the sound of the newborn baby crying his lungs out. But the house was silent.

"I'll send Eliza for the doctor," Hannah decided as she walked up the stairs.

Mama had fallen into a sound sleep, and Eliza was holding the bundle of their tiny brother. The baby was quiet and listless but beautifully and perfectly formed. Again Hannah felt a sick feeling of dread in the pit of her stomach.

"What shall I do?" she prayed silently. "What shall I do?"

126

"Feed him." The two words sprang into her mind. "Feed him."

It was almost as though the words had been spoken aloud. "Feed him." She looked at her mother sleeping soundly and knew there was no milk to be had from that exhausted, newly delivered body. As if her limbs were directed by another will, Hannah carried the baby downstairs.

She heated milk on the stove and added sugar, and then she held the baby in her arms and patiently, a few drops at a time, fed him several ounces of the sugared milk from the tip of a spoon. The baby, milk dribbling from his sweet, red lips, fell asleep, but to Hannah it seemed a reassuring sleep, and she felt a new vitality in his little body, as the muscles became more toned and vibrant.

Eliza left in the early afternoon for the trip to town on the old saddle horse, Enos. She would fetch Papa and the doctor while Hannah kept up her vigil beside Mama's bed. Hannah sat in silence, holding the baby against her body. She put him down only once, when she had to go downstairs to stoke the fires to keep the house warm.

When Hannah climbed back up the stairs from building the fire, she was greeted with a sound as welcome as the sun. The baby was awake, and he was bawling like a newborn calf. His cries were loud, demanding, and powerful, and Hannah began to cry, too, as she bounded up the stairs and took him joyfully in her arms.

Mama woke, and her face, white and depleted, became radiant with a celestial smile. "Is that my little Harold crying? Doesn't he sound like a grand boy?"

"Yes, Mama," Hannah laughed, "but he's not all that little. He is a great, healthy baby and manly already. I think he looks like a Harold."

Hannah held the baby so that her mother could see him,

and together they examined his plump, pink body. Harold complained loudly the entire time. The lassitude that had characterized him at birth was completely gone.

Twice more that day Hannah fed the baby with the sugared milk. She also placed him at her mother's breast, and her mother seemed to drink contentment as the baby drank nourishment. To Hannah it was the most precious sight she could imagine.

When Eliza, Papa, and the doctor arrived Hannah realized she was exhausted. The doctor asked the family to leave the room while he examined Julia. Hannah wondered why Papa could not remain. After all, this was Papa's wife! What right did a doctor have to know more of her than Papa did? But, it was the custom, and Papa left the room without complaint.

The family sat downstairs on the sofa waiting for the doctor's report, and Hannah fell asleep almost instantly. She woke when the doctor entered the room. His face was solemn.

"I am amazed that Julia was able to deliver the boy," he said, shaking his head. "A baby that large from a woman that small is a most difficult birth. I expect Sister Burgess had her work cut out for her, but she seems to have done a fine job. Julia is torn and bleeding, but I would have expected the forceps to have done a great deal more damage than is evident.

"Of course, we still have to worry about childbed fever, because most forceps deliveries result in that complication. Julia is not out of the woods yet. A few more days of watching and worry . . ."

Hannah said nothing, but Eliza spoke up. "The midwife didn't deliver the baby. Hannah and Mama did it. There were no forceps used."

There was a long moment of silence, and the doctor

stared at Hannah, stupefied, with a frown of indecision stranded halfway between anger and admiration. He could only sputter, "I've never heard of such a thing! Avoiding the forceps probably saved your mother's life. Hannah, you were very lucky that you did not kill both of them by interfering . . ."

"The important thing is," Papa took command of the situation, "that mother and child are alive. We should thank God."

Everyone in the room bowed their heads, and William gave a mighty prayer of thanks and supplication for the well-being of Julia and their new son, Harold, both sleeping quietly in the room above. Papa was, in spite of his worry, as pleased as punch to be the father of a boy.

In the weeks that followed, Harold flourished. The baby was the delight of everyone who saw him. Gifts poured in from every side, and the child grew strong, lively, and handsome. He had curling, dark auburn hair like his mother, and wide, interested eyes that took in each new experience as if it were a present just for him.

The baby's smile was dimpled and responsive, and he searched the faces of everyone who peered over his cradle to cluck and coo, as though they were wonderfully interesting and welcome in his little world. Hannah thought there had never been a brighter or more splendid baby, or one with a better disposition.

Julia, however, was not doing well. She nursed the baby and had begun to manage the farm again from the desk in her room, but her walk was slow and painful, and she was very thin and weak. Something inside Julia had not healed correctly, and the doctor said that nothing could be done. Hannah knew that her mother continued to bleed and that often she ran a slight fever.

Without saying anything, Hannah became adept at

reading the signs of her mother's recurring flareups. When her mother's eyes were dull and heavy and her cheeks had spots of red, Hannah knew Julia was experiencing one of the frequent infections that had begun to plague her.

"Please drink more water," Hannah urged her mother, who seemed to be fading before her very eyes. "The water will help keep your milk supply going when you have your fevers, and it will help to wash out the illness in your body."

Julia did drink water, and took alum and cream of tartar and other home remedies, and sipped the willow tea that gave her relief from pain. Still, Hannah knew her mother was slowly wasting away.

Adam faithfully continued his trips to the farm to visit Hannah, even though his work became more and more demanding as spring approached. Frequently he brought with him rolled-up sheets of drafting paper, and he spent much of his time working at the kitchen table on engineering specifications.

It did not take the eyes of a medical doctor to see that Julia was not doing well, and Adam could see that Hannah's mother was in great need of care. He accepted the fact that Hannah could not even consider leaving her invalid mother and the new baby. They both needed Hannah. Nonetheless, each time Adam kissed Hannah good-bye as he mounted Ensign for the long ride back to town, he felt as though his heart were tearing, and it became difficult to face the cheerless ride and the pain of farewell.

"It gets harder and harder to leave you, my darling," he whispered, his face buried in the mass of Hannah's hair, as the warm winds of March curled around them and pressed them together in the cool spring night.

"I know," Hannah whispered, "but Mama needs my

help, and what kind of marriage could we have if I deserted my responsibility to her?"

"Your mother could come into the city and live with us," Adam begged. "My house is big enough, and you could fix a place for her and the baby. She'd be comfortable." Even as he said the words he knew they were foolish.

"She wouldn't even move into the Big House with Papa," Hannah replied. "What on earth would make her move into a little house where she could not even be mistress of her own kitchen? No. An arrangement like that would be borrowing misery for all of us. The farm is Mama's home, and now that she is ill, she needs it more than ever."

Adam sighed and nodded, continuing to search in his mind for some solution.

"We could get married and move in with her for a while," Hannah suggested hopefully. "It wouldn't be for too long. There is plenty of room here."

Adam shook his head. "I couldn't possibly work in town and ride out to the farm every night. It would be no way to start a marriage to be together only on weekends—if that—and in someone else's house to boot. I don't think either of us would do well in those circumstances."

Hannah knew exactly what Adam meant. They were both used to independence and freedom of expression and thought. To begin their marriage under the watchful eyes of her mother would be awkward.

"We shall have to be patient a little longer," Hannah said, but there were tears in her voice.

Adam swung his leg up over the saddle and sat on his restless horse. "Look at Ensign pawing the ground!" he exclaimed. "He wants to be up and at it—on his way. I guess he and I are two of a kind. Patience is a hard lesson for the likes of us."

Until the horse and rider were out of sight, Hannah stood by the front walk, and then she turned toward the house with reluctance and a feeling of unease. "How much longer can I expect Adam to be patient and understanding?" she wondered. As handsome and eligible as Adam was, she was sure that the girls in town must be chasing him in every way possible. Constance, she knew, had never given up on the hope of winning Adam. It was too much to expect a marriageable young man to wait months and months for his wedding and watch while his intended bride became a dowdy, hermitlike drudge.

That was how Hannah was beginning to feel. She saw herself fading away like a sepia tint. Since the baby was born, she and Eliza had felt like prisoners at the farm, and the more that spring painted the world with warmth and vivid color, the more the two sisters yearned to be free and young and part of the awakening world.

Edgar's missionary farewell had been scheduled, and, on impulse, Hannah decided to surprise Adam and go into Ogden a day early to attend the reception, which was planned after Thursday's fast and prayer meeting at the chapel.

Tired from all the work required to get ready to leave and worried about leaving Mama and the baby in the care of Eliza, Hannah plodded into town on one of the work-horses from the farm. She slid off the wide, sturdy back of the animal and handed the reins to the stableboy. Then she walked slowly toward the front door. It had been months since she had been at the Big House, and it looked almost foreign to her, as if she were coming back from a long distance—from a long journey.

It suddenly occurred to Hannah that she was moving as slowly as an old woman. Every bone and muscle in her body seemed to be aching. "I'll go in and have a long, hot bath," she told herself. "I should have plenty of time before we need to get to the church."

The thought cheered her. Just as she put her foot on the first of the wide steps leading to the front porch, she heard the sound of laughter and voices. Looking up she saw Constance and Adam walking through the door. Constance's arm was linked through Adam's, and they were smiling at one another with easy familiarity.

Adam was the first to see Hannah at the foot of the stairs. She was frozen in position, her face white and strained, her hand clutching the stair rail.

"Hannah!" Adam shouted, surprised and disconcerted. After a moment's pause, he bounded happily down the stairs. "How did you get here? I was going to come out to bring you tomorrow! How wonderful that you could come sooner!" He bent to kiss her, but she turned her cheek.

Constance stood at the top of the stairs wearing a smug little smile. She was dressed in a green-sprigged poplin, with dark emerald braid and an elegantly draped bustle. On her head was a velvet bonnet with an emerald-dyed osprey feather curving around her smooth face.

"I rode old Caesar so that I could arrive in time to attend the reception at the Ward House this evening," Hannah told Adam coldly. "I guess I should have sent word that I was coming early."

"Nonsense," Adam replied. "It's the best surprise in the world! They never get to see enough of you in town, do they, Constance? And I—well, I can never see enough of you anywhere at all."

"We were just leaving to go over to the meetinghouse to make sure everything was ready for the gathering," Constance said, without any preliminary greeting. "Adam's been helping me with all of the arrangements." Constance moved to the stair above Hannah and smiled at Adam.

"He's a very great help to all of us. We don't know what we'd do without him."

"Oh," Hannah said, dully. The situation overwhelmed her. She did not have the energy or heart to respond. After all, this was where Adam lived and worked. His brief visits to the farm were just interludes. This was where he spent his days—here, in the city, with people who lived in well-run, spacious houses and laughed and talked and played. This was where he ate dinner, and conferred in Papa's impressive study, and attended church, and was entertained in the evening surrounded by girls who did not work like field hands, and who wore perfume and dainty shoes, and smiled and laughed. How long since she had felt like smiling or laughing? Hannah couldn't even remember.

How could she expect that Adam would remember her the way she had been the night of the party when he had first met her? Carefree, happy, full of hope and energy— that was how the world had been that night. As she stood looking at Constance and Adam, she suddenly realized that the world had continued much the same—but that she had changed and changed drastically. Adam and Constance stood above her bursting with purpose and vitality, sleek and well-dressed, and she stood at the bottom of the stairs with scarcely the energy to walk up them.

Constance gave Hannah a penetrating, triumphant glance. It seemed to be a silent warning and challenge: "All's fair in love and war." Hannah had no desire to compete. Her heart was as sore as if she had already lost the battle. Despair washed over her.

"You two go ahead and do whatever you have planned," she said quietly. "It will be some time before I'm ready to come."

"What is wrong?" Adam asked as the two of them walked home in the dark after the social. Hannah had sat quietly on the sidelines the whole evening. It had not been hard to remain unobtrusive, because Edgar was enjoying the spotlight and holding forth on his call to the eastern states. While he was in the east, Edgar expected to meet members of Papa's family and to see the old family properties in Connecticut, as well as obtain genealogical records. Edgar had already purchased the top hat, frock coat, and distinguished wardrobe of the Lord's elders and was practicing his most solemn and pompous expression.

Papa noted with concern that Hannah looked pale and withdrawn, but he had little time to talk to her with the press of guests. At the conclusion of the meeting and reception, Hannah stayed quietly to help with the cleanup. The other young people left early for another party, which Constance urged Hannah and Adam to attend, but Hannah shook her head and Adam remained at her side. By the time everything was in order, they were the last to leave the building.

"You've been avoiding me all evening," Adam said. "I don't know what's the matter. Are you sick? Is everything all right at the farm? Are you upset about something? Please talk to me and tell me what is wrong."

His voice was filled with concern, but Hannah did not even know where to begin or what to say, so she continued her silence. The spring evening had grown cold with the coming of darkness, and Hannah pulled her cape around her more closely, walking with a sturdy, determined stride. Adam's hand grasped her arm, pulling her to a halt.

"For heaven's sake, talk to me, Hannah. How can I help if I don't even know what's the matter?"

"I'm not a charity case, Adam," Hannah flung back. "If you think that all our relationship has become is that you are helping me, or pitying me, or whatever this is—well, then, our feelings for each other have deteriorated further even than I thought. If what is between us is not a bond of equals, if you don't feel that I am competent, capable, that I do not need to rely upon you to accomplish my responsibilities—then I do not choose to continue this charade.

"I saw how you laughed with Constance, how light-hearted you were with the girls in the choir. I saw them cluster around you and how happily you conversed with them. I do not wish you to come to me as if I were an obligation or an act of service. If your heart takes you in another direction, it is your heart you must follow. I will not become your duty!"

"Blue thunder!" Adam roared. "You are the most difficult girl in the universe! What a curse for me that I find you irresistible. This is a stupid conversation. Do you think any of those silly twits holds a candle to you? Of course I'm polite to them—I want them to be your friends when you finally come to live where you belong."

"I scarcely think you need to secure my relationship through a friendship with Constance," Hannah's voice had a sharp bite.

"Look," Adam took a deep breath and tried to rid his voice of impatience and frustration, "I am at the Big House on business all the time. Your father asks me to dinner. I can't ignore her. For heaven's sake, she's your family, and I figure she's a fact of our life."

"From what I saw, you were a long way from ignoring her," Hannah said. A spark of anger strengthened her voice, and her eyes flashed.

"Saints be praised! You are jealous!" Adam started laughing. "This is the best thing I have heard in months. It means you care for me. It means you're worried about keeping me. It means you think about me, and if I know you, it means you won't let me get away!"

In spite of herself Hannah laughed. "How can I let you

get away if I don't feel I have you in the first place?" she asked.

Adam threw his arms around her. "Oh, you have me all right, you darling girl, whether you want me or not. Nothing you can ever say or do will rid you of me. You must believe that, Hannah. You must." He threw the hood from her face and kissed her passionately. "Nothing in this world is strong enough to come between us except you, yourself, and your own proud, stubborn heart."

When Hannah returned to the farm the following week, the walls closed in on her more relentlessly than ever. Eliza was so restless that she paced the floors at night, and even little Harold seemed to resist the confinement of the quiet rooms.

Outside the walls of the farmhouse, spring sang its way into the mountains, canyons, and fields. It battered against the doors, but inside nothing changed, and the girls felt more and more isolated.

Finally, Papa rescued them.

"Julia," he said, when he visited the farm on the first day of May, "our little Harold is thriving, but you and my daughters look very peaked and pale. I think the thing we must do is change your location and plan a holiday."

With a weary smile Julia waved the idea away with her hand. "I don't think I'm well enough for anything much, William. You and the girls go, and I will stay here with Harold."

"No!" Papa's voice was rich with authority. "There is no point in arguing. I am going to take you into the Big House, all of you. I have employed the Thatchers to move out to the farm. I'm going to build a new house for them, and they will manage the property until you are feeling better, Julia. When you are up to it, you can come back and resume control of the farm—but with more help.

"We are about to begin our groundbreaking for the new reservoir in the canyon. The work load is going to be enormous, and I will not be able to make the trip out to the farm every week. Blast it, Julia! I want to see more of you. I want to see more of my son!

"Please, Julia, don't fight me on this." Papa's face was firm and pleading at the same time.

"This is my plan for you and the girls, dear. Then, in the middle of summer, after the reservoir construction is well underway, I want all of us to go on a first-class expedition to see the hotwater geysers in the Yellowstone. Just think! The first national park in the entire world, and it's practically at our doorstep. It will be a marvelous adventure, and the outdoor air will do all of us a world of good. Something wonderful to look forward to."

Hannah felt her heart beating. What a blessing it would be to be in town where Adam was. Adam's work would be demanding, but at least the two of them could spend their evenings and weekends together. Maybe, with all the extra help at the Big House and with a change of scenery, Mama would begin to improve. For the first time in months, Hannah's heart beat with hope. She and Adam might even be able to set a wedding date.

Everyone in the room knew that Mama was not happy with the idea, but Julia saw the flare of joy in her daughters' eyes and realized that it would be cruel and selfish to require them to remain at the farm. In her present condition she knew she could not manage alone, and so she agreed to the plan.

The Thatcher family moved into the farmhouse while their house was being built. Julia packed for the move to the Big House with the help of Hannah and Eliza, both of whom were so deliriously excited that Julia could no longer resent the changes that were being made.

138

When they were ready, Papa came for them, and with baby Harold held closely in Hannah's arms and sleeping like a rosy log, the three women rode home to the Big House in the beautiful caroche that William had bought for Julia so long ago.

CHAPTER FOURTEEN

Being in residence at the Big House was awkward at first. Anne felt threatened by Julia's being a permanent occupant, sharing the master bedroom with Papa. Technically Julia was, of course, the mistress of the house, and her presence threw Anne's ordered and comfortable existence out of kilter. Anne was apprehensive about the role Julia would expect to play in the running of the household. Would Anne have to relinquish the reins altogether or even move back into her own smaller home?

As the weeks passed, Julia's physical condition, in spite of the daily care of the doctor and the comforts and resources of the large, comfortable home in Ogden, continued to worsen. Many days it was difficult for Julia to leave her bedroom, and she took no interest in the day-to-day matters of overseeing the establishment, much to Anne's relief.

Hannah and Eliza were happy to help whenever Anne asked, but neither of them was inclined to change the order of things as they were, and so, gradually, Anne relaxed, seeing her position as head of the household was secure. In her relief, Anne treated them all quite graciously.

There were times when Hannah resented her older

half-sister's proprietary attitudes, and she still found Constance's air of superiority to be irritating, but the events of the winter had matured Hannah in ways that she scarcely understood. The insecure and prickly girl she had been when she had attended Uncle Abner's party all those long months ago no longer existed.

Hannah knew she was entering a new and different relationship with other people, with the Lord, and with her life, partly because of her experiences in caring for her mother, but mostly because of Adam.

She loved Adam with a fierce and undying commitment that gave her a sense of purpose and belonging. Her love for Adam and his love for her had quieted many of her old fears and insecurities. His love gave her the peace of mind to see the world around her more clearly. His love was the foundation of her whole sense of being, and it frightened her to have so much of herself dependent upon one person. Still, the gift of that love made her almost superstitious in her belief that she would need to repay the Lord for it—or it might be taken. Such a great gift would require a price almost beyond her ability to give, perhaps even everything she had to give.

In her breast burned a small, hot fire of resolve that since the Lord had blessed her so abundantly, she would live her life serving Him in whatever ways He needed her. She was convinced that her experiences with her mother and the birth of Harold were a sign from the Lord.

She had discussed her feelings with Adam. "I cannot understand why it is wrong for a woman to continue to be part of the social world when she is with child. Why should a woman who is expecting a baby be confined to her home as if it were too shameful to be seen or spoken of? Why is it that a pregnant woman cannot walk outside on the streets in daylight or attend church once her condition is physically observable? It is a terrible injustice.

"Childbearing is a process essential and natural to life. Children are the great blessing of the Lord, so why should the process of bearing a child be considered something sinful and embarrassing!

"Think of the women who must refrain from speaking of their physical problems because it is considered indelicate to refer to them! They refer to giving birth as 'confinement,' and confinement it is! There is no recourse even to discuss what ought to be discussed or teach what ought to be taught.

"How can women allow their bodies to be such a mystery to themselves? Adam, when I lived through this winter with my mother and realized how little anyone could help her because of this cruel veil of secrecy, I saw what great potential there is for harm in ignorance and silence. I felt the ghastly helplessness of my own ignorance. I promised myself then and there—I am going to learn everything there is to know about the bearing of children.

"I made this vow to myself and the Lord. I will never knowingly let another woman suffer as my mother did!"

Adam listened to her tirade with a quiet, indulgent smile. "The intensity of your feelings about this matter will fade, Hannah," he said. "You cannot change the way the world is. You have had a shattering experience, and your mother's continued frailty makes it seem even more unfair. But in time, I promise you, it will assume a gentler perspective."

"You are wrong, Adam," Hannah said quietly. "I think this experience has had a real purpose from the Lord in my life. I cannot—I will not—be dissuaded from my determination to study and learn. Sometime, somehow . . ."

He stopped her words with a quick kiss. They were

sitting out in the summerhouse at the back of the garden. It was late evening, but the sun was still lowering in the west, and the birds were singing their last song before going to their nests for the night.

"Enough," Adam whispered. "Let us talk of *us*. Of our future. Of our own children. Of wifery, not midwifery. When do you think we can announce our wedding day?"

She laughed. "You tell me. You are so busy blasting stone away to create that blasted reservoir that I scarcely see you, and when I do, you are covered with dust and dirt and have pebbles in your hair!"

Adam laughed. "In spite of the fancy title of civil engineer, the truth is you have promised to marry a man who is a glorified ditchdigger. Can you bear that?"

"Some ditchdigger!" she retorted, and her dark eyes shone like stars. "I have seen your drafted plans! You are creating a place where life-giving waters can be stored and used to nourish the people and the land—making this valley as productive, verdant, and green as Eden. Such a ditchdigger as you must have been made in heaven." Her admiration and love filled her face, and Adam stared at the wonder of this deep and complicated young woman who loved him with a fire as fierce as the sun.

"You are a strong woman, Hannah," he said quietly. "It is the thing I love most about you. You feel with a heart that is as strong as the mountains and as splendid and untamed as a river. But I want that heart for me, not for the world. I want it in my hands, in my heart, in my kitchen—in my bed."

Hannah blushed and hid her face in her hands. "Soon, Adam," she whispered, "soon."

Summer came in a blaze of sun and hot wind. Papa and Mama had decided that the wedding should take place the month after the family returned from their holiday in the Yellowstone territory. Adam and Hannah were impatient at the further delay, but they could tell William's anxiety about Julia's failing health, and his responsibility for getting the reservoir and canal construction effectively organized made it hard for him to add one more concern to his already burdened thoughts.

Somewhat reluctantly Hannah and Adam agreed to the chosen date, but they were delighted when William suggested that Adam should make the trip with the family entourage going to Yellowstone. At least they would not have to face another separation.

"I only wish the trip could be our honeymoon," Adam whispered to Hannah.

She laughed. "I wouldn't want to be on my honeymoon surrounded by all those people—and half my family," she answered.

William and Adam had organized the reservoir construction in such a way that the work could continue without their direction for the three weeks of the trip. Julia, although weak and often in pain, was looking forward to the fresh air and the prolonged time with her beloved husband. She would, for these few precious weeks, have his full attention—away from other people and the endless procession of his many responsibilities.

Little Harold was a dear, healthy, bouncy baby, and it was to Hannah that he turned when he was tired or needed care. Hannah held him, bathed him, rocked him, talked to him, and watched over him in his sleep. Julia, in almost constant pain, continued to breast-feed the child but could do little more for him than that.

When Julia held her baby son in her arms, her translucent face was transformed with love. Sometimes tears came to her eyes as though her secret thoughts were filled with sadness as well as joy. Hannah, watching, thought that her mother was trying to memorize the moments she had with little Harold, as though she understood there would not be very many.

The days until the family left for the long-awaited trip seemed to drag, and time dripped as slowly as water on a stone.

One afternoon Eliza burst through the kitchen and out the back door, letting the screen slam behind her. She was sick and tired of being cooped up in the house, where Anne was making raspberry jam. The kitchen was as hot as blazes and smelled of sugar and fruit, which was not a bad smell, except that the flies liked it, too, and they had become pesky.

In the early morning, Eliza had been sent to the raspberry patch and had picked berries until her hands and arms were a network of scratches. The sun had grown high in the sky, beating down mercilessly on her back.

Once the jam making started, Anne had turned into a general, ordering everyone around, boiling bottles and lids, and insisting that the sugar and lemon juice be measured just so. After a while, Eliza decided that she was tired of being treated like a servant by her own sister. She took off her apron and announced, "I'm going for a walk." Eliza was not asking for permission—she was stating a fact. Without a backward glance she headed out the door.

There was a cool breeze coming through the cottonwoods down by the irrigation canal at the foot of the garden. Eliza undid the top buttons of her blouse and threw back her head to let the wind dry her face and throat.

With quick precision she undid the long braid that was wrapped around her head and ran her fingers through her hair. As the soft curls escaped their restraints, the frolicking breeze blew them around her shoulders. It was good to be out in the open air, away from all the women in the kitchen with their solemn duties, their gossip, and their stodgy ways.

Eliza felt she had aged a hundred years in the past winter. She was tired of being confined in a house with a sick mother, a crying baby, and everyone old or middle-aged except Hannah, who was so busy mooning over Adam Fairfield that she might as well have been an old married woman already. She was no fun at all. She missed her old companionship with Hannah and knew that after she married Adam, it would be even less.

Whatever had happened to fun and parties and pretty clothes and all the things she had thought would be part of her life when she reached sixteen? Here she was almost seventeen, and nothing in her life was what she had hoped it would be. At the Big House, because of Mama's illness, there were no big parties any more, only occasional solemn dinners for stodgy old friends of Papa's or, worse yet, business receptions, where everyone talked about civic improvements, roads, and irrigation.

Eliza walked down the soft, clay path at the side of the irrigation canal, her hands thrust into the deep, patch pockets of her pinafore. She loved the color of her old coverall. It was a soft, periwinkle blue, and it matched the color of her eyes perfectly.

Before she knew it, she had walked all the way to the horse pasture, and, as she looked at the summer-green grass, she saw the shimmer of wild asters and columbine in profusion. On impulse she climbed through the fence to pick some flowers.

She was bending over, snapping stems and filling her skirt with summer's bouquet, when she heard the thud of a horse's hooves. In alarm, she stood up swiftly. The sudden apparition of her flying hair startled the horse and rider that were bearing down on her where she had stooped, unseen, to pick flowers.

Eliza leaped toward the fence as the horse swerved, reared, dumped its rider, and galloped away.

"Oh, my goodness!" Eliza screamed, racing to the side of the man who was sprawled, motionless, on the ground. "Are you hurt? Can you hear me? Are you all right?"

She stood above him, not daring to touch him, not knowing if she should stay with him or run for help. Her thoughts were in complete turmoil, and she was terrified.

Suddenly, the rider rolled over onto his back, opened his eyes, and stared up at her. She threw herself on her knees beside him.

"Is anything broken? What do you want me to do?" she fluttered helplessly.

"Kiss me better," the young man said, with a wicked grin. "It's the least you can do. After all, you gave Satan and me an awful start."

She pulled away and stood up indignantly. "I think you are perfectly all right, and I do not think you are funny, sir. After all, you are the one who almost ran over me."

He jumped to his feet, laughing. "Not at all. Here I was riding that brute, Satan, trying to tame the monstrous horse so your father can sell him, and what do you do? Lie in wait and spring out at us, knowing full well that animal shies at his own shadow."

"You were riding Satan?" Eliza was impressed in spite of herself. Satan was a two-year-old stallion her father had purchased the year before. The animal had a jet black coat with a jet black heart to match. In the open field he was magnificent to watch: head held high, mane flowing, tail switching, and hooves thundering. Whenever anyone approached, however, the animal threw its head up and

147

down, drummed and pawed, and ran in circles around the enclosure as though the fires of hell itself blazed in his nostrils.

"No one has ever been able even to break Satan to the halter. How could you have ridden him?" Eliza protested.

"Time and patience," the young man answered. "The same things I suspect it would take to manage you."

Eliza's eyes glowed like blue ice. "How dare you speak to me in such a way! I shall tell my father!"

Again he laughed. "Do," he said. "I think your father might agree with me."

Unable to think of an adequately demeaning response, Eliza glared at the man who stood before her, and for the first time she really looked at him. He was young, probably only a few years older than herself. His hair was thick and curly, the color of mahogany, and his face was deeply tanned with dark, upraised eyebrows and a wide, handsome mouth with a permanent half-smile.

When he grinned, his teeth were a startling white against the rich color of his face, and his body, though slender and compact, was graceful, muscular, strong, and quick. In a single fluid motion he bent down and picked up the battered hat that had fallen from his head. It was a Union cavalry officer's hat, now almost unrecognizable in shape and color, but, when he put it on his head and pushed it back, she thought she had never seen a look so confident, so devil-may-care—and so appealing.

"Who are you?" Eliza asked haughtily, unwilling to concede that she found him anything but irritating and impertinent.

"Joshua. Josh Foster," he smiled. "Just Josh."

"Well, *Brother* Foster," Eliza replied coldly, "why is it you are riding my father's horse? I do not recall seeing you before . . ."

148

Josh raised his eyebrows and regarded Eliza with an ironic stare. "No, Miss Eliza. You don't seem to see much that is not right beneath your feet. Perhaps that's why you almost got run down by a horse. Anyone else would probably have noticed that someone was riding in the field."

"How dare you!" Eliza retorted.

"I have been working for your father training horses for the construction site for almost four weeks. I have been in his house many times, and I have seen you running up and down the stairs, playing the pianoforte, arguing with your sister, and holding your little brother, Harold. You see, we have been in the same room together, and until you place yourself under my horse's hooves, you do not even bother to notice me. I think my point is well made."

Eliza gasped at his effrontery, but she found herself at a loss for words. Just as she determined to flounce away in dramatic dismissal, he caught her off guard by leaving first.

"If you will excuse me, I must go see if I can calm Satan down and retrieve my saddle. I do not think he will be agreeable to being ridden any more today." Josh turned to go, and Eliza felt she had been dismissed.

"You might at least apologize for nearly killing me," she demanded.

"Ha!" he retorted. "You ought to apologize for putting back a month my progress with Satan. You have spooked him right enough."

"You are the most arrogant, obstinate man I have ever met," Eliza sputtered.

"Thank you, ma'am." Josh doffed his hat and bowed with a swoop of mockery, and then he stalked off across the pasture toward the black horse that was still saddled, standing in the far corner of the field, shaking its mane.

CHAPTER FIFTEEN

"Papa."

Eliza walked up to her father as he stood in the stables overseeing the final outfitting of the wagon that was to carry Julia on the Yellowstone trip. William had had the conveyance made especially for his wife with reinforced springs and a thick, soft bed built into the wagon body so that she could lie down comfortably and still see the landscape as they rode.

The wagon was to be loaded on the train the next day when they boarded. They would ride the train north to Beaver, Idaho, and then they would begin the ride through the mountains into the Yellowstone.

William had thought of every comfort possible. He was taking his own crew of wranglers, mounts, and generous provisions. Once the Childress party arrived at the trailhead in Beaver, they would be met by Barrett Brothers Outfitting Company, which had made arrangements to complete their equipment, guide them, and supply extra crew. There would be hunting and fresh game along the way.

"Papa," Eliza repeated. Her father turned his head and smiled at her.

"All packed and ready to leave in the morning, Eliza?"

he asked exuberantly. He was as excited as a boy. "What an adventure we are going to have!"

"Yes," Eliza felt the contagion of his eagerness. "I am ready to go right now, if you like!" They laughed together.

"I was wondering about something . . ." Eliza spoke casually, as though the question had just occurred to her. "Who is that young man, Josh Foster? Where did he come from? I don't remember him from before."

Her father had gone back to fiddling with the harness, and he answered her question absently. "Fine young man. He worked for Uncle Abner up in Idaho this winter, and Abner converted him to the Church. Your uncle sent him down with a small herd of yearlings that I sold in Salt Lake, and then Josh decided to stay on with me for a while."

"Where did Uncle Abner find him?"

William bent down to inspect the wagon springs, and his voice was muffled. "Josh's father was killed in the War between the States. Boy's been on his own since he was a child, I gather. Made his way west with an army survey team and then hired on with Abner. I have never seen a man with a better knack for horses and livestock."

"No family or education or home, then?" Eliza asked primly.

William stopped his inspection and looked at his daughter closely. She looked as untouched, fresh, and beautiful as a morning sky. "The man has been a drifter by necessity since childhood." William's voice had a touch of remonstrance. "Perhaps the gospel, as he learns it, will give him a sense of permanence and family. As of now, I think he is a man caught between two worlds."

Eliza heard both the warning and the compassion in her father's words.

"Well, he is certainly arrogant enough," Eliza sniffed. "You'd think he owned both of those worlds."

William grinned. "I see. You've met him, I take it."

"He nearly ran me over, if you can count that as a meeting," Eliza spluttered. "He wasn't very nice about it, either."

"He'll have plenty of time to make amends. He is going on this trip with us."

"Well," Eliza snapped, turning on her heel, "as if I care. I don't care if I never see him again."

The Childress party made an impressive entourage as they boarded the Utah and Northern Railroad the next day. It was a warm day in the last week of July. William had chartered a stock car to accommodate Julia's special conveyance, the horses, the handpicked crew, and the provisions.

Members of the family were to ride in a private club car. The whole of the trip would take three weeks from beginning to end.

While William and Adam were gone, the black powder blasting on the reservoir was to continue, and when they returned, the men expected to begin building the dams and flumes of the water system. "What a summer to remember!" William exclaimed every time he contemplated all the life-long dreams that were coming to fruition.

"The greatest event will be at the end of it all, when we celebrate the wedding of our Hannah and Adam," he beamed as he patted Julia's hand and settled her comfortably on the leather seat next to the window. The train blew a warning blast.

There was a faraway look of sadness in Julia's eyes. "Yes, dear. We must not wait too long for that wonderful day." William felt a chill of fear as he looked at Julia's pale face. She seemed almost translucent. Why couldn't he find a way to give her some of his vitality, his health, his strength? It was so hard to watch her bravery as she wasted away before his very eyes.

The train gave a jerk and began to pull out of the station as he sat down next to her with a determined smile. "You are going to love Yellowstone, Julia. We all are."

When the United States Congress in 1872 had declared the whole of the Yellowstone Territory as a national park—the first of its kind in the world—the Washington legislators had envisioned the action as a means of preserving for all mankind the incredible geological wonders of this remarkable region. Yellowstone was truly one of the wonders of the earth.

Ever since William Childress had arrived in Utah with the first parties of Mormon pioneers, he had heard tales of the wonders of the hot springs, geysers, waterfalls, and boiling mudfields of the Yellowstone. Indian friends had told him tales filled with superstitious imaginings of this mythic region. Lewis and Clark and others had explored it with awe and had written elaborate accounts, which William had read avidly.

In the years since Yellowstone had been named a national park, roads had begun to be carved through the mountains, and army outposts and civilian rangers patrolled and protected the region. Although it was still a wilderness region, the park had steadily become more and more accessible. Now, many visitors went each year to drink in its wonders.

William had developed a growing hunger to see the magical place for himself, and, as always, he wanted to share the experience with those he loved. He had conceived the expedition as a gift to Julia. He was hoping against hope that the fresh air and the pleasant stimulation of new sights would prove beneficial to her fragile health. He had also heard wonderful things about the healing powers of the sulphurous hot springs and prayed that there might be truth in the rumors.

For two days they would ride the train to Beaver, Idaho, where they would be met by the Barrett brothers.

The motion of the train was surprisingly smooth, and Hannah and Adam sat next to each other, looking out at the thriving towns, green fields, large barns, and children playing around sturdy houses as the scenery flashed by. Hannah had not realized how Zion was thriving throughout the valleys of Utah.

At Brigham City the train stopped, and children came aboard, selling cool milk, peaches, apricots, and fresh bread. It made a delicious lunch. Adam laughed as peach juice dripped down Hannah's chin, and he wiped her face gently with his bandanna.

As the day continued, the train moved beyond the valleys to run along the base of the ridge of the mountains. The landscape became empty of people and human habitation.

As the sun began to set, the great outline of the Rockies clothed itself in blue and purple. Above the crestline the twilight sky, flaming with the last beauty of the sunset, began to grow dark, and the stars and moon shone in a world of midnight velvet.

"It is so lovely," Hannah breathed, her eyes intent upon the nighttime world. Adam, staring at her face in the dusky light, said, "No. It is you who are lovely." Hannah sighed with a feeling of happiness as though the train had become their own private world, and all was well.

Eliza, on the other hand, was bored and restless. Papa and Mama's berths had been made up, and her parents and everyone else but Hannah and Adam had retired. Hannah and Adam were mooning over each other, as usual, and Eliza was at loose ends.

Too wide awake even to think of going to bed, Eliza knocked on the portal beside Papa's berth.

"Yes, Eliza?" Papa asked, poking his head out between the curtains.

"May I take some of the leftover fruit and cake down to the crew in the stock car?" she asked. "We have so much left it would be a shame to waste it."

"That is thoughtful of you, my dear," her father answered, "but I think it would be more appropriate if Adam invited one of the men to come to our car to get the food. A stock car is no place for a young woman."

Josh Foster was the man who came back with Adam to pick up the food basket for the crew. Adam started to introduce Josh to Eliza, but Josh laughed and said they already knew one another.

"Well," he amended, "we don't actually know each other, but let us just say, we have run into each other before."

Eliza did not know whether to laugh or act annoyed.

"How are things in the stock car?" she asked.

"About the same as they are here," Josh answered. "It's the same train."

"I mean—are the horses behaving themselves, and do you have enough room . . ." Eliza's voice trailed off.

"It's a sight more comfortable than the floor of the desert," Josh said, "but I prefer not being boxed in."

"Me, too," Eliza answered, her restlessness showing in the quick agitation of her voice. "I feel so cooped up in this train I think I could scream."

"I know just what you need," Josh said. He turned to Adam. "Would it be all right if I took Eliza out on the observation platform for some air?"

Without waiting for Adam's reply, Eliza eagerly moved toward the rear door of the railroad car. Josh followed her quickly, and they moved out into the night air.

They stood with their hands on the railings of the deck

and watched the silver thread of the railroad track speeding beneath them like a living thing flowing out across the night as far as the eye could see. The rhythmic sound of the wheels and the vast silence of the planets and stars in the empty world were hypnotic. For the first time Eliza began to feel the wonder of the journey and a delicious sense of freedom and happiness. It was as if she had escaped from an old shell.

"It's glorious!" she exclaimed, closing her eyes and raising her face to the night wind and the soft air. "Who could imagine? It feels like we could go on like this to the end of the world and beyond—as though there is no place and no time and nothing but now and here."

Josh put his hands on her shoulders. "Open your eyes," he commanded softly.

Her eyes flew open, and she looked at him in gentle confusion, still bemused by the soft night air and the lull of the train.

"Why should I open my eyes?" she asked.

"So you can see me when I kiss you," he answered quietly, pulling her toward him. He kissed her as softly as the velvet night.

"It's time for us to go back in," he whispered, and before she could think or protest, he put his arm on her elbow and led her firmly back to the sleeping car.

Hannah was waiting up for her. Adam had already joined the men in the stock car, and the lights in the sleeping car had been extinguished. Eliza climbed into her berth without a word, and lay, fully clothed, with her wide-open eyes staring at the darkness, a smile of pure wonder on her pretty face.

At Beaver Canyon the Childresses got off the train with their supplies and men, and after a night's rest in a small log hotel, they met the Barrett brothers, who had organized their expedition into the Yellowstone and had completed the outfitting and other arrangements.

The Barretts regularly took groups through the Targhee Pass, which they advertised in the eastern papers as "The Shortest, Best Route to the Eden of America." Once through the pass and into the park, the Barretts knew the most comfortable places to camp and the best way to see all of the sights. They were efficient and experienced, and it took them very little time to prepare the Childress party to begin the final leg of their trip.

The distance from Beaver to Yellowstone was one hundred and ten miles. They would camp three nights through the pass and on the fourth day arrive in the park. With eager anticipation the party, with cook wagons, carriages, Julia's special wagon, and all the young people mounted on fine riding horses, turned into the Targhee and began the final assault.

The horses soon settled down to the journey on the well-marked road, and the miles passed. As the party meandered at a comfortable pace through the pass, the days took on a feeling of sameness. The mountains and canyons unreeled their spectacular and consistent beauty, and the cooling winds and the clear sunshine were like a tonic. The grandeur was almost hypnotic.

Because the horses and vehicles were in splendid condition, they moved with pleasant ease. Sometimes Julia felt well enough to walk for a short distance or to ride sitting in the padded seats of the wagon. The sun and air did seem to have a salutory effect on everyone, and the whole company became sun-bronzed, hearty, and quite merry.

Baby Harold became as brown as a nut, and his bright cheeks and sun-kissed hair gave him the look of a classical cupid painted by Raphael. Julia could not get enough of the rosy child. He played beside her in the comfortable wagon and slept in the warm nest of quilts that William had created close to her bed.

When Julia needed to rest, Hannah took Harold and carried him in a sling while she rode her horse or walked along the trail. Adam had grown accustomed to Harold's presence and had become fondly attached to the infant. Harold laughed and clapped his hands in happy recognition whenever he saw Adam approaching. With a happy shout Adam would clasp the baby in his hands and lift him high. "Ho there, little one!" he would laugh. "What have you been up to today?"

Hannah loved to watch Adam and Harold together. She felt it was a measure of Adam's goodness that the baby felt the joy of being with him.

As life on the trail grew more relaxed and natural, Adam decided to stop shaving. Baby Harold reached up and tangled his little fingers in the short beard that had grown on Adam's face.

"Ouch!" Adam groaned, gently untangling the baby's hand. "Maybe this beard isn't such a good idea."

Hannah smiled and took the baby from him. "Actually, I rather like it. Especially the mustache. It makes you look very handsome and not a little devilish."

Glancing around to see if anyone was watching, Adam bent over and kissed her on the lips. "Devilish, is it?" he said, chuckling. "So my bride-to-be has hidden depths. A taste for the forbidden?"

Hannah laughed. "Not at all. You shall be very bidden. Besides, it is one thing to look devilish—and quite another to act it."

The brush of Adam's beard as he kissed her made Hannah's heart skip a beat, and she had to work hard to keep her tone light and carefree. For Adam it was even harder.

His voice dropped to a whisper. "This is torture, Hannah! To know you are there at night, just yards away from me, with only the scrub oak and the thin canvas of our tents between us. I tell you, no man ever suffered more or worked harder for a bride since Jacob spent seven years waiting for Rachel."

Hannah reached over and touched Adam's hand with a light, dry touch that seemed to carry healing and peace. "Darling Adam, when we marry it will be with as great a love as Jacob and Rachel had. It will never die. Never. Not for all eternity."

Adam heard someone calling his name and looked up to see Joshua Foster beckoning to him. It was late afternoon, and the two men were responsible for selecting the camp- site and getting the train settled for the evening.

Quickly Adam kissed Hannah again. "Got to go, but first, I want to tell you, it seems like eternity just waiting for you. I love you, Hannah Childress."

That night a band of young men from Montpelier joined the Childress party as guests to enjoy a supper of spit-roasted beef, sourdough bread, and fresh peaches. The men were logging in the pass, and they conferred with William and the Barretts on their proposed route into the park. They confirmed the trail was clear ahead.

After dinner everyone gathered around the fire. A young man, Eldon Rich, who was a relative of Charles C. Rich and an avid explorer, stood in the light of the campfire and told the gathered company about the incredible sights they were about to see.

"You will see whole valleys where the earth is a thin crust, with great plumes of steam rising white against the blue skies. Everything smells like rotten eggs and salt water, and yet the air makes you feel strong and healthy.

"Some places there are bubbling pots of colored mud—pink, blue, yellow, and white, and it just plops and pops away like a thick, boiling stew. You'd fair laugh, it is so comical!

"There are hot pools that seem so deep they must go to China, and they are lined with rocks and minerals in colors you have never seen—as though the sunset had spilled its paintpot. But the most amazing thing you'll ever see is the dancing water that shoots into the air like the spout of a teapot boiling over. You have to see it! I cannot even tell you. It makes you feel the earth is alive!"

William's eyes were shining, and he drank in every word the young man was saying. Springing to his feet, he took the young man's hand in his own and shook it with enthusiastic vigor.

"I knew this would be the thrill of a lifetime!" William affirmed. He turned to the company seated around the campfire. "Since I was a little boy in Connecticut I have always had the feeling that I had a Heavenly Father who loved me and watched over me—over all of us on the earth. More than that, though, I have had the conviction that this earth, this very world on which we stand, is a special gift that he created and gave to his children—to me. I have always believed he wants us to love this world, to explore it, to go forth in it—to cultivate and savor it. That is exactly how I feel. I want to open my arms and fold the wonders in. I want to know everything that can be known and see as much as can be seen. I want to keep and ponder.

"Dear children, dear friends, this earth is a powerful and wondrous thing. The day will come when it will be celestialized, and it is here that we shall dwell. No moment of our lives that is used in understanding, developing, or appreciating the bounties of this earth will be lost."

Caught up in William's enthusiasm, the audience burst into applause. "Yellowstone, here we come!" Hannah shouted, and the company responded with three rousing "Hurrahs!"

"Tonight," William continued, "let us dance!"

One of the men had a fiddle and he began to play a polka. Adam caught Hannah's hand and spun her out in front of the wagons. Josh grasped Eliza and they joined in the merrymaking. Eventually everyone was wheeling and leaping and laughing.

In spite of the music and raucous voices, little Harold fell asleep in his mother's arms. Both of them were exhausted from the excitement of the day. Hannah saw that Harold was sleeping, so she stopped dancing to lift him from his mother's arms and carry him over to the wagon to tuck him softly in his bed. Julia walked behind, leaning on William's arm.

"What a lovely day, dear William," she murmured. "I am tired, but I seem to feel a little stronger each day. This wonderful trip is doing me a world of good. Perhaps in another week or so I'll even be lively enough to have a dance with you."

Tenderly, William smiled at her brave hope. "I'm sure we will dance many a dance together, dearest one. Tonight I pray that your rest may be as sweet as the joy you have given me in accompanying me on this holiday."

Hannah turned and smiled at her mother and father. "Harold's sound asleep. I'll rejoin the dancing again if it's all right with you."

"Of course, dear girl. Run along and have fun," Julia said, kissing Hannah on the cheek.

As the young girl slipped around the wagon, moving

161

toward the campfire, Julia turned to William. "Could you lie beside me until I fall asleep, my darling? It is such a comforting thing when I feel you next to me."

William enfolded her in his arms. "There is no place on this earth I would rather be," he whispered.

Josh had asked the young girl who helped with the cooking to dance with him, and Eliza, bored, walked away from the circle of the fire into the shadows by a stand of pines. She felt suddenly reluctant to rejoin the rollicking party in the firelight. It seemed everybody was paired off. She thought about her mother and father, so complete in one another, and of Hannah and Adam, who acted as if no one and nothing else existed when they were together.

Eliza sighed, feeling sorry for herself. True, Josh had kissed her, but she thought he was the kind of young man who made a practice of kissing every girl he could.

She stopped walking and leaned against a tree trunk. She was aware of the sound of the tethered horses cropping grass in a small enclosure beyond the trees. She could also hear the restless movement of the cattle and the murmur of the camp guards as they went about their duties.

A hand clapped her on the shoulder, and she whirled with a stifled scream.

"Didn't mean to scare you," Josh Foster said. "I just wanted to jolt you out of whatever spell you were in."

She pulled away from him, still shaking and somewhat disoriented in the darkness. There was enough light that she could make out his features, but still everything was distorted by the night and the shadows of the trees.

"I thought you were dancing," she snapped. "After all, you captured the hearts of every silly girl on the train who made eyes at you, and I thought for sure you'd be trying to add to your collection tonight."

162

Josh threw back his head and roared with laughter. "You are the skitteriest filly I have ever met!" he said. "Can't even say hello to a fellow without bucking."

His hand reached up and brushed the curls away from her face, and she could see why he was so good with horses. There was something gentling about his touch. With a sigh she felt herself grow quiet inside.

"Josh," she said, "what do you want to do with your life? Do you think this is enough? Wrangling horses and herding cattle and sleeping under the stars? This is fine for a holiday. But this is the way you've lived most of your life, isn't it?"

He laughed. "It is. And a finer way of life I cannot imagine. A good horse, a good supper, and a pretty woman. I think the Lord never made a finer combination than that for a happy life."

Eliza frowned. "I suppose that is all well and good as long as you are a lone man. But heaven help the poor pretty girl who thinks she wants to ride through life with you."

Josh laughed. "Yes. Heaven help her."

The fiddler had begun to play a waltz. The light of the fire was dying down, and nearly everyone had gone to the tents. Eliza could see Hannah and Adam walking hand-in-hand into the shadows, and she felt a pang of loneliness and envy. Josh bent over her, and his hand clasped her waist.

"Let's not waste a perfectly good waltz," he murmured, and she raised her hand to his shoulder. It was amazing how much taller he was than she, and yet how well they fit together. He turned her gently, and she felt her skirts brushing her ankles as they swayed.

"Oh, Eliza, Eliza," Josh whispered in her ear. "Heaven help us both."

CHAPTER SIXTEEN

The visit to Yellowstone surpassed everyone's imaginings. The first night the Barrett brothers set up camp at Firehole Basin. From that base camp the family visited the geyser meadow and got their first taste of the spewing hot waters flung from the heart of the earth. Two days later, William and Julia and a small party left to go directly to Mammoth Hot Springs.

A bathhouse had been constructed at the hot springs, and, while Julia lingered there, finding the waters as soothing and healing as William had hoped, the younger group spent their days exploring the more rugged regions on horseback. Their plan was to rendezvous with William and Julia in Mammoth in four days.

The guide for the horseback touring party was the youngest of the Barrett brothers. He led his charges across wonderlands of geysers, shallow brooks of hot water, and deep pools, fathomless to the eye, where brilliant waters seethed and boiled.

The young explorers saw cones and craters and rivers of dried minerals—beautiful shapes and colors that they never had dreamed existed. They walked over geyser soil that was neither wet nor dry, neither hot nor cold. It could not be described as mud, stone, or sand, but it seemed to be a mixture of a thousand ingredients—lime, clay, magnesia, brimstone—who knew what. As Hannah said over and over again, "This is splendid!"

Adam's scientific training made him look at these conundrums of nature with a hundred questions. Josh, however, looked at the unending spectacle with the eyes of a poet. He seemed to breathe into the experience an immediate, intelligent, and vivid appreciation.

One day as the four young people were standing by a field of mud paintpots that were bubbling and spitting in a dozen colors, Adam began muttering to himself. "What internal forces cause this? What chemical elements are in the mud? Are there reasons for the grid of fissures in this particular geographic location?" Adam was frustrated by all the unanswered questions Yellowstone posed to his scientific mind.

Eliza picked her way over to where Josh was standing in rapt silence. Holding her skirts above the seeping, sulphur-laden water that drenched the crust of the geyser field, she stepped close to him.

"You look like you are memorizing the whole of it," she said, the sweep of her hand encompassing the surrounding scene.

Josh glanced down at her. "I am," he answered simply. "I want it in my head, to pull out and look at again after we have left." He tapped his temple as though tamping the memory into his brain.

"Do you always do that?" Eliza asked. "Do you carry a picture book of your whole life in your head?"

"Yes, all the places and all the people worth remembering. When I leave them, I keep them in the pages of my mind."

"And have I warranted a page yet?" Eliza teased.

He put a hand on her arm and looked intently into her

eyes. "You do not need a page. I have no intention of ever leaving you," he answered. His voice was suddenly serious.

Blushing a furious red, Eliza whirled and walked away. "Such impertinence!" she exclaimed to no one in particular. Josh, hearing her, laughed out loud and walked back toward his horse.

"Time to be getting back, I think. Darkness is going to catch us before we reach the camp," he called. The touring party began to gather where the horses were tethered. It had been a long day, and there was still a considerable ride back to the campground.

The next day the men went hunting, and Adam shot a deer. That night the campers ate roasted venison, root vegetables, and wild blackberry cobbler cooked in a deep dutch kettle in the ashes of the fire. Everyone ate with huge appetite. The fresh air and the long, vigorous days made even the women eat like lumberjacks.

In such pleasant ways the days passed swiftly. Although the trails and roads were primitive, and some days the travel was demanding, still it was with a sense of regret that the group turned toward Mammoth Hot Springs and the reunion with William and Julia. Not that Hannah and Eliza were reluctant to see their parents; it was just that the time of their meeting marked the midpoint of the holiday. From now on every day would bring them closer to the end.

When the girls arrived at Mammoth Hot Springs, they were pleased to see that their mother seemed to be glowing with improved health. The warm waters did have an apparent recuperative power. Both Mama and Papa were happier and more at peace than Hannah could remember in a long time. It was a wonderful feeling and added to the sweetness of the evenings around the campfire.

"I declare," Adam sighed in repletion, stretched beside the fire on the evening of their last night at the Hot Springs, his riding boots toasting in the heat from the coals, "you ate four servings of bread and honey and more stew than I did. We shall have to get married soon, or you will be as plump as a summer bear."

Hannah was feeling too full of food and well-being to rise to the bait. "You would be mighty lucky if I did gain a pound or two. As it is you are getting a bag of bones for a wife," she responded serenely.

He looked at her lovely, slender form. Her long, graceful neck and the small curve of her waist were so beautiful to him that he could hardly keep his hands from reaching for her, even though they were clearly visible to everyone in the firelight.

Unaware of the storm of desire in Adam, Hannah sat, within reach, not looking at him. Her eyes were focused on little Harold. With a gentle, loving smile she was bending over the baby cradled in the basket formed by her knees as she sat cross-legged on a blanket. The child had just been fed, and he was playing with the curling ends of Hannah's hair. She was unbraiding the long, tangled plait and trying to brush it smooth.

"Speaking of bears . . . my hair is just like the fur of a bear," she said with a sigh. "I pick up burrs, thorns, leaves and twigs, and combing through my hair is like going through a thicket. I wish I could cut it all off."

"Heaven help you if you ever think such a thought," Adam said fiercely. "Anything as beautiful as your hair needs to be preserved—and appreciated. You do the pre-serving, and I'll do the appreciating."

Hannah laughed softly at his division of labor.

The darkness of the night lay around them like a shawl, and it drew them together into its silent and private embrace.

"Do you think Eliza and Josh are getting too close, Adam," Hannah asked in a soft voice.

"Why?" Adam asked.

"Haven't you noticed what is going on? They are together all the time. Their horses ride side by side, and they are always wandering off with each other. I do not think Papa would approve—and I know Mama wouldn't!"

"Your sister's almost a woman grown, Hannah," Adam replied. "She's got beauty and spirit. I expect she'll have a lot of young men following her before she's through. Don't worry. I have a hunch Josh can take care of himself."

Hannah clicked her tongue impatiently. "It isn't Josh I am worrying for, Adam!"

"I know your sister well enough to know that Josh is the one who needs our concern," Adam laughed. "You don't need to worry about Eliza. Your sister has a hell-bent-for-fire mind of her own. No one could talk her into anything she didn't want to do—not even someone as smooth-tongued as Josh. No. In the end, she will do exactly what she decides—and Josh will have to accept it. Seems to be a family characteristic."

Hannah did not laugh. "This is serious, Adam. Don't make a joke about it. I'm really glad we're back with Mama and Papa. After all, we don't know much about this man and everything is going so fast because of the unusual intimacy of this trip. I think I like Josh, but caution is called for, and caution is not a word that Eliza respects. She is still awfully young, and inexperienced . . ."

Adam patted her hand. "It's your parents' problem, not yours, Hannah. Eliza and Josh are just enjoying the trip— nothing more. I'm not sure they even like each other. Eliza seems to be quite impatient with him, and he treats her like a spoiled child of whom he does not quite approve. I don't think you need to worry about them falling in love."

168

The next day the Childress party traveled to Gibbon Falls and past Devil's Den before making camp in Elk Park. In the final days of the tour, they visited Norris Geyser Basin where the whole surface of the earth seemed ready to burst with heat and steam.

A massive plume of vapor filled the air, smelling vilely of sulphur, and fumaroles like frying pans sputtered and sizzled. The scene was splendidly intimidating and a grand finale to the whole spectacle.

All ten days in the valleys of the Yellowstone had been breathtaking, and when the family left to return through the pass to Beaver Canyon to board the train, the wonders they had seen seemed like a half-realized dream.

On the last day before the touring party was due to disembark in Ogden, everyone was sitting quietly, sunk in his or her own thoughts as the train wheels clicked the song of going home. Only one more night and the whole adventure would be a thing of the past—nothing more than a treasured memory. There was an air of melancholy in the silence of the group.

Josh came into the parlor car to report to William on the condition of the horses and the preparations to unload the wagon and supplies in Ogden the next day. After Josh finished his business matters, he asked William if he might have permission to go out onto the observation car with Eliza. William readily agreed.

Josh touched Eliza's elbow and led her out once again onto the platform. The train tracks raced below them, and the sun was setting in the west in a blaze of crimson and orange.

"Don't you feel like your eyes have been overstuffed with marvels? As though we have overeaten on beauty?" Eliza murmured, looking out at the majestic ending of the day.

"I expect these sights will have to last us through a long, dull, and barren winter," Josh replied, looking not at the sunset, but at her beautiful face, made bright by the rich colors of the setting sun. "For me, at least, winter will be long, dull and colorless. I head back to Salmon in three weeks, before the early snows. This year it will seem an empty place to me through the long months."

Eliza did not look at him. "Is it really only two weeks since we stood here, right here, together for the first time?" she said, musing softly. "It seems to me I have known you forever."

"Didn't you hear what I said?" Josh said harshly. "I said I am leaving."

"That's all right," Eliza said quietly, "because I'm not going to leave you."

There was a long silence.

"Did you just say what I think you said?" Josh asked, puzzled and disconcerted. "I am not a man to play games with."

"I know you are not," Eliza replied calmly. "I don't play games. I meant exactly what I said."

He grasped her shoulders and pulled her to him roughly, his voice edged with emotion. "Eliza," he said hoarsely, "you are too young, and I have led too wild a life. Your father will not see me as an eligible suitor for you, but maybe if I work hard and save some money and prove myself to Abner and the Church as an upright man— maybe in a year or two your father would agree to let me court you . . ."

Eliza reached her hand up and covered Josh's mouth. "I am not my sister Hannah," she said. "I *cannot* wait. I *will not* wait. Not one year—not two years! I want my life *now*. I don't want a courtship or a suitor—I want you. You are my life, Josh."

Josh groaned and crushed her mouth with his. "Eliza, we have to do what is right. We have to do it the right way so that there can be no regrets . . ."

"Yes, Josh," she whispered. "But our being together is right. The only thing that would be wrong would be for us to be separated. Surely you must know that. Surely you can feel that."

"I'll go to your father—I'll beg him to let us be married." Josh almost groaned again with the dilemma of his desire and his hopelessness.

"You can try with Papa," Eliza said quietly. "You can try. But if he says no it will make no difference to me. Whatever Papa says, we will leave for Uncle Abner's together."

Just then the door to the observation deck opened, and Adam and Hannah walked out. Josh and Eliza sprang apart, but not before Adam observed their tight embrace.

"What are you two talking about so seriously?" Hannah's forehead was furrowed with a questioning frown as she jolted through the train door onto the crowded platform.

Eliza laughed lightly. "About the poor buffalo in Yellowstone who do not know their time is past. Also about the setting sun—and what we will be facing tomorrow when we arrive home."

"Hm-m-m." Adam wore a bemused smile. "Talking about all that, were you? My! What a philosophical pair you are."

A month later, Hannah walked down the staircase of the Big House. Her sister Anne and her family were still in Saint George visiting relatives as they had been since the early summer. Several times they had delayed their return because of the pleasantness of the warm autumn weather in southern Utah. Hannah also suspected that as long as

171

Mama was in residence at the Big House, Anne and her family preferred to stay away.

Papa had said he did not think he would go to visit Saint George ever again because the lovely little city reminded him too much of his old friend Brigham and how much he missed him. Saint George and Brigham Young were inextricably combined in Papa's mind, for the prophet had loved the southern city with all his heart.

"What a mess has been left for poor President Taylor with Brigham's passing," Papa sighed. "The Feds won't give our new prophet any peace. Our government seems determined to harass the Church into the ground. It is a miracle to me that somehow President Taylor manages to lead us and inspire us, even from his hiding places. Sometimes I wonder if there is any place of peace on the whole of this earth for our dear church."

It was unlike Papa to be pessimistic, but since the family's return from Yellowstone, Mama's decline had been swift, and her advancing weakness was a shadow on everyone's heart. There was a terrible feeling of impending doom in the house, and the only two things that brought brightness were the happy cooing of baby Harold and the rush of plans for the elaborate wedding party that Papa insisted on giving for Hannah and Adam.

All the members of the community were to be invited to the reception at the Big House. Because of Anne's continued absence, the weight of the planning and arrangements had fallen on Hannah's shoulders, and for her it was a cheerless task on top of all her other responsibilities. Eliza was scarcely any help at all. Her younger sister was often gone for hours of the day and explained her absences with vague excuses. If Hannah had not been so busy and concerned with running the household, nursing Mama, and tending the baby, as well as trying to get ready for her October wedding, she would have realized that something was going on. Hannah felt twinges of worry about Eliza, but pushed them to the back of her mind in the rush and complexity of everyday living.

Today had been particularly trying. The doctor had told Hannah that her mother's kidneys were failing and that her blood was filling with poisons. Harold had become fussy and seemed hungry all the time. Hannah knew her mother's milk was drying up, yet she also knew it would break her mother's heart to know she could no longer nurse her baby. It was the one service she was able to perform for her beloved child.

"You will need to wean the child to a cup—and do so immediately," the doctor warned Hannah in quiet confidence as they left Mama's room. "You will have very little time to get him used to it."

"It will break Mama's heart to give up nursing him," Hannah replied.

"There is no choice," the doctor told her. "Your mother has lost her milk, though she does not realize it. The child is starving."

Now, in addition to her other duties, Hannah had to feed the hungry baby. It was a time-consuming and sad task as she thought of her mother lying pale and silent in the bed upstairs.

Although the hour was long past dinnertime, Papa and Adam had not returned from the reservoir site. Hannah had finally been able to settle her mother and Harold for the night and had completed the calligraphy addresses on the last of the wedding invitations. She had been working at the desk in her mother's small sitting room when a pang of hunger reminded her that she had eaten nothing since early morning. She was very hungry. With a flurry of skirts, Hannah walked down the stairs. Halfway down the stairs exhaustion washed over her, and, for a moment, the desire for sleep fought with the desire for food. Hunger won.

Just as Hannah's foot touched the bottom step, the front door opened and Adam came into the entry hall. He had obviously brushed off his workclothes outside on the porch, but rock dust clung to the creases. His face was gray with fatigue.

Hannah walked over to him and kissed him gravely. "We make quite a pair, don't we?" she sighed mirthlessly. "Are we going to have enough energy to get married?"

With a sudden burst of vigor, Adam wrapped her in his arms and hugged her passionately. "Absolutely. You may trust me on that."

Reluctantly he let her go. "Although I think I may need something to eat first."

"Me, too," she answered. "Let's go into the kitchen and see what we can rustle up."

"That's quite an offer from a woman who admits she does not like to cook." Adam followed her into the kitchen where a lone lamp glowed. They found some leftover chicken and homemade cottage cheese, and Hannah went to the larder for a bottle of pears. Adam got a fresh loaf of bread from under the clean cloth that covered the day's baking and cut thick slices.

For the first few minutes they ate in silence as they satisfied their immediate hunger.

"I have just finished addressing our five-hundredth invitation!" Hannah said. "Can you believe that in two weeks we will go to the Endowment House, and finally . . . all the waiting will be over."

"Two weeks," Adam repeated. "I wish it were tonight. I wish it were right now."

"I do, too, Adam," Hannah replied. "But Papa wants

174

this great party. He has done so much for us. It isn't too much to do for him."

She paused in sudden realization. "Where is Papa? Didn't he come home with you?"

Adam shook his head. "He left this afternoon and rode out to the farm at Riverdale. Harvest time is coming, and he wanted to be sure that proper arrangements were made with the tenants. Kind of sad to think of your mama's house empty."

Hannah nodded. "Sometimes I think of the farm waiting—hoping for us to come home. The truth is, the little girls who used to live there are gone forever." She stood up abruptly and began to clear the table. "This is far too melancholy a subject for a prewedding conversation. We're both tired. Did Papa say when he'd be back?"

"Sometime tomorrow. He didn't want to tell your mother where he was going. He thought it would make her too sad."

"She's asleep for the night," Hannah reassured him. "Papa should be back before she even misses him."

Adam stood up and stretched. "I must be getting home, or I'll be too tired to settle down Ensign for the night. I just had to fill my eyes with you before I went to bed."

"Well, don't remember me looking like this, for mercy's sake!" Hannah laughed, trying to straighten her hair and smooth her apron but giving up on the attempt. "If I don't get some beauty sleep, you won't have me for a wife! But Eliza is off at Phoebe Howard's house. They were making a quilt or something, and I probably ought to wait up for her."

Just then they heard the latch of the front door, and Eliza slipped through and began to run toward the stairs as quietly and surreptitiously as a thief.

"Eliza!" Hannah's voice cut sharply into the dim light

of the hall. "What on earth are you doing sneaking in like that? And why are you so late?"

Eliza whirled, and her face was flushed with surprise. "Hannah! I thought you'd be in bed! I didn't want to wake you."

Hannah strode out into the hall to give Eliza a piece of her mind and to demand some answers, but Eliza beat her to the confrontation.

"So, my dear sister, it's a good thing I did get home when I did! Just what are you and Adam doing alone in a darkened house? I don't care if you are getting married in two weeks. You know what Papa would say if he found you in such compromising circumstances."

"What are you talking about?" Hannah spluttered angrily. "Adam came to tell me where Papa was . . . and we both had not eaten supper . . . and . . ."

Eliza smiled and wagged her finger. "Excuses. Excuses. Sounds trumped up to me. No chaperone. No lights. Pretty irregular . . ."

"You are incorrigible!" Adam laughed. "You ought to have been a lawyer, Eliza. You could talk your way out of a rattlesnake hole."

"Good night, you two." Eliza ran lightly up the stairs. "As your chaperone, I give you five minutes, and that's all."

Hannah stood at the bottom of the stairs, shaking her head. "How did that conversation get turned around?" she asked Adam in confusion. "How did I end up being the one in trouble?"

Adam bent down and kissed Hannah good night. "Eliza's right. Even though we are going to be married, we have to avoid the appearance of evil. Believe me, this is going to be the longest two weeks of my life."

CHAPTER SEVENTEEN

The bridal dress was white, with a collar that buttoned high on the neck, seed pearls embroidered into the fabric, and a bodice that held Hannah like an embrace. At the final fitting she stood and stared at herself in the mirror, and for one instant, the heavy cares and concerns of the past weeks vanished. Suddenly, Hannah felt young and happy for the first time in months. She hurried to dress for the trip.

Adam was waiting in the circular driveway at the front steps of the Big House in the beautiful caroche, which was drawn by Papa's finest pair of matched grays. Papa had arranged for the young couple to ride into Salt Lake City in comfort and style where they were to be married at the Endowment House, spend the night, and return to Ogden for their splendid party the next evening.

Anne had returned home to Ogden, and, even though she still thought the timing of the wedding was inconvenient and ill-advised, she had, with her usual efficiency, taken over the plans for the reception. The only cloud over the day was that Papa's plans to accompany the young bridal couple to Salt Lake had been changed. During the night Mama had taken a turn for the worse, and Papa did not feel he could leave her bedside.

"With so much going on in the house, your mother needs someone with her every minute," Papa told Hannah, who reluctantly agreed. "I have taken a few days off from work at the reservoir because while Adam is away on his wedding trip, our work schedule is scaled back anyway. I will spend the time overseeing your mother's care myself."

Before stepping into the carriage, Hannah hugged Harold and handed him to Eliza, who seemed uncharacteristically quiet for such an exciting occasion. Eliza took the baby without comment, and Hannah was astonished to see tears streaming down her sister's face. Eliza looked strained and unhappy.

"Oh, Hannah," Eliza whispered, "I do so wish I were going with you."

"I know, dear sister, I wish so, too," Hannah answered tenderly, "but I promise you that on your wedding day I shall accompany you and we shall be together then. Perhaps the Salt Lake Temple will even be finished in time for your marriage."

At Hannah's words Eliza burst frantically into tears and turned her face away. Frightened, little Harold began to cry as well. The baby held out his arms to Hannah, who was more his mother than his own mother, and he began to scream as he realized she was leaving him. Hannah melted in sorrow and reached for the baby.

Adam, seeing her intent, jumped down from the carriage. Putting a firm hand on Hannah's elbow he lifted her into the carriage. "The sooner you leave, the sooner Harold will settle down, Hannah. You know he will be fine with Eliza."

In spite of her happiness, Hannah felt tears springing to her own eyes. "Oh, Adam, I don't know if I can leave. Everything is so topsy-turvy. Give me a few more minutes . . ."

"You can leave, my darling. This is our wedding day. There are plenty of capable people to take care of things here. We are going to start our new life together. Come sit beside me. That is the one place where you are essential and irreplaceable." He lifted her gently into her seat and then went to the other side and sprang into the carriage. Grasping the reins, he gave her a kiss on the cheek, took off his hat, and waved it to the family gathered on the steps.

"Until tomorrow!" he called. "Wish us luck."

Hurrahs went up from the family and workers gathered in the driveway. Flowers were thrown, hands waved. Hannah felt her heart lifting as the carriage began to move slowly toward the avenue. Suddenly, at the last minute, just as they turned out of the driveway, Eliza came running up to the side of the carriage. She had handed Harold to Anne, and now she was jogging beside the moving vehicle. The horses were walking slowly, and Eliza was able to match their pace.

"Hannah," Eliza gasped through the tears still streaming down her face. "You are the best sister in the world. I love you. I know I haven't been as much help as I should have been, and I want you to know I'm sorry. I'm really, really sorry. I'm sorry about everything. Please believe that I love you and—and—no matter what—I wouldn't hurt you—no matter what . . . Remember . . ."

"For heaven's sake, we'll be home tomorrow, Eliza," Hannah said. "I'm not sure what you're trying to say, but we'll talk then. We'll have so much to talk about. I love you too, Eliza. Good-bye, dear sister, until tomorrow. Take good care of Harold for me."

The horses turned out of the driveway and began to canter. Eliza stood by the gatepost, her hand half-raised in farewell or entreaty. She was almost out of breath.

"That's what I'm trying to tell you . . . I would if I could

. . . Remember, whatever else, I love you . . ." Eliza's jumbled words faded as the horses moved along at an increased speed.

Hannah twisted in her seat and watched the house growing smaller in the distance. She could still see the tiny figure of Eliza, standing by the gate, still waving. "What was it Eliza was trying to say?" she asked Adam. "I could hardly hear, and the baby was crying so hard, I could hardly think."

"I am sure it was nothing," Adam said. "She was just trying to express all the things that big occasions make us feel. Maybe she's beginning to realize what a mighty change this is going to bring into her life. After all, you won't be there to fill in all the cracks for her anymore, and she's going to need to take her share of the responsibilities."

Shaking his head, Adam dismissed the subject. "Take a deep breath, Hannah, and put it all behind you. Your wedding dress is wrapped in tissue and neatly boxed. We have all the necessary documents to admit us to the Endowment House, and we have each other. What a day! What a day! Let's just think about our wedding. We've waited so long. Just think about us for a while, Hannah. Do you think you can do that?"

With a dazzling smile Hannah turned and looked at this man with whom she had fallen instantly in love the first time she had seen him nearly a year before. "Oh yes, Adam," she breathed. "I think I can do that with the greatest pleasure."

But the truth was she could not rid her heart of the silent weight of the memory of her mother's pale and puffy face, or the dark circles under her mother's eyes, or the echo of baby Harold crying in Eliza's unfamiliar arms, or her father's worry-creased face, or Anne's disapproving frown. The press of her concerns would not leave her, and

180

somewhere on the perimeter of her worries she saw in her mind's eye the dashing smile of Josh Foster, and through it she heard Eliza's tears.

Papa had made reservations for their wedding night at the Continental Hotel. It was the most beautiful hotel in Salt Lake City, with a classic architectural facade, a cool piazza sheltered by tall trees, a wide, columned porch, and a magnificently appointed dining room. As the young couple entered the spacious lobby, Hannah was struck with the thought of how much the capital city had grown even in the few short years since her childhood.

Her father had arrived in Salt Lake Valley as a young man thirty years earlier, and he had described to her what a desolate and barren place it had been, with struggling dry farms and only a few log and adobe homes.

Now Salt Lake City was a bustling metropolis, with the great, egg-shaped Tabernacle at its heart, and the scaffolding of the mighty temple rising in the sky. Streetcars, carriages, clouds of dust, and crowds of hurrying people filled the broad streets. It was a place of vigorous commerce and explosive growth—a crossroads of the expanding nation.

Outside the city, spreading farms, watered by extensive irrigation systems, teemed with orchards, sleek cattle, and cultivated fields. The look of prosperity and civilization was everywhere. Indeed, as the prophet had said, the wilderness had blossomed like a rose, and still the Church was persecuted by the government and vilified in the press.

Hannah felt a little intimidated by the elegance of the crowded lobby, but Adam walked directly to the desk and registered as "Mr. and Mrs. Adam Fairfield." He paid a bellhop to drop their luggage in the room, and then he turned to Hannah.

"We must hurry directly to the Endowment House,"

Adam said, pulling his watch from his vest pocket and consulting it with a worried frown. "We are much later than we had expected to be."

Carrying the box with Hannah's wedding gown, they hurried down North Temple and entered through the gate at Temple Square. In moments they stood by the desk at the entrance to the Endowment House, along with a long line of other couples. The foyer and walkway outside the building were crowded with men and women, all looking worried and intense.

"We are very sorry, Brother Fairfield," the endowment worker said with a sad shake of his head. "We have dozens of couples waiting to be married and sealed. A large and unexpected attendance. We have more people in the building than the building can hold. There is no possible way that you will be sealed today. You will have to come back tomorrow. If you could have been here at eight this morning . . . ."

"But we have driven all the way from Ogden . . ." Adam began.

"Brother Fairfield, we have people here who have come from farther away than that. No. We cannot take one more couple for today's sessions. You will have to be on tomorrow's list. That is all I can do for you."

Hoping against hope, Hannah and Adam remained at the Endowment House until the sun began to set, and then, seeing the seemingly endless line of those who were still ahead of them, they realized the futility of the wait.

"There's only one thing to do," Adam said dispiritedly, "we will have to come back tomorrow morning and be the first ones here."

Emotionally and physically exhausted, they returned to the hotel. "Your dinner is waiting in your room," the desk clerk informed them. "Your father made all of the arrangements for your refreshment, Miss Childress, or rather, I should say, Mrs. Fairfield."

Hannah opened her mouth to correct the clerk, but then, realizing Adam had registered them as husband and wife, she became confused and said nothing, not really knowing what to say. How could she explain all the ramifications of their situation to an indifferent desk clerk when she herself had not sorted everything out in her own mind. What were they to do? She honestly did not know. Hannah was so tired, disappointed, and hungry that she could not think straight.

"Thank you," Adam said calmly. "We would like the key to our room, please."

The clerk handed the key to Adam with a knowing smile that made Hannah burn with embarrassment and shame. "Adam," she whispered, tugging at his arm as they headed for the stairs. "We can't go up to the room together."

"Of course we can," Adam's lips were next to her ear and he was holding her arm so firmly that she felt like she was being lifted up the stairs. "We do not need to explain our lives to hotel clerks, and we are hungry and tired, and it is our room."

When they entered the room they saw a small service table set with white linen, crystal, and silver. A roasted pheasant decorated with its own resplendent feathers, fruit compote, almond rolls, oven-roasted potatoes, creamed onions and peas, and meringue tarts filled the room with smells so enticing that neither Adam nor Hannah had any desire to address their problem any further before eating.

They fed one another with their fingers and licked their lips and laughed at the pleasure of taste and texture. At last, replete, they laid down the heavy white napkins, having wiped the corners of their mouths and the last sweet lick from their fingers.

"Oh, Adam," Hannah sighed happily. "It was all so delicious that I wish we didn't get full. Wouldn't it be fun to just go on eating and eating and eating . . ."

Adam was silent for a moment. "Yes, dear girl, but we are full, and you can't put off our dilemma by eating any more," he said solemnly. "You have to face it. We are here, together, and alone. And it is our wedding night . . ."

"No!" The word exploded from Hannah's mouth, more emphatically than she had intended. "It is *not* our wedding night. Not! Don't say it. Don't think it. We can't have waited this long only to spoil everything now on the very eve of all we have dreamed."

Adam pushed aside the table and caught Hannah in his arms in one stride. "You cannot know how I have dreamed! Here and now I take you for my wife! It is not our fault that our vows have not been finalized. This was our wedding day. Tomorrow's ceremony in the Endowment House will only be the outward evidence of what we have already covenanted in our hearts. We did all we could. Surely the Lord cannot expect us—you cannot expect *me*—to continue to wait. It is inhuman. This cannot be wrong. Surely the Lord will understand. He has put us together, here, now."

Adam pulled Hannah to him and pressed his lips to hers with a passion that made her head ring with answering desire. She wanted to give him everything he yearned for, everything she had to give. She loved him to the limits of her fierce, determined heart, and yet, at her solid, unyielding core, she felt the firm, hard voice of duty and reason.

With a small sob she pulled away. "No, Adam! You know this is wrong as much as I do. It doesn't matter if our wedding is one day away, or one year—until we are sealed by God, we are not married. No matter what our hearts say, we must wait. We must be careful, Adam, very, very careful, for the passions of one moment could destroy our happiness. If we do what is right, this will only be one, short, soon-forgotten night—but, if we give in to desire and circumstance, this night could brand our hearts with pain forever."

She was crying softly, almost silently, and Adam gave a ragged sigh and walked to the window. Staring out across the tree-lined street, he continued to breathe as though he had been running a long distance, but he said nothing.

After a long moment he said softly, "You don't have to lecture me, Hannah. I know the commandments. I also know the love and understanding of our Heavenly Father. The truth is not always black and white. Sometimes the human heart and spirit are part of the equation. Can't you believe in me enough to listen to me? Can't you hear the demands of desire without always erasing them with duty? Can't you trust me enough to know that I would never lead you astray? I only want you to feel as I do, until your love is greater than anything else, to the very limit of your being and beyond. You need to believe in me, Hannah. I would not lead you away from God. I only want to lead you into my heart—into our own life—our shared life. But you can't let go."

"Adam . . ." Hannah walked over to him and attempted to put her arms around his shoulders. Her warm, lithe body against his was like a jolt of electricity. He moved away.

"Don't make this any more difficult than it has to be, Hannah," he said roughly. "You may sleep in the bed, and I will not touch you. I will make a place for myself on the sofa. Let us pray this night passes somehow, because right now I feel as though it is going to be endless."

Feeling miserable and rejected, Hannah lay down, fully clothed, on top of the bedcovers. After removing his coat and shoes and taking a pillow from the bed, Adam threw himself down on the stiff, horsehair sofa. Neither spoke a word, and the room was full of their silence and misery.

Some time after midnight the moon rose, throwing a silvery sheen through the lace window curtains and onto the flowered carpet. Hannah was lying awake, listening to the sound of Adam's breathing, and guessed that he was awake, too.

"Adam," she whispered, "thank you for . . ." She did not know how to say what she wanted to say, and so she let the thought trail into the darkness.

There was a continuing silence, and for a while she thought she must have been mistaken—that Adam was, in fact, asleep. Then she heard his reply. His voice was husky and deep.

"I love you, Hannah, and I know you love me, but I also know your love will always come second to your sense of duty and right. There's a bit of the Pharisee in you."

She raised up on her elbow. "That's not fair, Adam. That's a terrible thing to say to me. You know we are doing the right thing!"

"Yes," Adam conceded, "of course I know this is the right decision—and I knew we would make this decision all along. I just wanted you to be tempted by our love. I wanted you to have to struggle with your desire for me. I wanted it to be as hard for you to resist as it was for me."

"Don't be silly," she said indignantly. "This decision wasn't easy for me. I love you—I want you—but I also know what the Lord requires. I do not struggle against things I know are my righteous duty."

"That is true," Adam said quietly. "You never struggle against duty, or obligation, or right. You only struggle against me. Against your love for me. Against putting love first."

Hannah felt tears spring to her eyes. "I don't know what

you're talking about, Adam. I truly don't. Please. Let's not quarrel. It will be dawn soon, and our real wedding day. Please be happy, and love me."

"That is all I ever want to do—all I have wanted to do for the past year, my darling girl. Why can't you believe in me? I would never ask you to give up your relationships and obligations to your family, or to God—I just want you to put them in a different order. I'll help you. You won't have to be alone anymore. Let me be the core of your life. Do you understand what I'm saying, Hannah? Let *us* be first in your life, and then everything else will follow in its proper order. Take that leap of faith—that leap of love."

"You are first, Adam. You are. It's just that . . ."

Adam turned over on the couch so that his face was away from her. "Yes," he said quietly in a resigned voice. "It's always just that something else . . ."

187

CHAPTER EIGHTEEN

Even though Adam and Hannah arrived at the Endowment House before the first light of dawn there was already a line of couples waiting in the anteroom. It was late morning before it was their turn to be married. Adam and Hannah hurried from the Endowment House, knowing they would have to travel at top speed to arrive in Ogden in time for the reception planned for that evening.

Hannah had removed her wedding dress and was wearing a dark blue traveling dress covered by a matching cloak trimmed across the shoulders and around the hood with black braid and tassels. The autumn day was brisk, but the sun was shining and the air was crisply pleasant. Her cheeks grew pink in the cold wind, but her eyes were pensive and unsmiling, and Adam's face also was quiet and unreadable.

Though they were now married, the lack of sleep and the emotional strain of the night before still lingered over both of them like a fine coating of dust dulling the brightness of their happiness. Hannah could not put her finger on exactly what was wrong between them. Somehow she felt she had failed Adam, and herself, but she could not define where or how.

She knew they had not really quarreled, and yet she had the feeling that they had laid open some gulf of pain between them that might be too deep and too real to overcome. It was something they would have to live over and through and cover up again and again.

She wanted to erase the whole memory of the night before. She wanted it never to have happened. It felt like something was broken and she did not know what it was. Adam was silent, concentrating on driving the team and keeping the carriage moving swiftly and steadily.

"I suppose if we are late for the reception, they can go on with the party without us," Hannah said, tentatively trying to find a neutral topic of conversation.

Adam nodded. "The bride and groom are not essential to the revelry of a wedding—although they do afford a good butt for humor."

Hannah sat up abruptly, as if stung, and answered hotly, "I don't like to think of our marriage as a joke."

"I'm sorry, Hannah. That was a thoughtless thing for me to say." Adam was genuinely contrite. "Our wedding has been so different from what I had expected that I'm having trouble being philosophical about it. That's no excuse for resorting to sarcasm, however."

A wave of misery washed over Hannah. Everything seemed to be out of kilter, as though her world had been jostled and things had fallen back not quite in the right place. Worse yet, she had no idea how to set everything straight. None of her inner self felt familiar or comfortable, and even Adam—dear, predictable Adam—seemed distant and changed. She hung her head down as the horses cantered along the roadway and lapsed into silence.

Though her shoulder was touching Adam's, an invisible chasm seemed to have opened between them. The future stretched in front of her like an unknown country, and a tear formed in the corner of her eye. She wanted desperately to talk, and yet for some reason, for the first time, she found it hard to think what to say to Adam, her husband.

What a shock to think those words. Her husband! She was married. Married to Adam. The word rang hollow and uncomprehended. If this was marriage, it was not anything like she had imagined, and already she was making a mess of it. Her heart felt cold and blank.

Conversation in the carriage through the long afternoon was desultory and formal, and the stiffness between the newlyweds continued as the afternoon faded into evening. Dusk was falling when they reached the wide curve of road that led into Ogden, and they drove past the trees and settlements of the outlying farms of the city.

"We'll arrive at the Big House too late for the buffet dinner," Hannah predicted, "but we will be in time for the dancing and the reception line. Papa will be so relieved when we arrive. He is probably wondering what has happened to us."

Abruptly Adam pulled the carriage off the road onto a grassy space under some cottonwood trees and reined the horses to a halt.

"That's what I'm wondering!" Adam exclaimed. "What has happened to us, Hannah? This is our wedding day, for heaven's sake! This is what we've been waiting for for nearly a year, and here we are sitting like two strangers. It's my fault. I was impatient and thoughtless last night. Please, darling, forgive me—because I am having a miserable time trying to forgive myself.

"I just wanted you so much—I do want you so much— that it clouds my judgment. I know I should not have pressed you last night, but I needed to know you wanted me, too, and in my need I was selfish and callous. I've been behaving like a lovesick schoolboy."

With a welcome feeling of release, Hannah laughed and turned toward Adam. "You are definitely not a schoolboy, Adam."

Adam laughed in response, "No, but I am lovesick."

With a joyous whoop that startled the horses, Adam reached for Hannah and pulled her eagerly into a passionate embrace. She leaned against him with relief and joy, and he kissed her travel-stained face and held her closer. Tenderly he parted her cloak and placed his hands around the small of her back. He could feel the fine outline of her bones and the hidden warmth of her body where it had been sheltered by the woolen fabric. Her face was cooled by the wind, and his lips caressed its coolness while beneath his hands her warm body was like a mystical covenant of the reality of their marriage. The seen and the unseen woman both at once, hidden and not hidden—and his. His own dear wife. It was so glorious he felt his heart almost burst with the wonder of it.

The horses moved restlessly, and Hannah almost lost her balance on the edge of the carriage seat. Adam caught her, but they were jostled apart and the spell of the impassioned moment was broken. Realizing as they glanced about them that other travelers on the road had an excellent view of them in their carriage even though the light was fading, and that carriages and wagons were slowing down to stare, Adam and Hannah sat back in their places and smoothed their clothing. With a sigh, Adam picked up the reins and urged the horses back onto the road.

"Whatever is happening at the party—we leave at midnight. At the stroke of twelve. Just the two of us, alone at last," Adam said huskily. "Agreed?"

Blushing in the twilight but feeling light of heart for the first time all day, Hannah nodded. She moved closer to

Adam on the carriage seat and threaded her arm through his. "Agreed," she whispered.

Even in that moment of sweet intimacy, some inner instinct told Hannah that they had not really solved anything. For the moment their love had built a bridge over whatever it was between them that had created the hollow, painful place, but she thought that until they understood better what had caused those bleak feelings they would occur again. She hoped she was wrong.

An hour later, having driven the tired horses as quickly as was humane, Hannah and Adam arrived on Childress Avenue and looked down the street toward the Big House with eager anticipation. The sun had set long ago, and the night was thick and black because the moon had not risen.

The wedding couple expected to hear noise and to see the house glowing with lights and music and people coming and going. Instead, the street was silent, and only a few muted rays of light shone on the porch and in an upper window.

Puzzled, Hannah strained to see the driveway. It was almost empty. Only a few riding horses and small carriages ringed the circle, and she wondered where the party guests could have stabled their horses and conveyances.

There was a peculiar hush along the whole of the street as though the night air had put a finger to its lips. No music. No laughter. No coming and going.

"Adam," Hannah gasped, and her voice was little more than a hoarse whisper. "Something is very wrong."

"Maybe your father cancelled the reception because we were so late," Adam said, trying to reassure her, but Hannah could hear the anxiety in his voice. Adam was already flicking the horses with the little buggy whip, speeding the caroche toward the house. Both of them knew that something had happened, and they both knew that knowing would be better than their present horrible uncertainty.

"It'll be all right," Adam reassured Hannah. "We will face whatever it is together. Try not to worry. Remember I am with you now."

But Hannah in her frantic fear could hardly hear him. The minute the carriage slowed in the driveway, not waiting for Adam to secure the horses, she simply threw her legs over the side of the carriage, hitting the ground with a thump and running up the porch steps without a backward glance.

"Papa!" she called frantically, as she burst through the entry doors. "Papa! Where are you? What has happened?"

William Childress was sitting in the front parlor. The bishop, the mayor, and the doctor were standing around him in solemn and silent brotherhood. Hannah burst into the dimly lit room, and, as she took in the scene and her father's grief-lined face, she threw herself across his knees and began to weep.

"It's Mama, isn't it?" she cried, knowing and yet wanting to be told she was wrong. "Is she much worse? Too sick for the wedding party to be held? I knew we shouldn't have gone. I told Adam we should have waited until Mama was better. I should have been here. I should have been here to take care of her."

Papa shook his head and looked up as Adam walked into the room. Speaking to Adam as much as to Hannah, he said with quiet dignity, "Your mother returned to the arms of her Heavenly Father at ten o'clock this morning. I was with her every minute, holding her hand. She left with a smile of peace that indicated true worthiness and acceptance. Her months of pain and suffering are over. If we weep, we must not weep for her. Only for ourselves. We shall miss her for the rest of this mortal span."

"Oh, Mama, Mama, Mama!" Hannah's cries were wrenched from her like barbed wire. "I should have been here. I should have been here to say good-bye. Why did I go? It was selfish—selfish!"

"No. No," William answered gravely. "Her greatest joy in her last hours was knowing that you and Adam had begun your life together. It would have been selfish of you to have stayed."

"But I was getting married almost at the moment that she died!" Hannah cried. "What kind of a daughter could do such a thing?"

"A righteous and loving daughter," her father answered firmly.

Hannah scarcely heard him. Standing up with a distraught air, she continued to berate herself. "I should have been here . . ." She looked around distractedly. "Harold. Who has Harold? Where is he? Oh, my poor, orphaned boy. And Eliza? Where is Eliza? Who is comforting Eliza?"

Adam walked toward her and put his arms around her gently. "You are tired, Hannah. I know this has been a shock, but try to be calm in spirit and mind. Hush yourself and think. Your mother was a great lady, but you know she has suffered mightily these past months. Her loving Father has taken her home. She is no longer in pain. All of us will miss her, but . . ."

"How can you know anything about missing her?" Hannah shot at him. "She wasn't your mother. You didn't know her when she was able to do everything—be everything. She was our whole world! Eliza, me—what will we do without her? Not even Papa knew her or loved her or needed her like we did. No one can pretend to know what I'm feeling except Eliza!" She paused and looked around her in confusion. "Where is she?" Hannah's voice rose on a note of hysteria. Suddenly she sensed that something more was wrong. Every eye in the room was on her, and there was a stillness that was as heavy as a suspended anvil.

Hannah's eyes flew wide open with alarm. "Eliza, Papa! Where is she? What has happened?"

With a groan William stood up and walked over to the fireplace. He leaned against the mantel and stared into the small fire burning in the grate. "I do not know where Eliza is, Hannah. I do not care to know." His voice was heavy and uninflected.

Adam moved quickly and put a consoling hand on his father-in-law's back. "Surely you cannot mean that," Adam said softly.

Still in the same deathly tone, William replied, "Some time last night Eliza left this house with all of her possessions. She ran away with Joshua Foster. They took two of my finest mounts, Satan and Lady, and they left behind a short note of explanation plus a promissory note for the price of the two horses. As though I would trust the word of a man to repay me for my horses when he has stolen my child."

William handed a piece of paper with Eliza's handwriting on it to Hannah.

The bitterness in William's voice was more awful to hear than the grief. He turned away to look at the fire again. "To think that I trusted that man. He wantonly and cruelly betrayed my trust. I shall never give it so easily again."

Tears filled Hannah's eyes, and she blindly handed Eliza's note to Adam, who read it aloud to her in a quiet voice.

"Dear Mama, Papa, Hannah, and Adam: This note is to tell you that Joshua and I have eloped. I know this will be a hard thing to greet you as your wedding party begins, but

195

do not be sad, because, in a real way, today will be my wedding party, too. Please, please, please try to be happy for me. And please try to understand.

"Papa and Mama, Josh wanted to tell you that we wanted to be married. He wanted to ask your permission, but I would not let him. Papa, you know you would have said no because Josh is not ready to go to the temple and you would have made us wait. I love Josh too much for that. I could not bear to have to wait. I'm not like Hannah. I never have been. I cannot put duty before love.

"So, even though I know I am hurting all of you, I still want you to know that I love you with all my heart—it is just that I love Josh with all my soul—and he is the choice I must make.

"Papa and Mama, I promise you we will be married in the temple as soon as Josh receives the priesthood, and then you can be happy for us, and forgive us. Until then, please just try to be happy. You don't need to think about me if it makes you too angry or sad—but I shall be thinking about all of you. Always. I will miss all of you very much. Love, Eliza."

Hannah snatched the note from Adam's hand, and through tear-blurred eyes, she read it again and again as though by the act of reading she could change what the words said.

"You mean Josh and Eliza are gone? Truly gone? And you don't know where they are? Where could they have gotten married? Have they left the city? *Are* they married? Did Mama know that Eliza had run away before she . . . she . . . Is this terrible letter . . . Is *this* what killed Mama?"

A fresh burst of weeping shook Hannah's frame, but she quickly controlled herself and continued in a voice of agony. "Does Eliza even know that Mama is dead? Has anyone ridden out to try to find her and tell her? Oh! What an awful mess. What is to happen to us?" Hannah buried her face in her hands.

Papa turned away from the fire and placed an arm across Hannah's trembling shoulders. "We do not know where Eliza is, Hannah, and I will make no effort to find her. She has made her choice, and she must live with it. She will reap what she has sown.

"I refuse to allow your sister's foolish and selfish actions to sully the memory or destroy the spirit of this sacred time of mourning for your mother. Eliza has always done exactly what she wanted to do. She has placed herself outside the circle of family and loved ones, and there she shall remain. No one is to speak of this matter again in my presence.

"Now, dear girl, you and Adam must rest and prepare yourselves. Tomorrow we will gather to say farewell to one of the greatest women of the covenant."

Hannah gasped. "But we can't pretend that Eliza doesn't exist! Mama's heart would break if Eliza did not attend her funeral. Eliza's heart will break when she discovers she was not told Mama died."

His face blank and hard, William turned away from his daughter and gestured to Adam. "I am too tired for further discussion, Adam. Please take Hannah to her room. Comfort her, help her rest. I have already taken the liberty of laying out mourning clothes for both of you for the services tomorrow."

Resisting Adam's guiding hand, Hannah whirled on her father. "No. I want to see Mama first. Where is she?"

"Her body is being prepared by the sisters. She is in her bedroom. Why don't you rest for a while before you go up?" her father answered gently.

"No! I must see her now. I will see her!" Hannah's voice broke and fierce, hot tears scalded her cheeks. "Oh Mama! Why wasn't I here?"

197

Adam supported her with his arm, and Hannah leaned against him as the two of them left the parlor, slowly mounting the stairs and entering the high-ceilinged bedroom where Hannah's mother lay on a downy pillow with her hands sweetly folded across her breast.

Although Julia's face was pale and cold as alabaster, it was the first time in months that the obscuring lines of pain and suffering were erased, and, in death, the exquisite composure and beauty of Julia's countenance had been restored to her every feature. Julia Childress was so beautiful that Adam felt his heart wrench with the loss of such a noble and exquisite woman—the blessed mother of the woman he loved. It felt to Adam as though the whole of the earth had become a little less bright and lovely because this great woman, whom he had come to know and admire during her months of endless suffering, would not pass this way again. His sense of loss was unexpectedly poignant.

To Hannah, seeing her mother's youthful, peaceful face was like experiencing the restoration of the mother of her childhood, only to realize that she had been snatched from her again for the remainder of her mortal life, not by pain this time, but by death itself. In the desolation of that absolute realization, Hannah thought immediately of Eliza, the only other constant in her young life. Both of these anchors of her life were lost to her now—lost in one fell swoop—lost to places unknown to her.

The room seemed to be shifting, and she saw the face of Adam swimming above her as her vision wavered. All of her past seemed to have flown from beneath her feet, and she felt as though she were hanging over a void. There was nothing left to cling to, no yesterdays, no foundation left at all, only this Adam—half-stranger, half-self—only Adam and the perilously fragile, uncomprehended promises of their long-ago, morning ceremony. Was it really only hours since she and Adam had knelt together at the altar? Who had she become at the moment those forgotten words were spoken? Who was she now? A child with no mother. No sister. Her father lost to grief and despair. Only Adam—but what did she really know of him? What bound them together? Not blood, not body, not experience . . .

Everything was whirling through her mind, and in the grip of her grief, fear, and confusion, Hannah mistily saw Adam reaching toward her as if through a veil.

"Lean on me," he whispered, but she stared at him without comprehension. How could she lean on him? He couldn't know—how could anyone know?—what it felt like to lose the place where your feet had rested, to be standing on nothing because no one, no one in the whole world, was there? There was no one . . .

She stared at Adam's face, trying to bring him into focus, but the room was spinning, and, as his hands moved to catch her, she stepped away from him and felt the room slide out from under her. As softly as the night, she slipped into blessed darkness, spiraling away until she knew nothing more.

When Hannah opened her eyes, she found herself lying in her bed in the little room that she had shared with Eliza. Adam was leaning over, chafing her hands in his, and her father and Doctor Morgan were standing at the foot of the bed. "Harold," she whispered and then sat up with anguished realization. "Harold! I must go take care of Harold. He must be frightened and confused."

"You fainted, my dear," Doctor Morgan said sternly, gently placing her back on the pillow and checking her pulse. "You are suffering from exhaustion and shock, and I insist that you remain in bed for the remainder of the night. I have prepared a sleeping draught for you, and I want you to take it. You will do no one any good if you destroy your own health."

"But the baby will not know where I am. He will need me to comfort him. He doesn't know anyone else," Hannah protested. Fresh tears sprang to her eyes.

"Harold is sleeping," Papa said quietly. "He is perfectly fine with Anne, although he clearly prefers you. Tomorrow will be time enough for you to go to him. Now please do as Doctor Morgan asks. We have a day of great demands before us."

Adam took charge. "William, you go rest yourself. I will finish making the necessary arrangements for tomorrow's services. Hannah will take the dosage as Doctor Morgan has prescribed, and we will behave in such a manner that we will be a credit to Julia's memory."

William embraced his new son-in-law, kissed Hannah on the brow, and walked from the room with quiet dignity. Doctor Morgan murmured some instructions to Adam for a moment and then followed. Hannah, knowing she was too shaken and tired to resist, sipped the small glass vial that Adam offered her. She gradually felt the lethargy of sleep and mourning turn her limbs to lead.

Adam bent and kissed her softly on the lips. "I will return as soon as I know that all the necessary arrangements have been made. The bishop, your father, and I will confer."

"Mama has to be buried at the farm. Tell Papa. She must," Hannah said groggily. The medicine was taking effect. "It's where Mama belongs. It's where she would want to be. I know. I know."

Once during the night Hannah came to the surface of sleep. Barely awake, she could still feel the fresh pain in her heart. Adam was sleeping next to her in the bed, and his arms were tenderly around her. For one moment she curled into the circle of his body, and a feeling of warmth, comfort, and belonging lulled her almost back to the edge of sleep. Just as she felt herself succumbing, a jagged reminder of her mother's death cut through her heart, and she was shocked to think that she had almost abandoned her suffering to the lure of Adam's embrace.

"What kind of woman am I that I could feel physical desires with my mother not even buried yet?" she berated herself and pulled away from the reassuring solidness of Adam's body. How strange that he could now lie beside her in her father's home and no one would think it shameful. But even knowing they had the God-given right to share this bed, she still felt a cruel, hot flash of shame at the thought that people knew they were lying together. It seemed like a desecration in her mother's house.

Not wanting to wake Adam, she inched over on her own side of the bed until her body was no longer touching his. She clung to the edge of the mattress, keeping herself tightly away from him. As exhaustion claimed her again, she thought she heard him moan softly in his sleep.

Hannah's father agreed that his beloved Julia should be buried at the farm that had been her home for almost two decades. The funeral was held in Ogden, but then the cortege traveled the slow miles to Riverdale, where a memorial service was held in the little chapel on the farm property. Neighbors, tenant farmers, and families from far and wide—the whole of the rural settlement—came to pay their respects to this quiet woman who had touched hundreds of lives and in her quiet, competent way had been the heart and soul of the small community.

Even William and Hannah were astonished at the steady stream of men and women who came to express their heartfelt admiration and to pay homage to Julia's memory. Standing graciously in the great room of the farmhouse, the family formed a receiving line and spoke to each one of the seemingly endless line of mourners. All day long Hannah held baby Harold, clinging to him as much for her comfort as for his. She would not let anyone else hold him or take him, and the child seemed relieved and happy to be safe in her arms.

Since the day of his birth, Hannah had been her baby brother's caregiver, and she was the only one to whom his little heart was completely bonded. Adam, watching her hold the baby, realized that the presence of the child was the only thing that seemed to give Hannah any comfort or solace. As hard as he had tried to reach her, she had rejected all his attempts to help her carry her grief. Now, with stoic patience, Adam stood by her side, exerting all his self-control to refrain from intruding on the solitary circle of grief and solace Hannah had drawn around herself and the baby. He would be by her side, waiting and ready for the time when she would turn to him and let him be the one to hold her.

In the weeks following the funeral nothing seemed to change or lighten in the Big House. The rooms and the people remained cheerless, silent, and gloomy. Adam and William went back to work on the reservoir and water conduits, trying to finish as much as possible before the first heavy snows began to fall and the ground froze solid.

In late November, after the construction was brought to a close for the winter season, the two men turned their efforts to designing improvements for the roads and bridges that fed the growing city of Ogden. The entire system needed to be redesigned and improved.

They were putting in long days with committees,

bankers, and engineers. The work seemed endless, but at least it gave them both a place to escape. Each was suffering in his own way: William, mourning the loss of his wife and silently agonizing over the defection and continued absence of his youngest daughter; Adam, puzzled and hurt by Hannah's detached grief. Nothing he did seemed to waken her to a sense of their marriage, to him, to their future, or to the desire to make decisions or change. She went through the days wrapped in an invisible shield that kept her apart from everyone, but from him most of all.

Remaining at the Big House was insupportable to him, and yet she would not even discuss the possibility of leaving. He loved her enough to wait her mourning through, but still he had a growing conviction that the current situation was not good for any of them. Her continuing presence in the Ogden home was beginning to wear on Anne and her family, who regarded it as their own.

Although Hannah sensed the growing tension between herself and Anne and was not deaf to Constance's scarcely tactful suggestions that maybe it was time for Adam and Hannah to begin a home of their own, Hannah nonetheless clung to her little bedroom. She had completely assumed the care of Harold, an arrangement which her father understood and approved, but she also continued to manage the household—or those parts of it in which she had an interest.

She countermanded Anne's orders to the hired help and supervised the organization of her mother's possessions and an inventory of the Big House. It was as though she was determined that everything remain exactly as it had been on the day of her mother's death. Everything was to be counted, identified, and kept in perfect order. Adam wondered if it was Hannah's way of making time hold still. She could not let go. Something was needed to move her on to the future, and yet nothing he said seemed to make any impression. Perhaps if Eliza came home. Or if they heard from her. Still the weeks passed, and there was nothing. Nothing.

Constance was being courted by the banker's son, and Anne rankled at the deep mourning with which Hannah had steeped the house. Black crepe was hung on the doors and windows, footsteps were muffled, and voices muted. Hannah walked silently through the rooms, carrying little Harold or holding his hands and gently guiding him as he took his first steps. She was as thin and silent as a ghost in her black mourning clothes. It was really too much, Anne thought.

"After all, dear," she said to Hannah one day, "we are Mormons, you know. Your dear mother has not ceased to exist but has only stepped to the other side. This profound mourning of yours does little credit to your faith." Heaven knows, Anne thought to herself, Julia was sick for so long before her death that the time of mourning actually took place in the months before her dying, and the household does not need to be shackled by unseemly grief.

The winter holidays were coming, and Anne was determined to do a little quiet entertaining so that Constance and her young man could be gently guided toward making a decision to become engaged. Anne and Cyrus were very pleased and felt the joining of these two young people would be such a fine and suitable match.

Anne and Constance both felt the Big House deserved some relief from all the gloom and doom of the past year. A little discreet entertaining over the Christmas holidays would not be inappropriate, but it certainly would not happen as long as Hannah hung about with her impenetrable sorrow.

William had become indifferent to his surroundings and

even when he was at home, he was secluded in his upstairs study. He had buried his grief and loneliness in his work. As far as he was concerned, the house had become nothing more than an office and shelter. He did not care what his daughters did with it.

Hannah appeared to be completely unaware of the passage of days or weeks. Time and other people were like dreams to her in her numbness. Adam's patience was wearing thin, and the stress of living among so many people in the Big House, his feeling of estrangement from Hannah, the constant presence of the baby, and the press of his work made him realize that a change had to be made before things eroded anymore.

He was painfully aware of how eager Anne and Cyrus were to have them out of the house, and he could not believe how inured Hannah had become to everything that was going on around her.

"I went over to our house today, Hannah," he said one night as they climbed into the narrow bed in their cold little bedroom. "I wanted this to be a surprise for you. I hired Sarah and Aaron Eldredge to put everything in order. They have painted and cleaned. The house looks like a new place. I can't wait for you to see it. I know it's small—but it's ours. Our very own. My parents have mailed us the deed for our wedding present." His voice was soft, but there was a firm edge to it.

"It's time for us to start our own life, Hannah. It's time for us to have our own home." He put his hands on her shoulders and held her. "You can't put it off any longer. Our life has to begin."

She pulled away from him, her head cocked, listening. "Do you hear Harold crying?" she asked. The baby slept in a small anteroom next to them. She began to get up.

"No," Adam said, pulling her gently back into bed. "He

is not crying, and even if he were, you are not going to evade this conversation. Now, Hannah. Now. I have tried to be patient and understanding, but the holidays are coming, and I want to have our first Christmas in our own home. For once, listen to me. We do not belong here. We are becoming unwelcome guests."

"How dare you say that!" she flared. "This is my home as much as anybody else's! How can I go and leave Papa and Harold?"

She sat up rigidly beside him, not yielding to the gentle pressure of his arms. "Hannah," he whispered, "you don't need to fight me. I am on your side. Everything I do, I do because I believe it is best for you. You must believe me when I tell you that if we are ever to be happy, we need to leave this place. Please, my darling, listen to me."

"I will not leave Papa and Harold." Her face was set.

"Your father and I have discussed this—" Adam began.

"Behind my back!" she flared. "How dare you discuss my life without my being present!"

"Hush," Adam said softly, pulling her toward him and gently stroking her hair as though she were a child. "Hush, dearest one. We talked of you with all the love in our hearts. We know you are grieving, and we only want to help. You do not need to worry about leaving your father. He is completely self-sufficient, and Anne gives him more care than one man needs. You may leave your father with complete peace of mind. He wants you to begin your own life.

"He does believe, however, that Harold belongs to you more than to anyone else. The baby feels that he is really your child, and you have earned him by love and care. Your father, who loves his little son with all of his great heart, nonetheless understands that it is you who should rear him. William has decided to let us rear Harold. When we leave tomorrow to establish our own home, we have your

206

father's permission—no, his heartfelt support—to take Harold and love him as our own."

Tears were running down Hannah's cheeks. Quiet, despairing tears.

"It seems Papa can lose his children with great ease. First Eliza, written out of his heart, and now Harold and me."

"That is not a fair or right thing for you to say, Hannah." Adam's hand tightened on her shoulder. "Look at me."

Reluctantly she raised her head and met his eyes.

"If you think any of this is easy for your father, you do not know a thing about the man or about the greatness of his heart. If you cannot see that he is making a sacrifice that tears out his heart when he sends Harold with you—if you cannot see that he sends you away because he knows it is the only way you will ever have a life of your own—if you think that he does not weep and pray for Eliza every minute of the day and night—then you are not his daughter—you are a counterfeit." Adam's voice was like steel.

"You have let your grief become a self-indulgence, and you are destroying yourself and everything your mother created—everything your mother loved. I cannot let you continue like this. Tomorrow we move to our own home, and I will not be swayed from that decision."

Hannah's eyes flashed with anger and defiance, but she said nothing. They lay side by side in bed like two stone effigies, until the warmth of the quilts and the long, drawn-out hours of the deep night pulled them into a dreamless sleep.

As he had warned, Adam would not be deterred. Their boxes were delivered to the little house on Park Street and unpacked by hired help. At the end of the day Adam, carrying Harold, with Hannah, silent and resentful, tramping behind him in the snow, walked through the shortcut across the Big House's backyard, through the pasture, and past the little stableyard into the back door of Adam's parents' house where they had spent their first pioneer days in the valley.

The house was brick with a sharp gable, a wide front porch, and a back wash-porch with a tongue-and-groove entry alcove addition. Even though the house was small, it had generous windows and touches of moulding and wood detailing.

The back walk had been shoveled, and smoke was rising from the chimney.

Adam's heart was beating with hope and apprehension as he threw the back door open with a flourish. Hannah stepped silently inside, her shoulders set with stubborn reluctance.

The house was freshly painted, and the pine floor in the kitchen had been stained colonial green, with lighter diamond shapes stenciled on it. The cupboards were ashwood and had been freshened with a light milk wash.

Green-and-white checkered curtains and a matching tablecloth brightened the room. A bowl of holly and berries and a shining brass lantern with a glass chimney added a warm, lived-in touch.

In the sitting room Adam had reupholstered the horsehair chairs and sofa with rich-colored tapestry and velvet. The rug covering the floor was a bright Aubusson with a repeating pattern of flowers and leaves. Upstairs, Hannah knew, there were two bedrooms and a small bath chamber.

Looking at the effort and money that Adam had spent, she wanted to relent and tell him what a fine job he had done in preparing their home. His face was so eager and expectant that he seemed almost as young as Harold, and yet some prideful, hurt, angry part of her would not let her speak the words of praise. She wanted to stay angry. Angry at the way the decision to move had been taken out of her hands by her father and her husband. Angry at the way her life seemed to be prescribed by others. Angry that the Lord had taken her mother and that her sister had deserted her. Angry that she seemed to be powerless to do anything about any of it.

Did Adam have no realization that by insisting on making this unknown house her home, he had torn her from her real home? He was not bringing her home—he was taking her away! Why should he imagine she should thank him for such a thing?

As they climbed the stairs, still silent, she saw the pictures Adam had hung in the hallway: a lovely, sepia daguerreotype of her mother, a silver-etched photograph of her father, and a framed watercolor-and-charcoal portrait of baby Harold which Eliza had sketched one summer afternoon. Nothing else she had seen had had the ability to break through her defenses, but as she looked at the pictures she realized how hard Adam had tried to please her. She felt the ice in her heart melt a little, and she gave him a tentative smile.

"Thank you," she whispered, pointing at the little gallery.

Adam nodded, and she saw a hopeful light come into his eyes. For a moment he looked just like the carefree young man who had walked to her across the crowded dance floor all those long months before.

Their bedroom was filled almost from wall to wall with a large brass bed. Over the headboard hung a joyous painting of sunset in the Geyser Basin of Yellowstone. The painting filled the room like a symphony.

"Where on earth did you find it?" she gasped, staring at the bold, splendid work of art.

"In a gallery on State Street in Salt Lake when we were

up there last week working on permits for the road commission. The minute I saw it I knew it was meant to be ours. Do you like it?"

"I love it," she murmured. "It is almost without form. Just color and light and feeling. What a remarkable painting—such an unusual style. I have never seen anything like it."

"I have," he answered. "Just once. In New York. By a painter named Turner. A painting of the Grand Canal of Venice at sunset. Nothing but plumes of color, and yet you felt as though you were standing at the very spot. The painting captured the spirit, the essence, the impression of Venice, more completely than any realistic image ever could."

"Yes," Hannah breathed, "that is exactly what this painting does."

Little Harold's room was clean and bright with a sturdy crib, a little rocking horse, and brightly colored alphabet blocks stacked in the corner. A white sheepskin rug covered the center of the floor. It was a small room but perfectly suited to the little boy.

Reaching out his hands toward the blocks, Harold struggled out of Adam's restraining arms and toddled a few steps across the floor toward his prize. Adam and Hannah watched with amused tenderness. Suddenly the baby lost his footing and toppled gently onto the soft rug. He rolled over and pulled himself into a sitting position. Seeming to forget the blocks, he looked back at Adam.

A dimpled smile wreathed the happy child's face, and he raised his arms, reaching to be picked up. "Da-Da!" he laughed, looking straight at Adam. "Da-Da!"

In a single step Adam reached the merry child and scooped him up, raising him high in the air and laughing.

210

Then he walked over to Hannah as she stood by the doorway smiling quietly at the scene.

"We are going to be happy here, Hannah. I promise you. Very, very happy. Just give us a chance."

CHAPTER NINETEEN

Gold had been discovered in Montana, and in the resulting rush of miners, Virginia City had become a boomtown. The rollicking, wide-open Montana city was directly on the other side of the mountain range from the Idaho settlements of the Salmon and Lemhi Valleys. A promising gold strike on the Idaho side of the slope made it desirable for the communities to be linked by some form of transportation.

As a result, the Red Rock Stage had begun regular runs across the Continental Divide, staggering over the perilous mountain trail between Salmon, Idaho, and Virginia City, Montana, with a hardy team of four draft horses and a high, sturdy stagecoach with rugged springs. At nearly every moment of the hazardous journey the lives of passengers and drivers were at genuine risk.

With the advent of the stage run, the Lemhi Valley was no longer isolated from the rest of the world, and an unreliable, infrequent mail link was established.

The week before Christmas a letter arrived at the Big House from Idaho. It was addressed to William Childress, and it was from Eliza. Having made its way on stagecoach to Virginia City and then by rail and personal messenger until finally it arrived, grubby and wrinkled, on the doorstep at Childress Avenue, the letter seemed almost a miracle to William. He read the pages of handwriting with joy and heartbreak, and immediately he thought of what this would mean to Hannah.

Because Hannah had been so offended by Anne and Constance's eagerness to have her leave, his daughter rarely visited the Big House. Since the morning when she and Adam had departed to set up house on their own, she had isolated herself from her former home and from the family. Hannah was hurt, proud, and stubborn, and her feelings had some justification, as William had to acknowledge. He understood that it would take a while for his daughter to work out all of her pain and confusion.

Rather than make an issue of her avoidance of the Big House, William made a practice of walking over to their home on Park Street. Even though he was always happy to see his daughter and her family, something about the feeling in her house always saddened and disappointed him.

It was not that Hannah was not a good housekeeper. Everything in the Fairfields' home was neat as a pin. Hannah, Adam, and baby Harold were always dressed in clothes that were impeccably clean. Like a dutiful housewife, Hannah made her own soap, baked their bread, separated milk, churned butter, and sewed practical pinafores, aprons, and coveralls for herself, Harold, and many of the young cousins and relatives. He could not fault the letter of her homemaking; nonetheless, he sensed some indefinable spirit missing from her labors.

If anyone in the family or the neighborhood was ailing or in need, Hannah was the first to visit, carrying broth and organizing the sick room in her confident, efficient way. She read the scriptures daily, to herself and to Harold, and she was rigid in her church attendance and service. Hannah did

213

everything that was right to do, her every action was fault-less and unselfish, but her heart seemed shuttered and unused.

William had been pleased when Hannah had been called, as young as she was, to be a counselor in the ward Relief Society. He observed her in her calling and was confirmed in his knowledge that his daughter was completely conscientious in her responsibilities. No one William had ever known met their duties with more meticulous devotion than his beautiful, dark-haired, serious daughter. So why did he feel so anxious about her?

She was also dutiful to her husband, Adam. William could see that Adam was fed, cared for, and well looked after by his wife. In every observable way Hannah was an ideal wife. She never complained about Adam's absences for business or church service. She accompanied him to church and to rare social events, always wearing the black of mourning, even on their early evening, family walks. Exquisitely proper, she held Adam's arm as they pushed Harold in his pram, and anyone seeing them together would have said they made a handsome couple. Still, something in Hannah's eyes made William feel sad and empty and, sometimes, when William came upon Adam alone in his office at the Water Commission, he would surprise in the young man's pensive face a haunted and unhappy look that made William's heart twist with pity for both of them.

Where was the exuberant, headstrong daughter William remembered as a child—fearless, impetuous, and full of fire? Where had that vivid spirit gone?

"Oh, Hannah!" William sighed. In a way he felt he had lost both of his daughters on that sad day in October when Julia died, Eliza had run away, and Hannah's wedding day had become a day of disaster.

William fingered the letter in his pocket as he strode

across the back field toward the Fairfields' home. Maybe something in the words of this long-awaited letter would help Hannah find herself. At least she could stop worrying about Eliza now, and that might give her a sense of relief. He could only pray that would happen.

As he walked up the front steps of the Fairfields' little house, William observed with dismay that even though it was almost Christmas, not a wreath or a ribbon could be seen. Yes, Hannah kept the house well—but she was doing nothing to turn it into a home. The house remained exactly as it had been on the day when Hannah had first reluctantly entered it under the duress of the decision thrust upon her by her husband and father.

His daughter was merely *existing* in this place—she was making no attempt to *live* in it, William thought sadly.

Suddenly, for no apparent reason, he remembered the long-ago night when he had given Hannah the beautiful ball gown. Happiness had been right there, within her reach, lying in the tissues of the dress box, right under her hands—and she had refused it, for what complex and internal reasons he could not comprehend—but she had not seemed to feel that happiness was her right. She had turned away and declined to accept it.

He recalled that it had taken her almost a week before she could bring herself to wear her dress, despite her promise to wear it at the family party the day after the ball. When she had finally put it on, she was dazzlingly beautiful in it. She had grown to love the dress and had worn it frequently. William could remember how Adam had looked at her in that dress, his eyes so filled with love that it had almost seemed an invasion of privacy to watch him looking at her.

Adam still looked at Hannah with eyes aching with love, although now he only did so when he thought no one was watching. He seemed to be waiting for something, some hidden signal from Hannah that she was ready to wear his love—just as she had needed to find the secure place within herself before she could wear her beautiful dress.

William shook his head. The girl was a conundrum to him, always had been. How he wished Julia were here! She was the only one who might be able to show him how to understand Hannah better and to find a way to help this little family. He sighed. Perhaps Eliza's letter might be a beginning. Hannah could at last rest from her worries and concerns about her sister.

When he entered the front door, William saw Harold in the small front parlor. The little boy was happily playing on the floor with some blocks and a stuffed horse in front of him. A coal fire was glowing in the grate, and Hannah was sitting on a slipper chair staring at the open Bible in her hand. There was nothing delicious bubbling on the stove, no smells of cinnamon or holiday baking, no tree or greens. Only silence, the contented toddler, and the empty feel of the neat, joyless rooms.

"Papa!" Hannah caught sight of her father standing in the hall and ran to welcome him. "Come in out of the cold. How good of you to come for a visit."

William stepped into the parlor, and his heart felt a pang of remorse as he saw his little son raise his head and smile at him with indifferent recognition, as though his papa were a casual acquaintance. Harold knew that William was someone he knew—not a stranger—but he did not understand that William had any role in his young life. The child called William "Pah-Pah," but he called Adam "Da-da."

The little boy seemed to look more like his mother every day. His child's face was already noble and manly, framed by dark auburn locks, and with bright eyes—so like his mother's—that saw the world and delighted in it.

Every night William prayed that he had made the right decision in giving Harold to Hannah to rear. Was it too much to have asked of the newlywed couple? Would Harold understand when he grew older that it was not for lack of love that his father had let him be reared by his sister but *because* of his love for him? Not a day went by that William did not miss his little son and worry about the arrangement he had made.

Did Hannah pour too much of her love into the child, and rob Adam of the time and attention that were rightfully his? That would be a cruel thing to have visited upon his beloved son-in-law. Still, both William and Adam had recognized that Hannah's love and loyalty to Harold was as fierce as that of a real mother. Hannah never could have accepted moving away from the Big House if she had been forced to leave Harold behind.

Another factor in William's decision was that his daughter Anne, at the Big House, had not wanted to rear Harold. Anne loved her little half-brother, but she had reached the point in her life where her youngest child was off to school and she finally had her days to herself. The thought of going back to caring for a young child had very little appeal to her. Anne was pouring her energies into seeing that Constance made a fine match, and she was also becoming very involved in civic and Church organizations. Her days were filled with meetings and socials, and she was not interested in going back to mothering.

But the compelling reason William had let Harold go was that Hannah was the only mother the child had really known. The baby had loved Hannah with all his little heart for his whole short life. She represented happiness and security to him. William felt that it would have been too

217

much for the little boy to lose both his real mother and the woman he thought of as his mother at the same time.

William sighed. As hard as it was to live with, he felt the Lord had affirmed the decision he had made. Still, as he looked at Hannah sitting in the clean, quiet room with the growing child playing quietly at her feet, he suddenly felt that Hannah must have long periods of unused time on her hands. Knowing his daughter, he wondered how well she was coping with the long, lonely days. Adam was often away for weeks at a time on survey teams, and one child scarcely provided enough work for a young woman as efficient and vigorous as Hannah.

"May I fix you something to eat, Papa?" Hannah asked, as William went over to Harold and lifted him onto his knee, kissing the sweet, warm nape of the child's neck and relishing the smell and touch of his beloved son.

"No, thank you, Hannah," William replied, taking a gold watch out of his vest watch pocket and handing it to Harold, who sat mesmerized as his father pressed the secret button and the watch popped open and began to play a melody in tiny chimes. The child laughed: delighted, amazed, and completely intent on the new plaything.

"I have come with good news," William said. "I think this will do your heart good, as it has mine." Without another word he handed Eliza's letter to Hannah. She looked at him with startled eyes as she recognized the handwriting. With trembling hands she opened the envelope and went to stand by the window to read.

The letter explained that Eliza and Josh had been married by a government clerk in Brigham City on the day they eloped. They had immediately made their journey up to the Lemhi settlement, arriving one week before the first blizzard of the season.

Uncle Abner had been angry with them for having left

home in such a cowardly manner but put Josh to work the very day they arrived because the range cattle had scattered far and wide and had to be rounded up before the weather closed in.

Eliza and Josh had a small log cabin inside the fort that had been left by a man who had abandoned the struggling settlement and moved back to Utah after the death of his wife.

"The Indians have mostly moved north. They think they will settle with their kin tribe in Canada. The government is putting much pressure on them to go to the reservations," Eliza wrote.

"Our biggest danger now is from penniless gold prospectors and angry mountain men. Most of the time, though, our real enemy is the weather, and we are getting better at outsmarting it. Our cabin is snug, and Josh has smoked a pig and salted down beef. I was able to buy flour with my garnet brooch, so we are ready for the holidays and the rest of the winter.

"Papa, I have prayed night and morning that you will forgive us. I know now that what we did was foolish, sinful, and selfish. We compounded our guilt by running away. Please, ask Mama to forgive us, too, although I honestly believe she has understood because, after all, didn't she leave her family and home for something she loved more than life itself? That's how much I love Josh—more than life itself. We are so happy together! Oh, Papa! Please be happy with us.

"We are reading the Book of Mormon together in the long winter nights, and Josh loves and understands what he is learning. Often he understands better than I do, and I believe he has an intuitive spiritual gift. We are trying to conform our lives to the principles of the Lord in every particular.

"Uncle Abner says we will be able to go to the temple in

no time. Hannah, I promise you, someday we will all be together in the temple, just as we always dreamed when we were little girls.

"Until that time, I love you—all of you. We are always together in my heart. Love, Eliza."

Tears coursed down Hannah's cheeks. "Eliza," she whispered. "My sweet, dear sister. She still doesn't know that Mama is dead. It will hurt her so deeply when she realizes . . ."

"I have already sent dispatches to Uncle Abner. He will know the right way to tell her. It will all work out," her father answered quietly.

For a long moment there was silence in the room, and then William continued speaking. "I have had to struggle to forgive your sister, Hannah. She hurt me more than I would have believed possible. I felt she had brought great shame to the family and to the memory of your mama, and that she had set a damaging example for the young nieces and cousins who admired her. My feelings toward Josh were even harsher, for I thought what he had done was unfor-givable and cowardly. Because he was older and experi-enced, I felt he had seduced Eliza away. I thought what he did was wicked and traitorous.

"But it was wrong of me not to go after them. I was wrong not to have brought them back to us with love and rejoicing. In my hurt and mourning, I forgot the lessons of the prodigal son and the good shepherd. Instead of me, it was Uncle Abner who had the wisdom to gather them in with love and forgiveness.

"Eliza and Josh may have things to repent of—that's between them and the Lord—but it is I who have more to repent of. Far more. Pride, selfishness, withholding love, anger, judging, lack of forgiveness—these are the greater sins, Hannah. These are the sins that even the Lord finds hard to forgive. I am full of such sins, and they are hard to root out. It is I who must beg forgiveness from them and from everyone whom I failed in this matter." William's face was lined with remorse.

"Papa!" Hannah protested angrily, "you have done nothing wrong. They were most wanton, heartless, and sinful in what they did. As though all of the hurt and shame they have caused can be wiped away with a simple letter? It is hard to do things the right way—to do our duty—and Eliza always wanted to take the easy way. Righteousness isn't fun or carefree. The Lord rules with a hard hand and requires us to keep the laws and ordinances. Are you implying that you do not regard their behavior as sinful? That they must not pay a price?"

William shook his head. "Hannah, my dear, have you not heard what I have tried to explain? Anger, pride, resentment, failure to love—these are sins against the Lord himself. The sins of the heart are the sins that keep us from the celestial kingdom—the sins that require us not only to repent but to change. Only the heart broken open and changed . . . the heart that does not judge . . . only that heart is worthy . . ."

Standing in the harsh light of the winter sun, Hannah looked like a statue against the curtains. Her lips were tight and her shoulders stiff with disapproval. She did not want to be lectured.

"I worry about you, Hannah. You are too thin," her father said, changing the subject. "I fear you are not eating enough. You are alone so much that I imagine you neglect to cook for yourself—which is understandable. As you know, Sister Lundquist was widowed this year and is trying to maintain herself by selling foodstuffs, so I've bought more preserves than I can use. Let me send some to you. I think they'll tempt your palate."

"No, thank you, Father," Hannah replied, her pride

221

stung. "My larder is well-stocked. Adam is an excellent provider."

"I know that, my dear," her father responded patiently. "It isn't that I thought you needed food—I just thought you might enjoy a treat. Sister Lundquist is an excellent cook, and her recipes are delicious. I'd like to fatten you up a little for Adam." He laughed.

"Are you implying that I do not feed my family well?" Hannah retorted.

"You are as touchy as a pill bug, Hannah, I swear," her father exploded. "No! I am not implying anything—I just wanted to send you a present. You don't need to get your back up."

Hannah sat down. "The truth is, I'm not a very good cook," she said with listless resignation. "I don't know how Adam puts up with me. Cooking seems such a waste of time to me. All the nourishment anyone could want or need can be had from a piece of cheese, a slice of bread, a glass of milk, and an apple. Why should I spend hours preparing a meal that is eaten in minutes? Where's the satisfaction in that?"

"So? What do you do with all the time you save by not cooking?" her father asked with an ironic smile.

"Don't try to provoke me, Papa," Hannah flared. "I am perfectly capable of admitting that I don't use my time well, but filling my days is the hardest thing of all. I can't find enough to do, and yet I still can't force myself to fritter time away with fancy cooking or handiwork. I read, ponder, fret, and take care of Harold, and do my church work, and clean and clean until I think I shall scrub my way to Kolob."

"And Adam?" William asked softly. "What time do you spend on him?"

She flushed a deep pink and turned her face so that she would not have to meet her father's eyes. "Adam doesn't need me. He works long hours, and he's traveling a lot. He's gone more than he's home. In this cold weather he sometimes gets stranded for days in Salt Lake. The state engineers have asked him to do some surveying on the Provo Canyon road after Christmas. I—I sometimes think it is a relief for him when he can get away. I'm not very good company these days."

William frowned at her words. "He needs you, my dear, believe me. Maybe you should try to think of ways to make him want to come home. Maybe your husband is the most important thing for you to ponder about."

In a stern, fatherly tone, William continued. "Your mother would not be happy with your extended mourning, Hannah. The time has come for you to take off that black dress! Go get some Christmas decorations for this house and bake a cake. I don't care if you know how to bake one or not. Read a recipe book along with all your other reading—"

Papa's voice had risen and, as he spoke, he snatched up one of the books piled neatly on the table by the fireplace. *Obstetrical Practices in Modern Surgeries.* He looked at it thoughtfully.

"I allowed one of my daughters to be lost for a while. I do not want to make that same mistake again." William's voice grew softer with a touch of genuine sadness. "Where have you gone, Hannah? Where is my wonderful, vibrant daughter hiding? What will make you come alive again, dear girl?"

Tears streamed down Hannah's face, but there was no sound of crying. Just the bleak, steady flow, and her confused eyes. "That's a cruel thing to say to me. Everyone wants me to be something—or somebody—else, but this is who I am. I don't even understand myself—only, I'm not hiding anywhere, Papa. But sometimes, sometimes, I do feel I am lost. I don't know where I am myself, anymore."

William put his arms around her and held her tightly for a moment. "It's all right," he said soothingly. "You have had enough emotions to cope with for one day. Eliza is found, and that is one less thing to worry you, so forgive your father for his unsolicited advice. Be happy."

He kissed Harold good-bye and walked down the front steps with a look of deep concentration.

"Frank." William was walking away from the long banquet table in the dining room of the Big House with his old friend Doctor Morgan. They had just enjoyed a lavish dinner in honor of Constance, her boyfriend, and his prominent family. Anne had invited an elite group of guests, and the party was walking upstairs to the ballroom for an after-dinner musicale.

"Before we go up to join the others, could you visit with me for a moment in my study?" William touched Frank Morgan's elbow and directed him toward the doors of his office.

"Of course," the doctor responded, following William into the room. "What is it you want to talk about? I actually don't think I can stay for the music anyway. Freda Chester is in labor and I need to get over to her house. But it's a first child, and since no one has come running to fetch me, I imagine it won't be born for a few more hours. I'll leave as soon as we've had our talk."

William began pacing in front of the fireplace. "Frank, my mind is heavy with concern for my daughter Hannah. She is a married woman now, and I don't wish to meddle in her life. Still, her husband is as dear to me as a son, and—I do not think that I am telling you anything you have not observed on your own—they love one another very much or I don't know a thing about love . . . but . . ."

Doctor Morgan smiled. "If you are going to be this

roundabout during our entire conversation, William, I think you may take longer than Freda giving birth to this baby."

Clearing his throat, William stopped pacing and turned to face his friend. "The issue, in a nutshell, is that Adam and Hannah are not happy. Or rather, Hannah is not happy—and because of her unhappiness, Adam is not happy. It's a terrible circle."

"What do you think is causing the problem?" Doctor Morgan asked.

William shrugged. "Who can know? I have never understood this daughter. She was not an easy child, and she is not an easy woman. She is so like her mother—deep, complex, brilliant. Everything in her life has to be thought through. At one and the same time she is driven by her intellect, by a compelling, unyielding sense of duty, by a need to contribute—and then—ah, well, who can explain it? She is also given to such powerful and impulsive emotions that the whole process of thinking becomes obscured."

Doctor Morgan nodded. "Life is much easier when one is not compelled to find answers because one is blessed with a mind that does not spit out questions. Questions! That compulsive need to know and understand! What goads our questing thoughts turn out to be! Far better to be a little mindless and complacent, I say, than to have a demanding intellect and spirit. Much easier to live that way."

William laughed without mirth. "Yes. But one does not choose one's nature, as you well know. We are what we are. Hannah is what she is. The girl was born with a mind that will not be stilled—and now in her loneliness, it has begun to turn inward. I am watching her draw further and further into herself. If things continue as they are presently, it will be disastrous for everyone who loves her. She needs a challenge that will draw her back into the world of people."

Nodding, Frank Morgan stood up. "I think you are

225

probably right in your assessment. She does seem weighted in mourning and confusion, but what do you propose to do? Surely she will come to see her self-absorption and work her way out of it on her own."

"I do not want to take the chance of waiting," William answered. "I have thought about it seriously, and I have come to the conclusion that I want you to take her on as an apprentice, Frank. As a nurse, as a midwife—call it what you will. She has an innate gift for healing and an understanding of the human body that is extraordinary. I want her to develop her skills and knowledge so that she can have something to engage her interest and bring her out of herself. Will you do it for me, Frank?"

Taken by surprise, Doctor Morgan stood for a moment sorting out his thoughts. "You are assuming she would even want such an occupation," he said reluctantly. "How can she be on call day and night as she would need to be, when she has young Harold to care for?"

"The boy is getting old enough to need to be around other children. It's not good for either of them to stay cooped up in that house day after day," William said. "She can make arrangements to bring him over to the Big House, or to stay with a neighbor. Saints alive! She could even hire a girl to watch him when she's called to a bedside— although in all honesty, what she really needs to hire is someone to cook!"

The two friends chuckled. They had both eaten at Hannah's meager table.

"All right, I'll give it some thought, William. I'll speak to Hannah and see if she is interested in midwifery." The doctor walked to the door and picked up his little bag. "I am a little worried, however, knowing Hannah, that if I take her on it won't be long before she is telling *me* what to do."

CHAPTER TWENTY

It was almost midnight when Adam rode up to the house. He fastened Ensign's reins to the ring of the hitching post and squinted through the darkness of the summer night to the shadowed outline of his house. No light showed in any of the windows, and the place had a vacant, unlived-in feel that made his heart feel heavy.

More than three years of marriage had passed, and still every time he came home his heart lifted with hope that things might be different. He dreamed in the long nights away that Hannah would be waiting eagerly at the door when he returned, that the lamps would be brightly lit, and that friends or neighbors might be visiting.

For a long time he had told himself that he would know when Hannah's heart and mind finally became focused on him and on their marriage. The talisman would be that he would walk into the kitchen and find a bouquet of fresh flowers arranged on the table. In secret he imagined this symbol would be the turning point of change and hope.

Earlier this year, in May, he had come home from a surveying trip in Provo Canyon to see the grass on either side of the front walk plowed up and shaped into planting beds. His heart sang with hope, and he ran into the house with a shout of joy. Hannah, coming out of the kitchen, gave him a questioning frown, and he flung himself across the room, picked her up by the waist, and spun her around.

"You are planting flowers by the front walk!" he shouted. "It is going to be beautiful! Flowers!"

He set her down and kissed her soundly on the mouth. She pulled away and crisply smoothed her hair and her apron. "Not flowers," she said calmly. "Medicinal herbs. There was no room for more herbs in the kitchen garden, and these I am planting require different amendments to the soil than vegetables. The front beds will work perfectly."

"Medicinal herbs?" Adam echoed bleakly. "In the front of our house?"

"Not any of the powerful ones," Hannah answered quickly. "Those can only be grown under controlled circumstances. There won't be any dangerous poisons. I am not foolish."

"No," Adam said. "Foolish you are not. Haven't been for a long, long time. A little foolishness now and then wouldn't hurt, you know." He gave her a pained smile.

She did not respond to his remark but looked at him clinically. "You look tired, Adam dear. Did you have a hard trip? I wasn't expecting you until the end of the week."

"We finished surveying earlier than I had planned, and I could not wait a minute to get home to you. I have ridden day and night. How are you? How is Harold?"

Those were always the first two questions Adam asked when he arrived home. More and more frequently as the months passed, the answer to the second question was, "Harold is spending the night with Papa."

Tonight it looked as if there would be no one to answer either of his questions. He let himself into the empty house wearily and walked across the stuffy, hot rooms until he reached the kitchen, where he lighted a lamp.

Carrying the light, he methodically went through the house from window to window, opening the bottom sash and letting the air of the summer evening cross-ventilate the silence. When he returned to the kitchen, he saw the note on the table:

"Dear Adam, I received a message from your runner yesterday that you might get home this evening. Harold is over at the Big House with Agnes and will probably spend the night."

Agnes was one of Uncle Abner's daughters who had come to Ogden to attend school and had stayed to act as nursemaid and household help for Hannah. Agnes lived at the Big House but spent most of her time at the house on Park Street when Hannah was absent.

"I am attending a confinement at Sister Green's," the note continued. "She has been having premature labor, and Doctor Morgan has asked me to monitor her condition for a day or two. She lost her last three babies to miscarriage. We are hoping with the help of the Lord to save this one.

"There is milk in the icehouse and johnnycake under wrap on the service porch. Fresh raspberries that Harold and Agnes picked today are on the dry sink. Please eat heartily. I will try to be home by morning. Love, Hannah."

Adam read the note ruefully and tossed it aside. "Hannah, my darling, you try, but you are never home. Not even when you are home." He sighed, reached over to the bowl of raspberries, and put one in his mouth.

How long since they had sat down together, the three of them—Hannah, Harold, and himself—at this table to eat together? How long since they had sat quietly for an evening in the front parlor reading or playing a game? How long since they had had guests in their home and laughter

229

bouncing on the walls? And even more painfully, he thought, how long since the two of us have forgotten time and the world as we have lost ourselves in each other's arms? How long? How long?

Adam was surprised to find tears standing in his eyes. It occurred to him that he was sitting in his own home, and yet he was desperately, miserably, hopelessly homesick.

Two and a half years earlier, when Doctor Morgan had first come to Hannah with his proposal that she train as a midwife, both Adam and Hannah, after long and careful discussion, had decided it was a great opportunity and a wise decision.

"I know I have not been the wife you have wished I could be, Adam," Hannah had said. "I have been locked in sadness over the loss of my mother and my sister, and I cannot find it in myself to fill my days within the walls of our house. The walls seem to close in and smother me. Try as I will, I cannot feel that anything I do is important—except loving Harold—and even he is getting so that he needs me less and less."

Adam kissed her then. "I understand. Until our own children come—"

"Oh, yes, Adam, yes," she breathed. "That will solve all my problems—but until then . . ."

That night, for the first time since they had returned to Ogden from their unhappy wedding trip, Adam had felt that the barriers had finally been removed between them. For a few hours Hannah's unhappiness and dissatisfaction seemed dissolved, and they came together in a mutual joy that seemed to wipe away the months of stiffness and emotional isolation. Once more Hannah was the passionate girl he had fallen in love with in an instant—for all eternity.

After that night Adam had been convinced that Hannah's weeks in training with Doctor Morgan would be very few and that she would discover, soon, that she was with child. But month after month went by, and with each month their eager hopes were dashed, again and again.

Adam grew to hate the sight of Hannah's sad eyes as she whispered to him that once more they were unfruitful. Sometimes he saw his sad, beautiful wife staring at her reflection in the mirror and pressing her hands against her empty womb as though she could bring it to life that way.

She asked for blessings. For her husband's blessing. For her father's blessing. For a blessing from the stake patriarch and finally from the patriarch of the Church himself. Over and over again the words of the blessings were the same: she and Adam would be blessed with eternal increase. Then another month would spell doom to the words of the blessings, and Adam watched in helpless sorrow as the months turned into one year, and another, and Hannah grew thinner, more distant, and more obsessed with caring for other women and bringing their children safely into mortality.

The changes in Hannah had been gradual. In the beginning Adam had felt that the excitement for the medical profession had given him back his wife, but as their third year together began, he had been forced to recognize that the demands of her work were slowly taking her farther and farther away. She was escaping him in her concern and service to others.

In the past year they had many confrontations on the subject. One night after Hannah had returned from a week's absence in the home of a family with eight children and a ne'er-do-well father, she had sat in the kitchen and ranted for an hour about her experiences. She was not confiding in Adam, or even really conscious that he was there. He could tell she was simply talking to relieve her frustration and to unwind so that she could rest. He was nothing more than a convenient audience. The realization shook him.

"I had to clean the house! Not a single member of that family had so much as picked up a washrag since Delia was taken to bed three months ago. The children were filthy. Dishes, windows—unwashed and stained—and no food to speak of. I told that no-good Benjamin that he'd better get out and find flour, bacon, and fresh greens, or he'd have me to reckon with."

As Hannah raged, Adam looked at her exhausted face. She was pale, thinner than ever, and her hair was skinned back from her forehead and held in a bun so tight that not a single strand strayed. It was as though she were trying to erase the woman in her.

"Darling," he had said softly, "come to bed. You are too tired to think."

"No," she retorted, "I am not too tired to think. That's my problem. I can never get tired enough to stop thinking. How I wish I could. I think all the time that the Lord is punishing me for something I am doing wrong. How can He send a perfect baby girl to a dreadful home like that? To a mother too tired and lazy to watch over the children she already has and a father who can't or won't provide for them? Why? Why? And here I am, as empty as a stone. Oh, Adam! I wish I were too tired to think!"

He held her then until he felt her trembling stop, and then he led her toward their bedroom. "My darling, we cannot know the reasons of the Lord. But we have each other. We have little Harold. Hard though it may be for you to believe, Harold and I need you very, very much. I promise you. There is enough need here in this little house to fill your life to the brim if you would only stop and look. Why can't you see it?"

She flung herself away from him, stripped off her clothes, and scrubbed her hands and arms fiercely in the bowl on the washstand. "The Lord has called me to do this service, Adam. I know it. If you pull me away from my duty to Him, then He will never listen to our prayers! If you strip me of my God-given work, then you bury me. You leave me alone all the time to go and do your work! Do you think your work is more important than mine? How else can I show the Lord . . . ."

Without finishing her sentence she threw herself on the bed and rolled over onto her stomach as though to hide herself. "I must sleep. I can't talk anymore. Edna Selkirk is going to have twins, and Doctor Morgan sent word that her water has broken. I may not get more than an hour or two of rest."

Adam blew out the lantern and came over to the bed. "Hannah, I have ridden forty miles to spend the night with you. Tomorrow the crew begins blasting to widen the mouth of the reservoir, and it may be days before I see you again. Please stay awake a little longer. I miss you so much."

He reached out to touch her, and he felt the heavy, regular lift and fall of her shoulders. She was already lost in a profound sleep. Long into the night he lay beside her, feeling the heat and sweetness of her body and feeling lonelier than he could ever remember feeling in his life.

It was Hannah who had detected that Edna Selkirk was carrying twins. Her finely tuned, gifted hands had explored Edna's swollen abdomen, and she had detected the separate motions, and eventually the separate heads, of the two babies. Under Hannah's watchful eye and with the advice of Doctor Morgan, the pregnancy had proceeded without complication, although in the final months Edna had stretched to such proportions that her skin felt as though it would split and her feet were two sizes too large for her shoes.

Edna's two older children were well-behaved and excited about the coming additions to their family. Her quiet husband beamed with a smug, self-congratulatory air, and everyone awaited the event with happy anticipation and a touch of apprehension.

Toward the time of delivery, Hannah determined something that gave her deep concern.

"I went to see Edna today," Hannah told Doctor Morgan at the end of an afternoon of visits to new mothers.

"Yes?" he said absently, anxious to be home. "We'll be delivering those twins pretty soon now, I imagine."

"I hope so," Hannah replied. "To tell the truth, I am growing concerned about the presentation."

Doctor Morgan gave her a sharp look.

"I think the babies are in a transverse lie. If we can't get them to change position, it could be disastrous to mother and children," Hannah said soberly.

Shoulders sagging, Frank Morgan chewed thoughtfully on his mustache. "What bad luck," he said sadly.

"Not luck!" Hannah said reprovingly. "The will of the Lord. But He has given us heads and hands to make things better—I know we can find a way."

Frank Morgan shook his head doubtfully. "Her womb is so overfilled, I think there is very little room and too much pressure for the babies to move around or change positions. We will have to hope that as labor begins the wee ones realign themselves. It can happen."

"And if it doesn't?" Hannah cried. "Do we just sit there and watch them all die?"

"I have explained to you, Hannah," Doctor Morgan said wearily. "Your most important role as a midwife is to try not to interfere with the natural process. The Lord is in charge of creation. Our primary role is to assist, comfort, and take care of the aftermath."

"I will not believe that is always true!" Hannah exclaimed. "What has the Lord given us minds and hands and medicines for? We are meant to help and to use His inspiration to do things better! I will not believe that it is His will that we stand by and watch this woman and her babies die simply because we are not wise enough, or brave enough, to prevent it."

Frank Morgan walked away. "Go home, Hannah, and rest. Your family needs you. And we are too tired to discuss this intelligently."

Since that conversation, thoughts of the Selkirk twins were seldom out of Hannah's mind. She visited the home regularly and each time did a careful external exam, praying for some indication that the twins had changed position, but the outline of the two heads remained side by side, firmly pressed against their mother's ribs.

The problem of the impending labor with its great potential for tragedy occupied Hannah's waking hours. She read everything she could get her hands on. Neither she nor Doctor Morgan had any idea if the twins were occupying one placenta or two, but if they each had their own placenta, perhaps it would be safer to try manipulating them.

For days her mind was so clearly occupied that Adam stopped even trying to carry on a conversation with her. He and Harold took long walks in the evening air, and Adam, knowing a little about the problem that Hannah was pondering, tried to be sympathetic and patient, but sometimes living with Hannah was like living with a ghost.

Uncle Abner's daughter Agnes was a sweet girl, plump and eager to please. She loved Harold, and the young child loved her in return, so Harold was never neglected. He was growing into a fine, happy boy, with long, sturdy legs, and a flashing smile that melted hearts. Even at his young age he had a natural flair for leadership, and he enjoyed the turmoil and excitement of the Big House with its bustle of people coming and going. There always seemed to be someone to play with at his real papa's house and lots of treats and laughing in contrast to the quiet and emptiness of his other house.

At night, when Hannah held the little boy and tucked him in bed, he still loved her with the single-minded devotion of a cherished child, and, when she was gone away at night on a medical call, he clung to Adam or Agnes and spoke Hannah's name. Still, during the day, Harold was a confident and secure little boy. He loved exploring the wide world and felt loved wherever he went.

Constance, who had married her young banker, was living in a lovely house in the newest section of the city. It was a house made of stone, with Greek columns, and a marble entryway. Hannah did not envy Constance her fancy house or her predictable husband, but she did envy the fact that Constance had already given birth to one child, Cyrus— named after her father—who was now two years old, and Constance was pregnant again. Hannah could hardly breathe with the pain of it.

For some reason Harold and his younger cousin, Cyrus, had formed a sturdy friendship. They played together in happy and total concentration, and Constance had grown to love Harold with the same indulgent and possessive affection she felt for her own son, Cyrus. It was hard for Hannah to see the eagerness with which Harold greeted the news whenever he was invited to Constance's house, and even harder to see him bound up the stairs without a backward glance at Hannah. The two little boys would run into the front hall together, playing before they had even had time to greet each other. Hannah, standing alone at the bottom of the front stairs, would wave to Constance in the doorway. "I'll pick up Harold as soon as I get back from this delivery," she would call.

"No hurry," Constance would answer complacently, unconsciously patting her burgeoning stomach with a happy smile. "He's welcome to stay forever."

Forever, Hannah thought. Harold would be welcome forever wherever he went in this world and the next. He was that kind of a child. So easy to love. It was almost as though there wasn't enough of Harold to go around for all the people who doted on him.

Hannah felt she was losing her little boy, and yet, if she were honest, she knew she had never really felt she had him. She had always known intuitively that she had only the loan of him, and now the debt was being called in. Like so many other things in her life, it was too painful to think about, and so she turned her mind back to the obstetrical problem of Edna Selkirk's babies.

She pondered the problem of the twins day and night.

One night Hannah had come home late from a long delivery. The newborn baby had been bathed, wrapped in warm flannel, and placed at his mother's breast. A competent and capable grandmother was taking care of the family, so Hannah had gratefully returned to her own bed to catch some sleep before dawn.

Adam was out of town with a survey crew for the irrigation canal, and Harold was spending the week at the Big House at William's request because William would soon be leaving for a visit to Abner's settlement in the Lemhi Valley.

Eliza had two children now. Their first baby had been born the March following Eliza and Josh's hasty October elopement. Hannah had bitterly counted the months between the marriage date and the date of the birth of the baby, and then she had immediately chided herself for her meanness. Nevertheless, she knew everyone else had counted the too-short months as well and had understood full well the sinful implication of that early birth.

Saying nothing about such matters, William was simply filled with eager anticipation to meet his grandchildren. He had written to ask Josh and Eliza to return with him to Utah to be sealed at the Endowment House, but Josh wrote back that he had a forestry contract he needed to fufill and Eliza was pregnant again and not feeling well. He explained that they would need to wait another year before they made the journey back home.

Even though it had begun under a cloud, Josh and Eliza's marriage continued to be filled with unselfish love and joy. They were doing everything they could to be forgiven of their youthful sins and errors. Eliza's remorse, Josh's heartfelt apologies, and the blameless nature of their current lives had helped Hannah to begin to understand for the first time the miracles of repentance, forgiveness, and casting away the burden of judgment. With determination, Hannah was trying to overcome her injured pride and hurt feelings and her self-righteous condemnation of her sister's actions. Hannah had begun to realize, as her father had said, that her proud and unbending heart was perhaps the greater fault.

When she read Eliza's long letters to her, she felt the underlying devotion and steadfastness of Eliza's love for Josh in every word, and her own heart felt a chill of remorse and guilt as she thought of her own confused heart and bumpy marriage. Poor Adam, Hannah thought, what a sad bargain he got when he married me.

A few nights before the twins were born, the dream came to Hannah in the middle of her exhausted sleep, as strongly vivid as though it were real. She dreamed she was standing in a tiny house in the middle of a valley. No, it was in the empty reservoir. The granite walls reached all around her like a bowl, and suddenly there was the sound of water rising.

In her dream she was a spectator, watching herself in the little house. She was sitting on a chair in the tiny room, with her legs entwined around the rungs so tightly that she was trapped. She could see the water rising all around the cabin. When the water covered the little house, she could feel herself struggling. The air in the house was compressed against her, and as the water surged all around, she felt as though her lungs would collapse. The outside pressure of the water seemed to push her down, down, down more tightly into the chair, and her legs felt as if they were in a vise. The pressure outside made it impossible for her to move.

Then, one of the walls of the reservoir split open with a loud crash, and the water roared through the breech, emptying the bowl of the reservoir in an instant. As the water poured away from outside the house, water rose inside, filling the little house, and suddenly Hannah felt herself floating free. When the outside pressure was released, the water inside the house became the freeing agent that lifted her from her cramped position. In a moment she had drifted to the ceiling of the little room. Free, fluid, and light as a feather.

Hannah jolted awake and sat bolt upright. She was drenched with perspiration, and her bedroom was filled with the sound of rushing rain. A thunderstorm crashed and flashed outside the windows, and she stared at the streaming water patterning the window with streaks of silver in the coal-black night.

For a long time Hannah lay in her bed, wide awake, listening to the sound of the water and thinking of the pressure of the water inside and outside the house in her dream.

"I am going to give her camomile and tramoli tea,"

Hannah told Doctor Morgan the next day. "It can't hurt her or the babies, and it may shift the pressure on her womb."

"I've never heard such a thing," Doctor Morgan said. "That will have a powerful diuretic effect. What if it starts labor?"

"The babies are big enough," Hannah asserted. "Onset of labor would be a blessing for the mother, and it might give all of them a better chance. We've got to try! We can't stand by and watch them all die."

Doctor Morgan shook his head. "You fly in the face of the very heavens, Hannah! You are always so fierce and so sure. Sometimes, though, great medicine takes that kind of courage. You are right, of course. It could do little harm, and the diuretic effect might be beneficial for the delivery. Edna is retaining fluids at an alarming rate."

"Sip just a little more," Hannah urged as she offered the herbal drink to Edna Selkirk. "A little more. It should help your body shed some of these excess fluids, and relieve the pressure in your abdomen. It will make the babies more comfortable." And, Hannah added silently, almost as a prayer, hopefully it will give them more room to move. Please, God, let them move.

For two days she gave Edna the astringent tea, and, in response, she saw the woman's hands, feet, and girth reducing as she shed the accumulated fluids. Edna's breathing was improved, and once again Hannah could feel the clear outline of the twins beneath her hands through the mother's skin.

On the third day of the medication, Edna began to have labor contractions, and Hannah, who had not left the woman's bedside day or night, sent for Doctor Morgan. The Selkirk children were sent to a neighbor, and Brother Selkirk went outside to wait for the doctor. Hannah looked at her patient and saw that Edna's eyes were dark with anxiety.

"I know they ain't sittin' right, Hannah," she said calmly. "I've known it fer weeks, but I didn't want to alarm anyone. You know it, too, don't you?"

Hannah felt tears rush to her eyes, but she firmly brushed them aside. "Now don't go worrying, Edna. We are going to do this. You and I and the Lord. Hold steady while we pray."

Clasping Edna Selkirk's hand, feeling the wringing-wet palm against her own, Hannah knelt by the side of the bed, and the two women took turns praying. Their words were slow, solemn, and rich with faith.

After the prayers were spoken, Hannah remained kneeling, in steady silence. A shudder shook Edna's frame, and Hannah opened her eyes and looked at the struggling woman. Although Sister Selkirk's mouth was tight with pain, her face glowed with courage.

"Now, Edna, this is going to hurt, but I am going to manipulate the baby I can feel on top and see if I can move his head toward the mouth of your womb. Do you think you can stand it?"

Hannah gripped the woman's hands more tightly.

"Now, Hannah. Do it now. The most important thing a mother does is head her children in the right direction." Edna smiled at her own whimsey, and Hannah thought it was one of the most touchingly brave gestures she had ever heard.

"Then let us do it, Edna."

The child had a mind of its own. Hannah prayed that a foot or arm had not already slipped into the birth canal. If that had happened the presentation was hopeless. But Hannah refused to give up hope—her dream had to have

241

been for a purpose. God would not let them fail. For two hours she manipulated the baby in the womb as Edna grew white with pain and stress. The baby's head remained hopelessly jammed somewhere between Edna's rib cage and hip bone. The second baby could not be felt at all, blocked as it was by the body of the first.

On the skin of Edna's poor stretched abdomen great welts, bruises, and streaks appeared where Hannah had tried every maneuver that reading and experience had taught her. Staring at the welts, Hannah wanted to cry and leave the room rather than continue to add to the laboring woman's agony.

Suddenly, as Hannah stared at the blossoming bruises, an idea she had read in an old medical journal came into her memory. "Grease!" she exclaimed out loud. "Grease!"

She ran over to the stove, where the lard drippings were kept in a can at the back. To Hannah, who was so meticulous about the cleanliness of all the procedures at a childbirth bedside that even Doctor Morgan lost patience, it was almost a sacrilege to take her scrubbed-clean hands and plunge them into the thick lard. But all her instincts told her to do it.

Coming back swiftly to the bedside, she smeared Edna's abdomen with the lubricant, and then, gently and firmly, she set to work once again on the round, hard spot where the baby's head stubbornly remained.

Slowly the unborn child began to respond to the prodding. For the first time, Hannah felt a gentle shifting, and then, almost as though the little body were on a fulcrum, she could feel the shape turn and move downward.

Edna gave a gasp of pain as the baby's head engaged and pressed into the birth canal.

Doctor Morgan arrived soon afterwards, and Hannah, again, stood by his side. She and the doctor worked far into the night as Edna gasped, groaned, and screamed while her suffering husband walked the barnyard, tying and untying a knot in the harness rope he carried in his hand.

The first twin was born face up, but with the head down. He was born squawling—as pink as a new shoat, and just as plump. The second twin was born feet first, a most difficult presentation, and for the first few minutes of the baby's life it was touch and go, but he finally gave a rasping breath and let forth a reedy cry that yet seemed to declare, "I am here, world, and I intend to stay."

Edna was torn, weak, and heady with joy. "They're alive!" she kept saying. "How can I ever thank you, Hannah? They are alive!"

"Thank the Lord," Hannah said. "Thank Him for the dream He sent to me, and the promptings He sent, and the doctor He sent."

"No," Edna whispered, "I will thank Him for sending you."

When Hannah returned home that night, as on so many other nights, Adam was not there. There was no one with whom to share her triumph. Oh well, she thought dispiritedly, I am probably too tired to tell about it anyway.

A note on the dresser said that Adam had been called out to administer a priesthood blessing. He had been called as a member of the ward bishopric. Because of his frequent absences from the city, it was an assignment he found difficult to fill. Still, when he was home he was a caring counselor and in his quiet way he had gained the trust and love of the members of the Church and community.

Because Adam so seldom spoke of what he was doing, it always amazed Hannah when individuals expressed to her their gratitude for her husband's labor on their behalf. She heard of money that Adam had contributed in time of need, healings performed by his faith, counsel given and received, and food or comfort given that had lifted hearts and changed lives. None of this did she ever hear from Adam but only from others who came to her with shining eyes to tell her what a wonderful man her husband was. She and Adam communicated more and more by notes left on the table or the dresser.

"Why do you not tell me of these things?" she asked him once, not meaning to sound accusatory but hurt and ashamed that she had to hear of his generosity and influence from other people.

Adam gave her his slow, steady gaze, and then he smiled with casual irony. "You know the rules. The right hand is not supposed to know what the left hand is . . ."

"Nonsense! I can quote scripture, too," she flared. "'They two should be one flesh.' And it seems to me a body should know what a body is doing . . ."

Adam grinned, and a mischievous twinkle entered his eye. "I like your choice of scripture a lot. Why don't we try it out?"

For all of her work with the human body, there was still in Hannah a strongly puritanical streak that was offended by casual reference to the physical relationships of men and women. She pursed her lips disapprovingly.

"You should not speak lightly of God-ordained things," she said primly.

Adam was hungry and irritated. Hannah had been gone all day and had arrived home as he had walked up the sidewalk covered with rock dust and with a mouth as dry as chalk. They were both sitting wearily on either side of the empty table.

"Is food God-ordained, too," he asked, "or is that something else that is being rationed in this house these days?"

He had not meant to sound petty, but sometimes

Hannah provoked him beyond control. It was like they were two business acquaintances living under the same roof. Sometimes the strain of wanting her nearly drove him out of his mind, and he could not imagine that she could go day after day, month after month, and not feel the hollowness of their lives as much as he did.

Even on those rare occasions when he could bring her to speak of their marriage, she insisted that they were doing the Lord's will and they had to make sacrifices to be worthy of His blessings. Adam felt she did not even hear his words, let alone the muted cries of his aching heart.

So time passed, but nothing in their marriage seemed to change.

Tonight, in the hot, muggy air of the early summer night, as Adam sat alone in the quiet house, he wondered how much longer they could go on like this: he, burying himself in his work because he could not abide the empty, soulless feel of his too-clean house; Hannah, wearing herself to a shadow, laboring to bring forth other women's children; and little Harold, loved by so many people that he and Hannah never felt they could lay claim to him. Yet they still loved the child as though he were their own, and they suffered at the loss of him.

Adam's last thought, before he climbed the stairs to his lonely bed, was of their own unborn babies. Where are they? he thought sadly. Why is it that everyone seems to have children like trees bearing acorns, and we remain empty and barren? The thought was a silent groan. Their barrenness was not for want of love. If love alone could create a child, his love for Hannah could have peopled a nation. He wondered for a moment if the unhappiness of not conceiving could possibly be the thing

245

that stood like a barrier between them and their dearest desires.

As time passed and their hope for a child grew dimmer, Adam's greatest fear was that their love was fading with their hope. To be empty of love would be an even more cruel fate than being empty of child.

CHAPTER TWENTY-ONE

Summer was definitely coming to an end. As a last outing before he left to return to Ogden, Eliza had taken Papa in the old buckboard up the Red Rock Stage trail to the top of the Continental Divide. With a beaming smile Papa stood by the small trickle in the high mountain meadow where Lewis and Clark had traced the fountainhead of the mighty Missouri.

Standing with one foot on either side of the little stream, Papa laughed and let the cool mountain breeze ruffle his thick, white hair. "This is the very spot where Lewis or Clark—I'm not sure which one—said that he had stood astride the whole of the Missouri river. It is a right powerful feeling!"

Eliza laughed in response to her father's enjoyment, but she kept her eyes trained on her two sons, playing in the profusion of late summer wildflowers on the slope beside them. A massive stand of pines, so thick and dark they looked almost black, flowed up and over the steep mountainside, and the wind played in the branches of the trees with the sound of a deep harp. It seemed to Eliza as though nature were an orchestra in this untouched majesty, and she sat filled with the vibrant sounds, her body like a tuning fork.

She was seven months pregnant but had gained very little girth, and so she was still quite lithe and agile. Agile enough to keep track of her lively sons, Reuben and Parker, who rolled and ran and played with the wind on the top of the world. There was only sky above them, and the rich gold and green of Lemhi Valley stretched below, bordered by the wide, blue turbulence of the boisterous Salmon River.

Parker, her one-year-old, staggered toward her on his chubby, unsure legs, and tumbled into her lap. She fluffed his golden curls and kissed him a hundred times on his face and arms and neck, until he pulled away, giggling and surfeited, and toddled off toward his brother, Reuben, who was examining a stand of Indian paintbrush with the curiosity of a pointer.

"I am so thankful that Josh brought me to this place," Eliza exclaimed. "Papa, it is like I found the Lord when I found this part of the world where He and He alone had walked. It seemed to us—to Josh and me—that when we climbed these untouched mountains and looked at the valley land, still as new as the day of creation—well, it seemed to us we could see the imprint of the Lord's hand. We have tried very hard to see Him in everything."

William looked at his younger daughter. Her face was more slender than it had been, but she had gained a sweetness and maturity that gave her a far greater beauty than the flashy prettiness of her childhood. When she looked at her children, or spoke of Josh, or asked questions about the family at home, he saw a softness in her eyes and a wealth of unfeigned love that suffused her with such loveliness that he thought his heart would break with the wonder of it. What a great woman she had become because she had discovered the gifts of the heart and she asked for nothing else.

When he had first arrived at Abner's little settlement and been taken to Josh and Eliza's home, he had been alarmed and dismayed. The house was nothing more than a rough, two-room log cabin of small proportion with a patch of a kitchen garden and a single clothesline behind it. Because of the limitations of space inside the fort, there was no front yard to the house and no plantings around the door, and the logs, unpeeled and rough, gave a hasty, temporary look to the structure.

Inside, the rooms were dark, with a beaten-dirt floor covered with hides; a large, stone fireplace that took up most of one wall; small windows—for safety during the years of Indian troubles; and the rafters lined with clusters of drying herbs and flowers, a salted ham, and ropes of onions and gourds.

There was a sweet smell of tomatoes and cloves cooking, and, even though the place was poor and simple, to William's surprise, Eliza had made it feel like a home. Pretty curtains at the window, a cluster of yellow daisies on the mantelpiece, and the happy voices of the bright-haired boys gave him an awareness that impoverished though they might be, Eliza and Josh had created a haven of love and happiness in this forgotten wilderness.

With relief and overwhelming admiration, he had shaken Josh's hand, clasped him in a fatherly embrace, reached down and lifted each handsome little boy into his arms, and then had enfolded Eliza with all the love a parent could feel for a child. "You have done well, my dear daughter. Your mother would have been so very, very happy to see the family you are creating. This home . . ." he looked about him trying to find the words to tell the young couple how much he respected what they had accomplished.

Eliza blushed. "I know it isn't very fancy, Papa. But we've done it on our own, and every year we'll put aside a little more, and some day we'll build a place you can be proud to visit."

Tears came to William's eyes. "You misunderstand, Eliza. I am trying to tell you that you have already done that! This is a home that is more fit than most palaces."

"Thank you, sir," Josh had said, and the young man's eyes shone with gratitude and affection. In his whole fatherless life he had never before experienced the unadulterated joy of having a parent express genuine pleasure. It was a most profound feeling, and Josh was caught off guard by the power of it.

The visit continued with great mutual love and delight, but after two weeks it was necessary for Josh to leave to go to work with the logging crew that he was contracted to. Josh had to travel across the mountains into Oregon, where lumber crews were pulling out huge timbers and floating them to rail and shipping heads. William remained to help Eliza and the boys for a short time.

With the discoveries of gold, the availability of land for homesteading, the completion of the transcontinental railroad, and the confirmed boundaries of the United States that stretched from sea to sea and from the forty-ninth parallel to the Rio Grande, the West had begun to explode with immigrants pouring across the face of the land into every western territory: by rail, wagon, and ship.

Lumber, cattle, land, gold, silver, sheep, and banking—everything was booming. Speculation was high, but so were hopes, and the West, still raw, new and forbidding, was nonetheless a place of opportunity for those who were willing to work hard and hazard the unknown.

In the years he and Eliza had been married, Josh had struggled fiercely to support his family without taking charity or asking for help from anyone. Whenever Uncle Abner had extra work he hired Josh, but Josh would not allow

250

Abner to pay him when there was no real work to be done. Because of Abner's large family, it was only at times of roundup and harvest that extra hands were needed.

The first year Josh had traveled all the way to Arizona and had worked on a sheep ranch, doing the shearing, sheep dipping, and lanolin extractions. He had hated the work, but by Christmas he had returned home to his wife and their little son, Reuben.

The rest of that winter he had logged a small piece of mountain property he had bought on shares for the profits from the lumber. It was grueling work in the deep snows, wrestling the fallen trees down to the valley, but he made enough to hold body and soul together.

In the following year he met the owner of a large Oregon lumbering establishment when a group of newly employed loggers passed through Lemhi on their way to Oregon. Since then, Josh had spent four months of the year working near the Pacific Coast. The pay was not lavish, but it was steady and honestly paid.

"This is the last year I will have to go away to earn a living," Josh confided to William. "When I come home in November, we will have saved enough money that we can buy a ranch. I want to breed the finest cattle in this country. My theory is that we can crossbreed and bring out the best beef characteristics, but at the same time try to develop an animal that has the hardiness and endurance of the buffalo.

"It's a dream, I know. But this land is made for grazing animals, and we can help the Lord by trying to create a breed that will be as graceful to the land as his original animals were."

William clasped Josh's arm and smiled. "What a remarkable young man you are! Who would have thought such dreams in that head!"

Eliza reached up and kissed her husband happily on the

251

cheek. "I would have. The minute I met Josh, I knew his mind and soul were far above the ordinary."

The boys, seeing the adults in a cluster, came running over and threw their arms around whichever pair of legs was closest. "Daddy! Momma! Bompa!" Reuben shouted in glee, jumping up and down, and everyone began to laugh. The tiny, dark room seemed alive with their happiness.

The sun began to go down, and Eliza felt the cold chill of the wind when the warmth of the sun was withdrawn. She sighed and began to pick up the picnic things.

"I fear the days of picnics are almost over. That wind has the feel of snow."

William looked up at the graying sky. "Soon, I imagine," he agreed. "My dear girl, are you sure you will not come home with me? It will be months before Josh makes his way back here, and you and the boys will be alone. We could take the journey in very easy stages, and once you are in Idaho Falls you can go the rest of the way to Ogden by train. I am sure you would be safe."

Eliza shook her head. "Thank you, Papa, but my home is here now. Even when Josh is gone, I like him to know that we are here, thinking of him, and keeping his home. It makes his being gone easier. It gives him the feeling that he is working for something real."

Again, William was amazed at the purity of the bond that existed between Eliza and her husband. It was something so fine and beautiful that he felt he could understand why exaltation would be an extension of such relationships. He also thought how sad it was that so few seemed to find their way to this level of mutual and unselfish devotion.

"It is hard for me to think of you here, alone, as winter closes in," William said sadly, "and yet I am touched beyond words by your decision."

They rode down the mountainside in the buckboard, moving slowly and carefully. The trail was rutted and uneven, but the surefooted horses picked their way meticulously, and the brake on the side of the wagon slowed the descent to a crawl. Nonetheless, it was a relief when William guided the team onto the valley road and clucked the reins to urge the horses homeward before the sun disappeared behind the crest of the mountains.

"You know I must leave. I have already stayed over-long, and my affairs in Ogden will be in disarray. Your little brother, Harold, has grown into such a fine, young lad, but I miss him—and he needs me. Hannah and Adam have done an excellent job rearing him through babyhood, but now he considers the whole of the family as his kingdom and realm. Truth is, I love him, and it pleases me mightily that he seems to have grown to love me in return. He knows I am his father, and, although he loves Adam, too, I believe he is sorting out his complicated relationships remarkably well."

Smiling, Eliza patted her father's hand. "I think you are telling me that you need to get back to your own son. That is a beautiful thing, Papa. After all, Harold was the last great gift that Mama left to all of us—but to you most of all. You deserve to love and miss him."

William nodded. Eliza understood him with surprising insight. He did not think he could have explained things to Hannah so well.

"And Hannah?" Eliza asked, as though reading his thoughts. "How is Hannah? Are she and Adam happy? Is she expecting a child yet?"

For a long moment William was silent. "She is a midwife, you know. Doctor Morgan has trained her, and she has a natural gift for the work. We will probably never know how many babies and mothers she has saved with

253

her skill and patience. Not only that but she seems to have a way of training mothers in the care and appreciation of their children. I often hear that families are much improved after Hannah has taken them in hand."

"But that is not Hannah you are telling me about!" Eliza exclaimed. "That is her work. I want to hear about my sister. About her heart and her life . . ."

Again William hesitated. "Adam works long hours," he said. "He is often away from home for extended periods . . ."

"Oh, like Josh!" Eliza was instantly sympathetic. "It is so hard to spend the days missing the one you love. But then, how sad it would be not to have someone you love to miss."

William spoke carefully, not wanting to sound critical and yet hoping to make Eliza see the situation clearly.

"Your sister fills her days with work, not with missing Adam. I think it is her way of coping with her compulsion to serve as well as her sorrow at being unable to conceive. She is trying to bargain with the Lord and run away from the pain—both at the same time—and in trying, she is pushing Adam farther and farther from her. I am worried for them, but perhaps I am overly concerned. They are two of the finest people I have ever known, and I am sure the Lord will bless them."

Eliza's eyes were dark with sadness. "He has blessed them, Papa. He is blessing them. But they need to slow down long enough to hear Him, to see Him, and to feel Him—to identify the blessings. The Lord will not demand their attention. He will wait for them to give it of their own free will."

The evening dusk was gathering, and William could hardly see Eliza's face. The little boys had fallen asleep on the picnic blankets, and the last rays of sunlight were touching the aspen trees on the ridge. William could see that the highest trees had already been touched with autumn gold, and he felt unaccountably melancholy, as he sensed the turning of another year, inevitably bringing change to each of their lives.

In a voice as soft as the night breeze, Eliza said, "Papa, Josh and I are so sorry for the wrong we did. Our shame and our sorrow felt like a yoke of lead around our shoulders, and for a long time that is all we could think about. When we married, and through those first months, we thought we would never be able to face you or Mama or any of the family again.

"We were brought to the depths of humility. All that we had to build upon was our love for each other and our faith in the Lord. Everything else was taken away, and our hearts cried for forgiveness.

"Nothing helped, and we felt hopeless and undeserving until the night our little Reuben was born. We were so ashamed about his 'early' birth that we did not even call anyone to help us. Josh delivered his little son, and when he placed him in my arms and that beautiful child began to cry, we knew that we would spend all the rest of our lives trying to be worthy of him. In that resolve we lifted up our hearts and eyes and realized that the Lord had been standing beside us all the time with his hands outstretched.

"We just have to stop—to be stripped of all the worldly distractions, to be rid of pride and self—and then we can see him. Really see, Papa. Can you forgive us?"

"With all my heart," William responded. "I forgave you long ago. And you, my dear daughter, can you forgive me?"

Eliza laughed merrily, and in the darkness her voice sounded just like the voice of his carefree, little girl. "For being the best father in the whole world?" she asked happily. "Oh yes, indeed. You are perfectly forgiven!"

When they arrived at Eliza's door, William carried the boys in and placed them gently in their beds in the little loft. He laid a fire for Eliza to warm the evening chill, and then he went outside to return the wagon to Abner.

As William led the team to Abner's door, he felt a chill of apprehension. Two lathered horses were tied to the hitching post, and light was streaming from the windows. William could see the heads of several people gathered around the table, but there were no happy sounds of a social gathering.

Hurrying into the house William noticed a sudden hush that fell on the gathering. Abner rushed to the door and put his arm around his brother's shoulder.

"Tragic news, I fear, dear William. I do not know how we shall tell Eliza."

"What is it?" said William, his voice choking on the words. "Not Josh."

Abner nodded, struggling with his emotions. "I feel I have lost a son. How I have loved that young man."

"What happened?" William steeled himself to hear the bad news.

Two young men had ridden all the way from the Oregon lumber camp to bring the news. The ride had taken them four days along haphazard trails, and they were exhausted and hungry, but their friendship for Josh had kept them going and given them grim resolve until they had finally made it to Lemhi.

"There was a new logger. Inexperienced," one of the men explained. "None of the rest of us would take on the greenhorn on as a partner or train him. Too dangerous, you know. Nothing worse than a bad partner. Well, Josh was the one who took him under his wing. The boy worshipped Josh, but the guy wasn't a natural lumberman, and he made a bad cut. Josh was on the other side of the tree. It was a

Methuselah of a tree—the size of a tower—and when it fell, it seemed to bring the sky with it.

"If it's any comfort to you, Josh didn't suffer. Not for a minute. The trunk hit him in the chest like a train, and he was dead before his next breath."

William shuddered. "Where is he now?" he asked.

The second man spoke. "We packed his body with pine boughs and resin cakes to preserve it as best we could. Knew you wouldn't want him buried in the wilds of Oregon. The camp manager made arrangements to ship it from the railhead as close to Salmon as possible. They'll need to haul it the rest of the way by wagon. It could take weeks."

"I don't care how long it takes. Or how much it costs," William said. "Please see that he comes home."

The men nodded solemnly. They had already made that commitment in their own hearts. The men had only one another to rely on, and what they would do for a friend, they knew a friend would do for them in similar circumstances.

Eliza met the unbearable news with a stoicism born of an eternal and undying love. "As soon as Josh's body is returned to us and buried here in this place that was our own shared heaven, I will come to Utah, Papa, so that Josh and I can be sealed to one another. It is the most important thing left to be done."

Her voice trembled, but her face was filled with courage. "This is going to be a long mortality without him, but eternity will seem short when we are together again."

Her loss was as deep and real as her love, and William knew the grief would lie in her heart, hidden and poignant, as long as she lived. Each of his youngest daughters had a gift for constancy that was awe-inspiring to William. He

257

often thought of the scripture that spoke of bonds "stronger than death." So they were.

"Please come home with me," her father pleaded, but Eliza remained firm.

"I must wait to bury Josh's body, and I must wait for our child to be born in this sweet, happy house, where I have lived the best years of my life. Only then will I return, Papa. I will raise Josh's sons in Ogden where they will have the strength of an extended family. I will secure our covenant bonds in the temple, and I will find a way to support my children."

"You don't need to think of such things!" William objected. "Of course you will come home and let me take care of all of you."

"Thank you, Papa," Eliza said quietly, "but it was important to Josh that we support ourselves. He felt that if we didn't, we were just pretending to be a family. I will not be so proud that I won't take help if we need it, but I will strive to be responsible for my own obligations."

"Darling girl . . ." William began to protest.

"Papa, our savings will get me to Ogden and help me settle in a house, and then we can speak of these matters further. I do have one request for help, though. Could you ask Hannah to come to me? I need her here to help me when I have the baby and to travel with me and my children. If anyone can help me bring this child—Josh's last child—safely into the world, it would be Hannah. Do you think she could come?"

"I am sure she will come, Eliza. With a glad and willing heart. She would do anything for you that she could. She loves you."

Hannah left to join Eliza in Lemhi as soon as William came home with the sad new of Josh's death. With Adam's love, prayers for comfort, and full support, she immediately packed her bags and prepared to take the train to Idaho. She would ride a single-gauge spur line to within a hundred miles of Salmon and then travel the last part of the journey by wagon.

"Are you sure you don't want me to come with you?" Adam asked. "I worry about you with winter right around the corner and all of Eliza's affairs to set in order."

"You are not to worry about us, Adam," Hannah replied crisply. "We will manage very well, and you cannot possibly leave your work for so many weeks. Papa has been gone most of the summer, and I know it has slowed the work on the reservoir. Until Eliza's baby comes there will be very little for you or anyone else to do, and you would be restless and idle. It's best if I go alone. I promise we will be back in Ogden before Christmas."

Her words were practical and were meant to be considerate of him, but Adam found himself wishing that Hannah would throw her arms around him and say that she could not stand the thought of being away from him for two or three months. He wanted her to beg him to come with her—and he would have gone without a moment's hesitation, no matter what heavy obligations he left undone. He would have gone even without her invitation, if only she had even smiled at him or looked at him with pleading eyes.

Hannah did neither. She prepared to make the journey, taking warm clothing for herself and Eliza's family and packing herbs, medicines, her obstetrical case, and several boxes of food supplies. On the surface Hannah was composed, organized, and methodical, but underneath her heart was torn. This would be the first time that she and Adam had been separated for so many weeks in a row. She had not realized until the reality of the trip dawned on her, how much she counted on the quiet evenings when they were both at home. How she would miss his loving words and encouragement that gave her relief from the pressures and stresses of their individual lives.

As she lay in bed the night before her departure, with her eyes open in the dark, she felt Adam's arm thrown across her waist, and his leg in its familiar crook against hers, and she realized how much sustenance and emotional reassurance she gained from the quiet, steady reality of his presence, even though she never acknowledged that reliance to herself or to Adam.

Why couldn't she tell him? she wondered. Why couldn't she just say how much she would miss him and how much her selfish heart wanted to beg him to come with her. But some level of pride and responsibility told her that their separate duties could not be shirked. Some shy and insecure corner of her heart feared that if she spoke her passionate need for him, she might be rebuffed. The rub of all these feelings, and the force of habit, kept her silent.

With stiff formality and yet genuinely shared compassion for Josh and Eliza, they accepted the coming separation. Just before morning, while it was still dark, Adam pulled Hannah into his arms and whispered his love for her. She almost broke down then and begged him to go with her, but her tears were kissed away, and her words swept away by his passion. Then she slept, and when she woke he was already dressed and ready to take her to the train.

When they said their good-byes with courteous tenderness, each of them was hiding an aching heart behind a strong and restrained expression. William, seeing Adam carefully assist Hannah into the coach, wanted to go to his son-in-law and lift him bodily onto the train behind his wife, but William knew that his interference would only make things worse.

Hannah arrived on the cold breath of an early winter storm, and when she saw the crowded, humble little cabin where Eliza and her children lived, Hannah, like William before her, saw that complete love could transform a woman and a house. The awareness of what Eliza had accomplished as a wife and mother smote Hannah like a blow. She thought of the beautiful Fairfield home that Adam had prepared for her, sparing neither effort nor expense, and she thought how her lovely little house remained unblessed by the warmth of her touch.

Eliza, in the humblest of abodes, in the deepest wilderness, it would seem, had given up everything, and yet, in so doing, she had gained everything important.

There was sorrow and mourning in the little cabin, but there was love and beauty, too. As the winter winds howled and the snows of the high mountain valley began to gather, many an evening after the boys were in bed Hannah listened as Eliza spoke of Josh and tears flowed down her sister's beautiful young face, but they were the tears of a woman loved and loving.

It was late in October before Josh's body was finally brought to the valley, and Uncle Abner and his sons carried the coffin, fashioned by the finest cabinetmakers the lumber camp manager knew, into the fort. The coffin had been in transit too long to be opened, so Eliza could not look on Josh's face one last time, but with the outriders who brought the body came a package of Josh's belongings. Eliza sorted through them, pressing his shirts to her face and breathing in the last trace of his smell, as though the fabric brought a small bit of his presence into her.

The grave had to be carved out of the frozen ground, but Josh was buried in the small graveyard behind the fort where lay the final resting places of Uncle Abner's youngest child, two unknown Indians, and the wife of the man who had owned Josh and Eliza's cabin. At the head of the grave they placed the marker which Uncle Abner had commissioned from a stonemason in Salmon. On the granite headstone was carved a line from Shakespeare: "Nature might stand up and say to all the world, 'This was a Man.'"

On the night after the simple service, a terrible blizzard struck, and Eliza went into labor.

A roaring fire in the great fireplace gave the room light and warmth, and the two little boys were fast asleep in the loft when Eliza came and shook Hannah.

"Something is wrong, Hannah," Eliza whispered. "My bedsheets are soaking wet."

Hannah sprang to her feet and looked at Eliza, who was standing in her white flannel gown. The back of the gown was red with blood.

"Lie down at once, Eliza," she ordered. "At once."

Fear gripped Hannah with cold claws. She had lost her mother and her brother-in-law, and she knew there was a real possibility she was about to lose the life of her sister and her baby. So much blood was not a harbinger of good.

There could be many reasons for the hemorrhage, but none of them were promising. Although Eliza had been experiencing labor pains most of the day, and by bedtime they had been quite strong—still, they had been erratic and of such unpredictable length that neither woman had felt it was true labor.

Now, with the sudden rush of blood, Eliza began experiencing powerful contractions, and, within minutes, she was bearing down.

Hannah washed herself and Eliza. The grinding labor pains were pushing the baby down the birth canal, but blood continued to seep onto the sheets, and Eliza was growing weaker.

Knowing she could do nothing until the child was born,

Hannah stood by the bed in an agony of suspense. She suspected that the placenta had been covering the mouth of the womb, and that the baby, in order to enter the birth canal, had ruptured it. If that were the case, the blood that was being lost was being lost by the baby as well as by Eliza as the placenta tore away.

"Please, Heavenly Father," Hannah prayed silently, "let me save them both, but, if I cannot, then let me at least save Eliza for her poor fatherless boys."

"I am feeling weak and light-headed," Eliza whimpered. "What is wrong, Hannah? What is wrong?"

"Nothing," Hannah lied. "The child is almost here. Push as hard as you are able, Eliza. You are getting thirsty. Here, let me moisten your lips." Hannah held her sister's head and gave her a sip of cool water. Eliza's skin had a deadly pallor, and her lips were shrunken and dehydrated.

Eliza smiled feebly. "What a good sister you are. And what a good midwife. I should have remembered from the night Harold was born."

Yes, Hannah thought bitterly, the night Harold was born, and Mama was hurt so badly that she died. Even though it took her a year to die, it was the night of Harold's birth that killed her.

How many times Hannah had gone over that night and wondered if her ignorance and inexperience had caused her mother's eventual death. It was a burden she carried always. If Eliza died under her care, Hannah honestly did not know if she could live with the pain of that guilt, too.

With a sudden contortion, Eliza raised her head and shoulders and with her last ounce of strength pushed her infant into the world. Swiftly, Hannah lifted the little boy into her arms, and her heart turned cold. The child was as white and still as ivory. His hands and feet were dark blue, and he did not move. Hannah saw the torn and ragged placenta, still bleeding, attached to the coil of the cord.

Hannah took the child and laid him on a blanket on the floor, and then she grabbed the placenta and lifted it high above him. The cord throbbed between the torn placenta and the baby as gravity caused the flow of blood to pour toward him. Hannah saw a slight pink flush touch the little cheeks. She continued to hold the cord above him, letting the blood reenter his circulatory system. Suddenly the perfectly formed infant stirred, took a breath, gave a little cough, and began to cry.

Wrapping the baby tightly to warm him, Hannah turned back to Eliza, who was lying white and still. Gently, Hannah delivered the rest of the placenta and pieced the shattered tissue back together to make certain that none remained in the mother. Then, with firm and knowing hands, she massaged the womb. At last she felt the muscle reflex that caused it to clamp down. The bleeding slowed.

For three days Eliza remained unconscious, and Hannah had to put the child to his unknowing mother's breast. When Eliza finally awoke, she looked at her tiny baby with eyes of joy.

"You saved us, Hannah," she said. "You saved us both. I knew you would. I am going to name this child Adam, after your dear husband who let you come to be with us. What great sacrifices you have both made. I will never forget our debt to both of you as long as I live. Neither will my son Adam."

The women and children did not make it back to Ogden in time for Christmas, as Hannah had promised. At first, Eliza and little Adam were not strong enough to travel, and then Reuben came down with the whooping cough and he, too, needed time to recuperate. Still, the week before

Christmas, Eliza was well enough to go out into the snowy mountainside with Hannah to gather greenery for decorating the log cabin.

Uncle Abner was planning a Christmas feast, and all of them were invited. It would be the first time the baby had been out of the cabin. Little Adam was doing wonderfully well. Every week he seemed stronger and was thriving in the snug warmth of his limited world.

Eliza was still weak, but she had resumed most of her duties, and Hannah had become the visiting medical practitioner in the community, not only to the cluster of families in Lemhi, but also in the town of Salmon, some ten miles away.

She delivered babies, treated coughs and sore throats, and bandaged burns and wounds. For the first time she set broken bones and had even amputated a toe. In the years she had watched Doctor Morgan, she had learned the method of many of his procedures, and, although she was not a doctor, her medical training far exceeded the home-grown remedies on which these outlying pioneer towns had had to rely.

Young Reuben and Parker had grown to love her as a second mother. Even if Hannah came home exhausted from traveling in the winter weather or watching beside a sickbed, after she had washed herself carefully, she would take the boys in her lap, rock them, and sing to them or tell them scripture stories.

"You know, Hannah," Eliza said, watching her tenderly one evening. "You are a natural mother. You have a gift with children, and you have tender, healing hands."

Tears came to Hannah's eyes. "I am beginning to think that I will never know if that is true or not. Maybe I am just meant to be a substitute mother. At least in this lifetime."

Eliza was quick with remorse. "I didn't mean to be thoughtless, Hannah. I'm sorry. But I have to tell you, I think the Lord intends that you shall be a mother. I can't tell you when or how—or why you must wait. But it will happen. I know it will—maybe not even in this lifetime . . ."

Hannah gave her head an impatient shake. "Eliza, you can't say anything to me that I have not said to myself. The words are fine—and probably true. They just don't give me any comfort."

Silence settled in the little cabin. Outside the wind howled, but inside the sap popped in the fresh logs, and the smell of hot cider and honey filled the air. Both sisters sat lost in their own mournful thoughts.

On Christmas morning Reuben and Parker were up with the first pink sliver of dawn. They skinned down the ladder from their loft and, ignoring the chill of the morning air, pulled their presents from beneath the tiny tree that Eliza and Hannah had decorated with painted pine cones, threaded holly berries, and popcorn.

Parker had received a little horse with wheels and Reuben had received a book with Bible stories and a set of tin soldiers. Both children were ecstatic. They sat sucking anise sugar sticks and placing their toys in a row across the sheepskin rug in front of the fire.

Adam woke and announced his demands for food with a lusty cry. Hannah, warmed by the cozy happiness around her, climbed out of bed and, without even pausing to braid the mass of curling hair that hung to her waist, threw a light blue shawl over her ruffled, white nightgown, and went to the swinging hook over the fire to bring the porridge water to a boil.

Among the treats she had brought in her food packages was a final treat she had saved for Christmas morning. She pulled four oranges out of her pocket.

"Aunt Hannah," Reuben said, looking at one of the golden orbs. "What is that? A new ball?"

Hannah laughed. "Better than that, Reuben. Oh, much better. You shall have the most delicious treat for breakfast this morning. Juicy and sweet—and so good for you."

The little boys held the oranges in their hands, sniffing at them, rolling them around, and poking their fingers at the strange, rough skin. Eliza, nursing Adam, formed a delighted "oh" with her mouth. "Hannah," she whispered, "you do know how to give the most wonderful surprises."

"I need to remember that," Hannah said soberly. "I am afraid I have let too many Christmases disappear without a single moment of surprise or delight." She sighed. "It just isn't the same without children."

"What about Harold?" Eliza asked.

Hannah shook her head. "I can't keep him away from Papa on holidays. It wouldn't be fair to either one of them."

Eliza frowned. "But you could go to the Big House. You and Adam. It is like your second home."

"No," Hannah said, "it is not. It is more and more Anne and Cyrus's home. Papa lives in his bedroom and study. Besides, it is too painful for me. Constance has two children, and they are the center of every eye. I know it is small of me in spirit and heart, but I cannot feel anything but hurt. If she had married Adam, he would have children and a loving wife instead of such a hopeless stick of a woman as I am."

Hearing the genuine pain in Hannah's voice, Eliza wondered if anyone understood her sister. "Take your heart to the Lord, Hannah," she whispered. "Let Him help you. But more importantly, take it to Adam. Have you told him what you are feeling?"

Hannah stood up impatiently and went over to the porridge pot. "You think I don't wrestle with the Lord night and day, Eliza? As for sharing with Adam, I don't need to give him my pain. He has plenty of his own."

"But you've got to share it," Eliza exclaimed. "Can't you

see that, Hannah? At least then the pain will have value. It will bring you together."

"Pain does not do that," Hannah replied dully. "It does not want to be shared. It does not want to be discussed. Pain wants to be hidden and forgotten."

"No," Eliza said firmly. "I know you are a much smarter woman than I am, Hannah, but on this one thing I know better than you. Pain is meant to be shared. You have shared my pain with me, and because of that I am healing. Believe what I am telling you."

Hannah turned her eyes away and looked at the boys with a determined smile. "It's Christmas morning, and we'll have no more talk of serious matters. Let's play a game of 'hide-the-spoon,' and then our mush will be ready."

Just then they heard the whinny of a horse, and loud feet stamped on the front step. A heavy fist pounded on the door. "Ho! Ho! Ho!" said a man's voice. "It is Saint Nicholas!"

Eliza carried the baby to the door and opened it a cautious crack. Then she gave a delighted laugh and opened it the whole way as a snow-dusted figure, dressed and padded with winter clothing, pushed through the doorway and slammed the door closed behind him.

Hannah, her face pink from the heat of the fire and with the steam of the pot rising around her like a halo, turned and looked at the visitor in genuine surprise.

"Adam!" she gasped as she recognized him. "Adam! Just what I prayed for for Christmas!"

He stepped between the startled boys and took her in his arms and kissed her rosy, beloved face.

CHAPTER TWENTY-TWO

In late January there was a long warm spell and with the help of Uncle Abner's equipment and crew, Hannah and Adam were able to get Eliza and her children across the valley and to the train. It took nearly two weeks, but just as winter came back for one last wicked blast, the travelers arrived in Ogden to the rejoicing of William and the entire family.

Young Harold was happy to see Hannah and Adam— he had missed Hannah especially, but in the time she had been gone, he had settled into the back bedroom at the Big House. His papa's house had become more of a home to him than the Fairfields', and William was so delighted to have his son with him every day that Hannah knew she could not fight the new arrangement.

Constance's boys were bosom companions to Harold, and they came to the Big House almost daily to play with him. In a few months Harold would be starting school, and Hannah knew that he had outgrown his dependence upon her. Or had she failed that dependence? It was a question too painful to be explored. Besides, whatever had happened, Harold was now his true father's son, and she and Adam took up the role of beloved extended family.

When Eliza arrived in her father's home, Reuben and Harold seemed instantly to recognize some unseen bond between them. The motherless four-year-old and the fatherless three-year-old were drawn to each other like brothers. In the next few weeks, while Eliza tried to make decisions about her future, Harold and Reuben, who were sharing a room, became shadows of each other. One would finish the sentences of the other, and the happy security of their relationship gave them confidence and an open, light-hearted engagement with the world as a whole. All the boys played together like exuberant young colts: running, chasing, and challenging one another.

They were splendid children. Eliza had a knack for rearing boys. She gave them enough freedom to let them be daring, but she gave them enough structure and direction that they were courteous and obedient as well. As for their education, she challenged their curiosity and created projects and experiences for them so that their minds were constantly busy. Before the thaws of May that first year after she returned to Utah, she taught both Harold and Reuben how to read.

During the brief weeks Adam had been with Hannah in Idaho, he felt he had never seen his wife so happy. Eliza had been caught up in the needs of the new baby boy and in the complications of setting her finances in order. Adam realized now that Hannah had been happy because she had been playing house, pretending that Eliza's children were her own.

In the mornings of those weeks in Lemhi, Adam tramped outdoors with Reuben and Parker to gather wood. They would come in with snow on their feet and stack the logs. Hannah had found it easy to kiss Adam spontaneously, as though the shimmering happiness of the little cabin removed the stiffness and formality from her nature.

The escape from her habitual armor of sadness and iron duty—as if she had given herself permission to playact and try on a different character—let the light and tender part of her nature which she had hidden away for so long come floating to the top. Just as in her dream.

Whatever it was, for three precious weeks that winter in the little log cabin, Hannah and Adam had almost felt as young, complete, and in love as they had felt during the remembered days in Yellowstone.

One night, locked in a tight embrace in the tiny, second room of Eliza's home, Adam whispered to Hannah, "I have been happier in this humble little place than I have ever been in my life, Hannah. Why can't it always be like this between us?"

Hannah sighed. "This isn't our life, Adam. We are borrowing somebody else's. Our life is an empty house on Park Street, and more work than either of us can do, and long, lonely nights, and . . ."

"Sh-sh-sh," Adam said softly and touched her brow with his lips. "Sh-h-h, my darling. Our life is each other. That is what you must remember."

With all his heart Adam hoped that the time in Idaho might have brought a meaningful change, but as soon as they returned and Hannah saw the clusters of children in the rooms of the Big House; as she watched Eliza gathering Harold, Reuben, and Cyrus around her to read to them; as she saw Parker wriggling from her grasp to go play with the other boys and baby Adam reach with equal joy to be held by Constance, Anne, or herself, indiscriminately, Adam realized that Hannah had begun inexorably to retreat into her work once again.

Before long she was finding excuses not to visit the Big House, and the demands of the world closed around them.

"I was called to do this work," she told Adam firmly as

271

she left for yet another confinement. "You cannot begrudge me the work of the Lord. I know it requires sacrifice for you, but it is what I must do."

Adam felt as if the sweet days in Lemhi Valley had never really happened. With a feeling of resignation he threw himself back into his own work.

When summer came, the days were long and hot. The dam and its controls were almost completed, but Adam was in the process of overseeing the building of the conduit canals and the networks of irrigation ditches, floodgates, and water mains. In July he visited both Chicago and New York City to see the water systems there, studying the newest innovations. In New York he saw the mighty Brooklyn Bridge rising like a cathedral out of the East River, and he thought it an engineering marvel.

For weeks before the trip he begged Hannah to accompany him, but she said she could not possibly consider it because of the number of cases to which she was committed. The Fairfields almost never saw Harold anymore. William had made a vacation trip to Saint George in the early summer, for the first time since Brigham Young had died. He had taken Harold with him, and the two of them had found that they loved the area with its great red rock cliffs baking in the heat and its cool, majestic canyons.

William's sense of adventure was piqued, and while in Saint George, he was encouraged by a friend to visit California and see the Pacific Ocean. When William returned to Ogden he arranged for tickets for Harold and himself to ride the train to San Francisco and then on to Los Angeles. Both William and Adam were gone for most of the summer, and when they returned, they were filled with the wonder of their experiences and talked of little else.

Hannah, listening to them, felt more and more isolated

and trapped in her cheerless and repetitive role. She knew her remaining at home was her own fault. She could have accompanied either one of them on their journeys, and yet, if she had, what would she have been? Just a pointless encumbrance. If she followed them into their lives, she could not be part of their work, and she would have abandoned her own. She would have become a cipher. She was not a woman who could fill empty days of an empty life with shopping, or touring, or basking on a porch. Even reading held little pleasure for her unless it had specific purpose. She wondered if she was somehow a damaged or incomplete woman.

When William and Harold returned from California, it was time for Harold to begin school. Eliza was still staying at the Big House, but now that baby Adam was healthy and robust, she was looking determinedly for a place of her own. As Hannah had before her, she felt increasingly uncomfortable and unwanted as Anne dropped hints about the inconvenience of Eliza's lively boys and the noise and confusion that Eliza's family brought to the ordered, elegant rooms of the mansion.

And so the year turned once again.

Hannah's twenty-fifth birthday was approaching. Four days before it, she presided at a birth that claimed the lives of both mother and baby. Of all the deliveries she had attended, this was Hannah's first loss.

The baby had been breech, and the mother was very young and extremely small. The girl's hips, as narrow as a young boy's, simply could not accommodate the needs of the struggling baby, and through a long and hideous night, Hannah watched as the unborn child, trapped in the process of birth, died. The mother, too, torn and bleeding, died of profound shock to her entire system.

"We could not have done anything more!" Doctor

273

Morgan said angrily as they walked out into the night, leaving the grieving husband in the care of his mother and father. Frank Morgan was angry at his own limitations, at the waste of such deaths, and at the agony of having to watch helplessly while such tragedies played themselves out.

Hannah walked silently for a few minutes. "We need to know more," she said grimly. "There is more to be known. I know that such presentations are being delivered, successfully, by caesarean section. I have read of it. The new ethers are safe for both mother and child . . . If we only knew more!"

Doctor Morgan, offended, stalked away. "We are not gods, Hannah. Go home and rest."

But Hannah could not rest. She felt she was a failure.

Days later, as Adam and Hannah walked to the Big House for the birthday dinner that her father was giving for Hannah, Adam turned to his pensive wife.

"You've been as quiet as a stump for days now," he said. "Are you still brooding over the loss of that patient?"

"She wasn't a patient!" Hannah flared. She had become quick of temper lately and hard to talk to. "She was a girl. A child, really. And she died a most awful death. She died with a dignity that a man could scarcely comprehend, and she deserves more than to be remembered as something as inhuman as a 'patient'."

"I'm sorry," Adam said quietly. "I really am sorry. I was trying to understand."

"How can you expect to understand?" Hannah replied sharply. "I don't understand myself. Even Doctor Morgan doesn't understand. Nobody does."

They entered the front doors in grim silence, and William, coming forward to greet them, could see the tension that separated them. He knew that Hannah and Adam were both in pain, and the awful irony was that the answers

274

they were looking for were as close as each other—if they could only learn to turn and look. But their eyes and hearts seemed to search in other directions.

After a delicious dinner, William rose from his place at the head of the mahogany banquet table and tapped a crystal goblet for attention. Everyone looked up.

"Today we celebrate the happy anniversary of Hannah's birth. Twenty-five years. I wish her mother were here to see what a beautiful and accomplished woman her daughter has become."

Hannah bowed her head and thought of her mother. Would Mama really be pleased with her, she wondered? Or would she say, "Hannah, you are twenty-five years old. Isn't it time you figured out what is of real value? Who you really are?" A tear slid from under Hannah's eyelid, and she let it fall, unimpeded, onto the starched tucks of her white shirt front.

"Your mama is not here in person, but it is she who is the author of this celebration. Not only did she give you birth, my daughter, but she has also given the crowning gift for this wonderful birthday." Papa continued talking, but Hannah could not comprehend what he was saying. He pulled out a letter and began to read.

" . . . the occasion of Hannah's twenty-fifth birthday, the farm and all of its adjacent and entailed properties will become the legal possession of my two daughters, Hannah and Eliza . . ."

Pulling herself out of her reverie, Hannah stared at her father uncomprehendingly. "What do you mean? What are you saying?"

Papa smiled. "The farm was always your mother's. The deed was legally hers—in her name. She wanted her girls to have it, but not until your own lives were settled. She felt

275

if you got it too soon, it would be a burden rather than a blessing."

He was beaming down at her, but Hannah felt as though she were in a fog, trying to see through to understand what was happening. "I have kept all the profits of the farm for you girls since your mama died. They are for you to use in any way you wish.

"The house is empty and has been completely restored. I've had it painted and fixed up so that you can decide to live in it—or get another manager. Whatever seems best. The property is yours, Hannah and Eliza. I know you will care for and replenish it with the same wisdom and success as your mother before you."

Hannah gasped. "I never thought . . ." she began.

Eliza jumped out of her seat and ran over to throw her arms around her sister. "The farm, Hannah. Our home! It is still there for us! Oh, isn't it wonderful! The dear old house, and the wash yard, and that wonderful kitchen—and the big old barn . . . Don't you remember, Hannah? It was all so perfect!"

At that Hannah gave a quick bark of laughter. "My recollection, Eliza, is that you couldn't wait to leave that 'pokey old farm' and get into the city."

Eliza laughed, too. "I'm wiser now," she said firmly. "And I have held on to the good memories."

"The good memories," Hannah sighed. "Yes," she repeated, "there were lots of good memories."

Because of Adam's work and Hannah's partnership with Doctor Morgan, it was impossible for the Fairfields to make their residence at the farm. Hannah and Eliza drove out to visit. The trees were bare of leaves, and the fields lay fallow, but they could see that their father had been an excellent steward of the property. More ground had been

276

broken. There were fields where wheat and alfalfa had been harvested and a newly fenced pasture with cattle and horses that had already grown their shaggy winter coats.

The house was as fresh as though it were new, and the sisters wandered through the rooms, recalling happier times. Eliza stood in the middle of the kitchen. "I remember the first supper I cooked on that stove. Applesauce and doughnuts," she said with a smile. "I did love cooking."

At the door of their mother's bedroom, they paused and stared at the empty bed, each sunk in her own thoughts. "Do you think you ever stop missing people that you love?" Hannah asked wistfully.

"You should not want to," Eliza replied softly. "Missing them is just another way of loving them."

It was decided, after long talks with Papa and Adam, that the best decision would be for Eliza to live at the farm. There was an excellent school in Riverdale now, and the community was growing so rapidly that it would soon almost adjoin Ogden. The decision filled Eliza with unalloyed joy. Surprisingly, she took an active interest in the business of the farm.

After studying the books, interviewing the farmworkers and tenant farmers, and consulting with her father, she planned the crops and drew up the breeding plans for the coming spring. Together, she and Hannah determined how to continue the profitability of the land, as well as ways in which to help the men and women who worked for them. They decided to sell a small, unarable parcel to a builder who was contemplating building modestly priced cottages for the workers who were coming in to work on the railroad and in the sugar-beet processing factories. The growth of the city was making land more valuable.

Early in March, Adam and Hannah finished putting away the last of Eliza's things at the farm and then walked into the kitchen where she was happily slicing bread and warming cocoa.

"This is an answer to my prayers, Hannah and Adam," Eliza told them. "I promise you, dear sister, that I will do everything in my power to be a good steward over our property. We will share all of the profits, and I insist on factoring in my use of the house, so that you shall have your proper share. Our mother has given us such a gift of meaningful labor and of sustenance."

The glow of Eliza's happiness made Hannah feel even more bleak and empty. As she and Adam jounced home in their two-seater buggy, she saw the years that stretched between now and those happy trips when he had come to fetch her into town and they, both young and eager, had felt the pull of their passion between them like the irresistible force of the tide. Now, each clop of the horses' hooves was an echo in the emptiness of her life.

Adam had the massive reservoir and the great skein of the water system to show for his years. Eliza had children and the challenge and visible harvest of the farm. Hannah had only the long hours waiting to see if nature would deliver a healthy child and then the repetitive tasks of cleaning up and completing what forces far beyond her control had caused to occur. And then, when help was desperately needed, she had only the feeling of helplessness and the pain of watching as her skills and knowledge failed.

A plan had formed in her mind, and yet she had not yet had the courage to discuss it with anyone. As she and Adam returned through the night to their house, Hannah knew that she had to do something or she would continue to be lost. Why had the Lord given her this one gift—the ability to understand the workings of the human body and to know how to care for it—if he did not expect her to develop that talent? Didn't the scriptures say that if the talent was buried, nothing would be given? And that which was given would be taken away?

Of course, what she wanted would be hard for Adam to accept, but, if he were honest, he was as capable of taking care of himself as she was, and his work kept him from home nearly half of the time. And since Christmas he had already accepted an assignment from the First Presidency to help solve an engineering problem in the foundations of the almost-completed Salt Lake Temple. If the difficulties of travel were as severe as they had been in years past, she might not see him for weeks at a time.

"Adam," she said hesitantly, "I need to go away for a while."

He reined the horses in, and she shivered as the night closed around her. "I haven't known how to tell you, but tonight as I saw how carefully Eliza is studying to manage the farm, and as I heard you discussing your trip to the East and all the things you have learned—I knew that I had to go."

"Go where?" Adam's voice was as cold and distant as the stars. She could sense the tension and stillness in his body. Was it anger or hurt? She could not be sure.

"Boston," she said softly. "Rowland House. It is a lying-in hospital. A teaching hospital."

"What do you mean?" Adam spoke harshly.

"I have to learn more," Hannah said desperately. "I'm a midwife. That is what I am, Adam. I'm not a mother, or a housewife, or a cook, or a seamstress—I am a midwife, and I need to know more. Don't you see, Adam? Just as you had to go study the best that is being done in engineering, I have to go learn what is best being done to bring babies safely into this world."

She was breathing heavily. "Adam, I promise you, they are performing miracles. Painless childbirth with ether.

279

Operations that save both mother and child. New antiseptic techniques, circumcisions, medicines . . . They are learning what causes over-large babies—diabetes and toxic poisoning. And they are finding ways to help. I have to learn more, Adam. I have to."

Without a word Adam snapped the reins, and the horses continued toward the town. For a long time he was silent, and then, almost so softly that she could not discern the words, he said, "I need to think. I cannot figure out what you are really saying. I have to think. We'll talk of this later."

Once the subject was raised, there was no stepping back from it. Hannah gathered all the necessary information. A midwife class was given at Rowland House starting every January. Doctor Morgan, although he clearly did not approve of Hannah's plan to leave her husband for a year, nonetheless wrote on her behalf, and she was assured that a place would be kept in the class for her.

Money was not an impediment. Hannah's share of the profits of the farm would more than pay her expenses, so it seemed to her that the gift of the farm had been a sign from heaven that she must go and complete her education.

Even her bishop, with whom she discussed the plan, told her that the need for midwives in the rapidly growing community far outstripped the number of qualified women and that the Lord needed sisters who were prepared to perform this essential service.

"The Lord has indeed given you a special gift, Sister Fairfield," the bishop told her, his lined and gentle eyes looking at her with grave respect. "But I must add that you can do nothing without the heartfelt support and understanding of your eternal companion. All the talents and gifts in the world are as ashes if we do not seek the seal of the Holy Spirit of Promise on our marriage covenant. My

280

dear Hannah, when we speak of first things first, that is my understanding. It is not so much what we *do* that qualifies us for the kingdom as it is the *order* in which we do it."

Stung by his words and feeling she was being chastized, Hannah replied stiffly, "I understand that, Bishop. Of course I would not go if Adam did not give me his wholehearted permission."

They discussed the subject long and late, and gradually through the spring and summer Hannah's insistence wore down Adam's despairing resistance. If she wanted to go so much, how could he hold her? He wanted her to stay with him, not because he forced her to do so but because she could not bear to be apart from him. He smiled to himself bitterly. If she did not feel that way after all these years, then what kind of a fool would go on hoping?

In the end, he acquiesced, and Hannah, not sure whether to laugh or cry, felt a sick hollow in the pit of her stomach, almost like a blow, and she thought she knew how a dog must feel when it chased a bicycle and unexpectedly caught it. Had she really expected him to say yes? Did she really want to leave everything she had ever known and tackle an unfamiliar world? Could she really find any kind of happiness in such a long separation from Adam?

The questions jangled in her mind, and then she felt the hurt and shame that he would actually let her go. What kind of love could he have for her if he would allow her to leave, even though she had cajoled and begged and pleaded? He couldn't love her as much as she thought if he could, on any grounds, agree to her leaving. Pride flared in her wounded heart, and her chin shot up.

"Thank you, Adam," she said coolly. "Then I shall make the necessary arrangements."

The autumn days seemed to fly past, and each day led them inexorably toward a departure that both regarded with bleak concern. Trying to put a lighthearted face on their decision, Hannah remarked, "The year is going to fly by! You will work on the temple all winter, and by the time you are back home, we will be almost half through our separation.

"Besides, in the spring you will come to Boston, and we will have the Eastern trip that you have always wanted to share with me. It will be great fun, and we will have so much to tell one another . . ."

"Of course," Adam nodded, but the light seemed to have gone from his eyes, and she could feel his sadness like a weight on her heart.

Eliza had candied the cherries, orange, and lemon peel. They had boiled in the heavy sugar water and then had dried for days until they were crusted with sugar. Their color remained as rich and deep as jewels. She had the precious fruits laid out on the table in lustrous heaps.

In her crockery bowl she had placed butter, flour, brown sugar, a touch of molasses, eggs, and generous portions of cinnamon, nutmeg, cloves, and allspice. Brother Heber at the mercantile had managed to order a precious paper of dates, and she had chopped them finely with the candied walnut halves she had roasted in the oven.

This was her favorite part of the process, when she folded everything together and then poured the fruit cake batter into the brown-paper lined, greased baking pans.

The oven was heated to perfection, and through the hours of the afternoon as the rich, holiday cakes baked, the house smelled like a feast. When the cakes were finished and cooled, she soaked them in lemony syrup, wrapped them in cheesecloth, and placed them in a dark cupboard to mellow and age. One week before Christmas, she would take them out and frost one of them with a thick, white marzipan glaze. For the whole of the Christmas season her guests would be treated to a thin slice of the wondrous treat, and a glass of hot, spiced cider.

The second cake she would not ice, but she would save it to serve with her rich, hot, creamy sauce on Christmas Eve. All the magic of the Christmas season was captured in the complex flavors of that once-a-year confection.

Eliza was humming to herself and did not hear Hannah enter the front door.

The house was alive with the work of Eliza's hands. She had patched a bright quilt that lay over the horsehair couch. Wreaths of winter bounties made the windows bright, and in the kitchen a new rag rug graced the polished pine floor and the table groaned under the happy load of newly baked apple pie, cookies, and chocolate cake.

"Hannah!" Eliza cried in unadulterated delight at seeing her sister. "Come in! What can I get you to eat?"

The smells of the house were irresistible, and Hannah realized that she was hungry. "I could manage a bite of something," she said, sitting down wearily. "I have been up all night, and there was little food in the house where I was attending."

"Is everything all right?" Eliza asked solicitously, as she pulled together a plate of sliced cheese and ham, a generous piece of apple pie, and a slab of warm, whole wheat bread. Placing a cool glass of buttermilk next to the plate, she sat down across from her sister, who began to eat slowly.

"Fine," Hannah responded absently. "The baby was healthy, and the mother came through well enough. I'll drop by to see them tomorrow. The Relief Society sisters arrived with dinner, and I felt it was best if I left and got some rest. The family lives down the road from the farm, so I decided I would come here."

"Eat," Eliza urged, "and then go rest in Mama's room."

For a few moments Hannah ate in silence, and the food

seemed to revive her. "The house looks wonderful, Eliza," she commented. "Better than it ever has before. You have a knack for creating a home—the curtains, the rugs, the decorations, the food. It's all so—so—remarkable to me. I can't imagine how you do it. I don't have the skills. Mama didn't. But you. You make it look so easy—and so right."

Eliza caught a tone of envy and defeat in Hannah's voice. "A home isn't about curtains and rugs, Hannah," she said quietly. "I do these things because they give me pleasure. They are what I have to give, but they are not what makes a home. It is the giving that makes a home. But you know that! You have so much to give—gifts that most of us can't even comprehend, let alone duplicate. You are such an extraordinary woman. Everyone thinks so."

"Yes," Hannah said, with irony twisting her mouth. "I know. I am so admirable. So respected. So impressive that no one wants to be around me very much. I need to be taken in small doses. You, on the other hand, dear sister, have people flocking to sit in your home. Even Papa would rather be here in the farmhouse than in his elaborate city house because you have made a haven."

Uncomfortable with the direction of the conversation and concerned about her sister's despondent words, Eliza tried to change the subject. "Well, maybe you'll come home from Boston with some new ideas for fixing up your house as well as new ways to deliver babies."

"Maybe," Hannah said, "but I imagine if I haven't learned yet, going to Boston isn't likely to help me."

Irritated by her sister's insistence on gloominess, Eliza snapped, "Well, I know that you can do anything I can do. It is just that you have never wanted to. Anything we do in this life takes thought and desire, and then the ability comes. A home is made out of thought and desire. A marriage is made out of thought and desire. A farm is made out of thought and desire—and so is a career in medicine. So is righteousness! Don't tell me our life isn't our own fault, that it is something that happens to us because of the way we are born. I don't believe it. I believe we create our lives out of the things we believe are important."

"So," Hannah said coolly, "you are saying that I will never be able to make a good apple pie until I think it is important? Well, if you must know, I probably never will think it is important. Something in me just can't."

"You misunderstand me, Hannah," Eliza flashed back. "I am saying to you that the apple pie is not the important thing. It is what it represents. And you can't have *that* until you think *it* is important."

"I'm too tired for metaphors," Hannah said dully. "Thanks for feeding me. I'm restored enough to make it home. I guess I'll be going."

Eliza was immediately contrite. "Oh, Hannah! I didn't want to quarrel, I just wanted to help . . ."

"It's all right, Eliza," Hannah answered. "I know."

"Please take home some of these cookies and a loaf of bread. Adam might enjoy them, and I've made far more than we can eat."

Hannah took the proffered basket. "I probably shouldn't take them. Adam might get to like such treats. Make him aware of what he's missing."

After Hannah left, Eliza sat down at the table and cried. "Can't you see that *you* are what Adam is missing, Hannah?" she whispered to the empty room. "All you need to make a home for him is to be there. That's the only home-making skill you'll ever need. Why can't you see that?"

CHAPTER TWENTY-THREE

Hannah sat in the gallery of the Rowland House surgery and listened as Doctor Stanholme discussed the use of ether in the process of delivering a baby. It had been nearly four decades since William Thomas Green Morton, a dentist, had discovered that sulfuric acid mixed with alcohol creates a gas that, when inhaled, produces a profound and pain-free stupor.

For years the medical world considered the concept of painless surgery as nothing more than witchcraft. It flew in the face of religion, science, and tradition. Even after such pioneers as Morton and Crawford W. Long had proven that surgery under anesthesia could be accomplished without pain and that the patient could recover from heretofore untreatable conditions, there was still so much prejudice and ignorance in the practice of medicine that the use of such powerful and unknown substances was frowned upon.

Gradually, however, the use of ether had been experimented with in hopeless cases and was slowly gaining acceptance. In the teaching hospitals of the great eastern cities, many new types of surgery were being attempted, but in the frontiers of America most rural doctors practiced medicine as they had from the traditions of centuries past.

Doctor Morgan, more enlightened and flexible than many pioneer doctors, had recently experimented with ether in performing a necessary amputation and was cautiously training himself on its uses. But when Hannah had suggested that she learn about the use of ether in obstetrical practice while she was studying in Boston, Doctor Morgan had been offended and angry with her.

"We are told by the Lord that he has ordained that women should bear children in pain and suffering, Hannah. How dare you think that you or any other medical practitioner has the right to make the Lord a liar? Surely if a woman tried to shirk her duty of enduring childbearing, both she and the child would be punished in ways we cannot imagine. If not by death, then by some other terrible retribution! As a physician and a man of God, I could not take upon myself such a responsibility!" Frank Morgan glared at Hannah. "If you are going to Boston to learn such godless ideas, then I pity you when you return, for no God-fearing man or woman will have anything to do with you."

Hannah was shocked. "The Queen herself was given anesthesia for her last child nearly thirty years ago! Surely the relief of agony and suffering in any circumstance cannot be wrong, and, if it can be proven that it does no harm to mother or child . . ."

"Hah!" Doctor Morgan exclaimed. "And how do you arrive at such a knowledge? By human experimentation. How many mothers and children will you sacrifice to the god of science to discover what the deleterious effects are?"

"Mothers and unborn babies who are certain to die without intervention cannot be further harmed by trying to save them by any means possible," Hannah replied promptly. "If even one such mother and child can be saved by the use of ether so that internal manipulation is possible, we must attempt it. Surgical removal of the child may even be attempted."

Doctor Morgan walked away in dismissal. "Removal of a child through surgery always results in the death of the mother, Hannah. Always. Remember that. Go to Boston if you must, Hannah. But strive to remember that you are a Saint, and the ways of the world are not our ways."

The echo of her cheerless farewell at the train station played in Hannah's mind as she sat listening to the long lecture on toxic poisoning in advanced pregnancy.

Adam, her father, Eliza, and Doctor Morgan—all of them had come dutifully to the station and stood on the platform, kissing her good-bye, lifting her luggage to the porter, and saying all the right, courteous words, but behind their eyes she saw puzzlement, hurt, and disappointment.

Even after all the days of travel across the endless miles of the nation, when Hannah had left the train in Boston, the shadow of those faces still haunted her. She was so uncertain she had made the right decision that she almost turned around to reboard the train and return to Utah. Only pride kept her from retreating.

The city was strange, crowded, and noisy, but she found a cab and gave the driver her new address. She had been assigned to a boardinghouse on Boylston Street, just two blocks from the lying-in hospital. Her room was clean, neat, and small, and the food that was served three times a day was bland and uninteresting.

When Hannah reported to the hospital her first day, she was issued her uniforms: three gray dresses with white collars and cuffs and three starched, white aprons. Until she was assigned to assist in operatories and labor rooms, which would not be for at least three months, she was to change her dress every other day and her apron daily. The hospital, for a small fee, laundered, ironed, and starched the uniforms. When she began working with patients, she would be required to change her uniform daily and her cuffs and apron after every delivery.

Hannah smiled at the thought of someone else doing her laundry because that was her best homemaking skill, and yet here in Boston she would have no home-related responsibilities of any kind. Her life would be the lecture hall and the hospital.

The days after she arrived were long and challenging. Winter in Boston was wet, cold, and dreary. The wind from the harbor blew across the city with a gray heaviness, and the streets were crowded with streetcars, horse-drawn vans, and carriages. The streetcleaners could not keep up with the traffic, and the smell of horse dung and wet sea air hung over the city like a pall.

Occasionally there was a crisp, cold day, with the sky as blue as bottleglass and the air singing with the wind coming all the way from Maine. On such days the gray miasma was scrubbed away, and the narrow streets and quaint, old, row houses and the great spread of Boston Common made walking a pleasure. If Hannah could manage an hour or two of free time, she tramped in her sturdy boots along the storied streets and thought to herself that her great-great-grandfather Elijah Childress had walked these streets when Boston was still a village seaport, nothing more. "When the weather gets finer, " she promised herself, "I shall go visit the town of Roxbury and see the place where Elijah and his family are buried."

But no matter how much she studied and worked or with what curiosity she explored the city, always, always, she missed Utah—her home, her family, Harold—and Adam. Day and night she found herself aching for him, yearning to see his face, to hear his voice, and she wondered how often he thought of her.

Her free hours were almost nonexistent. The hospital had two services: one for wealthy patients, who occupied private rooms and gave birth under the watchful eye of the best obstetrical physicians in the city; the other, a clinic, for the poorest of the poor—half-dead women brought from the tenements and the streets.

They came only when death seemed imminent and their time-worn, natural home deliveries with untrained midwives or members of the family had gone horrifyingly sour. Fear caused them to be brought to the door of the hospital.

Many of these patients died before they could even be examined, both mothers and children, but Doctor Stanholme, the director of the clinic, had done miraculous and terrifying things before Hannah's eyes that had saved and healed what seemed to be doomed cases.

Often it was the use of ether that made the difference.

Hannah roused herself to listen to the lecture and realized that Doctor Stanholme had begun a discussion of the use of ether in childbirth.

"For more than a decade now," he told the cluster of midwives who sat in the narrow chairs taking notes, "we have been able to use ether in the process of childbirth to institute procedures that overcome deadly presentations. We are able to manipulate fetuses in the uterus when the ability of the mother to feel pain has been stopped. We are even developing a method of surgical delivery when natural delivery is impossible.

"As you know, for centuries, it has been a common misconception that muscle tissue cannot be sutured. As a result, all surgical deliveries of infants have resulted in the death of the mother. Suturing was attempted on the external incision—closing the skin and tissue of the abdomen—but routinely the incision of the uterus was left open. The mother, if she was not already dead from the complications of the birth, would then die from internal bleeding or massive infection, whichever claimed her first.

"At this hospital, and at many others, we have flown in the face of conventional wisdom and are developing techniques of suturing the muscle tissue of the uterus when it has been necessary to remove a child surgically from the mother's womb.

"Such deliveries will always be used only as a last resort because they result most commonly in death—and in those few happy instances where we have been successful in saving the mothers, we have found sterility is common. In the rare case in which a woman has conceived another child, rupture of the uterus is almost inevitable. Nonetheless, we are beginning to save lives that would have most certainly been lost. Ether is what has made it possible to conquer that great enemy of women and men—pain."

In training the midwives, Doctor Stanholme allowed them to experience the inhalation of ether fumes. Hannah could forget neither the gentle darkness that had snuffed out her consciousness nor the total absence of awareness of the tight band that had been wound around her arm to show her that she could feel nothing during the interval of unconsciousness.

"Mrs. Fairfield." Doctor Stanholme fixed Hannah with his unnerving eye. She sat up straighter, wondering what she had missed or if she was being reprimanded. "Tomorrow we begin clinical training. You are assigned as my assistant. I will expect you to report to me at five A.M. Be prepared for twelve hours of duty."

It was April, and the months away from Utah had passed slowly for Hannah. Unused to being confined to study and classes alone, she had missed the turmoil, stress, and service of actual medical practice. The hospital required all of the midwives, regardless of their practical experience, to be schooled in anatomy, history, physiology, chemistry, and now, antiseptic procedure.

The first three months of their training, therefore, was academic. The lesson material was simple for Hannah, and she had added Latin to her curriculum on her own initiative. Of all the women in the group, she had scored the highest on all the tests. She was forthright and opinionated in class discussions, and, more than once, she had seen Doctor Stanholme's expression when he looked at her with disapproval or surprise. She was not sure which.

Now, at last, the director apparently deemed that she was ready to begin the practical, clinical work of modern obstetrics. She knew that Doctor Stanholme, like most medical doctors, regarded midwives as little more than servants—nurses, maids, factotums—who did the mindless and untutored work as a support system for the essential work and knowledge of the true physician. Yet the fact that Doctor Stanholme himself frequently lectured the class and answered questions made Hannah feel that perhaps he saw midwives, to some degree at least, as colleagues.

Most of her fellow students were planning to practice either in the inner cities or in far-flung pioneer communities such as her own. The women ranged in age from the early twenties to a graying, motherly woman of forty-five. A few of them were in the profession because they had to earn a living. Others were studying midwifery because they had a profound sense of calling and it was the only role open to women in the medical profession other than nursing. The older woman had come to study because she, like Hannah, had been trained as a midwife but felt her skills were inadequate. One woman was studying because she had given birth to a stillborn child and had, herself, been so badly damaged that she could never bear children again. She was on a burning crusade to see that such tragedies were prevented in other women's lives.

Although she was shy at first, Hannah, after a few days in the surgery, quickly found that she could work well with Doctor Stanholme. His orders were firm and clear, and he left her to work with the mothers using her own wisdom and experience.

Often Hannah could calm a hysterical woman so that she could communicate effectively with the doctor, and Doctor Stanholme recognized Hannah's unusual ability to bring order and confidence into the most chaotic of situations.

Hannah watched and learned from Doctor Stanholme's sure, deft, surgeon's hands. He taught her how to stitch up torn and suffering women so that they would heal with no ill effects. He taught her the slow, firm, effective moves of internal manipulation, and she became gifted at the skill because of her strong but slender hands.

Gradually, Hannah grew more and more confidant and occasionally was able to make suggestions when a presentation was one she had experienced before. Doctor Stanholme was a rare physician. In a profession where most men thought they were the complete arbiter—the final wisdom and subject to no entreaty or suggestions—he was smart enough and confident enough to listen to those whose opinion he respected.

One evening, after a particularly difficult labor and delivery by caesarean section of a woman who was almost certainly a prostitute, Hannah sat in the anteroom filling out the charts. Doctor Stanholme walked through the room and sat down across from her. "You did a fine job of assisting," he said. "There was so much infection and scarring in the birth canal that caesarean section was the only hope for either of them," he continued apologetically. "I only hope the child has not caught the infection."

Hannah shuddered as she thought of the poor, scrawny infant they had lifted from the mother's body. While Doctor Stanholme had swabbed and stitched the incisions, Hannah had washed the baby girl's fragile limbs. What kind of life could such an infant hope for? If the mother lived, she would drag the baby back to her hovel and treat it with the same filthy indifference she gave to her own hygiene. The baby would not live out the month.

As though reading Hannah's mind, Doctor Stanholme shook his head. "We can't save the world, Mrs. Fairfield. But every operation we do, every difficult delivery that we solve, everything we learn can help us to save one more baby. One more life. Whatever happens to that child we delivered tonight, her life has not been wasted."

In spite of herself, Hannah felt tears springing to her eyes. Even that woman whose whole life was sin and whose sinfulness would probably eventually destroy the life of her baby—even such a woman as that had been blessed to conceive. It didn't bear thinking about.

Hannah pressed the back of her hand to her eyes. "I apologize," she said, embarrassed by her open display of emotion in front of this highly trained scientist. "I am rather tired."

Doctor Stanholme pulled the chart out of her hand. "I'll finish this," he said brusquely. "You go home and rest."

She did as he commanded. Every night she returned to the boardinghouse too tired to think, too tired to be lonely or homesick. She was living through the days like a walking shadow.

Hannah had no idea how old Doctor Stanholme was. Around forty, she imagined. Not young, but not old. He was short and stocky with a head of thick, brown hair and a trim beard. He wore pince-nez glasses on a black ribbon attached to the lapel of his expensive suits. And, although his shirts were also tailor-made and dazzlingly white, he always had an air about him as though he were slightly rumpled. His clothing was clean and fine, but he did not wear it as though he ever looked in a mirror or paused to smooth out the creases. She thought that was one of the things she like best about him. His whole appearance seemed to say, "I exert myself day and night for the important things—the rest can go hang."

The other midwifery students talked about him among themselves. They said he came from a rich and established old Bostonian family and that he had disgraced the family by becoming a medical man, which they considered only one step above "trade." One of the women said he had been married unhappily as a young man and had left the exclusive and tight-knit world of Bostonian society because he did not wish to face the scandal and pain caused by that marriage.

Whatever the reason, he now seemed to make the hospital his life. Quite by chance, Hannah discovered that it was Doctor Stanholme's money that kept the charity part of the hospital in operation. Late one night, as she was filing charts, she had run across some financial records. In them she had seen the significant donations listed under Doctor Stanholme's name. She had told no one of her discovery because she knew she had seen papers that were not meant to be made public.

Hannah stepped out of her stained clothes and wearily put a nightgown over her head. As she reached down to blow out the lamp, she saw an envelope propped on her nightstand, and she recognized Adam's handwriting.

She and Adam wrote to each other faithfully once a week. Adam's letters were newsy, entertaining, and impersonal. Her own were the same. Just once, she thought, as she tore open the letter, I wish he would write that he misses me more than his heart can stand. Or I wish he'd tell me his house—his life—seem empty without me. But the cold thought struck her that maybe they weren't.

She drew the single sheet of stationery out of the envelope and read the first line. "I am coming to Boston. I have my train tickets in my pocket right now as I write. Meet me at the railroad station on May the first. Get some time off. We need to be together. Love eternally, Adam."

With a cry of pure joy she pressed the paper to her breast and slept through the night clutching it in her hand.

In May the New England woods bloomed. Blackberry vines formed carpets and runners of white blossoms, wild grapes twined the old rock walls with vibrant green leaves, and beech and bay trees wove a canopy of shade.

As Adam had requested, Hannah asked for two weeks' leave, and Doctor Stanholme, with a testy frown, had granted it. Knowing that her own narrow bed and boxlike room would provide neither comfort nor privacy, she splurged outrageously and arranged a hotel room at the Parker House. The expense was worth every cent.

At night they ate together in the fine old dining room, enjoying as many as five courses in a single meal. After one such meal—which began with oysters on the half-shell, clam chowder, thinly sliced melons, and lemon ice—and had continued with rack of lamb, carrot souffle, and scalloped potatoes, ending with meringue tarts and hothouse strawberries, Hannah sighed in repletion.

"You have been trying to plump me up since you first

met me, Adam Fairfield," she laughed accusingly. "Another week of this, and you will succeed!"

Somehow they were able to spend the days as though the rest of their lives had never existed—as though the rest of the world did not exist. They did not discuss Adam's work, or Hannah's school, or the family in Utah, or the strains of the past years. Both of them knew they were glossing over things that needed to be faced, and yet each was reluctant to spoil this infinitely precious piece of stolen time.

For the first time in her life, Hannah felt heedless. She wanted to be selfish and indulgent and full of worldly pleasure, as if she could wash away all the ugliness she had seen in the past weeks and years. It was almost like running away from all the misery in the clinic operatories and in the crowded streets of the city. A way to erase the memories of all the unhappiness she could remember in the pioneer rooms of families who struggled to put each morsel of food into their children's mouths. A way to ignore the memory of her own failures as a wife and homemaker.

Somehow, when Adam stepped off the train, she wanted him to be the only thing she had to see and the moment in front of them the only moment she had to know. She gave herself permission to forget duty and purpose and family and eternity and, for this short, precious time, simply give herself to the present.

The headiness of their desperate passion and the strange transformation in Hannah puzzled, concerned, and thrilled Adam. He did not think for a moment that Hannah was basically changed. He knew that neither of them had faced any of the real issues of their marriage.

His instincts told him that Hannah was close to some breaking point, and her carefree behavior was a reflex, a safety valve to help her survive. Still, the days of their reunion passed with an unforced gaiety, and Adam took each day as a gift.

Together they explored the museums and historic monuments of the old city. They walked the Trail of Liberty and stood quietly in the Old North Church. They hired a chaise and visited Bunker Hill, the harbor, and Haymarket Square, where they ate huge steaks cooked over an open fire. Their fellow diners were the tradesmen who brought their goods to the open stalls.

One afternoon they walked the quiet enclosure of Harvard Yard, and Adam remarked that it had some of the cloistered feeling of Temple Square.

It was the first time Hannah made any inquiry about his work. "How is the temple progressing?" she asked, but he sensed her indifference to the answer, and so he passed on to another topic, and they continued their pleasant stroll in the warm, spring air.

As the two weeks of truancy from their responsibilities drew to a close, he felt her anxious restlessness, and he knew they needed to find a way to share their inner lives and thoughts before he had to leave. If he left now with this sense of unreality between them, he did not know whether they could ever find their way back to each other again. He could almost sense their lives spinning separately, alone, and in different directions. They would still be married, but to him sharing a house, or sharing a bed, did not mean a marriage.

They were resting on the satin sofa in the sitting room of their suite. Adam was holding Hannah's hand, and she was leaning against the frame with her eyes closed, as still as a painting. She was more beautiful than the day he had met her.

"Hannah," he said gently, "I have to leave in two days. Let's talk about ourselves. Let's talk about these next few months. About our work. About where we are going with our lives when all of this is over."

He felt her stiffen. "What do you mean? We've been talking for two weeks!"

"Yes," Adam said gently, "about food and art and history, but now I want to talk about *us.*"

"Haven't you been happy?" Hannah asked urgently. "Hasn't this been what you've always wanted? No distractions, no quarrels, no separations?"

"Yes, my darling, darling girl. This has been what I have wanted—you in my arms and in my eyes. But I am leaving, and I need to take something more to sustain me through these long months. I need to feel we have some kind of shared vision—some future. I need to know this is worth it."

"What is worth it?"

"This being apart. This lonely existence that we are both enduring. This feeling of a desert in the places in our hearts that should be filled with living water—you know what I mean, Hannah. This terrible gulf between us. Don't pretend that all is well."

"But I thought," she began, "I thought this had been such a perfect time together that you would believe in us again. That you would forget and forgive . . ."

"Hannah," Adam said, and his voice was patient and tired. "There is nothing to forget or forgive. Taken first to last, every day of my life with you is more precious than all the riches of the world without you. But, Hannah, we need to at least try to find our way through this forest that has grown up between us."

"You can make love to me as you did last night and then tell me that you . . ." she raged, hurt and cornered by things she did not want to face.

"Please, my darling girl, don't think I am talking about

our love for one another. The passion I feel has never quenched or dimmed. It is that passion that makes me yearn to hold your heart, your mind, as well as your body—not because I want to control or change you but only because I want to feel a part of the whole of you. I want to be your support, your protection, your comfort . . . your friend . . ." Adam stopped. He did not know how to go on.

There was a long pause, and then he said, "I am finished with my work on the temple. Next week I will reopen the house on Park Street because we are starting the last section of the reservoir. Remember that rocky spit of land that comes down off the granite ridge? It is going to be a bear to remove, but when it is gone, we will have a basin large enough to serve the valley for generations."

Adopting the tone of his new, impersonal approach, Hannah sat up and said in a pedantic voice, "I have finished my formal classwork, except for Latin, which I'm studying on my own. We are now into clinical practice, and I am learning the use of ether and assisting in operations and surgical, obstetrical techniques. Although I will not be able to perform such procedures—since I will not be licensed as a doctor—I will be qualified to judge when such procedures should be undertaken, and I will be able to supplement the surgeon's work."

"Well, is it worth it?" Adam asked. "Are you learning enough for it to be worth being so far from home and all alone?"

"Worth it!" she cried. "I learn more in a week—I see more complicated deliveries and solutions—than I could learn in years of normal practice. If I am ever to be a viable midwife, it is not only worth it—it is essential!"

"Doctor Morgan feels you were perfectly competent before. He's afraid you are learning things that you do not need to know and that it may cloud your judgment and

300

make you less capable rather than more," Adam said carefully.

Hannah was outraged. "Doctor Morgan is a fine man, but he is an outdated and narrow-minded doctor. The world of medicine has passed him by, and he doesn't even want to acknowledge the progress."

Adam was quiet for a moment. "He saves many lives, and his wisdom and compassion are worth a great deal more than any advanced technique, I should think. I think it is rather arrogant to demean such a good man."

With a slight blush, Hannah bit her lip. She had not meant to say unkind things about Frank Morgan or imply that she knew more about medicine than he did, but she knew she was right in charging that his resistance to change could cause needless suffering.

"I'm sorry, Adam," she said. "I didn't mean to sound arrogant, but it is true. Medicine is changing. Almost daily. Things that were impossible only a few years ago are becoming routine. Ether is going to make an enormous difference in the way we practice the healing arts. Surgery will become more and more common—and we will learn the mysteries of our bodies."

"You think the Lord will approve of all this?" Adam asked.

"He approves of you blowing up His mountains to build a reservoir so that people can have water. Why should He not expect us to learn how to care for our bodies more effectively? Who knows? The day may even come when we can know why you and I cannot . . ."

She did not finish the sentence, and the pain of her unanswered prayers filled the room. Adam put his arms around her. "It always comes back to that, doesn't it, Hannah? You won't believe that our love is enough. As much as we want children, the truth is, that as long as we have each other, we are a family. You are my wife. I'm your husband. Those are important things. But somehow they are never enough."

After that they spoke no more of such things. The two remaining days were tinged with the sadness of their impending separation and with unsaid thoughts.

When they kissed good-bye at the railroad station, Adam held Hannah to him with an embrace so strong and filled with longing that she could not breathe. Wearing her gray uniform and starched apron, she stood watching the train until it was out of sight, and then she went straight to the operatory at Rowland House and reported to Doctor Stanholme for work. She worked harder than ever, studied endlessly, and filled her days as though she were driven.

Through the long, hot weeks of summer, Hannah toiled in the clinic. She scrubbed and sterilized instruments, washed the delivery tables and stirrups, and watched at the bedside of mothers who had gone septic.

She held babies and mothers, stitched torn tissue, timed labor pains, and waited through the long hours while babies went through transition and struggled to be born.

She observed ether, both the use and the abuse of it. She began to recognize both the blessings and limitations of the substance, and more and more she came to understand the physiological and emotional process of birth. With each new understanding she gained, Doctor Stanholme observed how her intuitive skills helped her to make brilliant medical decisions.

Time and again he found himself listening to and watching this slender, beautiful young woman and feeling he had gained an insight that would make him a better obstetrician. He knew part of the reason for her uncanny accuracy was that she was a woman—and an articulate one at that. Not for the first time he wondered about her marriage and the fact that she had no children.

He asked her if her husband had enjoyed his visit to Boston, and she answered briefly and courteously that Mr. Fairfield had found it very pleasant. That had been the total of their conversation on the subject. Even though they worked together daily, Doctor Stanholme and Hannah still spoke to one another formally and with professional respect.

All that changed one hot day in July. Hannah was assisting in a delivery such as Eliza's had been. They had managed to save the mother from bleeding to death, but the baby had died.

After the delivery, Doctor Stanholme asked Hannah to take the mother's pulse while he signed the chart. As she stood beside the bed, the room began to tilt, and for the second time in her life, she fainted. When she revived, she was lying in a bed in the private part of the hospital, and Doctor Stanholme was sitting quietly in a chair beside her.

"Back with the living, I see," he said heartily, as she opened her eyes. "You gave us quite a start, pitching forward like that."

"I don't know what happened!" she murmured. "I am not the fainting kind. Perhaps I am more tired than I realize."

"You mean you seldom faint?" the doctor asked, with quick medical instinct. "Have you ever fainted before?"

"Only once that I remember. When my mother died."

"And never again? Not from exhaustion, or hunger, or sudden change of position?"

"No," she answered.

"Then I think perhaps we should give you a medical

exam. Something may be wrong," Doctor Stanholme suggested with a worried line between his brows.

"I don't think so," Hannah said slowly. "I have no symptoms that I can think of, except occasional nausea, which I attribute to the dreadful food at the boardinghouse, and a feeling of tiredness that seems to have grown out of all proportion."

Doctor Stanholme sat beside her for several more minutes without saying anything. Then he asked, "How long ago did your husband visit in Boston?"

"Almost three months ago. You know that, Doctor Stanholme. Why do you ask? I certainly don't need to worry my husband about this little incident."

"I think perhaps you do need to contact your husband. Great balls of fire, Mrs. Fairfield! You are the most competent midwife I have ever known, and you can't even diagnose yourself!"

All the air went out of Hannah's lungs in a rush. Her mind began swirling frantically, and suddenly, with a mad, disbelieving certainty, she knew it was true. After all these years, she was going to have a baby.

"It can't be true," she said, staring at the ceiling, afraid even to admit the possibility for fear the idea was a fantasy. "It can't be true."

"I'll warrant it is true," Doctor Stanholme insisted. "Use your head, girl."

Even while her spirit refused to take it in, her mind knew without a doubt. She could not even have imagined such a thing, and the idea was so new and so unexpected that she could not feel anything, only a vast, yawning corridor. Somewhere out there, in all that amorphous unknown, maybe the happiness that had eluded her and Adam for so long would be waiting.

"I must send a telegram," she whispered. "I must."

But she did not.

That night she had a small show of blood, and when she told Doctor Stanholme about it, he put her to bed immediately. She did not write Adam to tell him anything that was happening. If she lost this baby, she felt, it would be better if he never knew. Facing the agony of uncertainty every day herself, knowing what a gashing pain it would be if she miscarried, she was determined to save Adam the same crushing grief. She did not want to give him a rush of false joy, only to dash it with the awful news that they were still childless.

Doctor Stanholme kept Hannah at the hospital. She was fed and pampered, and for the first time in her life she lay still, not rushing to the next appointment or the next responsibility. Day after day she lay in the bed, doing nothing but praying that the fountains of her body would heal and hold her baby in the cradle of her womb and nourish him until he could be born, healthy and whole.

Her prayers were sweet to her, and she wove her hands across her body as though she would hold the child and keep him safe. In her prayers she spoke to the Lord, until one splendid night she heard His Spirit speak to her.

All through the years of her life she had prayed to the Lord and had pleaded with Him and instructed Him, but now she realized she had never taken time to listen to what He wanted her to hear.

It was a quiet miracle. In the long and sleepless hours of the lonely night the Spirit whispered in her ear. He spoke the same words her father had spoken to her when she was a child: "It will be all right. Everything will work out."

Did the Spirit really speak in such humble, daily words? Yes, she suddenly understood, He did. He spoke in words she could hear and understand because He wanted her to feel comforted and secure.

Sometimes in the long hours when she prayed, she thought she saw Adam's face, and she wondered if there were times when she was not really praying but was carrying on a conversation with Adam. Adam. How she had resisted him and failed him, and now she carried a part of him within her. It was the first thing that had ever happened in her life that filled her to the very brim. Had he always had the power to do that for her, child or no child? If she had let Adam into the innermost parts of her mind and heart, if she had dared to share her insecurities and suffering with him, could she have been filled with peace and purpose long ago?

Late in September, after the hospital was quiet for the night, Doctor Stanholme came in to see Hannah. She had been up for most of the day and had felt strong and well. She had even worked in the clinic for a few hours taking medical histories.

"The nurse says you are the picture of health," Doctor Stanholme said. "The staff is beginning to think it is time I released you from the hospital. I must say I think they may be right. Since that first week when we laid you flat, you have had no difficulties of any kind, and my observations say that this pregnancy is progressing famously. If things continue like this, I should think by St. Valentine's Day we will have a rollicking baby on our hands."

Hannah nodded her head. "I think so, too. I have been walking every day and have felt no concerns. I would say the pregnancy is well established." She could not stop the sweet, bemused smile that lighted her face, and Doctor Stanholme reached for her hand.

"You are happy about this, then?" he asked. "You and your husband?"

She flushed. "I—I have not telegraphed my husband yet. I did not want to raise his hopes on a false promise. But now, of course, I will send him word. Yes! Yes! Of course, we are pleased beyond measure."

"Hannah." Doctor Stanholme flushed. It was the first time he had called her by her Christian name. "If there is any difficulty between you and your husband, if you feel any reluctance to return to him, I wish you to know that I have grown to feel an overwhelming admiration and affection for you."

The doctor stood up and bit his lip, and then he looked at her with fierce intensity. "What I am trying to say is that you could have a great career here. A great life. You are one of the finest medical practitioners I have ever observed.

"If you stay, I can get you admitted to medical school. I will be your mentor. You could be on staff here or at any of the great teaching hospitals. Do you understand that you are not an ordinary woman, Hannah? It seems to me there is little to pull you back to the barren West. Stay here where you can change the course of human suffering.

"If you do not wish to return to the West, to your husband, you must know that I would happily fill the role as protector and provider for you and your child. Hannah, this child does not mean that your life has to end . . ."

"No!" she exclaimed, before he could say any more and embarrass them both beyond recovery. "No, Doctor Stanholme. Please. Not another word. I am afraid that the unorthodox pattern of my life may have given you some false impressions of my true feelings.

"I appreciate your concern for me as a colleague and your generous and complimentary assessment of my skills, but the truth is, I am very much in love with my husband. Perhaps more in love with him than even I realized.

"As for this child—this pregnancy is an answer to a lifetime of prayers. This child is not the end of my life, Doctor Stanholme. It is the beginning.

"It is my failure that you have not seen this in me. It is my own continuing failure that I have not known it in myself.

"You have been my mentor, my guide, Doctor Stanholme. You have taught me about medicine and strength of character and generosity. And you have saved my baby for me. I will never be able to repay what you have given me." She took his hand in hers. "Nothing I have learned, nothing you have taught me will be wasted. What I need to do now is build a life to use it in."

The silence in the room stretched like a filament of silver between them, and then the moment broke. Doctor Stanholme lifted her hand to his lips and kissed it. "Wherever you go, Hannah, whatever life brings you—and I hope it is happiness—remember that I am here."

She gently removed her hand, and he turned down the gaslight and slipped out of the room. In the dim light of the hospital room she leaned back against the pillows. The hand he had kissed in farewell lay softly on top of the sheets, and suddenly she felt a flutter—no stronger than the whisper of a butterfly—but she knew immediately what it was.

"Oh, my little one," she whispered in the darkness, "tomorrow we shall be on our way home to your father."

CHAPTER TWENTY-FOUR

Some childlike and superstitious part of Hannah had made her always distrust happiness. She had read the scriptures that asserted that mankind existed so that they might have joy and have it more abundantly. She had studied the passages that promised that if she cast her burdens upon the Lord, He would defend her. Still, there was a shadow of feeling in her that always feared that when things were going well, when blessings were poured out, that the Lord would counter each blessing with a trial. It was her nature to fear the trial so much that she also feared the blessings.

Yet her joy at being pregnant had been so fresh and unexpected that she had not countered it with any foreshadowing of sorrow or tragedy, and once she felt the baby move within her, healthy and strong, she was confident that it was her new beginning.

When she left the hospital, she returned to her boardinghouse to pack her bags and arrange for train tickets to Ogden. As she entered the front parlor, the landlady glanced up and, seeing Hannah, reached into the mailbox.

"This came for you about an hour ago," the woman said. She handed Hannah a yellow telegram envelope, and it felt hot and foreboding in her hand.

The last spit of rock had given Adam and the construction crew trouble all summer. Blasting crews kept quitting in frustration and fear, and Adam kept trying to read the rock better so that the blasting could fracture more of it away. In spite of persistent effort, the stubborn spine of the mountain refused to be broken. When this last section was removed, it would form the deepest part of the reservoir.

The granite and limestone they were loosening, cutting and blasting away, was being hauled to building sites up and down the state. It was infuriating to Adam to be so close to the finish and then be stymied by such a seemingly trivial geographic outcropping. The ridge was deep and hard and beginning to feel endless.

Day after day Adam returned to his empty, joyless house, so tired that he could hardly carry food to his mouth. William, knowing the strain his son-in-law was under, had asked the cook at the Big House to provide dinner for Adam every night, and so, when he came into the house, no matter how late the hour, there was always something on the table for him to eat. If it hadn't been for William's thoughtfulness, Adam would probably have gone hungry. He had become indifferent to everything but the reservoir, it represented so many years of his life.

One evening William visited Adam.

"Did you enjoy your visit in Boston last spring?" he asked.

Adam nodded. "You have a beautiful daughter, William. She is a woman like no other. What can I say? She is my life, and when I am with her, I am as alive as this life will ever let me be. When I am not . . ."

"Poor Adam," William said with tender humor. "You should have fallen in love with Constance. Now, there is a predictable and understandable girl. But no, you had to choose Hannah. She is like that impossible granite ridge you are trying to blast into submission."

The two men laughed. "I wouldn't have chosen any differently, even if I could have seen the end from the beginning. I didn't have the power to make another choice anyway. She simply took my heart and has never given it back."

"Well," William said comfortably, "you still haven't seen the end of it all. Not even close to it. You are still so young, both of you. Things will change. They always do."

Adam shrugged and was silent.

"Speaking of change," William continued, "I want you to be the first to know, Adam. Things for me are not the same as they used to be. Anne and Cyrus and all of their grandchildren are filling up the Big House, and I feel more and more a visitor in my own home.

"Eliza is so busy rearing her boys and running the farm that I never see her, and the long Utah winters are beginning to wear on me. My responsibilities in the town and Church have been given to younger men.

"When Harold and I were in Los Angeles I visited a little town by the ocean called Laguna. There are several Mormon families who have small farms there, a few artists, and a lot of fresh air and space.

"There's a fine little school, and Harold and I were quite taken with the whole area. I am thinking that if I want to stay healthy and strong to raise this son of mine to manhood, I might be wise to seek a gentler climate. So, the upshot of the matter is that I am going to begin spending my winters in California, starting next year. I have bought a little cottage, and it is all set.

"I'm waiting until Hannah comes home and your reservoir is finished, and then I am off. No more snowstorms or blizzards or chillblains for me."

"Won't Harold miss the family?"

"Yes, I've worried about that," William responded, "but he will be here each summer, and now that he and Reuben are in different schools, they hardly see each other during the winter anyway. I don't think he will be too unhappy. If he is, he'll tell me—he's like Hannah that way—and I'll rethink the matter."

Adam nodded. "Your last winter in Utah? Hannah's last winter in Boston—and hopefully my last winter of being alone. There is a lot of change looming over us. I've made a decision, too. After this reservoir is finished, I am going to refuse any contracts that take me out of the city. There is enough expansion and construction going on here to fill my time."

With a glad cry, William stood up and shook Adam's hand. "That's a good decision. You and Hannah need time to be together. Here's to a winter we shall be glad to see come and go."

Adam did not confide in William that he was worried about Hannah. Her letters had a peculiar closed sound to them, even more than usual. She wrote with less frequency and seemed to have very little news to share. He wondered if she blamed him for having spoiled their two heedless weeks together by trying to resolve long-standing issues. Something in him had an unsettled feeling about her, and his instincts made him long to be with her and be reassured that all was well.

Why couldn't he learn to be wise enough to let her be herself? Why did he always have to try to force the bud open rather than waiting for it to blossom on its own? Of course, in his own defense, he had to admit that she was taking so long to open to him that he was justified in feeling, at times, that it might never happen.

Adam stilled his anxieties with the thought that in only

three more months Hannah would be home. Another Christmas. He was determined this one would be the happiest they had ever known. Without requiring anything of her, he would fill the house with the feelings of his own love and celebration, and he would show her that all he wanted was to be near her and to have her happy. He would show her that he did not want her to change or try to be like other women. He loved her as she was.

His Christmas gift to her would be his promise that he would not accept any work that took him away from her. Perhaps if they could spend more time together, their lives would be blessed with the feelings of belonging and security that they both longed for. He hoped his decision would seem like a gift to her.

September had come, and the reservoir was not finished. It was later in the season than Adam had planned, and if the snows began to fall, it would become too hard to work on the mountain laying charges and even harder to haul away the loosened stones. They had only two to three weeks of certain weather, but after that it was anybody's guess. Adam woke early in the morning determined to make progress.

He had ordered some explosives that were packed in tubes in a new agar suspension. The new product was supposedly very safe. The only way this form of dynamite could be set off was by detonation, but there had to be a spark along with the blast. The new explosive was set off by a detonating plunger, but the detonator was attached to a fuse. The spark of the fuse plus the blast of the small detonating charge worked together to create the explosion. Simple detonating force alone could not cause the sticks to explode, so the fear of jolting or jiggling them—even the concerns about heat—were nullified.

In the years of construction on the water system, there

had been remarkably few accidents, but the handling of blasting powders and explosives was always an anxious and dangerous activity, and Adam was always looking for ways to minimize the potential for injuries on his projects.

The September morning air was cold, and when Adam arrived at the reservoir, expecting to see men swarming up the last hump of rock that stood between the work crew and a completed, smooth-walled reservoir, he saw instead a few desultory construction workers standing around the foreman's shack.

"What's going on here?" Adam asked, irritated that the work had not begun as he had ordered.

"The blasting crew arrived, took one look at the new stuff, and said they didn't know how it works. They aren't goin' to use it until someone shows 'em how," the foreman growled.

Adam strode around the corner and found the explosives men sitting on some rocks, staring at the ground.

"What's all this about?" Adam asked testily. "I've ordered this new stuff for your safety, and now you are refusing to use it?"

"Don't know nothin' about it," one of the men said sulkily. Blasting crews were always a hard lot to work with. They risked their lives every day, and so they considered no man to be their master. They were superstitious and cautious, and if they had bad feelings about a job or a boss or the omens of a day, they simply walked off the job.

"We ain't messin' around with stuff we ain't never seen before," another added.

All the impatience and frustration that Adam had felt in the years he had been straining to complete this job welled up inside of him.

"Then come with me, and I'll show you how it's done.

Have you at least drilled the bore holes?" His voice was terse with disgust and command.

"Yep," one of the men said laconically. "Them holes are all ready for the charge. If we lay it right, and it's a big enough blast, it ought to be the last bang. By nightfall your reservoir will be in fine shape."

"Then let's get on with it," Adam said. "It's about time."

They moved around the gaping hole that would be filled with the water that would bless the lives of generations yet unborn. Carrying the box of explosives, they moved from bore hole to bore hole, tamping in the explosives, setting the fragile line of the fuses, and connecting them one by one to the detonator on the other side of the rim.

At last there was only one final bore hole to reach. The hole had been drilled too small, and the dynamite resisted entering the hole. The man who usually held the tamping rod had gone across the reservoir to connect a fuse. Adam, anxious to finish the job, nodded to the worker who was wielding the sledgehammer that pounded the tamp.

Taking the wooden tamping rod in his hands, Adam pushed it against the stick of the explosive where it protruded from the bore hole. He nodded to the man with the hammer to hit the end of the wooden tamper and push the dynamite deep into the bore. There was no need to fear the stroke of the hammer. The new explosive could not be set off by the hardest blow because it required a spark to create detonation. The tamping rod was wood and could not create a spark.

What neither Adam nor the man with the sledgehammer realized was that the rock around the bore hole contained flint. Bright, hard, metal-bearing flint.

Billy, the hammer man, stared at his boss standing in front of him holding the tamping rod, and he felt a shudder

315

of nervousness. What was a boss doing down here getting his hands dirty and working on things that belonged to the labor crew? Billy wondered irritably. This boss had power to dock his pay or even fire him. But he didn't belong down here working with the crew.

When Billy was working with Sam, he never had to worry about hitting the old geezer's hands with the hammer. Heck, every tamper-hog in the world had his hands whacked at least a dozen times a week. But hitting the boss would be another matter. Billy felt weak in the knees. He gulped for air and held his hammer higher.

"Billy," Adam said impatiently," I can't hold this rod much longer. Will you please tap the hammer?"

Afraid not to do as he was told, Billy swung the heavy hammer forward, missing Adam's hands, missing the wooden tamp rod, but hitting the end of the dynamite and the surrounding flint with a resounding metallic blow of the sledge.

Sparks flew out from the stone, and the whole of Adam's world erupted in a black and scarlet void.

CHAPTER TWENTY-FIVE

"Talk to me as though I were his doctor and not his wife," Hannah told Doctor Morgan. He had met her at the train in his buggy and was hurrying her to the house where Adam lay.

"Your father wanted to take him to the Big House, but I knew when you came home you would want to nurse him, and so I arranged for him to be taken to his own place. Your father took over the work at the reservoir, and it looks like they will be able to finish before the snows. He thought it would be the best way to help," Doctor Morgan told her.

"How is he?" Hannah said quietly. "I want to know exactly."

"Let me put your mind at ease on this, Hannah. His life is not in danger, but he has sustained injuries of significant proportion. His right hand is mangled, he has lost considerable muscle tissue from his right hip and leg, his right eye is severely damaged, and he is still concussed and delirious.

"I think he cannot hear very well, but I do not think the damage to his hearing is permanent. Every day there has been some slight improvement. Yesterday I noticed he opened his eyes and turned his head when the nurse dropped a pair of scissors."

"Will you need to amputate? Is the damage to his leg or his hand that extensive?"

"I can't make that decision with certainty, because there is always the possibility of infection, but I believe that if we can protect the wounds, they will heal enough that he can keep the limbs. Of course, he will walk with a limp and his right hand will be useless. And there is no hope for sight in the right eye."

"I cannot wait to see him," Hannah whispered. "Can't your team go faster?"

Adam was lying on the bed. He was as still as death, and the cold, bright light of the autumn day slanted across the woven coverlet like bars. Everything was so white. The walls, the sheets, the pillow, the bandages, and Adam's beloved face—white as the padded bandage that covered one eye and half his head.

She knelt beside the bed and took his strong, uninjured left hand in hers and held it against her cheek. "I don't know if you can hear me, Adam, my darling, but I am here. I am home. I am with you. It's going to be all right. It's going to be all right. Everything will work out."

She murmured the words like a litany. They were her promise directly from the Lord, and she believed them. She willed Adam to hear and believe them, too.

The first time she changed the bandages she saw what terrible work the explosion had done. It had torn his fine hand with an attack like that of a clawed beast and had left the tendons, muscles, and bones hopelessly mangled.

Doctor Morgan, using the blessed balm of ether, had operated for hours, trying to put the hand back into some kind of order, but she knew, looking at it, that although it might be able to be used as a lever, it would never have

318

manipulative skills again. The nerves were damaged beyond repair.

The leg and hip were lacerated and gouged, but the wounds were clean and uninfected. Hannah could tend them with such care that all her medical skills would ward off the specter of infection.

The eye was blasted, and she saw the tears that ran from it continuously. She knew the eye would stop weeping eventually. It was a natural physiological response to the terrible injury, but as she looked at the stricken eye, she thought that the tears were absolutely right. How natural that the eye should weep for the end of its sight.

Hannah had a cot installed next to Adam's bed. She changed his bandages and his sheets, she washed him as if her were a baby, and, in the moments when he roused to wakefulness, still not knowing where or who he was, she fed him spoonfuls of nourishing broths and spoke to him with loving insistence.

"Adam. Adam. It's Hannah. I'm with you. Wake up, Adam. Wake up. We need you to wake up and help us. You have work to do, my darling. We have work to do. Together. Wake up, my dearest. Adam. Adam."

Sometimes he mumbled, and once he called her name, loudly and distinctly. Another night she woke up to hear him calling to the construction crew. "Let's get that last bit of mountain blasted out of here! Come on. Let's finish this job. Get going, men. Get going, men . . . get going. . . "

She put her arms around him and soothed him. "The work is done," she said. "It is all finished. This is Hannah. I am here, Adam. Wake up."

Every day he seemed to grow more alert to his surroundings. One morning she put up the blind, and the sun filled the window. For the first time he turned his head, and she saw his uninjured eye focus in the light. The maple tree outside the window was ablaze with gold and scarlet leaves.

"Autumn," he mumbled. "Hannah home soon." He smiled and closed his eyes.

That night he woke up shouting. "Get away!" he shouted, "get away! It's going to explode! The mountain! It's going to explode!"

He was thrashing back and forth, and his face was wet with perspiration. His voice was hoarse with desperation. "Get the men out! Get them out! Hurry! The mountain!"

"Adam," she cried, holding his shoulders and trying to calm him. "Adam. You are here. In your bed. This is Hannah, Adam. Hannah. You've been hurt. You must lie still."

He stopped shouting, but he still thrashed against her restraint. "Darling," she cried, "listen to me. You are home. This is Hannah. You've been hurt. You must lie still."

She said each word with powerful clarity, and yet her love filled them with more emotion than she had shown in their tenderest, happiest times. "My love. You must lie still. I am here."

He gave a great sigh and became quiet. His unbandaged eye closed again, but this time the tone of his body against hers was not the rigid stillness of unconsciousness but rather the graceful relaxation of true sleep.

His hand was in hers when she fell asleep, and she woke to the motion of his fingers stroking hers. Looking across the small gap between her cot and his bed, she saw his head turned toward her and his good eye staring into hers.

"Hannah?" he said softly. "Then I wasn't dreaming? You are really here?"

She burst into tears and sprang from her bed to put her arms tenderly around him. "Yes, my darling, darling husband. I am truly here. And so are you. We are here, in our own home, and we are together."

He smiled wistfully. "Did it take an explosion to get us here?"

She smiled, but the tears would not stay out of her eyes.

"How bad is it?" he asked, and she could tell he was already on the verge of going to sleep again.

Rest would be his best healer, but before he slept she wanted him to know. "Not bad at all. You have to try very hard to get well quickly. I'll need help with the baby," she smiled.

He didn't say anything.

"Did you hear me?" she asked, afraid that he was still confused. "You are going to be a father!"

"I heard," he said. "I just thought maybe I was still dreaming."

"No, dearest Adam, it is true. It is a dream. But it is true."

She bent to kiss his dear, ravaged face, and he held her with his lips. "My darling girl," he whispered. And then he slept.

William explained to her that it was a miracle that Adam was alive. Fortunately the bore hole that held the charge had been situated so that the explosion did not fracture the boulder. All the harm had been done by the concussive force of the explosion and a few small, dislodged pebbles. The hammer man had escaped with ringing ears and cuts and bruises.

Adam's hand had been smashed by the splintering of the tamping rod, and his eye had been destroyed by a rock the size of a fist that had blown away from the ridge. What had saved his life was that the force of the explosion expanded out into the great hole of the reservoir and was dissipated in the open air.

"You don't need to tell me it is a miracle," Hannah breathed. "It is a second chance, and I don't intend to lose it. No more mistakes."

William smiled. "Hannah, of course you'll make mistakes. Life is made up of a million decisions, words, choices, and priorities—mistakes are inevitable. The only real mistake is not learning from them."

"He's doing better every day, Papa. Yesterday he sat up and fed himself with his left hand. He is already practicing writing with it. It's going to take a while, but he will be able to master it. Fortunately, he has significant ambidexterity."

Harold was sitting in the room over by the window playing with a new puppy. "What does that word mean, Hannah?" he asked, and she realized he had been listening to the conversation.

"It means that Adam was always quite capable of doing things with either hand, and it will be a great blessing to him now that his right hand is hurt."

"Oh," Harold said. "He's going to be all right, you know, Hannah. I pray for him every day."

Hannah went over and hugged the boy. He had their mother's eyes and aristocratic features, and he had Papa's warmth and sturdy vigor. "He prays for you, too, Harold. You do know how much we love you, don't you?"

Harold squirmed under her embrace. "Aw, Hannah! No need to get all squiffy about it."

Laughing, Hannah released him. "Sorry, Harold. I guess I just feel squiffy whenever I see you."

Adam was physically strong, muscular, and resilient. His recuperation moved forward with gratifying speed. With Hannah's expert care he came through each crisis and grew stronger by the day. It was several weeks before the ringing in his ears grew quiet, and his hand ached so viciously as it began to heal that he found it impossible to sleep.

At each plateau, however, Hannah and Adam worked together to solve the problems, and slowly they found a way through. When Adam's hand pained him, she soaked it alternately in bowls of hot and then cold water. Gradually the injured nerves subsided. She gently massaged the scarred skin on his hip and leg with pure lanolin so that the tissue would not become hard and inflexible. They created a series of exercises that stretched the injured muscles and kept them from contracting and shrinking.

The days flew by as Hannah and Adam concentrated on the healing process. By Christmas, Adam, weak and thin, was able, with the help of Hannah and a crutch, to walk outside to a waiting carriage and go to the holiday party at the Big House.

Hannah's dress was garnet red velvet with a white spray of lace at the neck and wrists. It had been sent to her by her father. "This is my Christmas gift to you, dear daughter," the note from Papa read. She recognized the square dress box. It reminded her of a long-ago party. "I want you to be the prettiest girl at the ball. I know you will be the happiest."

The dress was cleverly made with a high waistline, a full, gentle gathering that flowed to the floor, and the suggestion of a train in the back. It almost disguised the fact that Hannah was happily, thoroughly, and completely with child. When she put it on and turned so that Adam could see her, he had beamed with pleasure.

"You will be the loveliest woman there, Hannah," he said. "But the dress does not make the woman—the woman makes the dress."

When they arrived at her father's house, Hannah paused at the foot of the porch and looked up at the gleaming windows, the festooned doors, and the warm, buttery squares of light on the newly fallen snow. It was a beautiful house, beginning to show its years, and long since eclipsed by the mansions of newcomers with wealth from mining, railroading, or land speculation. Still, she felt, for the first time, that she could look at it without the old resentments and discomforts. It was a place where her family lived and had lived and would always be a part of her.

Suddenly, though she was looking forward to the party, she realized that she could not wait to get back to her own comfortable little house. "My goodness," she thought with a sense of wonder. "This isn't home to me at all any more."

When they entered the foyer, the guests surged around Adam. Many of them had not seen him since the accident, though he had been bombarded by notes from well-wishers, gifts, and offers of help.

Looking at him, Hannah could not help but think how handsome he still was, even with his ravaged eye, which was now covered by a jaunty eyepatch that gave him a rather devil-may-care look. In spite of his injured leg, he still stood tall and straight, and his wide shoulders and powerful face belied any signs of weakness.

As she observed his friends and members of the family clustering around him, Hannah felt a twinge of concern. She could tell that the excitement and noise were tiring him, but even more concerning, she realized that he suddenly seemed conscious of the scarred and unusable hand that hung at his right side.

Several people made the mistake of reaching to shake hands with him, and she saw them flinch when they caught sight of his poor, disabled hand. When Adam saw their looks of surprise and revulsion, something dawned in his eyes that she had not seen before. She watched as he lifted the broken hand and pushed it deep into his pocket, out of sight. The light went from his face. He rested his crutch against the wall and sat heavily in the chair behind him. Responding mechanically to the words of welcome and concern, she saw him visibly droop.

"Papa," she said softly, "I think maybe the idea of bringing Adam to this party was a little premature. Adam is still recuperating, and it is probably too much for both of us. Would you forgive us if we wish you a merry Christmas and go back home."

William was instantly solicitous. "Of course, Hannah. Let me help you get him into the carriage."

When Hannah suggested to Adam that they leave he did not object, and they were driven home. Adam was very quiet as he struggled up the stairs with the crutch and the banister as aids. By the time he reached the top, he was perspiring heavily from exertion, and Hannah fussed over him.

"Here, dear, let me help you take off your suit. It was too much for you. I should have been wise enough to take it in smaller stages—but you fooled me. You have been doing so well!" She tried to get him to smile, but he shook his head and turned away from her.

"I can undress myself," he said. "You don't want to muss your party dress. I know I'm a cripple—but I'm not helpless!" It was the first time she had heard the sound of bitterness in his voice.

"No, you are not!" she snapped. "You are not a cripple, and you are not helpless, and I won't stand here and listen to you feel sorry for yourself because somebody was surprised at the mess a stick of dynamite has made of your hand. If you can't overcome the squeamishness of other people, then you are crippled indeed!"

Adam sat down on the side of the bed and began to

remove his shoes with his good hand. His shoulders were shaking. Hannah stood in the doorway, alarmed. Was he crying? Had she been too harsh? After all, he had lost a hand, an eye, and the partial use of one leg. Perhaps he did have the right to feel sorry for himself.

She walked toward him, filled with remorse, ready to cradle him in her arms and beg for forgiveness. Then he raised his head and fixed her with his sapphire blue gaze, and she realized he was laughing. Laughing!

"Hannah," he said, "I should have known better than to think I'd get sympathy! I must be getting better! This is a sure sign. You are so tender with people when you think they are in pain or dying, but once they are healed, you expect them to measure up."

The relief of his laughter was too much for her, and she stamped her foot impatiently. "Really, Adam, I thought you were downhearted, and here you are making a joke of serious things."

Adam reached up and pulled her down onto the bed beside him, and they sat, looking out the window at the moon-bright snow and the crystal-spangled sky.

"Christmas again," Adam whispered. "I was going to give you a present this year. I was going to promise not to work outside of Ogden, not to accept a contract that would take me away from you ever again."

He paused. "Now, I'm not so sure that is a gift. Am I going to be your patient for the rest of our lives, Hannah? Is it only that I was wounded and injured that brought you back to me? Will it be my disabilities that keep you here? I don't want you to feel sorry for me. I don't think I could live with that."

"Adam." Hannah stood up with her back to the window so that all he could see was her silver outline. Her face was in darkness.

"I was already on my way back to you when I got the telegram about your accident. I did not come home because you were hurt. I did not even come back because of the baby. I wasn't even sure that I might not still lose the baby and never conceive again.

"It wasn't any of those things that brought me home. I came back to you. It was as simple as that. In the long nights that I lay in bed trying to preserve this child, I had time to think, and I realized that every thought I had came circling back to *you*.

"I confused sewing and cooking with making a home. I wasn't good at those things, and so I felt a failure. I felt trapped. There was one thing I *was* good at—making people well. So I thought if I did that, you'd be proud of me, and I'd have some value, and we'd be happy.

"Then we just seemed to grow further and further apart, and finally I thought I might as well make a life for myself. We could still be married, but we would each find our own way.

"One night, lying in bed and missing you, I understood. I can't find my own way without you. Any way that I go it has to be with you and through you and by you. That doesn't diminish me or my talents in any way. It just means that I have to put first things first.

"We made a promise to each other and to the Lord, and somehow in the confusion of our wedding day and the heartbreak of the years since, I forgot that promise.

"Adam, forgive me. Forgive me. Let me come home."

He opened his arms, and she took his injured hand in hers and kissed it. She kissed his face, and his other hand, and then she kissed his lips, and she felt the completion of a love that would last for eternity.

Two months later, when William Adam Fairfield was

born, a red-faced, uproarious, opinionated infant with a shock of black hair and a body of remarkable strength, Hannah looked at the baby boy with such wonder and amazement that Adam had to laugh.

"My dear, one would think you had never seen a newborn child before!" he exclaimed.

"I am thinking that the Lord made us wait for a child because He knew we would have to be very wise and vigorous to raise such a one as this!"

Smiling indulgently, Hannah raised her hands, and Doctor Morgan placed the indignant child next to his mother.

"It's a pity you couldn't have been the attendant at your own delivery," the doctor smiled. "You are the finest midwife I have ever seen. A pity to waste such a gift."

"There is no waste at all in this world," Hannah said calmly. "It is a matter of doing things in the right time and the right order. All that I have learned the Lord will put to use in His own time. In the meantime, I have other things to learn."

She held the baby against her and traced the velvety softness of his head with her lips. Adam came over to them. He still walked with a limp, but he was already hard at work drafting the plans for the roads of a new building development on the north of town and was supervising the laying of the water mains. His left hand was becoming more and more adept at every task.

She lay there smiling up at him, and his presence filled the room like music. The days stretched like a path started at daybreak, wandering out of sight to who knew what but offering all the wonders of the journey.

"Who knows, Adam?" Hannah said. "I may even learn how to cook."